Through the Mist

by

Michael Keene

First published October 2007 by
Collective Publishing as an eBook
ISBN 13   978-1-905909-001
ISBN 10   1-905909-00-4

This edition published March 2008 by
Purple Velvet
being an imprint of
Collective Publishing

ISBN 13   978-1-905909-018
ISBN 10   1-905909-01-2

Edited by Freya Heims
Designed & Typeset by Palladio Design
Front cover image © Kevin Russs
Back cover image © Dmitry Zaltsman

Printed and bound in Great Britain by
Printondemand-worldwide
Peterborough PE2 6WA

COLLECTIVE PUBLISHING
Fareham, Hampshire, PO15 6QH
United Kingdom

www.collectivepublishing.co.uk
info@collectivepublishing.co.uk

Foreword

It would have been impossible for me to
write this book when much younger as I
know now that... *one has to experience life
- before one can write about it.*

For a number of years I was a successful
fashion photographer before becoming a
travel photojournalist.

With my first two ebooks successfuly published, 'The Loch
Keeper' & 'Poor Rich Guy Matthew', I set about writing
'Through the Mist', which has developed into a trilogy.

Having met so many gay people through my photography, I
had no problem in finding images of the main character for
my book - *Nigel*. Although fictitious, I know him well.
Through my travels across Europe, I also knew the locations I
would take Nigel to in his desperate search for his sexuality
and the problems and humour he would embrace.

I started writing the book five years ago. But, before that I
spent many years of travel away from home. I could not have
been able to do this without the love and support of my wife
and family, to whom I thank.

Unlike my previously published books that were rejected
several times, much to my frustration, by various publishers,
the first of this trilogy 'Through the Mist' was received first
time when submitted to publisher Pauline Andersen. I quote
her email to me. '*I read the story twice - and couldn't put it
down*'. I thank Pauline for all her encouragement and hard
work in collating my writing and the preparation of graphics
plus her deep belief in my portrayal of the lifestyle.

Michael Keene, Author

Through the Mist

by

Michael Keene

CHAPTER 1

It was a nice thought, but why a diary this birthday? I suppose being eighteen one is expected to write things down.

Nigel was at a crossroads in his young life. Birthdays had always been great to look forward to, but this one seemed different.

He took a slow look around his room. Apart from being a bit of a mess, it was the same room that had seen him grow into his youth. It was a good place to be alone in, detached, with his parents, and young brother's rooms being just along the landing.

Yes, the toys had gone. They had been replaced with books of varied reading. He also had a fine collection of sports cups and medals on display. He hadn't done badly in the sporting department. His mind flashed back to some of the tennis, squash, and badminton wins. He was quite proud of these. As he lay there with these thoughts, his hand moved across his well-toned body, then down to his calf muscles. He was in good shape.

Good job the diary had not been around for some of the past times he'd shared with his room.

His smile reflected his thoughts. It's good that his room could not talk. There had been many shared secrets, with the fun, laughter, music, moods, guilt, and the hidden books. They were good growing up days. Oh room, we could certainly tell some stories, he thought.

Now eighteen, with that topless poster behind the door, and the full size nude on the other wall, these were the OK things now.

"Do you really have to have things like that around." Mum would say, looking around his room.

Dad, on the few times he felt it was his duty to visit his room, just to talk about nothing, would on leaving, just give a glance at the poster. He would pat Nigel's shoulder in a knowing manner. It was his way of showing his understanding of teenage life.

As for his younger brother Dean, he would just stare at them. And on leaving, he would ask if there were any good books he could take away to read. Being only thirteen, the answer was always a shake of the head, followed by a firm "No."

The body building weights would annoy Mum. She claimed that they were far too heavy for an upstairs room.

"Just look at the marks on the carpet."

Nigel found that the workouts offered relief from the pressures of growing up.

Dean would come in at odd times. He liked to work out with Nigel, but mostly he found himself helping to replace the weights on the racks. He was well developed for a lad of his age.

Cuttings from bodybuilding magazines were stuck around the gym area of the room. Dean would remark on these and would tease Nigel about them. But they had just as much a place in his life as the topless posters.

Nigel often found himself questioning his feelings about these as he could relate to both.

This was a bloody difficult age to be at. So many mixed feelings and emotions to deal with.

Maybe the diary was not such a good present after all. His private life could be at an end!

His thoughts were broken as the door opened. Dean's head appeared, and then quickly withdrew again. With the door partially open, Dean called out to ask if he could come in.

"Yes, but what do you want?"

"Just a chat."

Pulling on his briefs, Nigel pulled the door fully open.

"Hope I didn't disturb anything?" Dean asked, smiling. He gave his brother a wink.

"Very funny. I can take them off again if you like. Come on in."

Dean cleared his throat.

"Can I talk to you in secret?"

"You know I can't keep a secret, but try me."

Dean's face was not smiling at the thought that Nigel might laugh at the question. Nigel was thinking that as this happened every so often, he was in for a mind bender. These were going to be the left over questions after Dean had put them to the test of his friends.

Pulling on a sweater, Nigel sat down on his bed to wait for the question.

There was a long period of silence. Dean just stood there with his hands stuffed in his jeans.

"Now, don't laugh. I think I have a problem."

"Where, in the head? Sorry, that wasn't fair." Nigel said.

"Christ, it's bad enough having to come to you. If I can't talk about it, I could go mad."

Nigel, putting on an older brother look said, "OK, lets hear it."

"Well, you know we all have nights." Dean was looking down at the floor with this question.

Nigel assured him that he understood by letting out a snigger and giving a nod of the head.

"Well I've been dreaming a lot, and have a problem."

Nigel sensed the questions to follow. He thought he would ease the situation a little. "So you've had a little hard on, is that it? We all have those," he said. He was feeling the big guy now, and a little smug with it as well.

"Well, yes, but nothing happens... nothing at all. Nothing comes out. My mates all talk about it...well, you know?"

"It's called masturbating." Nigel thought it best to be direct and to the point.

"I know what it's called, but nothing happens."

"Dean old mate, you're just thirteen. Some guys can do it when they are younger than you, some have to wait until they're older. Don't worry, the feeling's the same, but your sperm isn't quite ready yet."

"Do you mean spunk?" Dean asked.

"Call it what you want, it's the same thing. You will have it one day, honest."

Dean, who had been sitting on the end of the bed, stood up ready to leave now that his question of life had been answered.

He turned, and looked at Nigel. "Thanks," he whispered.

Nigel stood up to put his arm around his brother. It seemed ages before they moved. This was to be an important period in their lives.

"Go on, you'll be OK my man."

Dean reached the door. He turned and stood with his head just looking back inside the door.

"You don't have to put your pants on for me, unless you're shy or something."

This was to be the first of many a male bonding session with his brother. Nigel felt good about this.

CHAPTER 2

"This is nice," mum said, "us all sitting down for a meal to-gether."

Most days, meals were a dash and grab time. Not the best way to communicate.

"Could I have some wine please?" Nigel asked. Dad glanced across at his wife. This was his usual checkpoint before giving an answer to questions of such great importance as this.

"Yes, sure you can, as long as you buy the next bottle. Why start now?" he said.

Nigel had already thought this question out in advance.

"Well. As I am planning a trip to France this summer, I thought I should get in training."

There was a silence that seemed to drift over the meal table at this point.

"When did you come up with this idea?" Mum asked.

"Only the other day."

"It's not that far away, and it's easy to get to. I'm only going for a month."

"What will you do when you get there?" His parents were almost in unison on this.

"I will just bum around a little." Nigel looked across at Dean, half expecting him to comment on this, but no.

The meal came to an end. Mum seemed more than a bit upset about this. With the washing up finished, Nigel tried to escape to his room. Dad had other ideas.

"Sit down. Let's talk this over. Another wine. Red or White?"

Well at least this was a choice, Nigel thought.

"I know you are not going to like what I'm about to say, but when I was your age, I was out at work, earning my keep. And let's face it, you are only just eighteen. So, what makes you think you can go off around the world on a free passage?"

Nigel sat for a while. Dad thought that this was so he could consider the question. But the silence from Nigel was only from frustration.

"Well, am I going to get an answer, or not?"

Taking another swig of his wine, Nigel could only think of the modern day term.

"I just want to chill out, and find myself."

"Where in France will you go? And what will you do for money?"

"Haven't really thought much about that yet. But I just know that I have to do it. And when I come back…"

"Oh you intend coming back then?"

Nigel gave his Dad a glare…

"As I was saying, when I come back, I think I will be ready to settle down and study, or find a job."

"Who will go with you on this trip of finding yourself, may I ask?"

At this point, Dean came back into the room, followed by his mother.

This seemed to be the right time to hit the fan again.

"Who with?" He looked around the room. "Well, Dean of course. He will be old enough by the summer."

"What? You think fourteen is old enough?" Mum shouted. "And who is going to look after him?"

At this point, Dean felt that he had become a man within the hour. "I can look after myself." And with a quick glance over at Nigel, "I'm not a kid any longer, and I did well in French last term."

Nigel nodded at this statement, trying not to smile. "We'll get on fine. It will help us to get to know each other better. It's only for a month."

"We've had him for fourteen years, and we still don't know him," Dad was heard to mutter. And with that he made towards the stairs, followed closely by Mum.

"Well, that went well, don't you think?" said Nigel.

"I'm not so sure that they thought so. And if you don't mind, how about asking me first, if I would like to go next time?"

"Well, do you want to come or not?"

"Just try and stop me." Dean giggled.

Monday's at college were never good. But, as it there was tennis at the club later in the afternoon, this did make for a better end to the day.

With his college clothes dumped in his room, Nigel changed into his jeans and sweater. He checked his tennis bag, and with a shout of "bye," to mum, he headed off to the club.

The grass courts looked good. He liked playing on grass. It was fast, which suited his game. Good first serve. Then up to the net and volley the ball away. That was his style of play. Yep! He felt good today.

He put his bike into the rack. Then he quickly checked around to see who was there. This was almost a routine with him.

"Hi Dave. Hi Mike. Are you playing anything special, or are you down for a knock?"

"Hi Nigel. Do you want a game? Big Dave is coming down." This was good news, Nigel thought. This would be a great doubles game.

"Well get changed man, else someone like Sue will turn up and bugger the system up."

Now Sue was OK. She had everything a guy could hope for in the looks department, but she was not too good at playing tennis.

Nigel was at a stage of getting into his shorts when he had a vision of Sue on court. Not a good time to have thoughts like these. Sue was an expert at putting guys off their game. He had been on both sides of the net with her seductive moves. He'd had the full treatment. Her routine being anything from undoing the last button of her tennis top just to let you have sight of her cleavage, to grabbing your balls with a smile of innocence on her face. Nigel had found that he was at the top of her hit list for this.

"Come on Nigel, for Christ sake. You've been sitting there with one leg in your shorts and a grin on your face for ages. You should always share your thoughts with your mates."

"Not these ones. Anyway, where's Big Dave?"

The tennis proved to be good. They had played together so often, that they knew each other's game off by heart.

"Wish you wouldn't try and take all the shots. But then, you do need the practice." Mike said.

"Well, someone had to take the lead. At times, I thought I was playing a mixed foursome." Nigel said, blowing him a kiss through the air.

The showers were hot. "Bloody hell! Pass the soap Nigel, or are you on that gel stuff, *as seen on TV?*"

"Well at least I have the body for it."

"True mate. You should offer it to Sue."

"Maybe she doesn't use gel," Nigel shouted over the noise of the showers.

Nigel finished showering first. As he passed Mike's shower, he made a grab at the hot tap and turned it off. He also managed to snatch his towel off the bench, and ran out holding it high above his head.

"You bastard, I'll get you for that."

Running into the changing room, Nigel flung the towel out of the top window. Mike made a dash to retrieve it. He ran outside in his naked state. This turned out to be a big mistake.

Moments later, he returned, towel between his legs, only to tell his captive mates that he wished it could have been handed back by anyone else other than Sue.

"I suppose she put it between your legs as well?" Nigel laughed.

"Not much else there, so I bet she thought it was the best place for it." This was Dave's contribution to the scene.

The two Dave's went off in Big Dave's car. Nigel and Mike decided to walk together.

"I wish you had a bike Mike. It takes so long to get home. I'm bloody hungry."

"You can go on if you want. I'm not in a hurry."

"Ah, you're all hurt now." Nigel put his arm around Mike's shoulders. "Come, smile for Nigel."

They walked along for a while like this. It felt good. On reaching Mike's house, they stood talking for a while.

"Good game this evening. I expect you know my parents are not taking their tennis holiday this summer. So that's fucked up my play away time. What are you doing for a holiday?" asked Mike.

"Going off to France, with a pack on my back."

"You lucky bugger. Don't want a mate without a bike to join you?"

"Well I think Dean is going to come with me. Mum and dad aren't too keen though. They think he's too young to go abroad."

"How long are you going for?"

"A month."

"Oh man. What I would give to do that?"

They both exchanged looks. There was something special about their friendship, thought Nigel.

"See you tomorrow. Be good." Nigel smiled at this parting comment.

Nigel gave some thought to Mike's comment about going with him on his trip. It would be great if he could make it. Although they had been friends for years now, Nigel had never talked about his sexuality. He wasn't sure, but there were times when he found himself being attracted to other guy's. The posters and pictures of body builders hanging in his room, he had to admit, had stirred him more than once. It would be nice to be able to relax with Mike and find out if it was natural to feel this way. Maybe Mike had the same thoughts himself...No, not Mike, surely?

Maybe, if Mike did take a break with him, it would be the right time to talk about things like that?

There was definitely something going on in his body lately. He fancied girls, he knew that, but why this appeal for another guy? This had to be sorted out before he went mad thinking about it. Yes, Mike was the one to confide in. Oh, if only he could get him to travel to France with him.

CHAPTER 3

After tea the family took up their usual positions in the lounge to watch TV. Dean moaned about what he was forced to watch. Dad could watch the programmes and read the paper at the same time. Mum always took up a position on the couch, leaving a place for Nigel to sit. This was her way of keeping in touch with him.

"How did tennis go?" asked Dad.

"Good," was the reply.

"What are the courts like this time of season?"

"Fast."

The conversation faded out at this point.

"Do you see much of Mike these days?" asked Mum.

"Yes. We played tennis this afternoon."

"Of course, his parents play a lot. Don't they take tennis holidays?"

"Yes Mum. But not this year."

"Oh, what a shame. Mike used to enjoy going with them, didn't he? So what's he going to do this summer for a holiday?"

"Don't know. But I think he would quite like to come with me to France."

"That would be nice. That's if you're still going. It would be nice company for you."

"What about me then?" Dean demanded.

"I've told you, you're too young to go." Dad almost shouted across the room. "And as for you young man," looking at Nigel, "you might just be lucky enough to get away with it, eighteen or not."

"But it's OK for Mike, if he was going I suppose?"

Dad looked over the top of his paper. "If I am not mistaken Nigel, Mike is coming up to nineteen?" He sat back in his reading position, having made his point clear.

"I'm going to my room. Love you lots, all of you. Goodnight."

Nigel splashed water over his face. He stared into the mirror above the washbasin. There were signs of stubble appearing on his chin now. Man, are you growing up to be a good-looking guy. He smiled to himself.

Pulling his jeans and top off, he stretched himself out on his bed. Face down at first, then twisted over on to his back.

His thoughts went back over the day. College was becoming boring. The sports were OK. Mike was the only guy that could extend him at tennis though. Thank Christ for Mike.

And, as for the girls, well, we have a problem here old man, he thought. Quite a few to choose from. The problem with girls is, they don't want to just be friends, they get too serious, and I'm not ready for that yet.

His mind now turned to his sex life. Should he have had it off a few times by now? I'm sure Dave and Big Dave, as well as Mike must have had it away a few times. Dave says he has had at least three girls. He was boasting that only the other week, but he'd had a few beers, and that always gets him shouting his mouth off.

As for Big Dave, I'm sure that the stories about having it away in the shed were made up. Oh, come on, there's too much junk in there for a start, and the size of him...no way. Mike doesn't talk about that side of his life much. That's why I like him a lot, he thought. Yep, I like him; he's my type of guy.

Who would I choose if I were about to have sex with someone? Well it would most likely be Sue. She was up for it with him all the time, any time.

His thoughts started to stir a reaction in his groin. He rolled over to enjoy the thought of Sue and himself having sex together. He smiled to himself at his sexual arousal. He had learned to enjoy such situations like this, and felt pleased with himself that he did not have a guilty feeling about his reactions.

Now, with briefs removed, he was free to roll around on his bed. He looked down his body. He was still wearing his white tennis socks. They made him look more athletic, and added a look of extra strength to his legs. He was in no hurry to arrive at his destination, he was proud of his control. If only he could ask others if they could go through the same slow process of control. But it wasn't possible, as nobody seemed to be able to talk about things like that, or confide in others.

He stroked his shaft. It was firm and awaiting his commands. His thoughts returned to Sue. Why did he need her at this point? This was not a time to be sharing his actions with anyone. He rolled around his bed. Should he get a tissue or two, or should he just let in flow across his now taut stomach muscles. He lay on his back as he reached the point of no return. The flow seemed endless. He just lay there watching the spurts eject higher up his body. The tensions were now released, and his stomach taut no longer. He felt good. It flashed through his mind; he had just shared another experience with his room. How many times had he shared his sexual pleasures with his room? After a while, he found himself drifting off to sleep.

The slight knock at the door made him stir. There was no panic. He wasn't the intruder. It was his room after all.

"It's only me mate." The voice belonged to Mike. "Can I come in? Your mum said that I could come up."

"I'm not really ready to receive guests. Give us a moment."

He started to wash himself down at the washbasin. Mike poked his head around the door.

"Sorry old mate, have I come at a wrong moment in a guy's life?" They both smiled at this.

"Yes you have, but come on in. I'm not rushing around for you. Close the door."

"I think I know what you have been up to," Mike said, sitting down on the bed. They both smiled at the situation.

"Bollocks," said Nigel. "I'm not getting dressed for you." He wrapped a towel around himself, and joined Mike on the bed.

"I feel a little overdressed," laughed Mike. "I thought that I'd ask if I could join you on your world trip. I've got a tent, and I gather you're roughing it."

"Fucking great! Shit, yes. I'd like you to come with me. No, joking apart, bloody great. But there's loads of planning to be done."

"I'm your man." Mike raised his hand to give it five. The two locked hands, then Nigel threw his arm around Mike's shoulders to show his feelings. Mike gave Nigel a hug too, just to show their bonding. They stared at each other, and both smiled at themselves.

They talked well into the evening. The break came when Nigel got up and started to pull the duvet over himself.

"Well at least I don't have to get undressed for bed."

"If you are going to be like that, I'm off. See you then. I'll close the door on the way out."

"Cheers." He gave a wink.

Later, Nigel made his way down the landing towards the bathroom. He hadn't reached the door, when Mum appeared up the stairs.

"Goodnight. I do wish you would put something on, it isn't that warm." Her look said it all.

On his way back to his room, Dad appeared. "Did you see Mike? Nice chap. Goodnight."

He was standing at his washbasin, and just about to clean his teeth, when there was another knock at the door.

It was Dean this time.

"Nig, (that's what he called him) are you really taking Mike with you?"

Before Nigel answered this one, he climbed back into bed.

"I think so. He said he would like to come."

"What about me then?"

"Well, it's not for me to say. You know dad's dead against it, and mum is worried."

"What do you think then?" The question was asked with a look that could have crushed even the hardest of people.

Nigel invited him to sit next to him on the bed.

"I know it's hard to understand, but we would be away for a month, and we would be living rough."

Dean pulled a face. Instead of getting onto the bed, he turned towards the door, slamming it shut as he left.

Christ, what an evening thought Nigel, putting his head back on the pillow in order to reflect upon it.

How very different were people's reactions. First there was Mike. He came into his room, just after he'd jerked off. He had found him naked but this didn't present a problem. They had both shared feelings of emotion as to their friendship towards each other. The bond was a great feeling to have. Was it right for a guy to embrace another, or was that not normal? These thoughts raced through his head.

Then there was mum. She wasn't too happy seeing him walk from his room naked.

Dear old dad. Not sure that he cares too much. He thought that he would have liked to have been a fly on the wall when dad was his age. I bet he could pass on some tips, but dad's seem to find that hard to do. Maybe it's so the sons don't get the wrong image of them. Yeah, that's it.

As for Dean, he has problems of his own. He wished that he could get closer to Dean. He should wander into his room someday just to find out what makes him tick. Yes, that's the answer.

Nigel met Mike after college. They walked together on their way home. The forthcoming trip was the main topic of conversation.

"So what do we do when we get over there? And how are we getting there?" Mike asked.

"Glad you asked me that. I've got so many ideas running through my head, it hurts."

"Well, Nigel old mate, it was your idea. Do you want to hear some of my mine, or are you going to be the leader all the time?"

"Don't talk daft. This is our adventure, not just mine. Tell you what, let's get together this weekend and make some plans. Where shall we meet, your place or mine?"

"What about mine?" said Mike. "How about I ask my old man if we can use his camper van? It only stays in the back garden most of the time, and I'm sure he won't mind us using it."

"Great. So, it's all round Mike's place then. Phone me later this evening."

Nigel went straight up to his room to change. His mind was full of the venture ahead. I can't sit by the phone all evening, he thought. So what could he do? He felt on edge. But why?

"Nigel. Could you give me a hand?" shouted Mum. "I want to move a few things into the shed."

"Sure thing. What wants lifting then?"

"That lot over there in the boxes."

"Right, no problem."

Mission over, he joined Mum in the kitchen. Taking a can of coke from the fridge, he perched himself on a stool.

"I might be staying at Mike's over the weekend, so can I take a few cans with me?"

"Yes. Is that all you want to take with you?"

"A few beers and some wine would be nice."

"I don't think so. You see, that's why I worry about France."

"Oh Mum, I'm a big lad now. I can handle things."

"I worry about the stories I hear, like drugs, sex, Aids. Oh, and not to mention all the other things you teenagers get up to."

"I don't have problems like that to deal with Mum. I rarely drink. I don't smoke, and I don't take drugs or get involved with girls."

"And, that's another worry I have. I never hear you mention girls."

Nigel gave her a cuddle. "You are the only girl for me. You leave all the others standing."

"You can't get round me like that. Do you get involved in things?"

"OK. I've had sex a few times, after too many beers though. And yes, I have had the odd joint."

"What's a joint may I ask?"

"Mum, you must try to keep up with the latest trends," he giggled.

"Maybe. But that's all the more reason to worry about you."

"Well, at least you haven't asked me about my gay life yet."

"Don't you start on that one my boy. The times we live in are bad enough without you coming home to tell me that you are…oh, you know?"

"Mum, I'm a good-looking healthy guy. Girls fall all over me all the time. I'm good at sport, good at college, have a great mum and dad. All I'm asking is to be able to be given a little space to find my direction in life. Trust me."

"I do darling, I do." There were tears in her eyes. They embraced. Not a word spoken.

He felt good about having a relationship so close with his family.

The phone rang. Nigel dashed into the hall to answer it. It was Mike.

"Hi, old mate, the camper's on. And guess what? My Dad suggested that he would even trust me with it to take us around France."

"Bloody hell, that's brilliant! What can I say? Now we really have some serious planning to do."

"I gather you're not too keen on the idea then?"

"Mike, you're such a prick sometimes."

"Well, that at least makes me useful, unlike someone I know. Must go. See you tomorrow."

"Did you hear that Mum?" Nigel called out.

"Yes, I did. I wish you wouldn't use those sorts of words."

Nigel shouted, "Sorry," and dashed up to his room.

Old room of mine. Have you ever seen me so happy?

I must start to fill in my diary. This would be a good place to start. His thoughts were so mixed. All he could do was crash out on his bed, and try to sleep.

He was just drifting away when he heard a knock at his door. It was dad's voice, requesting the password to enter.

Turning over, Nigel granted an entrance.

"Sorry. Did I wake you?"

"That's OK."

Nigel rested against the headboard. Dad sat on the edge of the bed. There was a silence, which seemed much longer than it really was. Dad was looking around the room whilst Nigel stared at the ceiling.

"I hear that you are staying at Mike's place over the weekend?"

"Yes, we are planning for our trip." Nigel thought he would get this in first, just to ease the pain Dad was going through in trying to open up a conversation.

"What can I do to help?"

"Money, understanding, and your blessing would be nice for starters." Nigel looked him direct in the eyes with his reply.

"Fine, I'll pay for your return ticket. I'll also give you a loan, let's say, £750. You can pay that back when you make your first million."

"I don't know what to say. Dad, I love you."

"Good. That's what it's all about. Family bonding, and all that."

Now came the serious bit from Dad. He cleared his throat.

"Are you going prepared. I don't mean food and things. I think you know what I mean?"

At this stage, Nigel thought that he could make it difficult for him...but no.

"Yes, I have been going over the things we should be taking. I will be very careful. But Dad, it's months away yet. Everything will be past the sell buy date by then. So I won't buy them just yet." He smiled at his answer, thinking it was rather good.

"Oh, very dry. Who's growing up fast then? Beyond this, is there anything you would like to ask your Dad? You know, well let's say, if I were you, and you were me, what would you like to know about life? Are there things that might be a problem at this time to you?"

"Christ Dad, I think we have done quite well up until now. We are a close family."

"Good. Then I feel quite happy. Feel free to come to me if there is a problem. Good... Good."

With that, he went to the door. He turned, winked at the topless poster, and left, closing the door behind him.

Well that was something. Bloody difficult being a dad I suppose. He's great really. Christ, a return ticket, £750 to spend. I'll break the news that that includes the camper later.

The week seemed very long. It was only Thursday, and not a tennis evening with the guys.

After walking around the house several times, and being told he was annoying, he packed his tennis gear, and headed for the club.

There were no cars or bikes around, but it was early yet.

The changing room was all his. He had just stripped off and had started pulling on his shorts, when there was a knock at the door. Bloody hell. Just like home, he thought. There was another knock.

"Come in. It's not locked."

"Hi Nigel. Thought it was you in here. Remember me, I'm Sue."

"Sue, this is the guy's changing room. Remember. Guys in this room, and girls in the other one."

"Yes, but we are the only ones here. I felt so alone. Go on, you can finish dressing, although I don't mind you as you are. I only wish I'd come in sooner, I could have helped you undress."

His face turned a little red. He hurried to pull on his shorts but his hands wouldn't function.

Sue moved across the room to offer a helping hand.

"Come on Nigel, there's no one here. You might like this game better than tennis. And if you're as good at this as you are on the court, we could extend our membership."

Her body came into contact with his. All the time she was talking, her hand ran down his bare chest, then into his shorts. Sue looked into his eyes, which were now glazed and his vision gone.

He knew there would be days like this. This was one of them. 'This is the test my boy'. These were flashes through his mind, even though Sue was undoing his zip.

Her breasts pushed against his chest. He could feel the hardness of her nipples. Oh God. His mind going in two directions. One being the feel of her breasts, the other following her hands into his briefs. He only wished he knew what command his brain could send to his hands, which remained motionless at his sides. Sue smiled at him as she worked on his erection. He felt a sudden rush of fluid. Sue withdrew her hand, and wiped his released manhood across his bare chest. She then kissed him on the lips. He stood motionless. His arms still stiffly by his sides.

Sue walked towards the door and looked back at Nigel. He was still in a state of extreme shock. "We must do this more often."

With that she walked through the door, leaving it wide open.

Nigel just stood there. He could not believe what had just happened. He hadn't even touched her. He had completely frozen.

The sound of voices soon returned him to earth. Players were heard entering the clubhouse now. He hurriedly pulled his shorts up and put on his top. He had no time to tidy himself up.

"Hi Nigel. Make up a four?"

"No thanks, I've just been playing."

He sat down for a moment on the bench. Players were now changing. Their voices seemed to drum through his head. He had to get out of there fast. He stuffed his clothes into his bag, and left. The journey home on his bike was far from steady. He was still in shock.

"Don't slam the door like that. If you are in a mood and you think you have problems, then take a seat and listen to mine." Mum stood there, hands on hips, watching him.

"Sorry. I'm going up to my room."

Nigel hadn't even changed into his jeans and sweater in his rushed exit from the club. He looked down at his tennis shorts as a reminder of the changing room encounter. Although he wanted to undress, he felt a strange urge just to lie there on his bed. He placed his hands inside his shorts, then felt his chest. He could still feel the fruits of his brief experience.

'So you blew it', he thought. 'I will never play tennis again. And for sure, I will never play mixed doubles with Sue. Christ, what a prat she must think I am. I could at least have lasted a bit longer than ten seconds. I bet I have set a new world record. I can see it now. Guinness Book of Records. *Mr.Nigel Wood. World record for the shortest wank. Ten seconds flat.*'

He lay there in the same position for ages, not wishing to move. Everything racing through his mind. Bloody rotten being eighteen. Too many problems to deal with. And for sure, he could do without a Sue in his life right now. Let's be honest, she hardly had time to touch me before it was all over. Come on room. You know me better than that for staying power.

CHAPTER 4

The phone rang. Mum called him to the phone. "It's Mike" she informed him.

"Hi. Yes great. I'll be ready if you can collect me in your old man's car, I'm not a proud man."

"Now, are you sure you have everything. I know what you are like. Do you think you will be warm enough? It's only a camper," mum said, looking concerned about his weekend.

"Ha. So who's a big boy now?" Dean stood there smiling.

"I'm fine Mum. Just keep an eye on my little brother here. Keep him out of my room, you know what he's like."

"I've read all your dirty books anyway. You can't keep secrets from the great Dean."

"Are you going to help me with my gear to the car, or are you going to just stand there annoying everyone?"

Mike pulled up in the car. He looked at the two loaded sports bags that Nigel had struggled to get to the gate.

"Is that all you are bringing to the big meeting?"

Nigel flung the two bags in the boot. "Lets' go man. Head for the great hunting lodge, or camper to you."

Mike drove off, trying not to crunch the gears.

"I'm looking forward to this. Haven't looked forward to anything so much since...oh, beating you at tennis."

"As I can't remember that far back, I'll give you that one."

The car pulled into Mike's drive. They carried the two bags round to the camper that was parked in the back garden. Nigel remarked about the swimming pool looking clean. "I bet it's cold though?"

"No, it's heated."

"Well this is base camp. Go on in." Mike pulled at the sliding door. "See, there is quite a lot of space. We have an upstairs bedroom, and one downstairs. They are both doubles. Take your choice."

"Can't we just settle in first. We can sort out the sleeping later, can't we?"

"Sounds fine to me Nigel. You're the boss. It's your chill out adventure."

Beer cans opened and feet stretched across the bench seats,

the weekend was about to start.

"Well, what do you think of it then?"

Nigel looked around the camper.

"So where is the cooker then?"

"I'll give you a conducted tour. Pull that flap down, the one on your right. See, cooker, grill, and a sink. Behind that seat there's a cupboard to hang clothes. The couch that your bum is on, has storage space underneath."

Nigel looked up above his head. "What's up there?"

"Another cupboard."

"Where's the toilet and shower?"

"Toss off. You go outside for the loo, and I chuck a bucket of water over you for the shower. That's the best I can do for you. If you open that cupboard door, under the sink, this might make up for the lack of a toilet."

Nigel leaned forward and pulled the handle. "Man, it's a fridge for the beer."

"Well that and a little food I guess. And, if you lift that up, we have a table as well."

They both laughed. Their eyes met. "Mate, this is going to be a great adventure." Nigel said.

Mike put his hand out for Nigel to grip. This seemed to bond their friendship even more.

They had a couple of beers to help wind down, and then decided to have a take-away for their evening meal.

As they walked towards the shops, Nigel could not get the tennis club scene out of his mind.

Mike had known Sue as long as he had. He felt that he had to share what happened with someone. Not that it was anything to boast about, but more to find out if this had happened to the others. Life never told you about things like this. But how do you ask someone. Was Mike the one to ask? He could be trusted, as a best friend should be.

"Mike."

"Yes."

"Mike…"

"Look old mate, you've got the name right, but you don't have to keep on repeating it to me."

"Sorry."

"Is that it then?"

"No. Just shut up and listen."

"Go for it Nigel. The world awaits."

"Well, I went down to the club, just to play against the practice wall. I knew there would be hardly anyone there."

Nigel then went on to tell the whole story. He tried to keep to the point without adding to it. All the time he was telling the story he kept his head down, looking at the pavement. At odd statements he gave Mike a glance, just to see his reactions.

After telling the whole sequence of events, he finished off with…"I just stood there like a prat."

There was a long silence. Nigel waited for Mike to start laughing or come out with one of his funny remarks.

By this time, they had reached the take- away. Mike entered, without a word. Nigel elected to stay outside. His feelings were very mixed now, and he was feeling an even bigger prat.

Mike stuck his head outside the door. "What are you having?"

"Anything…what ever you're having…Thanks."

Mike came out holding the food. "Hope you like what I like? Come on, let's get back."

The two walked along for quite some way. Then the silence broke.

"I'm glad you told me about Sue. Do you know what, that makes me feel very special. Not many blokes would have the balls…sorry; wrong term to use…would have the guts, to tell that to anyone. Yes, I feel special."

"Mike," muttered Nigel…but it was clear that he had not finished.

"No. Shut up, it's my turn. I wish I'd had a mate to talk to. We've all had fuck ups in our lives. Did you expect me to laugh, or what?"

"Not sure what you would do."

"Well for sure you couldn't have had it off in the changing room. So it hardly matters if your arms worked or not." There was a slight smile that went with this statement. "And as for the time it took for you to shoot your load into your pants, so what!"

Nigel had no idea how to react. He just flung his arms around Mike, pulling him to his chest.

Mike, with his free arm, did the same.

They stood there for a moment. Mike then broke away. "Get off you daft sod. People might get the wrong idea about us. Anyway, you are squashing my prawn balls."

Nothing more was said between them until they got back to

base. There were strange feelings going on inside Nigel, ones that he had never experienced before. It felt so good; he was wishing it to last.

"Well this looks over the top to me. Much too much for me. Do you want some more?" Mike asked.

"No thanks. Do you want more beer, or are you having some wine?"

"Thanks." Mike said. "I"ll have wine."

"Red or white?"

They spread the maps out across the table. Mike decided that it was best to draw a straight line on the map, starting from home, down to Portsmouth. Once they hit Cherbourg, it seemed to be quite straightforward, Nigel suggested.

"It looks like a straight line across to the South West coast-line. About three days steady driving," said Nigel, looking quite smug in having worked it out by measuring with his thumb.

"You haven't seen me drive the camper, old mate. It's a pity you don't drive as well. And it's sad about your map reading. One good thing though, we should be OK in finding Cherbourg with a captain on board."

"Very funny."

With the map reading finished, Mike thought that they should sort themselves out for the night.

"Well, choose your pit. Upstairs or down?"

"If I have a choice, up top," Nigel said, looking up at the raised roof bed area.

"You can grab a shower. There's one in the cabin by the pool. You go first. I'll make the beds up, it might be too much to ask of you on your first night."

Nigel found his way to the shower. It was nice and hot. His old man must be loaded, he thought.

He grabbed up his clothes, looked to see that no one was around, and nipped across the lawn in his underpants.

The light was on in the camper, with curtains drawn. Nigel pulled the door open. Mike was standing there with a towel wrapped around his waist.

"This looks like home. I like the camper with the lights on."

"Yes. I bet it could tell a few stories."

Like my room, thought Nigel.

Mike went off for his shower, and Nigel climbed up into his sleeping bag up top. It felt snug and warm. This is the life, he thought.

His mind flashed back to Dean. Maybe it would not have been the same being away with him on this adventure. He felt comfortable with Mike. With Dean though, he would have felt the father figure.

You can't relax in that situation, he thought.

Just for a moment, Sue came into his thoughts. Just think, if it were her he was going away with, he would have to think of his every move, being a female. But with a guy, you don't have to worry about what you do or say. But then, it would be nice to have a nice warm body to cuddle up to at night...His thoughts were broken as Mike opened the door.

"Christ that shower was hot. You OK up there?"

"Yes thanks. I might even get some sleep in. It's great."

Mike was jumping around, trying to get into his bed. The camper rocked with his every move.

"Are you sure you are comfortable now?" Nigel asked.

Mike rolled over to on his back. Looking up, he could see Nigel's face peering over the edge of his bed.

"Mike."

"Yes."

"Thanks for lending me your ear about Sue and me. You don't have to answer this, but have you ever been in the same situation?"

"Now. I could give you a load of crap talk that you hear from other guys. We both know it's crap."

"No, I mean yes. I know what you are saying, but cut out the crap and answer the question...as a true mate."

"Well, I have had it away. But it was the biggest let down ever the first time. It was over so fast. I'd hardly started. What's more, she wanted to have another go. Shit, I couldn't raise it again. I felt my ego slide out of the car window."

"A car?"

"Yes. My old mans car. Maybe I could feel him looking over my shoulder, or should I say, bum."

"Is that the only time?"

"No. I've had a couple of goes since, but to tell you the truth, I don't think the situations were right for me."

"Why not?" Nigel asked, looking more than interested.

"Well. Picture the scene. It's a hallway. Her Mum and Dad were in the next room. It was one of those back against the wall jobs. Christ, it slipped out, and I heard her shout out. Funny really, I just pulled up my jeans, tucked it away, and ran home.

As for the other time, I prefer not to talk about it".

"What about you then. Have you had your end away?"

"Not much to tell really. I did have a blowjob after badminton in the church hall with a woman that was old enough to be my mother. And that's about it really. It means I attract the older woman I suppose. This may sound bloody daft, and I don't want you to laugh, but in my younger days, I was chatted up by other guys. I think they thought I was gay."

Mike kept a straight face. "And how about now?"

"I've never talked about this with anyone before, it makes me a bit scared in a way."

"Why?"

"Well, I don't want to loose a friend like you. Sounds bloody daft and girlie when you start talking about it. Shit, what must you be thinking? Must be the wine, I don't know. All I know is, it feels right talking it through with you."

"That's nice. Give us five." Mike raised his hand up towards Nigel's outstretched hand. "No problem. I know now why you want to get away to find yourself. As for the girlie bit, don't talk a load of balls. What's wrong is that people don't know how to open up with each other. That's how life gets screwed up."

"Thanks mate. Let's hit the sack before I make a bloody fool of myself."

"That goes for me too." Mike said, pulling himself into his sleeping bag.

"Goodnight mate."

"Goodnight, and thanks again." Nigel said. He was just drifting off when he heard Mike again.

"First one awake makes the tea."

The morning greeted Nigel with sunshine on his back. He slowly opened his eyes. It was a while before he could work out where he was. His thoughts flashed back to Sue and the chat with Mike last night.

"Come on. You can't lie there all morning. Take your tea."

"Thanks Mike. Didn't hear you making the tea down there."

"I cheated. I went indoors to make it. My parents came home late last night, so I made them one as well. They must have thought it was their birthdays again."

"It tastes good. It's nice and warm up here. I think I could live like this."

"Well, don't get too settled. Mum is going to spoil us with

breakfast. She said it would take about half an hour. So, if you want a swim, go for it."

"What about a costume? Never thought to bring one."

"Thought of that. You can borrow one of mine. There take your choice." Mike said, chucking a couple of pairs up to him.

Nigel eased himself down from his bed, trying to balance his mug of tea at the same time.

"Well, that was a sight the world should have seen. Hair's a mess, pants half way up your bum, and a balancing act at the same time. Bloody brilliant."

Pulling his costume on, Nigel opened the camper door. This is great. The sun is so warm, feels good. With that he took a running dive into the pool. Mike followed, swimming the length of the pool underwater. He was a good swimmer.

Hanging onto the rail at the other end of the pool, they both looked back at the camper.

"This is really living." Nigel said.

"Yep." Mike agreed. "It's a pity we have to go to college."

"Go on, let's do ten lengths and out," suggested Nigel.

"Right. Bet you don't even make the distance."

They both thrashed around in the pool. The water turned into waves as they raced each other up and down each length. Mike finishing first, waited for Nigel to join him at the shallow end.

Nigel pulled himself up alongside Mike. They sat there on the edge laughing and panting with the effort that had gone into the challenge. They both had super fit bodies. In many ways they could have been brothers.

"Come on you two, breakfast is ready," mum shouted from the kitchen. "Do you want to come indoors or are you having it in the camper?"

"Indoors please. That's if you don't mind a tramp at your table." Mike shouted back.

"We've put up with you all these years, so why ask today?"

Nigel thought this very funny. "I think she knows you well. You've met your match mate."

They hurried into jeans and sweaters and joined the family at breakfast.

"Did you sleep well?" asked dad.

"Yes thanks, Mr Alby."

"Call me John. I hate the formal names. I hear you are off on a trip of a lifetime?"

"Well yes. And can I thank you for your offer of the camper."

"You can."

"Well, thank you. And you as well Mrs Alby."

"That's Ann to you," She replied.

"Right. Thanks."

"Don't you think he says "thank you' so nicely," smiled Mike.

"At least he has good manners. Now eat up." mum said.

"Sorry mum."

"Don't you think he says "sorry' so nicely," Nigel said, looking across at Mike, giving him a wink.

"Game set and match, I would call that," said John.

"When I was your age, I went off on an adventure."

"Really Mister Alby, sorry John."

"Yes. It was called the army. Just for two years. Very enjoyable it was too."

"Oh Dad. Don't let's have that one over again." Mike pleaded.

"Wasn't that called national service?" Nigel asked, wishing to sound worldly.

"No. I made the mistake of joining up to get a career. I lasted two years, then asked if I could leave." He smiled at this.

"Dad. Do we really have to go into this again?" pleaded Mike.

"No. Only getting at you both. I wish I could have done what you are about to do. To go off and find myself. Sounds great."

"Well, look who you found…me. Saved you all that trouble." Ann said.

"That's another good reason you should go. So as you can get away from getting involved with women. They only want to settle down and put a rope around your neck. It's called love by them."

"What do you call it then?" asked Ann.

"Blackmail."

"Come you two. You make it sound like hard work being married." Mike said, looking up across the table at his parents.

"It is." John then got up from the table, giving Ann a kiss on his way out.

Breakfast over, the two returned to the planning of their adventure.

The route being mapped out in more detail than the evening before, with the vote going against the tunnel and in favour of the ferry crossing, based on this being good for the soul. These were Mike's words, which Nigel thought were just right for the summing up of the venture.

They spent the rest of the day writing endless lists of items that they would be taking with them whilst lounging on the lawn and drinking beer.

Around eight in the evening Mike got the car reversed, assuring his Mum that he had not had too much to drink. Then, declaring himself sober, he drove Nigel home.

They sat in the car upon safe arrival outside Nigel's house. There was a long silence with neither wishing the day to end.

"It's been bloody great." Nigel said, breaking the silence.

Mike nodded. "Don't go all daft again. See you at the club."

"I just hope you defend me from Sue."

"Don't worry. I'll get her to work on me next time."

"Then I hope you last longer than me."

CHAPTER 5

With the summer nearly at an end, Nigel started to think how he was going to pass the winter months. He was able to pick himself up with the thought of the coming summer in France.

He had two main sports to play the winter away, badminton and squash. Now with the tennis season finished, he could at least get away from Sue.

He did, however, have to attend the end of season prize giving. He had two cups to collect. One was for winning the men's singles and the other for the men's doubles with Mike.

Friday, the night of the presentation, Mike called round in his car.

"Hey! Who's the best-dressed guy in town then?" Mike asked.

"Well you can't claim first prize for that, so it must be me."

Mike, looking at his bow tie in the car mirror, suggested that Nigel might like to rethink that one again.

"It's going to be one of those evenings, is it?"

Mike said "Yep it could well be."

Looking over the table plan together, they found that Sue had been placed opposite them, on the same table.

"Well what a lucky boy you are. It's funny how life seems to play tricks like this on a guy. You will have her right in your sights Nigel, old mate."

"Oh shit. I could do with a drink. What are you having Mike?"

"Two largers it is then. Grab those chairs over there." Mike sat down. "Hi," said a voice over his shoulder. He didn't turn around, but he knew that it was Sue.

"There you are Mike me boy, get that down you. Seems to be a full house tonight. Don't turn around, but Sue is sitting just over there, behind you."

They had only just started their drinks, when the announcement came over the mic. "Please take your places for dinner."

"Hi," said Sue to everyone around. This was followed by another "Hi," to Nigel direct. He returned this with a nod of the head.

Nigel had only just started his soup as he felt something touching his groin area. He put his hand under the tablecloth. It was a foot. He looked up, as he kept hold of the foot. Sue was staring right at him. She had a smile on her face.

"Have you lost a shoe?" he asked.

Sue leaned forward. Her voice was just loud enough to be heard by him. "Yes, but have you lost anything worth having lately?"

Pushing her foot away, he tried to join in a conversation with Mike, just so he could take his mind off this little sex kitten. Shit, will she never give it a rest, he thought? Nigel drifted off into his own little world, even though Mike was chatting to him. But with Mike, he only had to grunt the odd word here and there, and Mike was quite happy in believing he was being listened to.

He was thinking that there must be more to life than the scene he was involved in now. What about college, the tennis club, badminton and squash? Was this enough for him. Was this going to be his lifestyle forever?

It would be easy to let Sue teach him about sex. But surely life was not just about all these things. There must be something else that he had yet to find. He thought about his home life and parents.

He was lucky to have parents like his. And there was Dean, poor sod; he had all this to come.

Mike shook his shoulder, bringing him back to earth. "They are dishing out the cups in a minute. Look as if you're interested, for Christ sake."

The club Captain introduced the president in a loud voice over the mic. The guests had to listen to about twenty bad jokes, mixed in with a back history of the club.

The Captain managed to wind him down and remove the mic to attach to the stand. This was done with a smile. He then went on to say some nice things about some of the cup winners. The presentations got under way. The winners of the mixed doubles being the first up on the stage.

Nigel was hearing most of this, but strangely, as if he was listening through a funnel. His hearing cleared as he heard the Captain announce the award for the most popular player of the year… he waited, surely not…it was, Sue!

She glided to the stage with all the poise of a model on the catwalk.

"There you are mate," Mike joked, "see how lucky you have been to have, er…" Nigel dared him to continue that line of chat.

"Don't say another word." Nigel said, giving Mike a look that could kill at ten paces.

The Captain then announced the presentation of the men's singles winner. After a few nice words, he invited Nigel to collect his winner's cup. He walked towards the stage feeling that this was all very false.

The Captain asked him to say a few words.

"Er, well, thank you. I'm very proud to have won this cup this season. And I hope to defend it again next season. Thank you."

"Well, a man of few words." Mike said, taking hold of the cup as Nigel sat down again.

The Captain announced the winners of the men's doubles.

They both walked towards the stage to receive the two cups. "You can do this one." Nigel said, pushing Mike forward.

Mike moved forward to the mic. He managed to drop his medal on the stage, and nearly let go of his cup trying to pick it up. "I never could hold on to two things at the same time," he was heard to say over the mic. This was greeted with loud shouts from the other members. Mike, now bright red in the face tried to explain himself. Nigel took hold of his arm, leading him away back to their table.

"Well that beats my speech. Come on, let's grab a drink."

Mike asked him if he was going to stay to the disco. He thought for a moment. "For a while."

The music was loud, and the lighting Nigel found was not helping him to relax. He was deep in thought again. He could understand why youths took to drugs and got stoned out of their minds.

How else could they stand the noise level? It helped them to travel to another planet. He was wishing that he were on one now. He found it strange that everyone believed they were enjoying themselves at events like this. He felt it to be a bloody false world he was living in. Surely there was more to life than this?

He could see Mike dancing. It was hard to make out with whom, but he guessed it was Jane. If it was her, this narrowed the field down a little. Where was Sue? She must still be around waiting to grab him. He went into panic mode. His reaction was to grab the first girl available to dance with.

"Hi Jean." He held his hand out, inviting her to dance.

"I thought you would be with Sue."

Choosing not to answer that, he led her through the mass of bodies onto the dance floor. They danced away, getting parted quite often.

Jean was nice. She was always there in the background at college. And at the tennis club she joined in most events, but was never pushy. Nigel had always liked her.

After dancing for quite some time, they decided to take a break. "Would you like a drink?" Nigel asked her.

"Thanks, a coke would go down nicely, with ice please," she said, feeling for his hand so as not to be parted through the mass of bodies.

"Two cokes please, one with ice." He had found a barman at last.

"Thought you would be on lagers?" Jean smiled.

He returned the smile. He thought he would have been well tanked up by now. But this evening he was not in the mood for beer drinking. Maybe it was Jean saving him from the clutches of Sue that was having a calming effect on him.

"Shall we take these outside?"

Jean nodded. "Yes."

As he fought his way through the packed bar area, he glanced around for Mike. There he was, arms around a girl. It wasn't Jane though. By the look of him, he thought, I doubt if he knows who he's with. Well that's my lift home gone.

"God, fresh air." He was not sure that he could take much more of the disco.

Jean had found some steps to sit down on. These led to the parkland behind the hotel. She patted the step next to her, but Nigel decided to stand for a while.

"This coke's very welcome. Thanks," said Jean.

"You're welcome." He smiled.

"I like it when you smile."

"Thanks. I didn't know I was on your college list of studies. Would I get high marks if I were?"

"I think you might make eight out of ten. Come on, sit down, it's too much looking up at you all the time."

He sat on the step just behind her, so that she could lean back against him. "That's nice," she said. "I like a man to take the lead."

"OK then. How is this for starters? Why did you say that about Sue and me back there?"

"What did I say then?"

"You said you thought we'd be together."

"So I did. Everyone knows that she has the hots for you. All the girls back away because of her. You must know your'e a wanted man?"

Nigel blushed at this. Jean seeing this laughed and laid her head back onto his chest.

"Sue means nothing to me," explained Nigel. "Let's not spoil the evening talking about her."

He was suddenly aware of the warmth of her body leaning against him. She turned and eased up to sit across his legs, facing him. Placing her arms around his neck, she gently brushed his lips with a kiss. He felt he was being invited to take this further. It was nice to have a girl suggest the moves, but then invite the guy to make the moves.

His kiss sent a message through her body. He felt that, and felt he was in control.

They carried on kissing as he felt her breasts pushing into his chest. She then unbuttoned his shirt down to his waist and he felt her hand explore his chest, finding his nipples to touch and pinch, driving him a little wild at the sensation.

His erection was well on time, yet she never took advantage of the fact that she was astride his lap. This was a new experience for him, one that was taking him to new heights. His hand slipped under her loose top. Her breasts were not large, but just as he liked them. They were sporty ones, he thought, the ones with those small boyish nipples that stood proud when touched.

After they had explored each other, and at the point when he thought that he really should cool off before things got out of control, Jean made the first move to control the situation. She stood up, adjusted herself and looking down at Nigel, offered her hand to help him up.

"Not just yet," he laughed. "It's not quite the same for a guy," looking down at his erection.

Once he had composed himself, he stood up to take hold of her hand. They slowly made their way back to the disco. Not a word was spoken between them; it had been a nice experience.

The heat of the dancing bodies hit them as they entered the hall again.

"Shall we get our coats and things and get out of here?" Nigel asked.

"Well my Dad is picking me up at eleven."

"So, you don't want me to see you home then?"

"I would have liked that if I'd known I was going to be with you."

"Well, maybe next time." Nigel felt a little down. It could have been a great end to the day.

"Yes, great." With that, she took his hand. "At least you could walk me to the car."

"Do I get my kiss now, or do I perform in front of your Dad?"

Jean gave him a kiss on his cheek. "There, I don't want to be seen as being over keen."

With that she ran towards her fathers car. Nigel just gave a wave as she drove off. He felt gutted.

He returned to the disco. His head was spinning. I must find Mike, he thought. Yes, find Mike.

The heat and noise was too much for him. He looked around asking people if they'd seen Mike. "Yes, I saw him over there." Someone shouted, pointing across the hall.

Nigel found him. He made a grab at his arm. "Mike, are you OK?" he asked.

"Yes. I've been looking all over the place for you. I've had enough. Let's get out of here." Mike said. He looked hot; his eyes showed the signs of drinking.

Leaving the cups in the hands of the Club Secretary, they walked outside to find the car.

"Give me the keys," Nigel said. "You're in no fit state to drive."

He waved to a taxi. Opening the door, he shoved Mike inside the cab.

The journey home was quite a laugh. Nigel had to keep pushing Mike into a sitting position. They arrived at Mike's house. Getting out of the cab was even more of a laugh. Mikes legs were not going in the same direction as his body. Somehow they got to the front door. On finding the right key, Nigel opened the door, and pushed Mike upstairs and into his bedroom. The noise of this disturbed the household.

Mr Alby appeared on the landing to help. "Don't worry Nigel; I'll tuck him into bed. This will cost him dearly. At least two car washes."

"Thanks. Are you sure you can manage? I'll get on home then."

"Right. I'll be fine. Goodnight."

Nigel leaned over the slumped body of Mike. "Who's a silly boy then?" But Mike could only manage a silly grin back by way of a reply.

Nigel kicked his feet along the pavement as he walked home, deep in thought. The evening's events spinning around in his head. This led to his thinking about life in general. What was happening to him? Did every guy go through the same emotions?

He reached home. Taking his shoes off, he climbed the stairs, trying not to disturb the rest of the household. Once inside his bedroom, he striped off his clothes, just leaving the bow tie. Standing to look in the mirror, he twirled it around. He stood there looking at himself.

Oh my god, he thought. Maybe what he was looking at was a clue to the mixed feelings he was having about life. Who was the guy in the mirror?

After a while, he opened his door and walked along the landing towards the bathroom. A pee and shower were required.

He heard Dean's door open. "Very nice. It was one of those parties was it?"

Nigel smiled, as he remembered that he was naked, and still wearing his bow tie. He raised two fingers to Dean, entered into the bathroom and locked the door.

The shower felt good. His thoughts were taking him back to the quick encounter with Sue in the changing room. Events such as that seemed to unfold a pattern in his life. He was not sure that he could handle his life being like this forever, as all he seemed to be doing was to masturbate in his room or in the shower. He relaxed against the tiled wall as he released himself of the sexual frustrations of the evening. Was this to be his life? Surely there were going to be times when he would feel complete. There must be a time in a guy's life when the right girl comes along, just so that he could experience and enjoy the ultimate act. He longed for the feel of that rush through the body of his stored up load. It happens on the videos he'd seen, but maybe that was all an act. He watched his love juices flow away once again.

His mates had boasted of their moments of passion. Christ, he thought, I wish I had someone that could be trusted, someone that could help clear his mind. Maybe he was worrying too much about the recent encounters he'd had.

He reached for a towel to dry himself off. At least he felt relieved of some of his frustrations now.

Crashing out on his bed, he lay there knowing that it was going to be a long restless night, as his mind refused to switch off.

Leaving sex aside, life seemed to be full of people just going through the motions of living. Surely there must be more to it than this. Look at college. They are not really interested in where you end up in life. The tutors just push you through a tunnel and out into the big wide world once they have done their bit. Next one please...thank you...next.

Look at parents. They go through the same old routine. But, I am lucky, he thought, Mum and Dad have sheltered me from things, maybe a little too much, but I love them for it. Soon they will be sending me out into the world to do something with this life of mine, he thought, but what?

Look at my social life. Yes, sports are about the only thing I am good at. I'm not having much luck with girls though. And although I have quite a few friends, Mike is the only one that I can really trust.

If you go to a disco or nightclub, everyone seems to think drugs are the in-thing. His mind continued to run around in a mist. Finally the long day caught up with him, and he drifted off into a deep sleep.

CHAPTER 6

It was the weekend again. Nigel had made entries into his diary about the events of the past weeks.

With the diary updated and the secrets he'd shared with his bedroom, he was feeling a little more stable today.

Mike arrived. He looked a little under the weather. The past evening had taken its toll on him.

"Fancy going to London this afternoon?" Mike asked.

"Yes, why not."

"We could go up on the tube, take a look around for a bit and then go to Zigzags. Haven't been there for yonks."

"Sounds good to me."

"Right. I'll go home and change. Meet you at the tube then."

London to Nigel was always an adventure in a way. It was the mixture of people and the life of the big city that interested him.

They got off at High Street Kensington as they liked to walk the rest of the way to Oxford Street.

"One day man, I'll have enough money to buy some of the gear in these places." Mike said, as they were looking in Harrods' windows.

"Even with money, some of the gear in there isn't for me."

"Look at that bum." Mike giggled. "Man could I walk along-side that. Christ, would we turn a few heads?"

"What, you or the bum?"

"Well if it were you, it would be, look at that bum, with that bum."

They walked along in a good mood, every now and then turning to admire the odd sight of female form, always followed by a witty remark from one of them. This always made their day.

They lined up outside Zigzags, ready for the bouncers to frisk them.

"OK gents. No drugs or weapons on you. In you go, and no trouble."

"Well, he could only have searched you mate," Mike said.

"Go on funny man, why is that then?"

"Well he searched you, and couldn't find your weapon. They

45

should employ Sue on the door."

"Oh stop, you are so funny…ha, ha."

The place was packed and the DJs music loud. As for the lighting, this always had a strange effect on Nigel. He felt as if he'd already drunk several pints before the evening had even started.

Mike looked around. "There's a lot of talent here tonight."

Nigel looked, and nodded in agreement.

Moving to the bar, Mike brushed passed three girls. They were looking and laughing together.

"Hey, do you want to buy us a drink?"

Mike looked at them. "Not really, we are only here for the beer."

One of the girls looked at him. "Well I expect you and your friend will have a good time." She blew him a kiss and added, "He's got a nice bum. It's a pity it's only yours to share."

Mike was about to shout his mouth off at this, but Nigel pulled him away towards the bar.

"Well they have us worked out." Nigel suggested.

"I hate girls like that. Christ, they piss me off. No style. It's sad, really sad."

Nigel once again gave a nod in agreement. There was not a lot to add. It only went to confirm what he was beginning to feel about life and the world in general. Turning slowly around, he could feel eyes watching him at the bar. He looked across to a small group of guys, just to the left of him. Not wishing to show that he'd noticed them staring at him, he glanced around past them, and then turned to lean on the bar again.

"Don't look now, but I think we may have trouble with that group of nutters behind us, just to our left."

"Here, take your beer." Mike said, handing Nigel a wet glass. "Thanks."

"Can I look now?"

"Yes, but don't make trouble."

Mike turned quickly; making out he was brushing his trouser leg down.

"I think the blonde one is nice too." Mike said, laughing.

Nigel turned, and looking directly at the blonde guy in the group, received a wimpish wave back.

"Yes, I believe I've scored again. Fuck me will it ever go away?"

They decided to join the dancing masses in the hope that they would get involved and chat up some of the female talent around.

Everyone just moved around in groups. They moved a few paces every now and then; there were no partners, just mass movements.

Nigel and Mike drifted apart. His body heat was reaching boiling point. The volume of the music beat through Nigel's head. He felt that it was almost like a drug, and his mind began to feel like a cotton wool punch bag.

He became aware that a girl was following him around in his drifting movements around the floor. Each time he raised his head for air, she was there. She smiled. He smiled back.

"You have gone," she shouted above the music.

"It's the noise, I'm Ok really. Do you mind if I try to dance with you?"

"Well, you may not have noticed but, I"ve been following you around hoping that you would ask me."

They danced together for quite sometime. Nigel thought she looked about eighteen or nineteen. The dress she was nearly wearing showed her figure off well. She had the sort of figure that he liked. The dark hair and red dress suited her. As they could only shout to each other over the music, he had no idea where she came from or what type of girl she was.

Their bodies touched several times. He put his arms around the back of her waist, pulling her closer to him. She made no attempt to pull away.

They were now getting tired. Their heads rested on each other's shoulders, as they swayed with the music.

"I don't know your name yet." Nigel whispered in her ear.

"Is that your best chat up line then?"

"It gets better after a drink. Can I get you one?"

"Yes, and the name's Tina."

They pushed their way through the crowd to get to the bar, with Tina trying to hold onto his hand.

"What are you going to have?"

"Just coke with ice for me."

Nigel ordered the two drinks, and they found a wall space to lean against. Nigel placed himself against the wall, giving Tina the choice of leaning against him or against the wall. The test worked out well, she rested her body against his, and he enjoyed the feel of her against him.

Tina explained that she was there with some friends, but not with a boyfriend.

Nigel told her that it was the same for him. He was just there with Mike, but no girlfriend.

He felt her move her body on hearing this. There was a slight pressure to his crutch area. His first reaction to this was to ease her off. He had been going through a period of let downs, and he was not sure he could take another right now.

He seemed to have little choice. He felt his pride and joy stir, and he thought that he should at least enjoy the situation, yet at the back of his mind, this was going to be one of those cheap thrill jobs that he was getting into again.

Tina gave him a peck on the cheek. "Don't get too involved tonight, I was just testing you out."

"Testing me out for what?" he asked, pushing her away.

"Just to see if you were gay or not. My friends bet me that you were."

"Point me in the direction of your...what did you call them? Friends, and I'll bloody well prove them wrong."

She turned and pointed across to a group of guys standing together along the same wall.

"What, those wankers?" Nigel laughed.

"Yes. Don't get up-tight, they are only having a bit of a laugh."

Nigel looked again at them. He caught sight of the blonde guy again. Taking her hand, he walked up to the blonde guy. His expression changing as he drew closer. He stood directly in front of him. The moment was tense.

"I understand you have sent one of your friends to test me out?" Nigel said, his voice quite calm.

"Not really. It was my way of getting to know you though."

"Do you want to know more?"

"That would be nice. I'm Wayne."

His mind was in a spin now. What was he thinking?! This guy was gay, and here he was now, about to put himself to the test. Wayne was keen on him, that was only too clear. Was this the way that gays acted? Did they pick up guys just anywhere? Should he punch him on the nose and run? So many questions ran through his mind, but something at the back of his mind was telling him that this was a chance to test out his sexuality. Too many times he had been thought of as being gay, through his good looks. So this could be the time to put this to the test.

"How well do you want to know me then?" asked Nigel?

Wayne moved closer. Their bodies were now touching.

"I don't know. I just think we could get on fine. I don't come to these sort of places just to dance."

Wayne offered his outstretched hand to Nigel to hold. "So you are out to find a guy tonight, and I'm that guy, am I?"

Nigel was now feeling very tense. What should he do? For Christ sake Mike where are you, he thought.

Wayne leaned forward to place a gentle kiss on his newfound friend's lips. At the same time, he took Nigel's hand that he'd been holding, and introduced it to his erect penis. Nigel felt a shudder run through his body. He had just experienced the feel of another guy's erection.

Neither of them moved. They stood together, staring into each other's eyes. Nigel now felt a hand on his own rising erection. Their eyes now drifted apart.

"There," said Wayne, "I know now that you have mixed feelings." He planted another kiss on the lips, and slowly pulled away from their body contact.

Nigel just stood there with frozen body and arms at the thought of what had just happened. His thoughts flashed back to Sue at the club that night. He moved his arms, just to test to them out. Yes, he could move them.

"I think you are a nice guy Nigel, but I am not the type that fucks up a young guy's life. I think you should find your friend, and go home. This is not the place for you."

Nigel walked away like a lost puppet. His mind now completely gone. He roamed around to find Mike. How the hell was he going to find him in this jungle of bodies? He had to go to the toilet first. Mike could wait.

He leaned over the basin, splashing cold water over his face. Looking up into the mirror, he could see the face of a confused guy. He found it hard to get his thoughts into gear. He knew that he simply had to get out of there.

After a while, he found Mike chatting up a girl, as was his style. Nigel went over to the bar and pulled at Mike's shirt, begging him to follow him.

They got outside. The fresh air started to clear his head now. Mike just followed him. Not a word being spoken. They both walked along with hands stuffed in pockets. They reached the tube station, and just as they were about to pass their tickets through the machine Mike started to shout out. "Hold it. What the fuck is up with you?"

"I don't want to talk about it."

"Well, thank you very much. I await your statement."

The tube train rocked them around. Mike could see that Nigel had one big problem to deal with. Being the friend that he was, he could see that he didn't want to talk about it that evening, so he remained silent for the rest of the journey.

On reaching Nigel's home, turning to Mike he asked, "Do you think I'm gay?"

"Yep, that's why I tag along with you. Bloody hell, what have you been at tonight?"

"Nothing, no…it's just that…oh shit. I'll tell you tomorrow."

Mike turned round and headed off home.

Nigel went to his room and quietly closed the bedroom door, trying not to disturb anyone. The last thing he wanted was having to talk to anyone.

There was not going to be much sleep that night. His mind was a mess. He had so many worldly things to put right. There were so many unanswered questions. He just had to get out of his clothes and take a shower. He managed to reach the bathroom without waking anyone.

The shower was inviting. Once again he was aware that he was washing off the evenings sexual encounters. He must be the only guy around that never gets to complete the sexual act.

He let the water flow into his mouth. He stood there, mouth open to the stream of water. Bloody hell, he had been kissed by another guy.

Should he work himself off again? Surely, all of these situations he had got himself into, and all the uncompleted erections were not good for a young guy?

He returned to his room, and crashed out on his bed, his thoughts became very active.

Was life like this for every guy of his age, or was it just him that attracted attention from both sexes? He had the pick of girls he knew, and there were a few that turned him on. Yet there he was, at the night-club, being kissed by another guy, and what's more he was getting a reaction to it all. Did that mean he had enjoyed the experience, and did this make him gay?

He started to drift asleep with his mind still active. The world was too big for him to deal with at this time. Life was good, but with all these emotions to deal with as well, he simply had to get away to clear his head.

CHAPTER 7

He awoke the next morning with a slight headache. Looking at the clock he had time enough to be able to lie there for a while longer. His thoughts started to roll through his head again.

One of the things that he hadn't thought about at the time was why did Tina find it funny leading him on like that? As when they were dancing together, she seemed nice, the sort of girl that he could get to like. She'd made the first move to see if he fancied her, and she soon found out. He smiled at the thought.

It must be that he was not as street wise as others. He had a lot of growing up to do.

His thoughts then turned to Dean and his small problem in life. It was not that long ago that he'd also gone through the same stage as him, suffering from the same fears at eleven or twelve. Now he was at that next stage in his life. As everything functioned in his body, as it should, maybe he should just enjoy the experiences as they presented themselves.

He could work everything out except the reaction he'd had at being kissed by a guy. Gay guys did this, but let's face it so do footballers, only to them it's called bonding. The more he thought about this, the better he started to feel. He had enjoyed the sexual contact with Tina, and strangely enough he had not disliked the experience with Wayne.

"Nig, do you want a cup of tea in bed, or are you getting up now?" Dean shouted out from the landing.

"Thanks, I was getting up anyway. I'll be down in a moment."

He pulled on his jeans and a sweater, splashed his face with water, brushed his teeth, and joined the family downstairs.

"Well, good morning. What time did you get in last night, or was it this morning?"

"About one, I think."

"Did you have a nice time?"

"That's a leading question." Nigel said, looking down at the floor with his answer.

He felt mum's eyes giving him the once over. "Are you getting enough sleep, you look a little pale?"

"Oh Mum, I have just got out of bed, and I've had a late night."

"Well you look pale to me."

As they were united as a family insisting that he looked pale, he kept his head down and just grunted the odd reply during breakfast.

"Nig. What goes on at a night-club, is it the same as a disco, with lots of girls?"

He decided not to answer this from Dean. Dad reminded him that he had been asked a question.

"Sorry little brother, I was thinking how to answer you. Yes, it is a little like a disco, but they are that much older."

"Do they have drugs and things?" asked Dean again. He was on a roll now with his questions.

"Yes, there are drugs around if you want them."

"And do you?" asked Dad.

"No, I don't take them."

"Have you ever taken them?" asked Mum.

"I have had the odd funny fag, that's all."

"What's a funny fag?" asked Dean.

"Bloody hell, do I have to have this as soon as I come downstairs?"

"Well, you do look pale to me." Mum said again.

Dad came to the rescue by changing the subject. Good old Dad thought Nigel. I guess he knows what I'm going through. He must have been young once after all.

I wish I could ask him outright about some of my problems. I bet he would skirt all round the questions. I doubt he could offer advice though. Maybe one day I'll ask him. The thought though of going through a session with him…shit; he could not handle that.

On the way up to his room, Dean passed him on the stairs. "Nig, can I come and have a chat later?"

"Problems?"

"Sort of."

"OK, later on this evening." He gave Dean a pat on the bum to help him up the stairs.

Not wishing to stay indoors, Nigel thought about calling in at Mike's and maybe kick a ball around in the park.

"Hi Mr Alby," he shouted down the phone, "Is Mike around?"

"That Nigel? You do sound posh over the phone. I'll see if he's out of bed."

Nigel could hear him thumping down the stairs; he was not light on his feet. Nigel used to kid him about this on the squash court. He could always hear him, even if he couldn't see him.

"Hello, is that Nigel?"

"Yes, sorry if you thought it was Sue calling you."

"Oh, very witty for you mate. So you are speaking to me this morning then?"

"Sorry about the mood I was in, but there was a good reason for it. I'll tell you all about it when you're ready to have a mind bender."

"I'm at your service. But that's not why you are phoning me?"

"I thought a kick around the park would be the sort of good for you, seeing as you have just got out of bed."

"Are you going to call for me then? I'll be ready by the time you get round here."

Turning to go upstairs again, he saw Dean bob back into his room. He gave a knock, and pushed his head around the door.

"Wish you would knock."

"I did. I was going to ask if you would like to come and have a kick around in the park with Mike and me?"

"There has to be a catch," said Dean. "Do I get a chance to kick the ball, or do I just fetch it when you get tired?"

"Look, do you want to come or not?"

"Please."

"Five minutes then."

The two walked to Mike's house bouncing the ball between them. It had been a long time since they'd been out together, Nigel thought. He was a nice guy to have as a brother. This would be a good time to ask him his problem. He posed the question.

"Oh it's nothing really. You know what we talked about in your room that time?"

"Yes."

"Well, I don't think I have that problem any longer now."

"You mean it's happened? Great, I told you it would be OK one day soon. So no more problems then?"

"Well, I think Mum is worried. I tried to put my sheets from the bed in the washing machine."

"As you always do."

"You know I don't, but I didn't know what else to do."

Nigel laughed aloud. He took Dean around the neck to ruffle his hair. "Don't worry; Mum has been through all that with me. I was advanced for my age."

Dean gave him a friendly punch on the arm. Nigel was thinking that life was quite tough at that age. Guilt was something hard to handle.

The three of them kicked the ball around for about an hour. Although they had been up half the night, they were feeling quite fit. Dean ran out of puff, the excuse being that he'd hurt his knee playing hockey at school. "It was OK yesterday, but it's hurting today," he moaned. Both Nigel and Mike smiled at this, and continued playing.

"How about going to my house?" Mike suggested.

Nigel had had enough of the running around, and thought it would be a good idea. "It's about time you offered, it's ages since I've been invited into your sin bin of a room."

They reached Mike's gate. Dean decided to go on home. "I'll take the ball with me, see you later."

Mike opened his front door. "Go on up. What do you want to drink?"

"Anything, as long as it's cold."

Nigel settled down on the chair at the computer desk. Looking around, he could see that Mike had the same style of room as his. The posters were a bit naff, he thought. He looked at the football poster of Chelsea stuck on the wall. They hadn't been to see them play for ages.

"Here you are old mate, one coke out of the fridge." With that he bounced on his bed. He looked at Nigel. "So?"

"What do you mean?"

"So what was all the silence about last night then?"

"This could test our friendship." Nigel said.

"Try me then." Mike settled back on his bed. "Come on man, let it flood out."

Nigel then went through the evening's events. His voice lowered when he got to the sexual parts. This only resulted in Mike asking him to repeat these, pretending he could not hear. Mike remained silent, with his face never changing expression. He just fixed his eyes on Nigel, but offered no help.

"Is that it then?" Mike asked.

"Yes. What would you have done?"

"Kicked him in the balls," came the swift reply.

"Is that all the advice you can offer?"

"Well. If you let a guy you don't know kiss you, then let him play with your prick, what do you expect me to say?"

"I suppose I'm asking you if you've ever had the same feelings?"

Mike thought for a while. "Are you asking me if I have had feelings for another guy?"

"Well yes. That's what I have a problem with, and I want to know if this is normal?"

"I think every guy has moments in his life that questions his sexuality. The problem is, nobody really wants to talk about it. Well, they want to talk, but who with?"

"But you haven't given me an answer yet."

"OK. I've had a couple of locker room situations. I was only fourteen, and I was just curious."

"Did you have any feelings for the guy at the time?"

"Yes, but not after I had tried my luck."

"Why?"

"Because in both cases, I ended up with a bloody nose."

There was a long silence, and then they both laughed.

"Nigel old mate. What I think your problem is, is that you have to find yourself. Get your life sorted out. You are living in a mist."

"Living in a mist." Nigel thought that was very true.

During the rest of the winter months, they both made their plans for the venture across France.

They were agreed that they would go across from Portsmouth to Cherbourg. This, they had worked out, would take them about five hours, long enough to collect themselves.

As they got closer to the date, the two mums started to overdo the food provisions they had taken on as being their contribution to the journey.

Once Dad had revoered from the shock of paying for the ferry crossing, his efforts were directed at the camper. Being one of the old VW camper models, he wanted to check it out. In the end he had given it a complete overhaul. Mr. Alby remained in the background, after all it was his camper, and to have someone do all the hard labour seemed a good deal to him.

Dean was keen to show that he could carry out such technical things as, playing the radio, checking the tapes. He was quite often removed from the driver's seat.

Mr. Alby was heard to give some sound advice on first aid. This was based on his stay in the armed forces. He even gave advice on drinking water.

So it came to the last weekend. The planning now over with,

and the families now feeling very uptight about it all, the time had now come for Nigel to go out into the big wide world to find himself.

Both fathers felt that a swift half at the pub would be the right thing to do in the way of a send off.

The pub was crowded. Once they had decided who was getting in the first round, they found a table and settled down to the birds and the bee's bit.

"Well, let's drink to the mission," was the opening remark from Mr. Alby.

They all clanked their glasses to this, with both Mike and Nigel sitting back for the profound words of advice that were to follow.

"Now I'm sure that you don't want me to delve into your private lives?" said Nigel's Dad.

"No," came the blunt reply from Nigel.

"Now hear what has to be said." Mr. Alby said.

"Dad. We have about twenty packs of the bloody things between us." Nigel burst out.

"So you think you are going to be that lucky do you?" smiled Mr. Alby.

Nigel asked as to why things like this were so important. On sitting back in his chair, he wished that he had not thrown this question into the arena.

The evening went on like this, with both Nigel and Mike trying not to explode with fits of laughter. Sure, they could understand their parents concern and some of the points raised during the evening even made them sit up and think. One comment, made by Mr. Alby registered with both of them. *"Life is cheap.'*

Once all the talking was over with, and some of the good advice received, they made a move to go home. It had been a good evening. Both dads, having already made several trips to the toilet, made one final visit. The lads waited for them to return. They seemed to take ages.

At last the door opened. They could be seen giving support to each other across the bar.

"Your dad's not looking too good." Mike said.

"Must have been the sandwiches as he always told me that he could hold his beer."

Nigel went across to help his dad. "Are you OK?" he asked.
"I'm fine."

"Good, because you were telling us earlier never to drink with strange people."

They all left the pub, each trying to convince the other that they were not the worst for drink. On reaching Mike's house, the four stood by the gate to say goodnight. This being repeated several times, they parted company. Mr. Alby was heard to shout out, "Nigel, don't they sell them in France any longer? They used to be called French Letters." Nigel turned to see Mike pulling at his Dad's jacket, heading him towards the house.

Nigel and his Dad walked with arms around each others' shoulders, not always in step. They reached their front door. It was sad to see a man trying to get his key into a lock when drunk. After a few attempts, he passed them over to Nigel. A couple of goes without luck, he decided that they were not the right keys anyway. He put his hand into his own pocket and found his own set. Turning the key, they staggered inside.

"Night son."

"Goodnight dad." He watched him safely into his bedroom before crashing out in his own room.

CHAPTER 8

Looking at his clock, Nigel could not believe he had his eyes open before the alarm went off. He'd set it for four thirty, just so it gave him enough time to get into shape for the journey ahead.

No time to lie there thinking. It was too late to have negative thoughts. The ferry was due to depart at eleven. So, a quick shower, followed by toast and coffee, then away.

As he approached the kitchen, the smell of fried bacon reached him.

"Mum, you are great. You should still be in bed."

"Couldn't sleep, so I had to do something."

"I bet you are going to worry for the whole month."

"Yes, I'm sure I will. Can't help it."

Dad appeared, already dressed. He was in the doghouse over his drinking. Mum had made it hard for him. The only way out for him now was to mow the lawn, and finish painting the window frames. Mum had a way of getting things done. Let him have some fun, then hit him with the guilt.

Mum kept going through the checklist of things still to be put in the camper. Right through breakfast questions were fired at Nigel, and his parents going over the items on the list, with each question being answered with just a nod.

Mike arrived with the camper. He quickly explained why he was so early. His parents had been driving him insane.

"Mine too. Have we got everything?"

"Don't you start that as well, else I'll go on my own."

Nigel dashed upstairs to collect the small bag with all of his personal items in. He stood there in his room for a moment. He started thinking about the adventure. What would the stories be on his return? His diary should have some good content after one month away. Looking at the poster behind the door, he blew her a kiss. "See you, take care of my room." With a deep breath he headed downstairs and out into the drive. His family lined up to say their goodbyes.

"Dean, go back and put something on, this is the front garden." Mum demanded.

"They won't know they are my underpants," he said, standing there with arms folded to keep warm.

"They might not know, but I do."

Nigel gave him a hug, and suggested he went indoors.

"Have a good trip Nig. See you in a month, you lucky bugger."

"That's enough of that kind of talk," said dad.

Nigel had a feeling that they should make a move. The family was getting uptight. So with kisses all round, including Mike, they set off down the road, waving out of the windows until the family were just dots in the distance.

As Nigel was the navigator, he suggested that they headed for the M3.

Mike gave a salute in agreement.

There was a burst of conversation at first. This was the nerves showing through. They were both feeling a little tense as they tried to cover up the thought that they were now on their own.

The odd question flashed between them such as, "have you got your passport?" Always a good way to calm the nerves.

They reached the M3 and read the signs directing them to Portsmouth.

"Right, keep over to the right. Bloody hell, that guy behind must have given birth," Nigel shouted.

"You only have to say it once. It would help if you could give directions a little earlier…Sir."

They arrived at the port with an hour to spare. They were directed into line after showing their tickets. "All went well and according to plan," suggested Mike.

"Yes, but that always makes me concerned. With my luck, we could land up on the wrong ferry. I don't go with all this going well bit."

"Come on mate. Who got you down to Portsmouth in one piece? Your navigator."

"Yes sir."

The ferry was not that full. They went up on deck to watch the sights as they sailed away leaving England behind.

They both leaned over the side of the deck rails as Portsmouth drifted away into the mist. They stood there, each locked in their own thoughts.

Nigel was the first to break the silence. "I think this is going to be a bloody good time. I feel as free as a bird, and what's more, I'm with my best mate for a month. Fuck me, life feels good."

"Stupid sod. I'm really looking forward to this. And what's more, I'm waiting for my best mate to buy me a beer."

The crossing was calm. They drove off the ferry with the time being just after four o'clock.

"Just don't say it...I'll remember to drive on the right." Mike said, with a look of concentration on his face.

Following the other cars in convoy, they headed out of the port. They just caught sight of directions to St,Lo. The camper liked the open road. The engine's roar was sounding sweet.

"Where should we pull in for the night?" Nigel asked.

"Let's leave it till about six to look for a campsite."

Nigel looked at the map, reporting to the captain that there were several sites on the route they were taking. The sun was still very warm. They saw signs coming up for camping. As it was just after six, they decided to pull in and inspect the next one on their right.

They could see that there were a few caravans parked already. They pulled up at the main entrance, and walked over to the reception office.

Nigel thought that he would take command and ask if they could camp for the night. He did this in a mixture of English spoken with a French accent, which made Mike smile. As the answer was in good sounding English, they both felt that this was going to be the right place to stay on their first night in France.

The camper rested in a nice position, away from the other caravans, but near the toilets.

"Nice one Mike, couldn't have done better myself."

"That comes with experience. One day you'll learn the art of driving. Come on, give me a hand to push the roof up." Nigel got at one end, and on Mike's count of three, the roof was raised.

They decided to eat light. The meal on the ferry was quite enough.

"Where did the wine get put? I feel the mood coming on for a relaxing session with the aid of good wine."

"You mean you want to get pissed?"

"Could be." Nigel smiled.

They talked and laughed well into the late evening. Nigel thought that they should head for the South Coast, and then head across to the boarder between France and Spain. Maybe, they could go into the Pyrenees. "It's supposed to be lush green countryside, and even snow on the mountain peaks." Mike agreed.

They flung their sleeping bags onto their beds, found their towels, and headed for the shower block. They found the gents showers around the back. The heat hit them as they entered. They found two cubicles next to each other. There were one or two others in the showers.

Nigel stripped off having turned the shower on. He stood under the jet of water and it felt good. Mike complained that he had no soap, and asked Nigel to share his.

"You won't want to share this now, I've just soaped my bum."

"Well, I'm sure the world wishes to know this. Come on pass it over, I'm not proud."

The plastic bottle of soap, having been tossed over the top of the cubicles a few times, landed outside in the washbasin area. As they were finished, neither was bothered. Nigel thumped around in his cubicle, trying to get one leg into shorts. He felt the weight of the plastic bottle on his back as it was tossed back to him.

"Thanks Mike."

"What for?"

"For throwing the soap back, nearly knocked me for six, you prick."

"Wasn't me."

They went to clean their teeth at the washbasins. A couple of basins along, a man turned and smiled. He collected his towel, headed for the door, and wished them "Goodnight." He spoke in perfect English.

"Bloody hell, he must have heard us." Mike said. "But don't worry, you only told him that it was your bum you were working on...it could have been..." Nigel cut him short.

They got back inside the camper, both feeling tired. It had been a long day. They pulled the curtains closed.

"This feels nice and cosy." Nigel said. "If it's warm now, in this part of France, what's it going to be like when we hit the south?"

Nigel leaned over the edge of his upstairs bed, watching Mike wrestle into his sleeping bag.

"Well that was a sight well worth seeing. Good job you've got pants on and the curtains are closed, else that guy in the showers might have got the wrong idea about us."

"He should be so lucky." Mike said.

"Talking of showers. Do you think they are all like these here?"

"I doubt it. I've heard that they have mixed ones." Mike answered.

Nigel laughed at this. "You must be joking; I'm not going to show off my manhood to all the French females. Sod that."

"They may not all be French."

"Tell me you are pulling my pisser."

"Well, I'm not sure about the showers, but some of the loo's are shared. We will have to wait and see. I can see it now. Women running out across the campsite shouting, "Nigel's got a big one."

At this point the conversation started to get out of control. Mike suggested that he could see Nigel taking showers in his underpants for the month. Nigel then suggested what Mike could stuff down inside his pants, so as to compete with him. Nigel kept on the longest. His voice getting softer as he started to drift off to sleep.

"Good night Mike."

"Good night my old mate."

The sun was streaming into the camper. It was hot already. Nigel had spent most of the night lying on top of his sleeping bag. He had no idea how he had managed to get out of it without falling down onto Mike's bed. It took a few moments to work out where he was. It seemed strange that he should be waking up in the camper, as all the material things he was used to seeing were missing. The poster. She would be missing her morning kiss. He couldn't dash along the landing to the loo; he would have to cross the campsite. Would the toilets be mixed? He didn't know this yet; Last night he "d just had a pee in the shower. This time, he wanted a dump.

He leaned over the edge of his bed. Looking down, he was greeted by a grin from Mike.

"Morning."

"Morning, Nigel, old mate."

Mike slid along his bed. He could reach the stove from his bed. He lit the stove and put the kettle on the gas ring. This task done, he turned over onto his back, so that he could chat to Nigel.

"Did you have a good night?"

"Not bad. Must have crashed out as soon as my head hit the pillow."

"Me too."

Mike had made the tea. He stretched up to pass the mug to Nigel.

"I think I'll have to make room for this before I drink it." He eased himself off his bed, with his back to Mike. Pulling on his jeans, he turned to reach for his sweater that was screwed up in the corner of his bed. Turning again, he bent down to slip on his trainers. Mike watched with a grin on his face. Nigel then pulled on the sliding door to open it.

Mike made a remark. "What did you say?" asked Nigel.

"I said, it's a good job I know you well. First, you stick your bum in my face, and then you turned to thrust your manhood into me, and if that were not enough, I'm presented with your bum again when you put your trainers on. Go on, run for the loo, don't want a flood in here as well."

Nigel pulled the door closed. He stood for a moment to look around. It was early, and people were walking towards the toilet block. He followed, trying not to run to show that he was now desperate. As he approached, he started thinking again. Would he have to stand in front of women, in full view, having a pee?

He walked around the back of the block. He could hear the showers in full flow. There were hardly any sounds of people talking. That's because they were all in their own cubicles. Surely then, the toilets would be the same. To his relief, he saw signs displayed for ladies and gents, with arrows pointing in two directions. He stood there, looking along the row of guys peeing, giving nods to those who caught him looking in their direction.

Mission over, he returned to the camper to have his tea. Mike was still in bed. With the door shut again, Mike made a move to get up. It was his turn now.

"What about the toilet situation then?"

"Well, you were right. I caught a couple of women looking down at me, and when I'd finished, I received a round of applause."

"You wish." Said Mike.

"Well you wait and see. I know you won't get the same reaction from the women as me, but you can dream and hope for better times."

Once they'd had breakfast, they hit the road again. The sun was low and bright, and already quite hot.

"If we head across to Orleans, we could reach Moulins by about four o'clock, or we could drive on to Roanne."

"If only you could drive, then we could drive through the night,"

Nigel reminded him that they were there for a month. "So what's the rush?"

The sun was getting hotter. They travelled well to reach Moulins by four, but Mike decided to travel on until about six o'clock. They missed the turn off to Roanne, and having discussed who was to blame for this, decided that they might just as well head for Lyon.

"Look," shouted Nigel. "There's a sign for camping, look coming up on our right. Must be just around the bend."

Mike heaved at the wheel. The camper managed to stop at the entrance, wheels dragging at the gravel drive. They both nodded that this would be an OK campsite. Nigel set about doing his routine bit of getting out of the camper to go through the booking in procedure. He felt that this improved his French.

They selected their spot to park for the night. As Mike was a little spaced out with all the driving, Nigel prepared the meal. It was still very hot. Being lazy, they could not be bothered to get the table out, so they sat down on the grass with their backs leaning against the camper.

"Tell you what. I saw a bar up the road, just around that bend you nearly didn't make, back in the village centre. Let's go and sample the local brew, shall we?"

They hid their money in the camper, locked the door and windows, and headed for the village.

"I've got about five hundred francs. What about you?" Mike had about the same on him.

The walk did them good. The sun was going down now, but it was still very warm.

Their thoughts and conversation being about home. They talked about Dave and Big Dave, and joked about what those two would have been like on this adventure. Nigel thought about Dean and how let down he had felt about being told he was too young to travel across France. And, as ever, the conversation got around to Sue. Mike thought that they could very well have let her come along with them, then they could have shared her. The thought brought laughter and a few smutty comments.

All this came to a halt. They were being approached by a group of teenagers. Mike suggested that they kept on talking and to keep their heads down till they passed them. They drew level, and to Mike's horror, Nigel gave them a friendly wave.

"Bonjour," said Nigel, smiling.

Mike gave him a nudge. "Fuck me, that gave the game away. I told you to keep your head down. And if you don't mind me telling you, you sounded as much like a French guy as my prick."

"Well, as I've never had a conversation with your prick, as you put it, what was wrong in me saying *"Bonjour"*?"

"Well, for starters, that's good morning. And, if you hadn't noticed, it's fucking evening. And if you don't mind me keeping on, apart from them thinking we are a couple of English prats and easy pickings for them, there are four of them against two of us. Not my kind of fun evening."

They hurried into the bar, seeking safety.

The bar was quite small. There were small tables lining the walls. They became aware that the eyes of everyone were on them. The conversations died.

They both leaned on the bar for what seemed ages. The barman stood looking at them as he continued to clean a glass time and time again with his tea towel. He kept holding it up and looking through it at them. At last he threw the tea towel over his shoulder and walked slowly along the bar towards them to take their order.

"Two beers please," Nigel mumbled.

Mike quickly repeated this. "Deux beers, s'il vous plait." He then turned to Nigel. "You're a bloody liability, that's what you are…you're a disaster."

"Well thanks." Nigel grinned. He watched the barman place the glasses over the water cooler. The beers were then drawn into the glasses and placed in front of them. Mike paid him, trusting that he gave the right amount.

The beer was ice cool, and went down a treat. They sat up on the high bar stools, one of which Nigel had collected from the other end of the bar. He said, "merci beaucoup" to the guy standing by the bar.

"I like the way they cool the glasses before they pull the beer." Nigel said.

Mike agreed. His thoughts then raced back to the clubhouse bar at home. These thoughts brought back a vision of Sue again, so he quickly dismissed them.

As they sat there, they had the feeling that the people in the bar were starting to gather around them. They soon found themselves surrounded by about eight or nine young French guys.

Mike leaned over to Nigel. "For fuck sake drink up fast. Don't show them that you are about to panic. Walk to the door slowly, and then run like hell.

They managed to look quite cool in walking towards the door. Once outside they walked a few paces, then, as if a starter gun had been fired, they ran for their lives. Just for a moment, Nigel had started off in the wrong direction. He turned and then caught Mike up.

They rounded the bend in the road, and looking back, they found they were not being followed. They reduced their escape to walking pace.

"Well, that was a close shave Mike, old mate. What caused that?"

"They don't come closer than that," Mike suggested. "I think they just wanted to take us on just for kicks, it's best not to get involved."

"Don't look now, but I don't think we are out of trouble yet." Nigel nodded ahead in the direction of their campsite. There were the group of teens they passed on the way to the bar, waiting outside the entrance.

"Oh fuck." Mike said. "This is trouble."

"Bloody hell, come on Mike, let's walk right through them, it's got to happen."

They decided to walk through the centre of the six of them, sooner than split up or go around them. Once in the middle of them, they had to stop. Looks were exchanged, and then the pushing started.

Before it got into a full-scale scrap, they heard a loud drowning voice that could be heard over everything that was going on. It was the French owner of the campsite. And with a few loud commands, the group broke up and started to move away. There were a few pushes and shoves before Nigel and Mike reached the entrance to the camp.

They both thanked the owner; both relieved that they had come out of it without a beating.

"No problem they are just bored. They do this every summer," he explained in perfect English.

Offering their thanks again, they headed for their camper. Mike opened the door and slumped down on the bench seat. Nigel grabbed a couple of beers and joined him.

"Christ what a day. That could have been trouble Mike, old mate."

"If you don't mind me correcting you again...that was trouble."

Nigel thought for a moment. "Why do people have to be like that? I'm getting pissed off, as it seems like wherever you go, there's trouble. It's a fucked up world."

Mike agreed. "Nothing seems to make sense anymore. There must be places that are trouble free?"

They talked around this subject well into the night. The beers now having their effect on them, not only the amount they were drinking, but on the number of times that nature called.

This found them standing side by side, peeing in the bushes behind the camper. It was too far to the toilets for the number of visits they would have made.

They found a tap for drinking water just a few paces from the camper. With teeth cleaned and water splashed under their arms to freshen up for the night, they retired, ready to sleep.

Mike suggested that as it was an effort to push the roof up for Nigel's bed, they could crash out on his double bed.

Nigel agreed. He yanked his jeans off, found his sleeping bag, which was under a pile of clothes, and climbed into it. He watched as Mike removed his jeans and climbed into his sleeping bag.

He had kept his pants and tee shirt on as well. He asked Nigel to move across and let him in.

Nigel thought that it was going to be too hot during the night. They were both exhausted from the day's events, and were almost asleep as soon as their heads hit the pillows.

It was gone three o'clock. Nigel lay there awake. It was hot, the sweat rolled across his body. He looked around him. The camper was a mess. With the washing up not done, he could also see the empty beer bottles lined up on the work top and the bottle tops that had not reached the bin when thrown still scattered around. Their clothes were in a heap...it was a complete mess.

He thought of home and his bedroom. If he was there now, and it was this hot, he would be striped off, and lying on top of his bed.

This was too much. Not wishing to awake Mike, he tried to undo his sleeping bag zip. It was not easy in such a confined space. Each move was carried out, an inch at a time, his body, now sweating in an unbearable way, with one last final tug he was free from his bag. He pulled his T- shirt off and used it as a towel to wipe the sweat from his face and body. He collapsed face down on top of his bed. He had thought about taking his pants off as well. If he were at home he would"ve done so by now. But as he was sharing with Mike, it made him think twice about this. Being a young healthy guy, most mornings greeted him with an erection. He was unsure about the Mike's reaction if he was seen like this, so he decided to keep his pants on. With his thoughts about life's problems still on his mind, he drifted off to sleep again.

Mike was the first to stir in the morning. It was coming up to eight o'clock and time for early morning tea.

He rolled over to nudge Nigel. He was still lying in the same position, face down on top of his bed, and as expected, having to hide his early morning erection.

"Bloody hell, that was a hot one," Nigel said, clearing his throat.

They looked around at the mess the camper was in and decided that they would have to keep this in check for the rest of their adventure. So with breakfast over, they cleared up the camper.

Pulling on their shorts and T-shirts, they headed for the showers. Nearly everyone was taking a shower at the same time, so they had to wait a while to grab a cubicle.

When Nigel returned, Mike was already seated in the drivers seat ready to go. Nigel checked around to see if they had left anything. With the engine turning over sweetly, Mike put it into gear and they headed for the open road again.

They travelled at a steady speed. The sun was getting hotter. Nigel remarked that his left arm was getting browner than the rest of him as he always had the window down to rest his arm on.

Le Puy was their first stop. They had lunch and a beer to wash the taste of garlic away. Although there had been a lot of chat between them, the last evening's events were not mentioned.

The scenery was beautiful. "Look over there to your right," Nigel said, pointing in the direction of a river that unfolded with the bend of the road. "It looks inviting. Shall we try to get down there?"

"Looks good to me." Mike agreed. "I could do with a swim right now, I'm bloody hot."

As Nigel's map reading was on the up, he announced that it was the river Ceze. We are getting near a place called Barjac."

"Are you sure this is the place?" asked Mike.

"It could be the river Ceze."

"Come on navigator, be a little more positive. Is it, or is it not?"

"Yes. Positive."

They seemed to drive around in circles for ages before they saw the sign directing them to Barjac.

"Look, there's a sign to a campsite over there." Nigel shouted, jumping up and down in his seat.

The little track led them down a steep incline and down to the river. Nigel did his duty again by leaping out of the camper to enter the reception. Mike waited for his return, smiling as he saw Nigel waving papers and maps in his hand.

"Looks like a nice place."

As soon as the camper was parked, they both changed into their swimming costumes and headed for the river. They returned the odd wave to people sitting around their caravans and tents. The campsite looked quite crowded, almost to the point that they had to weave through gaps between caravans, but nobody seemed to mind.

There were quite a few people swimming in the river. Mike thought that they should leave their towels and trainers in a spot they could keep an eye on them.

"The last one in makes the evening meal," shouted Mike.

"You're on," shouted Nigel, as he was already on the run.

They both dived in, and swam quite some way under water. When they broke to surface, they were near the other bank.

"I think you are in for the cooking, Nigel old mate."

"Don't really mind. This is great. I'm going over to the other bank."

Mike joined him. They sat there looking around. The river was not cold, rather more refreshing. In the distance they could see what looked like white cliffs towering over each side of the river. Trees lined the banks as far as they could see. The water was deep enough to swim in, and they could see that there were signs of white water downstream flowing around carved rocks standing proud out of the water.

"Look Mike, I can see canoes, lots of them."

Mike stood up, and shielding his eyes from the sun with his hand, agreed that he could see them as well. "We'll have some of that tomorrow, that's if they hire them out."

"I tell you what Mike..."

"What?"

"We have got to get in some serious sunbathing. Look at the colour of some them."

"Give us a couple of days, and we'll leave them cold."

They dived in again and swam around for a while. Both tried to duck each other. Mike almost managed to pull Nigel's costume off, but on listening to his begging him not to, he gave up.

With this Nigel went under the water again, made a grab at Mike's trunks, and with one swift tug of them, he swam to the surface to wave his success in the air.

"You bastard." Mike called out.

Nigel headed for the bank. He took in quite a lot of water through laughing so much.

Mike swam around, found that he could stand up, and started to walk towards the bank. He stood there with the water level around his navel. First he made threats, then came the pleading.

Nigel was enjoying the situation. After a while, he chucked the trunks back to him, but only after making Mike promise not to do anything back at him.

They sunbathed attempting to at least get a start with a tan, with the evening meal being the next priority.

"I don't know about you Mike, but I hate having to walk around in a wet costume?"

"Got no choice, unless you want to get arrested mate."

They sat there outside the camper in the evening sun. "That was a nice meal. Couldn't have done better myself," Mike said.

"Well at least I don't have to wash up. Pass the red wine over."

Feeling relaxed and at peace with the world now, they settled down to one of their deeper conversations. Although they had talked in the camper earlier, there had still been no mention of last night. Nigel had felt restricted in sharing his sleeping quarters with another. It was not just Mike; it was about being with another person. Was this a normal feeling and did Mike feel the same?

"Mike, you know last night?"

"What about it?"

"Well when we shared your bed."

"What about it?"

Nigel was feeling that his timing was not quite right. He shouldn't have raised the question. As they were going to spend a month together, there was plenty of time. But the point was, this was going to nag away at him. If only he could only relax more. Christ, he thought, he is my best mate I have shared most things with him.

"And, the point you were trying to make was?" asked Mike.

"Never mind, it will keep."

On being a little more organised tonight, the roof was already raised for Nigel's bed. The sleeping bags laid out, and the camper nice and tidy. They were now ready to go to the clubhouse for a quick drink before turning in for what was going to be another hot night.

"Your turn I think," Mike said.

"Deux beers, s'il vous plait."

"I bet you are English?" said the barman.

"How did you guess?"

"Well not very good French. Anyhow, I'm Dutch. What's more, I can spot and Englishman from ten paces."

"All you Dutch speak very good English," Mike commented.

"Mostly."

"In that case, do you know where we can hire canoes from?"

"Yes you can from here. Just put your names down on the list over there, and give me a deposit of 200 francs."

They both said "Thank you." They drank up their beer, and went back to the camper for the night.

CHAPTER 9

The sun streamed down into the camper. The patterns from the curtains danced around with their movements in bed.

Nigel thought back to the night in the bar. He was pleased that they hadn't stayed too long; as for some reason he was not able to relax. Once again his mind went over what was fast becoming a big problem with him. He was not at ease with himself or life. There seemed to be so many unanswered questions. How could he feel restricted in the company of his closest friend?

He had observed the people in the bar, they all seemed to have to drink so much before they relaxed. He had listened to conversations. Some German, some French, and quite a few Dutch. He liked the Dutch they were friendly. There were a couple of girls from Holland he would have liked to chat to. Mike had made a pass at one of them, and it had to be the one he liked. He had tried to tell Mike that she was too tall for him. Mike responded by suggesting that they were all the same height lying down.

"Are you going to get out of your pit?" Mike asked.

Nigel leaned over the edge of his bed, asking if that was a greeting. Mike was lying there, naked on top of his sleeping bag.

"Good morning. I see you are up with a bright start." This was the only thing that he could think of saying at the time. He was feeling overdressed wearing his briefs and T-shirt. Now he really was feeling confused. He moved back from the edge of his bed for a moment. The camper started to rock with Mike's movements below him.

Nigel looked again. Mike was standing up trying to pull on his briefs.

"Don't pull the curtains yet. Don't want to show my all to everyone."

"Sorry," said Nigel. "I was only taking a peep outside. It's going to be another hot one." He then went into thought mode again. Mike hadn't been bothered about lying there naked in front of him, yet he had been concerned that others outside might see him. So that meant that he was comfortable in his company like that. Maybe he didn't have to ask questions now, all he had to do was to relax and be natural.

"Come on mate, we have a canoe to catch."

Nigel scrambled out of bed, pulled on some shorts, shoved his feet into his trainers, and dashed after Mike as he was heading for the toilet block.

After a good breakfast, they collected what they thought they would need on their canoe trip. Things like, towels, bottled water, a sweater and swimming trunks. No jeans, just shorts, as it was going to be too hot.

As all the canoe's looked the same, they just choose the first one that was handy. They lifted it between them the same way they had seen the experts on tele do. Mike took the lead by walking into the shallow water until it reached his knees, and then remembered that he was still wearing his trainers. The trouble was as Nigel was holding the rear-end, he had to follow.

The canoe rocked around in the water. Mike told Nigel to hold her steady. He then placed one foot in the canoe, lost his balance, and fell backwards into the water. As it was not deep, he just sat there. Nigel was pissing himself with laughter.

"Would you like me to get in first?" asked Nigel.

"No."

Mike tried again. He managed to get in this time, not quite as the textbooks advise, but he got in. Then, with a smug look on his face, he took hold of one of the paddles and suggested that Nigel joined him. With a lot of luck Nigel managed to get in first time, almost without a problem. He sat down and removed his trainers, which he had been reluctant to let Mike know he also had been wearing to launch the canoe.

They pushed off, weaving their way downstream through the rock formations.

Mike suggested that it would be better if they did not both paddle on the same side, that way they might actually go in a straight line instead of circles. This being agreed resulted in them canoeing in a straight line, and looking more professional. They soon gained confidence, so much so that they felt they had enough control over what they were doing that they could take the chance to wave back to others canoeing in the other direction. They felt good.

The scenery was beautiful and the sun was getting hotter on their backs. They had paddled for about an hour when Mike suggested that they stopped for a swim. They drifted to the bank, finding the water quite shallow. The canoe grounded to a halt and they attempted to get out.

"You get out first, and I'll get out next." Mike suggested.

Nigel, placing a leg over the side of the canoe, got out and started looking around. Mike remained seated as he watched Nigel search around inside the canoe.

"What the fuck are you doing?"

"I'm looking for the other guy."

"What guy?"

"Well, you told me to get out first, and you would get out next...so I thought there was a third guy around, and I'm fucked if I can find him."

"Oh, we are so bloody funny. If this is going to be your mood of the day, I might go back."

"Well, you can bugger off, and take your mate with you."

They both stood on the bank to look at the view. The white cliffs made a brilliant backdrop. It seemed so peaceful. They listened to the sound of the water swirling around the rocks. There were sounds of birds singing their tunes to each other. These were sounds they had never taken time out to listen to before. They stood there listening for ages; it was a new experience for them.

"Well, how about this swim then?" Mike said, as he waved to a group of passing canoeists.

Nigel collected their costumes and towels from under the canoe seats. Mike had overlooked that they were still wearing their shorts. They headed for some bushes to change behind.

"Pity there are so many canoes going up and down, else we could have taken a dip without these," Mike said, trying to remove his shorts under his towel.

"Not a perfect world," said Nigel. He was making a mess of changing. One leg refused to go into his costume. He was hopping around on one leg. Mike enjoying the scene gave him a gentle push, which shot him through into the bushes. He stood on the bank, one leg in his costume, and one leg free. He hurriedly pulled his costume on, looking to see if he had been seen by anyone.

"That could have been a sight for the world to see." Mike laughed. "Come on, put it away man, and let's have this swim."

The water was warm, and this was just what they needed at this moment. They fooled around in the water. The bank on the otherside was just right for diving off of. They had competitions as to who could dive and stay under the longest. After they had used up their surplus energy, they lazed around on the grass bank to sunbathe. Their suntan was now passable. After a couple of hours of this, they decided to get on their way again.

There seemed no point in changing back into their shorts, as their costumes had dried on them.

This time they mastered the art of getting into the canoe. Paddles in tandem, they headed down stream again.

They had canoed for about half an hour. Nigel was aware that he could hear laughter, which sounded as if there were crowds of people ahead. As the river had many bends, it was hard to work out where it was coming from. They were certainly happy voices, he thought.

"Can you hear that in the distance?" he asked Mike.

"Yes. Sounds as if we're coming to another campsite, or there is a festival going on."

Their rate of knots increased. They were ready to take a break again. "Hope we can get something to eat and drink at whatever is going on up there."

As they rounded the bend, Mike thought he saw movements along the riverbank ahead. But as they were some way away, he was not sure whether his eyes were playing him up.

"Nigel old mate, I don't want to excite you too much, but I swear I saw a group of people up there, and they were all naked."

"Just a few kids mucking around I expect." Nigel suggested.

"No, look through the trees to your left. See them, tents, caravans and loads of people. I swear they aren't wearing anything."

"What the tents?"

"No, you prick. There are people running around naked. Look Nigel, see through there."

"Bloody hell! You're right. I saw them. And look up stream."

They could not believe their eyes. They rounded the bend in the river, and before them was a sight that was about to bring another dimension to their lives.

Before them, left, right and centre, were what seemed to be hundreds of naked families, swimming and playing in the river and up on the banks.

Their canoe came to a holt as it just drifted without direction whilst they collected themselves.

Nigel was the first to break the silence. "Think we should turn around and go back?"

"Why?" asked Mike.

"Well it looks private to me."

They both sat there as the canoe still drifted towards the scene. They could see to their right, youngsters climbing the white cliffs where they stood on a ledge, all bunched together. Others sat around on other levels watching and waiting their turn to dive or jump off into the river below.

The scene was unreal to them both. Should they go on, or turn back?

Nigel took control. He started to paddle forward again.

"I gather we are going through this little lot then?" Mike muttered over his shoulder. With that he started to paddle as well.

There seemed to be such a mix of people. It was very much a family reserve. They paddled slowly through the nude swimmers, and kept to the left bank in order to avoid the youngster's jumping and diving off the cliffs.

A swimmer surfaced just in front of them. He was able to stand in the water. Seeing the panic on Mike's face in trying to avoid him, the man took hold of the front of the canoe, and directed it around him.

"Thanks. Sorry about that." Mike said.

"No problem. Are you from the other campsite?"

"No not really. We were just out for a paddle. We came in this direction by mistake. Is it private?" Mike enquired.

The man smiled. "The campsite is, but the river is not, it's free to everyone."

"Oh, that's OK then. We thought it was private." Mike added.

At this point, the man was joined by two youth's. They were about twelve or thirteen, thought Nigel.

"Are you Dutch?" one of them asked.

As Nigel had been feeling out of things up till now he answered, "No, English."

The man and the youth's were now joined by a group of their friends. Even the mother made her way down into the river. This is turning out to be quite party, thought Nigel.

There was a short burst of talking in Dutch. The man, who was the father, explained to the group that Nigel and Mike were from England, and just passing through.

"So you are not naturists then?" asked the mother.

"We are not what?" Mike asked.

Nigel gave Mike a shove on his arse with his foot. "Naturists." he said.

"No, sorry," answered Mike.

The father laughed at this, and told them not to worry. There were many people that came in their canoes and were amused to find so many nude people around.

"I'm not amused," said Nigel, "I think it's great, I had no idea there were places like this."

The mother suggested that they might like a drink. "You both look hot."

With the canoe being pulled towards the bank by the youngsters, they were not able to take a vote on this, so they both just sat there until the canoe grounded.

The father looked on amused. "I think the lads want you to join us. You are very welcome, our tents are just up there."

They both tried to get out of the canoe together, which only resulted in a complete mess. Nigel decided to sit down again and let Mike crawl out first. Mike then stood there looking around.

"I don't mind you holding the canoe steady while I get out," Nigel said.

"Sorry old mate."

The father and the lads stood waiting for them to join them.

"I don't believe this is happening to us." Nigel said.

"Neither can I. Pinch me please. Tell me it's all a dream." Mike added.

They followed their newfound friends along the riverbank passing couples and families sunbathing nude around their tents. They both returned the waves and smiles that greeted them.

They approached the tent. "What would you like to drink. We have beer, wine, coke or orange?"

They both agreed on coke. "With ice?" the mother asked.

"Please," Nigel said. Mike gave a nod. He was still looking around.

Mike asked if the canoe would be all right with all their things in it. The father assured them it would be fine. He offered them a seat. The rest of the group sat down around them on the grass.

The father made some introductions. His name was Erik, and his wife's name was Anita. As he could not remember all the youngster's names, he pointed to one of his son's. This is number one son, Jon, and the other son's name is Jack. The rest of the group called their names out in turn. Both Nigel and Mike shook each of their hands in turn. It was too much to try to remember all of their names.

They drank their coke, it went down well. They also took up the offer of some Dutch chocolate spread on a kind of biscuit.

"Are we going to get into trouble by just walking into the campsite like this?" Nigel asked.

"Not at all," said Erik. "You are very welcome, and as long as you are in our company, you will be fine."

Anita suggested that they might like to look around. Mike asked her if there were any rules that they should know about.

Anita smiled. "There are a few rules. The first one is that you do not go in the swimming pool wearing a swimming costume. Another rule is, you should always sit on your own towel when you sit down on chairs."

Nigel made a move to stand up. Anita laughed. "You are still wearing your costumes, so you are alright."

With that, Erik suggested that they collected their own towels from the canoe; he would then show them around the campsite.

Nigel nodded at Mike. They offered their thanks for the refreshments and started to walk back to the canoe. They waved again to the same people that they saw on their way in.

Nigel broke the silence first. "I can't believe that this is happening to us. We only came out for a paddle up the river. I just don't believe this."

Mike suggested that they just went with the flow.

On reaching the canoe, they just stood there looking at the scene around them. Mike summed it up with a profound statement. He estimated that there were at least a hundred in and around the river, and they were all naked. So if it was wrong, then there were a lot of folk doing it.

"The thing is, Nigel old mate, do we do a runner, and paddle like hell out of here, or do we join them?"

Nigel gave this some thought. At home he would be nude in his own room, it made him feel free. Apart from walking to the bathroom naked, he had never experienced being nude with others around. How would he react to this?

"Well, take your time." Mike said.

"What if we do strip off and I get an erection, I could be evicted surely?"

"Well, that goes for me as well." Mike suggested.

They both decided that it was worth taking that risk. Nigel, with one quick tug at his costume, stood proudly naked for a moment. He then grabbed his towel just as a precaution. Mike looked around just to see if anyone was watching. He then removed his costume as well. They each took a deep breath, and then headed back in the direction of Erik and family.

"This feels bloody great," Nigel said, flinging his towel over his shoulder.

"Well you had better keep one hand free," Mike suggested, "look around you."

The people that they were now passing for the third time waved to them again. Most smiled a knowing smile. Nigel was thinking that they must all have gone through the same experience when it was their first time being nude in front of others. He was also aware that they were not staring at them; they just carried on sun bathing.

Erik and Anita were waiting for them. They had been watching the scene, and there was a slight clapping of hands from them. Nigel thought that this was not just a welcoming to a new lifestyle, but he felt that this was a sign that they had just passed their first test of social freedom.

Erik led the way to show them the campsite. They were joined by the small group of youngsters which helped them to feel more relaxed.

They walked up a steep pathway leading to the first of three swimming pools. They tried not to stare at the nude sunbathers as they passed them. It was beginning to feel quite natural to Nigel now. His thoughts returned to home again. How would he be able to explain this to mum?

Erik, who suggested that they should take a swim, cut his thoughts short. He then showed them by example by taking a running dive into the pool followed by his two sons.

Nigel, not waiting for a second invite, made the perfect running dive into the pool. Mike decided that he would do a bomber and landed at Nigel's side. Once the waves had settled down, and he had surfaced; the two of them swam several lengths of the pool. They held on to the edge at the deep end, gasping a little from the effort they had put into this display. They tried to sum up their feelings.

Nigel said that he had never felt so free in his life before. "It feels great swimming in the nude, doesn't it?"

Mike agreed. He also suggested that if there were signs of having an erection, the pool was the right place to get this under control. They both looked down into the clear water just to check this statement out. The others joined them swimming, and they fooled around in the pool for quite a long period. Nigel was thinking it felt good.

They collected their towels, spread them out on the pastel coloured paving slabs around the pool, and settled down to sun-bathe.

"Well, how was that then?" Erik asked.

They both answered at once. Erik listened, and smiled. "I gather you are not too keen about this naturist way of living then?"

"Truly, I have never felt so free as this before, it feels great." Nigel answered.

"Where is your camper?" Erik asked.

Mike told him that it was parked at a campsite upstream. "It's about an hours paddle time in the canoe. That reminds me, we should really think about getting back."

"Is it a nice campsite?" Erik asked.

"Quite nice, but nowhere near as nice as this one." Nigel replied.

"Then why don't you bring your camper over here tomorrow and stay for a while?"

Mike looked at Nigel. "That would be great, but is that possible to arrange?" he asked Erik.

"In Holland, every thing is possible. And when we are in France, we make it possible," came the reply.

They sat around the pool a little longer soaking up what they were seeing around them. Nigel kept shaking his head and saying, "this is great." He watched the mix of people enjoying the late afternoon sunshine. He remarked to Mike about the various shapes and sizes of the naked bodies lazing around. "And look at the youngsters, not a care in the world," he remarked.

Mike agreed that the whole scene was hard to take in all in one go, but he could get used to it.

They started to make a move. Thanking Erik for the invitation to join them the next day, they made their way back to the canoe.

Mike remarked that he would not have believed that he could walk around naked, surrounded by so many good-looking nude females, without having a permanent erection on.

Nigel laughed at this. In his mind he had been thinking the same. Yet there he was, naked, and free to walk unashamedly amongst other nude people. It was something out of a storybook.

They made a better launching of the canoe. Although they were paddling upstream now, they seemed to have renewed energy. There was about half a mile to go before they rounded the bend of the river that took them into the area of their campsite.

He was still trying to get his head around the days events when Mike broke the silence.

"If we are going to join Erik and family, we would have to get our bums brown quickly, or else everyone will know that we're newcomers."

"True. Is my bum really that white?" Nigel asked.

Mike inspected it. "In my opinion, it could be a better match to the rest of your body."

"Well thank you."

They clambered out of the canoe, clutching towels around their middle sections, dived into the bushes, and pulled their shorts on. They were getting quite expert at this now.

The canoe glided into the shallow water where they had to return it to . The attendant asked them if they had had a nice day. Nigel answered, "you will never know."

"Shall we eat at the clubhouse tonight, or shall we cook?" Mike asked.

Nigel thought it would be less bother to eat out.

They unlocked the camper; the heat hit them, so they quickly opened up all the windows to let the air flow through.

Mike opened up the fridge and passed Nigel a beer.

"I can't sit in here." Nigel remarked. He climbed outside the camper, and sat down on the grass. "Shit, it's uncomfortable in these shorts."

"What a day." Mike said, joining him on the grass to drink his beer. "I feel I have visited another world."

"Well, we have." Nigel said.

"What did you make of it?" Mike asked.

Nigel smiled. He knew that they would get into deep discussion on this one. So before it got too deep, he suggested that they went for a shower. They could then have their meal, chill out with a bottle of wine and discuss the day. Mike agreed.

Mike asked for a clean towel from the cupboard. "I think I'm going to change into my other shorts and T-shirt, so if you find them with the towels, chuck them to me please."

Nigel decided that he would have a change of things as he had been wearing the same shorts for a couple of days. He thought that he was in need of a clean T-shirt also, as the one he had been throwing around in the canoe looked disgusting.

"Close the curtains your end mate." Mike asked.

"Oh, come on," said Nigel, "nobody is going to look at you

changing.

As they headed for the shower block, Nigel thought, here we go again. Men in the men's, and ladies in the ladies. It was not like that at the naturist campsite. He was not sure, but although he had only been there a few hours, he was positive that he saw everyone going into the same shower block together. That would be a good point to discuss tonight.

The showers were full. All the cubicles were in use. Mike ran to the first one to become free, giving Nigel a V sign as he did so.

Nigel had only to wait a little longer for a cubicle to become free. He stripped off, letting the jet of hot water shower down on him, it felt good. He looked down at his backside; he would soon get the tan to catch up on it, but what about his front. Sunburn on his dick. Bloody hell, he would have to watch out for that one he thought.

They both met up outside. Mike remarked that he thought Nigel looked a lot better now he was clean and dressed ready for the evening. "You scrub up well," he said.

The meal was good, and the wine went down well. Nigel tried to swing the conversation around to the events of the day. Mike would not talk on this, as he wanted to save this till later in the evening.

On the way back to the camper, they both went for a pee. Nigel thinking again about what he thought the arrangements at the naturist camp was for this. He was sure that they shared the same toilet block. He wished now that he had paid a visit there.

Although the sun had almost gone down, it was still very hot even though it was nearly ten o'clock. They passed one or two caravans with people sitting around outside drinking. Although they had given several waves and nods to people, there were only a few that bothered to wave back in return.

As it was still hot, they decided to sit outside the camper. Nigel opened the first bottle of red wine, ignoring the comment about room temperature. They then settled down for the rest of the evening's summing up of the day and a little male bonding talk. Both of them agreed that they would not hold anything back, as after all, they had come away to find themselves on this adventure. At home, they found that there was always pressure on them, and they never felt free to talk about each other's problems. Now was the time that they could feel free to open up with each other.

"I think I want a couple more glasses of wine inside me first." Mike said, opening the first bottle of red.

"That goes for me too," Nigel said. "But I don't want to get too pissed, because I really do want to have some true answers from you." With that, he finished the first glass in one gulp, and held it out for a refill.

"Are you going to be embarrassed by all of this?" Nigel asked.

"I doubt it. But I don't think I would open up to anyone else other than you. I value your friendship. I only wish other people could be like us now. Fuck me, everyone so strung up about life."

"So where do we start?"

Mike suggested that they should sum up the trip so far.

Nigel thought on this one for a moment, then said, "Great."

"But don't you feel we should have relaxed a little more by now?"

"Do you mean with each other?" Nigel asked.

"Yes. Fuck the others. I'm talking about us."

"Well we have only been away for a few days, so it's hard to be that relaxed."

"You are the one that doesn't care a fuck at home. I can think of many a time when I've caught you in your room, and you carry on as if I weren't there." Mike said, with a smile.

"Is that a bad thing then?" Nigel asked, as he tried to think of a time Mike had caught him off guard.

"Not a bad thing at all. I always felt that we shared a special trust, and that means a lot to me."

"So what are you getting at. You must have a reason to bring this up?" Nigel asked.

"Well, let's go back over the last few nights. I don't know about you, but I felt that you were a bit concerned about being in close contact with me?"

Nigel thought on this. "That's funny, I have been feeling the same way. On the first night, I kept my pants on. I wasn't sure what you would think with me being starkers. Then when I looked down at you, bloody hell, you were wearing nearly all your gear, plus you curled up in your sleeping bag. So who's the reserved one now?"

It was Mike's turn to think on this now. "Yep, you're right, I didn't know how to handle the situation. Funny really, we've both been thinking the same things about each other."

"Right, said Nigel. So let's agree, sod the world then, and what we do in our camper is up to us."

"Agreed," Mike said. He then went on to give his views as to what he thought about the rest of the world. He felt that it was in a mess. The powers to be, tutors at college, and all the others that made up the rules, had no right to tell him what he could or could not do with his life. So, when it came to what he wanted out of their friendship, there was only one other person that had a say about it, and it was his mate Nigel. With that he sat back, smiled, took another gulp of wine, and looking at Nigel said... "There."

"I'm not sure that I can beat that." Nigel was feeling quite special now.

They were silent for a while, just looking at each other. Mike broke the silence. "More wine?"

Nigel held out his glass. "Please." He was not sure that Mike could handle the questions that were burning inside him though. What if he took it the wrong way? How could he explain about the sexual feelings that he had about people? Females were no problem. It was all right to have sexual feelings towards them, but what about having similar feelings towards another guy? Maybe Mike had the answers to some of these questions now, having heard his rules about life. He was going to have to chance his luck with whatever he asked Mike. The next few minutes could have an effect on his life.

"Come on mate," Mike demanded. "I've done all the ground-work, and you have just been sitting there. If you have to take that amount of time to sort out your questions, then you can't think much of me as a friend. Just go for it, or we can change the subject."

Just at that moment, a group of campers passed. Mike gave a wave to them. One of the men walked over to them hands in pockets. He stood there for a moment, cleared his throat, and in an educated English speaking voice addressed them both. "We are in that caravan over there. I trust you are not going to stay up most of the night making a noise? We have to make an early start."

Mike remained sitting. "I don't think we are making any noise at all."

"Well, we could hear you from up there."

Mike asked him if he could make a suggestion.

"What's that then?" the man asked.

"Why don't you piss off now? This would do us all a favour."

"That way you could be making a very early start." Nigel added.

The man then, in true English fashion, turned and walked away muttering about the youth of today. "Rude little buggers."

They both sat back laughing at the old guy. "See what I have been saying?" said Mike.

"Yes. So you can add to your list, 'people', what's the matter with them?"

"Let's get back to what we were talking about." Suggested Mike.

"It's not that I'm so mixed up, it's just that I want to talk things through with someone that I can trust to give me straight answers and not to laugh at some of my problems."

"Well we have come to the right part of the world, that's good for starters surely. And what's more, we have landed up in a naturist reserve. So old buddy, you had better get yourself sorted out with your sex life at least, as once you get amongst that lot, you will never know who or what you are."

"Well let's sort that one out first. Are we going to join Erik and family tomorrow?"

Mike had no problem with that question. "Now that I have got over the shock of finding myself amongst a mass of nude people, I think their way of life looks great. It sure beats college."

Nigel thought that it was time to hit Mike with some of his mixed feelings about life. Getting up from his chair, he suggested that they settled down in the camper for the night, and they could then talk on in bed.

Mike agreed, and he thought that it was best to be lying down when the wine kicked in.

They went through the routine of pushing the camper roof up. Nigel then climbed up onto his bed. As it was hot, Mike had thought about leaving the sliding door open, but that would put them in the spotlight to the rest of the campsite, so he closed it with a thud.

"I bet we don't have the same problem at the other site." Nigel said.

"Hadn't thought of that. What about having to share the loo's with women?" Mike asked.

"And what about sharing the showers then? Bloody hell, I don't think I will be able to handle that."

"Handle what?" asked Mike.

Nigel just smiled.

They thought that the swimming was the easy bit to deal with. But as their thoughts raced away with them, and their minds invented funny situations that they dreamed they could find themselves in, plus the wine beginning to have effect, their laughing began to give them pains in their guts. Nigel pleaded for them to stop.

The laughter went on well past midnight. Nigel was aware that he had been talking for a while, but there was no response coming from Mike below decks. Looking over the edge of his bed, he looked down only to see that Mike had drifted off into slumber land. So much for question time he thought. He had fucked it up again. Mike had given him the opportunity to talk about his sexuality…and he'd fucked up by talking about everything other than that. He reached down to remove the glass Mike was still holding, then crawled back on top of his own bed, falling asleep, almost within seconds himself.

CHAPTER 10

Nigel felt a tug on his pants. "Come on mate, do you know what time it is?"

He guessed that it was about eight o'clock, but when he was told that it was nearer ten, he shot up on his bed, hitting his head on the camper roof.

"Tea, and a tablet for your head Sir." Mike said, handing him a mug of tea.

Pulling on their shorts and T-shirts, they headed for the showers. Mike thought that they should hit the road before eleven thirty. Nigel agreed.

As the showers were empty at this time of day, they decided to have a sing along. This consisted of singing, then at the end of each chorus; they banged on the cubicle partition between them, keeping in time with each other.

On their way out, they passed the man that had been giving them a lecture last evening. They both felt a little sheepish.

"Thought you were leaving early this morning?" Mike asked him.

The man turned, looked back, and with a look of thunder on his face said, "Piss off."

"I love it," shouted Mike, as he waved to him over his shoulder. "Have a nice day."

The camper ready for the road, with breakfast only consisting of toast and coffee, they set off to experience their new lifestyle.

The entrance to the naturist campsite was easy to find. Although they had to drive down narrow roads, they kept seeing signs that read FFN. They were quite small, but could be seen placed in the grass verges and hedgerows en route.

The road that led to the main entrance was about a one in seven. Mike did a good job in getting the camper around the narrow bends. They stopped at reception. Nigel decided to stay in the camper and let Mike do the booking in routine this time. He watched him enter the office, and it dawned on him that Mike was the only one wearing anything. The scene was quite novel, Nigel thought.

He sat there looking around at the scene. If all the women

are like those two over there, reading the postcards from the small bookshop, then they were in for a good time, he thought. Bloody hell, good looking, and with all-over tans, beautiful.

Mike appeared from reception. He glanced across at the two young women, and smiled, as only Mike could.

The two women had said something to Mike, so he went across to speak to them. Nigel could not hear from where he was sitting. Mike was smiling a lot. Bugger, thought Nigel, he gets all the fucking luck. Look at him, smooth bastard. He watched as Mike walked back towards the camper.

"That was nice," Mike said, as he opened the driver's door.

"I bet it was, I could tell from your face. What was all that about then?"

"It was a bit of a downer really. They told me that I looked a new recruit. Do I look new?"

"Yes." Nigel said.

They looked at the map of the campsite. "If we go down this road, we should come to a track on our right, which leads down to the river. With any luck, we should find Erik and family." Mike said. He looked up from the map. " You haven't been listening to a bloody thing I have been saying, have you?"

"Yes I have." Nigel muttered.

"You fucking well haven't. You've been staring at the two women. You could go blind you know."

"I'll take my chances on that one." Nigel grinned. "So everything was OK then. Can we stay?"

Mike nodded, and then produced two cards. They were about the size of passports. "These make us members of the naturist movement". He passed them to Nigel to look at.

"So how much did you have to pay for these then?"

"Well, let's put it this way, you now owe me seventeen quid."

Mike released the hand brake, and the camper rolled down the steep road leading down to the river. They saw the track on their right. It just about took the width of the camper, with the bushes brushing against the sides.

They looked around for a level pitch to bring their camper to rest on. Mike drove forwards and backwards a few times, as Nigel waved his arms around giving directions as to the right spot. With the engine still running, Mike looked out of his window, and beckoned Nigel over to the camper. Once they were close enough to hear each other over the engine, Mike caught hold of Nigel's ear, pulling it towards his mouth he uttered words of simple meanings. "Look mate, this is a camper, not a fucking aeroplane, so cut out the fucking arm waving crap. Just tell me when we are level."

Nigel suggested that he found his own level. He then sat down to watch with a big grin on his face. After another few attempts, Mike switched off the engine, swung his legs out of the driver's seat, kicked the door shut, and joined Nigel.

"What a master." Nigel said.

"What a prick." Mike replied.

"Is that it then? It doesn't look very level to me, but then you're not a pilot."

"And you are not a prick, because they are useful."

They locked the camper up and started off to find Erik and family. They passed the same people as they had passed the day before. Once again, waves were exchanged.

Erik got up from his seat to greet them. The whole family was seated at the meal table.

"Well, you did come then? We thought that you might change your minds."

Mike said that wild horses would not have held them back from coming. Erik asked him to explain this. Mike decided it was not that easy. He wished he hadn't said this.

Anita invited them to join them for some food. Erik interrupted her. "You can only join us if you remove your clothes. And what about the towels? Remember? Naturists have a code of conduct, so the quicker you learn them, the more you will enjoy your stay."

"Sorry," Nigel said, removing his things on the spot. Mike had walked on a little. He stopped, removed his clothes as well. With shorts and T-shirts now removed, they headed back to the camper to collect their towels.

I guess it's no clothes from now on, thought Nigel. Maybe this was the freedom of body and mind he was searching for.

"Does this feel strange to you?" Mike asked.

"It did yesterday, but strangely, not today."

They once again passed the same people, and more waves were exchanged between them.

When they returned to Erik's meal table, the food was already waiting for them. Placing their towels on their chairs, they sat down to enjoy the meal and company. They now felt comfortable.

As they started to eat their meal of various meats and a salad,

Erik started to real off some of the simple polite rules of naturists. These included, towels on chairs, no costumes in the pool, no clothes to be worn when the weather was good, and it was polite to keep the noise down after ten o'clock at night.

"Is that it then?" Nigel asked.

"Yes, just plain simple polite rules." Erik replied.

"Where have you parked your camper?" Asked Anita.

They pointed down towards the riverbank area.

"That's fine. It's near the toilets, and you have running water there as well, and an electric link up. You see, you are fast becoming naturists, as you are beginning to work out the easy route of living." Erik laughed.

Anita suggested that Erik walked down to double check that they were going to be comfortable where they had parked. Erik summoned them to walk with him back to the camper.

The three of them stood inspecting the campers position. Erik suggested that the camper be turned around. "You see, you want the sun to be entering your sliding door side in the mornings, and then the sun would also be going across them during the daytime. In the evenings, it would still be warm in your eating area."

With this, Mike climbed into the driving seat again, started the engine, and reversed into the newly selected position.

"There," said Nigel, "If you had listened to me in the first place, you would have known what I was trying to tell you."

Mike looked to see if Erik was looking in their direction, but as he was more interested in looking over the camper, Mike was able to sneak in a one-finger gesture to Nigel.

"There, I will leave you now. If you want anything, you know where we are. Just be good, and the owners will allow you to stay."

With that he headed back up the track, leaving them to soak up their new nude freedom.

They sat outside the camper, looking at the view. They looked out across the river to the other bank. There was a backdrop of white cliff face, with ledges that formed small tracks that climbers over the years had worn away on their route to the top. At each level they could see youngsters, teenagers, and a few brave parents, jumping and diving freely nude, into the river below. They watched what was almost a relay of naked body's climb out of the river and clamber up the cliff face again. Nigel remarked that they reminded him of ants in the way they formed a con tinuous trail. Just in front of the camper lower down the grass bank, naturists lazed along the narrow beach. Every now and then, they would wade into the river to cool off, then return to watch the diver's from the cliff face.

"What a brilliant sight." Nigel said, as he sat there watching the scene. Turning to Mike he said, "Who would have thought that we would have been sitting here together, in the nude, like this. Only a week ago we were stacking all our designer gear away in the camper, thinking that we were going to kill all the women with our good looks and flash gear around France this holiday. But not us. Here we are, sitting here naked together, enjoying the freedom, and what's more, we haven't even unpacked any gear."

"Do you know, Nigel old mate, I can't believe that I could be sitting here, sun on my manly torso, stark naked…and not even a hard on. What's more, it feels so bloody natural." He laughed at this, then placed his arm around Nigel's shoulders, giving him a hug. "Yes, bloody great."

Nigel's reaction to this show of friendship caused a slight stir in his system. The body contact made his thought process activate again. The feel of Mike's body against his *should that stir him?*

This was certainly going to be a testing ground for his sexuality. In a way he was glad that he had not got into talking about his feelings last night. There would surely be a right time to pose the questions about life to Mike.

"Who's for a swim then?" Mike stood up to stretch his naked body. Nigel looked up at him. He had the type of body that other guys would kill for. Just watching Mike like this gave him a strange feeling inside, but he had to clear his thoughts on this one. Mike was a bloody good friend, and he didn't want to mess with the thoughts that ran through his head.

"Are you coming for a swim, or are you going to sit there in thought for the rest of the day. What are you thinking about anyway?" Mike asked.

"I was just thinking about what your mum would say if she could see you now." He lied.

"I can hear her. Get yourself covered up, there is someone at the front door." Mike laughed.

They ran down the bank together, dived in and swam to the opposite bank. There were not too many people in the river now, as it was lunchtime. They clambered up onto the bank and stretched out to soak up the sun.

"That was a bloody nice feeling swimming starkers like that." Nigel said.

"Yes. Makes you think about what you've been missing all this time."

Nigel sat up to look around. "Look at those two." He pointed up at the cliffs. Mike turned over to see. There were a couple of youth's standing on a ledge. To their right, there was another group about to join them. As they gathered on the ledge, they all greeted each other with a kiss on each cheek.

The sight of this fascinated Nigel. He had just seen kisses exchanged between both sexes. To the youths, this seemed quite natural. Back home, maybe two girls might exchange a kiss, but for two guys to do the same. No way! Maybe this was part of the answer to the question of his own life.

"Are they all French, do you think?"

"I would think there is quite a mix of continental blood up there. It's nice to see scenes like that though," Mike said.

With that, they heard shouts of joy, as one by one, the youths splashed down into the river below. Some dived, and others just jumped. There was a lot of messing around once they were all in the water. Then the process repeated. One by one, they climbed back up the cliff face and onto the ledge again. Then with shouts of encouragement they dived back into the water.

"Do you want some of that?" asked Mike. The look on Nigel's face was more than a verbal answer.

They both stayed in the sun for most of the afternoon. They took several swims to cool down, but the main purpose was to get their bums brown.

Nigel looked down at himself. With continual turning over, he was getting an even suntan. He turned to Mike. "Look, my balls feel as though they have been in the sun, and look, my dick has stood up to the sun quite well. I expected to be suffering."

Mike said he would prefer not to have to inspect his private areas, then added, "but I am quite pleased for you."

They were now feeling famished. So with one final swim, they headed for the camper. They felt that they were beginning to fit into the scene now. They returned the greetings of the naturist families they passed. Some waved, others just smiled.

They had only just opened the camper door, when they heard voices.

"Hi. Are you staying long?" The question was in English.

They both turned to look out of the door to see three girls standing there. Two had fair hair, the other was quite dark. They all had good figures, and looks to match.

"Don't blink," whispered Mike, "I think we're in luck here."

Nigel just stood there, mouth open, as he tried to answer the question. "About a week." His voice sounded like a young choir-boy. He cleared his throat, "About a week."

Mike corrected this right away. "A week at least or maybe a couple. It depends who we find here...I mean, what we find here to do. Is there much going on?"

"Our parents have asked us, to ask you, if you would like to join them for a drink?" one of the fair-haired girls asked.

"Oh, you're here with your parents then?" Mike said looking out through the camper door. He returned a wave from a couple sitting outside the next caravan.

"Yes, we have the caravan next to theirs."

"That's nice," Nigel said, his voice now returning to normal. "What are your names? I'm Nigel and this is Mike." He said.

The dark haired girl introduced herself as Nina. Her two friends were sisters, Jodie and Ariel.

Nigel and Mike shook hands with the three of them. It seemed the English thing to do.

Nigel guessed that they were all around seventeen. He should have been feeling self-conscious, standing there in the nude, shaking hands with three naked girls, but he didn't. *Strange* he thought.

"Well, are you going to join us for a drink?" asked Nina.

"Thanks." Mike replied. He nearly suggested that he would put something on, but stopped in time to remember where they were. He closed the camper door and locked it.

"Now we know you are new." Ariel said. "You don't have to lock up at naturist campsites. Naturists are very trusting, and can be trusted also. Never a problem," she added.

They went across to be introduced to their parents. They were offered a chair, but they sat on the grass seeing as they hadn't brought their towels with them. Nigel smiled about the fact that they were learning the rules fast.

The parents asked how long they had been naturists. Nigel suggested that they couldn't claim to be naturists yet, and then went on to explain how they had canoed around a bend in the river, only to find another world awaiting them.

"Did you not know about us then?" the father asked.

"We had no idea that places like this existed." Mike told him.

"You must call me Jon," said the father. "And this is my wife Tina." He then started to introduce his daughter, only to be told that the introductions had already been done.

"Sorry, I must be feeling too relaxed." Jon said.

As they talked, Nigel was aware that he could see movement in a small hike tent pitched at the side of the two caravans. He watched as a young guy crawled out. He was about eighteen. His long black hair was pulled back into a ponytail. His body was lean and very tanned. He had one of those faces that told the world that he was his own man.

Jon looked over his shoulder at the youth. "This is my number one son, Josh."

Josh smiled at the introduction. And with a slow movement of limbs, offered a handshake.

He sat down on the grass, crossed legged next to Nina, and then proceeded to roll a cigarette. Nigel watched this. He thought Josh was clever by using just one hand to roll it so neatly. And with a lick of the paper, the job was completed.

Both Nigel and Mike were asked a series of questions about England and what they were going to do in life. Jon seemed very interested. Nina suddenly asked if they were going to the bar later in the evening. "There is always a disco going on each evening."

Mike asked if this was an invite?

"You don't have to have invites, you just turn up," Jodie said.

Nigel suggested that they should eat first. "If it's OK with you all, we will join you at the bar later."

Tina asked if they had enough food. "You are welcome to join us to eat."

Mike suggested that they should use up some of the food they had with them, just in case it went off in the heat. Some of it has to be eaten by tonight. He thanked Tina for the thought though.

Saying their thanks for being so friendly, they made a move towards the camper. "See you later."

They sat down in the camper, and started to prepare the meal. "Fuck me," Mike said. "I think we're on to a good thing with this lot."

"So which one is yours then?" asked Nigel.

"Believe it or not, I think it's going to be Ariel. I think there was a little bit of the hot's for me there."

"Well, that's fine by me. It leaves me free to tackle Nina."

"Well, the way you were staring at Josh, I thought it was going to be him. You almost made a pass at him."

"Now what makes you say that?"

"It was the way your eyes never left him, from the time he crawled out of his tent, till we left."

Nigel chose to ignore this.

After a smallish meal, and with the washing up done, Mike suggested that they went for a stroll along the riverbank. It was still so very warm.

Nigel took a quick look along the stretch of river they had been lazing around that afternoon. The banks that had housed so many families were now quite deserted. He was not sure that he wanted to go for a walk.

"If you don't mind, I think I would like to chill out a little. I would like to catch up on my diary."

Mike picked up his towel, and headed towards the river. "See you later then."

Nigel settled down on the couch. It felt great just to lie there naked. The sun still being warm with a stream of sunlight sprayed across his body, this was heaven, he thought. What had he been missing all his life?

He jotted down some of his thoughts in the diary. Some of these thoughts started to make him feel horny. As nobody was around to witness this, he felt a great sense of freedom. He continued to write, and he enjoyed feeling this way. After all, he was not offending anyone, and he was quite proud of his manhood. Some girl was going to be lucky one day. At home, although he had the freedom of his bedroom, this was so much more relaxing, and what's more, felt very natural.

After a while laying there, he suddenly felt quite tired. He lay back on the coach and drifted off into a light sleep. His diary slipped to the floor.

Mike walked along the riverbank. Nigel had been right; there were very few people around now. He looked way into the distance where he could just see a couple making their way back to the camping area. He stood alone. How great it was to have this feeling of naked freedom. Here he was, standing on the bank of the river with the sun streaming down on his nakedness. This was really living, he thought to himself.

Across the river he could see some rocks standing proud out of the water. He took his watch off, flung his towel on the bank, and let himself ease into the river. He swam towards the rocks, the current guiding him towards them.

He swam around to find a foothold, and pulled himself up onto a flat surface. These rocks he thought, had supported many a naked body in its time.

He lay down to catch the remaining sunshine. The sun was now very low in the sky. The scene was so perfect. He looked down into the clear water where he could see fish swimming around the rock, making their quick dashes to the surface catching the insects that dared to settle on the surface. He felt that he was living in a world of his own now, yet surrounded by a new way of life.

Nigel was not sure how long he had been asleep. He heard a movement outside the camper. Someone was knocking. He sat up, trying to collect his thoughts, and leaning forward, he stuck his head outside the door. It was Ariel.

"Sorry, were you asleep?"

"Drifting, but that's OK. Come in and take a seat," he said, moving across to make room. Thank God his erection had retreated, he was thinking.

Ariel sat down, not alongside him, but on the other couch. She looked around. "This is nice. Who sleeps where?"

"This is Mike's bed down here, and I sleep up top. It's all we need really. Not too much to have to clean up."

"I've come to talk about tonight. Do you mind if Josh joins us?"

"No problem. Why do you ask? I thought everyone could go?"

"Yes, but Josh is a loner really. I didn't want you to think he was joining us to be our big brother. It's just that he finds it hard to make friends on his own. But he's a really nice guy, maybe too nice, I think."

They talked for a while before she decided that she should get back. Halfway out of the door, she turned and said, "I can see Mike in the distance, so you wont be on your own for long. See you later."

Mike arrived. Pulling the curtain to one side of the door to peer in, he gave had that smirk on his face that suggested everything. "Have I interrupted anything? How was it for you then?"

"You have a dirty mind. It was nothing like that, we were just talking."

"I'm your best friend, you can tell me."

"Did you meet anyone down by the river?" Nigel asked.

"Only the fish," replied Mike. He still had that smile on his face. Nigel wasn't sure what that meant.

Mike was keen to find out what had been going on in the camper. He kept firing questions at him.

Nigel thought about stringing him along with a story line of some sexual encounter with Ariel, but decided not to. He did tell him that they were going to be joined by Josh for the evening.

"Strange that she had to come and see you just to tell you that." Mike said. "Are you sure you are telling me everything?"

Mike got a couple of beers out of the fridge, then spread himself out next to Nigel.

They both lay there silent for a while, taking stock of the days events. Nigel was the first to break the silence. "I just can't believe all this. Here we are, lying naked together; door wide open for all to see, but nobody takes any notice. What's more, there's been a nude girl sitting where your bum is now, and we were just talking. I just can't get my head round this."

"Did you have your legs crossed?" Mike asked.

"No, felt quite at ease about sitting here with her, I don't think she looked at my dick."

"I can understand that," joked Mike.

"No, really, I didn't get a reaction with her. Ariel has a smashing figure and good looks, but I didn't get aroused. Explain that if you can."

"Maybe I should remind you about the reason why we came away on this adventure. Correct me if I'm wrong, but wasn't it to find out about your sexuality and fucked up thoughts on life?"

"Yes, I suppose you are right."

"Well maybe you're about to find out that you could be more attracted to people like Josh?"

Mike looked Nigel straight in the eyes at this statement. He laughed. "Oh, come on, I'm only joking man."

Joking or not, Nigel's thoughts flashed back to the night club situation back home.

He had not backed away from contact with Wayne, the blonde guy. But then there was Sue, and how he had reacted to her. Christ, I have a lot of things to sort out in my head, he thought, but now was not the right time to hit Mike with his problems.

Mike looked across at him. He could see what Nigel was going through in his confused mind. It was not for him to push the situation. Nigel had to open up to him first.

"Come on, it's shower time," Mike said, breaking the silence.

As they approached the shower block, they could see everyone going into the same entrance.

Mike smiled at the expression on Nigel's face. "Well, will you be able to handle this one?"

Nigel watched as families entered through one door, carrying just their towels and toilet bags.

They both followed what everyone else was doing, trying not to give the impression that this was their first time in a mixed shower.

So, with trainers off outside the entrance, they both took a deep breath and entered the steamy showers. People were hanging their towels on one wall lined with hooks. The showers were in a line along the other long wall. Everyone just mixed in together. Men, women and kids, just standing in the line of showers. There were no cubicles. As soon as a shower became free, Mike made a dive for it. Nigel's turn came next. They both stood there under the hot jets of water, trying not to stare.

Nigel started to soap himself down. The scene around him was very strange at first, and far from the tennis club showers at home. He looked to find Mike in the long line of shower jets. There he was, just as he thought, soaping himself and chatting to the person in the next to him. The noise of the chatter of voices was a little overpowering, but everyone seemed to be in a happy mood.

Nigel showered himself as he would at home, yet when it came to soaping his private parts, he turned towards the tiled wall at first. Then as everyone else was moving freely around, he just went about tackling his private parts, and nobody even looked. They don't know what they are missing he thought, inwardly smiling to himself.

As he stood there, under the shower washing the soap away, the rather plump lady next to him tried to strike up a conversation with him, but it was not in English. Nigel smiled, hoping that he did so in the right places. He added the odd nod. He thought he was doing quite well, as the lady continued to chatter away, smiling back at him, as she sloshed vast amounts of soap over her large body and between her crutch area. Nigel could hardly contain himself at the sight.

Mike had finished and Nigel joined him to towel himself dry. They both smiled at the scene. It was happy, healthy and natural Nigel thought.

Slipping their trainers on outside, they made their way back to the camper. They talked about what they had just witnessed. Nigel kept on saying that he couldn't believe this was happening to them.

They nodded and waved to families sitting outside their tents and caravans. The smell of the food being cooked almost made them hungry again. "Shit, do I feel good right now," remarked Nigel.

The first priority when they reached the camper was a glass of wine.

"Bloody hell. I'm glad that Big Dave is not with us. He would have disgraced us in the showers. I still can't get over how I controlled myself amongst all those women."

"I didn't know where to look at first," Mike added.

"Tell you what," Nigel said. "I was wanting to have a pee in the shower, but thought twice about it. And that's another thing, there is only one toilet block for everyone. Did you see the urinals for the men? I had to laugh at the way the blokes just stood there pissing in the troughs, everyone could see the line of bare bums lined up...shit, that's funny."

"I don't think I will have flashed it around so much in my life." Mike laughed.

"Doubt if anyone would notice it anyway." Nigel added.

It was getting on for ten o'clock. They could hear the music drifting across from the disco.

Mike said he was going to wear white socks with his trainers.

"People will say that I look like a Greek god."

"People will say you look like a prize prat."

"I think we should take towels to sit on"

Mike laughed at the thought of going to a disco at home in the nude. Nigel thought about the dancing naked bit. He was sure that he would be chucked out.

"Did you see the girls leave for the disco?" Mike asked.

Nigel said he hadn't seen them since they were having a drink with their parents. "Well, apart for Ariel. But let's not go into that again."

Nigel wore his white socks and trainers as well. They looked good walking together, towels flung across their shoulders, which helped to make their naked bodies look even more tanned. They looked the part.

They strutted towards the bar. The disco was in full swing. Suddenly Mike took hold of Nigel's arm, pulling him up sharply.

"What the fuck's up with you? You nearly pulled my arm off."

Mike pointed ahead. "Look at that," he muttered. "Everyone's bloody dressed. Fuck me, they've all got clothes on!"

Without a word being spoken, they both turned around, and at first they walked at a normal pace, then as if a whistle had been blown, they ran full pelt back to the camper.

Door flung open, they dived inside. The door then slammed shut, they both fell about laughing at the situation.

"Shit. What a couple of prize prat's. Bloody good job the girls didn't see us." Mike giggled.

They had another wine each, just to help calm them down. Mike ploughed his way through his clothes pile. He decided that he would wear jeans and T-shirt. Nigel thought that he looked good in shorts and tight fitting T-shirt. Now they felt dressed to kill.

Entering the bar area, trying to look as cool as possible after their balls up of accessing what they thought the night life was like, they ordered a couple of beers. Nigel, looking around, spotted the girls and Josh through the crowd.

Everyone was dressed in casual gear. Nigel and Mike were feeling that they were really raw recruits to this lifestyle. Mike laughed. "But it's going to be fun learning."

Josh and the girls had taken over one of the tables, so they made their way through the dancers. It was quite packed. Nigel estimated that there were at least a hundred or more there. The music was not what he would have played back home, as some of the numbers were quite oldies, but good to dance to.

The girls made room for them around the table. Nigel felt that they must be interested in them, seeing that they had reserved them a couple of chairs. They sat down next to each other, not by choice, but that was how the chairs were placed.

There were bottles of red wine already started on the table. As they had ordered beers at the bar, there seemed no point in changing their drinks just now.

"Do you always drink beer in England?" Ariel asked.

"Quite a lot. You see England has a lot of pubs, and after football matches, everyone goes to a pub to drink beer." Mike thought that this would get the conversation rolling.

Josh looked up from under his long shoulder length hair. "What is a pub?" He asked.

Mike explained that it was a better type of French bar.

"That's why you can only afford to drink beer." Ariel suggested.

At this point, Nigel thought that he would change the subject. He had been watching Nina. Leaning across the table, he held out his hand, asking her if she would care to be kicked around on the dance floor.

"I would like to dance with you, but I prefer you to go and kick someone else...if that is what the English do at disco's."

He took her hand; it felt soft and warm in his. He led her through the tables and onto the dance floor. It was quite crowded, and they found it difficult to find a space to be together. As they were not playing the type music that made for close contact, they just shuffled around, trying to keep together.

He wanted to get close to her, as he had a nice feeling about her. They found it difficult to talk over the loud music, but he was able to watch her move around. Nina had a nice body, the type he liked in a girl, she was a little tomboyish he thought. She wasn't quite as tall as himself, which made him feel good, and in control.

The mood of the music changed at last. A slower number was played. Nina moved towards him, he didn't have to make the first move. This was a good sign, he thought. She moved close up to him, her body felt warm and soft. He placed his arms around her body. His hands ran up her back to clasp around her neck. She was not wearing anything under the long knee length T-shirt, he was sure of that because he would have felt the top of her panties, and the strap of a bra, but no, his fingers never felt them.

As they swayed with the music, he could feel her nipples brushing against his chest. This was going to be the test he felt. His mind flashed back home. Sue entered his thoughts, but only for a moment. He quickly cleared her from his mind. Here he was with Nina, a new girl. It was his first time with her. He kept saying to himself, "don't mess this one up."

He held her close. It was hard not to react. Nina smiled at him, she could sense his reactions.

Nina rested her head on his shoulder. Nigel responded, and their heads rested together.

He felt her hand caress his bum. It was only for a brief moment, and it felt good. This, he felt, was an invite for him to return the move. He slowly moved his hand down the small of her back, then came to rest on her nice firm rounded bum. There was a reaction that ran through her body as he caressed her in return.

Looking down at her, he could see that he had made the right moves, and the evening was only beginning.

"Why did you ask me to dance with you, and not the others?" Nina asked.

"I felt comfortable in asking you. When we met earlier, I just had that feeling about you," he replied.

"And now, what are your feelings?"

Nigel thought that this was a good time to express his manly control to her. "I'm finding it hard to keep myself under control. It's so warm, and you are dancing so close, it's not easy for a guy to have that amount of control."

"That's nice," said Nina, "but don't think I'm an easy good time holiday girl, I don't go with anyone, but you can enjoy the evening."

Nigel assured her he was not the type to have one night stands. "But," he added, "I'm just a healthy guy on holiday."

Nina pulled herself closer. Nigel, having been given permission to relax, did so. His hand, which was still active on her bum, pulled them even closer. His control gave way to a perfect erection.

Nina clearly enjoyed the firmness of his manhood. As for Nigel, he was thinking that he had not enjoyed such a hard on as this for ages. He just hoped that this was not going to be a repeat of the Sue experience.

Mike and Ariel joined them on the dance floor. Mike was already locked in position. Nigel looked across at them. He felt that they were right for each other, and that he was going to be in luck tonight with her. That was the difference between them. Mike was able to handle a one-night stand. At least that's what he thought.

Jodie, he could see, was dancing with a young guy. They were not dancing that close, so there couldn't be anything going on between them, he thought.

He looked around for Josh, but couldn't see him anywhere.

Nina suggested that they took a break. "Let's go and have some of the wine. Oh, I forgot, you are on beer."

With that, she danced them in the direction of their table. This came as a relief to him as he had not got control of his manhood at this point. Nina smiled. "See how I am looking after you."

Nigel was relieved to not be being exposed to the others. He sat down, pulling his chair well up to the table. Nina poured the wine.

They talked for ages. Nigel told her about his sport, and Nina, he found out, was the creative type, doing a graphic design course at college.

Nigel thought that he should apologise for his uncontrolled behaviour on the dance floor. Even though Nina smiled at this, he was still not able to relax. He had only met her a few hours ago, and he reacted like that. "Nina," he blurted out. "I hope you don't think I was trying it on just now. I don't know what you must be thinking. I'm not really like that."

"Well. You are new to this way of life, it takes time to get used to the lifestyle." Nina gave his hand a squeeze as she tried to reassure him.

"Thanks for understanding," he said.

"Josh doesn't have the same problems though. This was his first time at a naturist holiday also. But it's more difficult for him,' she said. "You see he is gay." She gave a nervous laugh at this.

"Gay." Nigel looked around. He was aware that he had just shouted that aloud.

"I expect he'll be sitting around on his own, smoking. That's his biggest problem, we all wish he would stop it. Do you smoke?"

"I've tried it a few times, but not hooked on it." Nigel replied.

Nina asked if they could dance some more. He nodded, thinking that this time he would try to have more self-control, or at least try to.

They danced for about another hour. It was a nice mix of music. On the slower numbers, he did behave himself when they came into close contact. They went back to their table to finish up the red wine. This time he managed to stand there drinking without having to cover up his manhood.

He looked around the dance floor for Mike, but he could not see him or Ariel. He caught sight of Jodie as she drifted over to the table to join them. Nina and Jodie entered into a conversation. Nigel caught little snippets of this. It sounded as if Jodie had not been having a good time.

Nina turned to Nigel. "Jodie has asked if she can walk back with us to the caravan. Is that OK with you?" she asked.

Nigel nodded a yes to this. He was thinking that this was quite a good idea really, as he felt a little insecure about his self-

MICHAEL KEENE

control.

They headed back towards the camping area, chatting about the evening. The night was still very hot, and Nina, who had been wearing a T-shirt, removed it. She looked good walking along in the moonlight. Nigel, almost without thinking, removed his T-shirt and shorts. It made him feel so good and free. Jodie had already removed her sarong from around her waist. She looked relaxed.

Nina suggested a swim before bed. So they set off along the riverbank. Jodie made the first move, and with a running jump hit the water creating waves that splashed against the bank.

Nigel took hold of Nina's hand, and with a running jump together; they landed next to Jodie. The water was fresh; it brought new life to their bodies after the long dance session.

They played around for what seemed ages, trying not to shout and disturb the other campers. The two girls were trying to duck Nigel. Jodie, having decided that three was a crowd, swam off up river leaving the two of them to play together. After a while of fooling around in the water, reality set in as Nigel began to realise the implications of being in such a situation, alone, nude and free in the moonlight, with a sexy girl he hardly knew. The playing stopped, and they found themselves panting for air from all their efforts. They were able to stand up, as the river was not that deep where they had been playing. Nina curled her arms around his neck. He felt the body contact. With her legs around his waist, and arms around his neck, he swirled her around in the water. He had at last found a freedom that he had never experienced before. Yet he was not being aroused by these actions. She seemed so happy. They made no attempt to make any sexual moves that might destroy the sheer enjoyment of just being nude together.

Nina, her limbs still wrapped around him, planted a sweet soft kiss on his lips. "Thank you for this evening. Please take me home now. I want the evening to stay as a memory forever, just as it is."

"Me too." Nigel whispered, giving her a peck on her cheek.

They collected their things, and walked towards the caravans. Nigel felt quite relieved that the evening was ending like this, it was a nice feeling.

Jodie had gone ahead to her caravan. They both stood there holding hands, with their clothes having just being dumped on the ground. Neither made a move to embrace. They just looked

106

into each other's eyes.

Nina broke the silence. "Good night. And thanks again." She leaned forward to give him another soft kiss on his cheek. "See you tomorrow."

Nigel just stood there watching her enter her caravan.

He turned, and walked towards the toilet block. Apart from wanting a pee, he thought a shower would help clear his head.

The shower block was empty. He stood there under the stream of hot water jetting down over his body. Looking to see if the coast was still clear, he directed his pissing into the drain grill. He stood there with hands behind his neck, letting the free expression of nature take place. It felt good. Oh God, this was an unbelievable experience he was having.

As he had no towel with him, and it was very warm outside, he started to walk back to the camper, using his T-shirt to dry off a little.

Opening the camper door, he was not sure what to find. He had thought that Mike would be in bed with Ariel. He poked his head inside; he had been wrong, as the camper was empty.

He climbed up onto his bed. It was too warm to get inside his sleeping bag, so he lay back letting his thoughts run through the evening.

Where was Mike? Looking at his watch, it was nearly one o'clock. I hope he's OK he thought to himself. Yes he would be all right in a place like this.

His thoughts returned to the evening. He smiled to himself about the way they had turned up at the disco naked. Fuck, we could have looked bloody stupid if anyone had seen us.

He thought about how he had reacted when dancing with Nina. They had been dressed, yet he had been turned on by her. Had she enjoyed his hard on? He thought so, because she did lead him on.

His thoughts then went to the swimming. They had stripped off, and he had enjoyed the feel of her being wrapped around him, but he didn't get an erection. Something not quite right about this he thought.

He tried to work out the set up between the three girls and Josh. And what about Josh being gay?

He sat up. He was now getting concerned about Mike. It would have been good to be able to chat these things over with him. There were so many questions unanswered. His thoughts went back to the late night swim. Why had he not taken advantage of the situation? He hadn't even got a hard on. Surely this was not normal, so what was wrong with him? He thought then of what Big Dave would have done. He would have been in the river or on the bank, humping away most of the night. He smiled at the thought.

He was now very tired, and wishing that Mike would come back. He left the camper door open for him. His mind started drifting as his tiredness overcame him. It had been a great day, yet the problems about his sexuality still ran through his mind. He would have to get this sorted in his head soon; else he would surely go nuts.

His sleep was disturbed on hearing the camper door being closed. He half opened his eyes. Mike was trying to creep in without waking him. But as he was not really awake, there was no chance of conversation between them.

Mike looked up at the bunk above him, just to check that Nigel was in bed. He gently ruffled his hair, and gave him a pat on his bare bum. He then fell on top of his own bed, it had been quite a day for him too. As it was nearly three in the morning, he was glad that he did not have to listen to some of his mate's questions about sexuality.

CHAPTER 11

It was the movement outside the camper that woke Nigel first. Leaning over to look out of the window, he could see that there was a car towing a caravan away. There was alot of shouting and laughing going on as campers could be seen running alongside the departing car. Nigel thought that it was a bit much making all that noise so early in the morning. He stretched himself over the edge of his bunk bed, reached for his watch. Shit, it was ten thirty.

Mike stirred. "Hi yer."

"Hi yer too."

"Have a good time last night?" Mike asked.

"Very good. Doubt if it was as good as yours though. What time did you get in then?"

"You sound just like my old man. About three."

"If I were your old man, you would be grounded."

Nigel got down from his bunk. Sitting on Mike's bed, he started to poke him on the chest in fun. For a moment there was silence as they looked at each other's uninhibited nakedness. This was a new experience for both of them. Mike smiled at the situation, then playfully made a grab at Nigel's neck, pulling him down onto his bed in a headlock. He said he wanted the truth, and nothing but the truth, before he would let him go. This resulted in a friendly mock fight. The camper started to rock around as they wrestled. Nigel broke away from the headlock and fought to sit astride Mike. He held him down, with his legs across Mike's chest. The sweat was already pouring off of them with their efforts. "So, who has been a naughty boy then?" Nigel asked. His face being just inches away from Mike's as he asked.

"Give me a kiss, and I'll tell you." Mike said, pouting his lips.

Nigel thought for a moment with Mike still locked under him. Here they were, for the first time during their friendship, locked naked together. They both smiled. Mike must have been thinking the same.

Nigel made no attempt to move off Mike. He planted a kiss direct on his lips. Mike never pulled away or even moved. Nigel stared into his eyes to see if there was a reaction to this. But no, only a smile. They stayed motionless for a while, and then Nigel started to release the body lock. Guilt now entered his thoughts. He was feeling bad about letting his feelings show.

"Don't move away." Mike said. His voice was calm.

Nigel felt his body freeze on him. He had not expected this kind of reaction. He sat astride Mike again, not knowing what to do next.

"I thought that you might the beat the hell out of me for doing that." Nigel said, looking back into Mike's eyes again.

"I've been waiting for you to make your move. You have taken a bloody long time in breaking the ice. There had to be a first time."

They stayed locked together for a while. Nigel was thinking to himself, what if anyone should see them? He posed this question to Mike.

Mike grinned. With his arms stretched out across the bed he said, "Do you know what, I really don't care a fuck."

"What do you mean when you said that there had to be a first time, and waiting for me to make my first move. How did you know this?"

Mike cleared his throat. He was not sure that he should tell how he knew about Nigel's feelings.

"Well, when I came back and found you and Ariel in the camper, after she'd gone, I found your diary on the floor under the front seat."

Nigel felt a rush of embarrassment through his body. "Did you read any of it?"

"Only the juicy bits."

Nigel's mind flash over what he'd written in the diary. He had mixed feelings about Mike having nosed into his private world. He thought however, it might be a good thing if Mike had read it, as when it came to the big question time, this would at least tell Mike where he was coming from.

"So why having read my diary did you encourage me to kiss you. Why didn't you stop me, or at least turn away?"

"Don't you see. You told me about the guy at the nightclub, and how you just stood there. I've also read some of your diary, and I don't regret that. So, putting that all together, I thought that if I blew my top, how the hell would you know what it felt like? At least you now have part of the answer, if and when you want to talk it over."

Nigel thought that this made sense, yet he was still in a confused state of mind. He climbed off of Mike, yet he wanted to remain having body contact with him...it had felt good.

"Lets make some tea, then you can tell me about last night." Nigel suggested, putting the kettle on the burner.

Mike announced that his first priority was to have a pee. Nigel joined him, letting the kettle boil itself until their return.

They had a kind of breakfast, and several cups of tea and coffee. Mike also drank half a carton of orange juice...informing Nigel that it was rich in vitamin C.

They were now ready to tell each other their experiences of last evening.

"You can start." Nigel suggested.

"Well, after the dance, me and Ariel were going for a swim. But on the way we had to pass Erik and Anita's caravan. Erik invited us in to join them for a coffee. It was about two in the morning before we eventually left for our swim."

"Did you go swimming at that time then?" asked Nigel.

"Yes. We swam to the rocks. You know the ones I told you about."

Nigel nodded.

"After the swim, we picked up our clothes and came back to her caravan."

"And then what?"

"Nothing really. We sort of kissed goodnight. She went in, and I came into the camper and crashed out. Fucking boring really. Sorry mate, I wish I had a better ending for you."

"I think you are a sad man.' Nigel said, smiling.

"So how did your evening go then, big boy?"

Nigel went on to tell what had happened to him. He told Mike about his erection on the dance floor, and how he had felt a prat having to be led back to the table to hide his stiffy.

Mike laughed at the scene. I can see you out there now. "Bloody hell, it's a good job you were not dancing in the nude. Just as well we came back to put some gear on."

"Funny you should say that." Nigel quickly said. He then told Mike about his swim with Nina, and although they had been swimming nude, and even when she had wrapped herself around him, he never got a hard on. "How do you explain that?"

"Maybe you have been born a true naturist. Taking your clothes off it's less of a turn on, but with just even a few clothes on, bingo, your prick gets out of control."

"Does it effect you the same way?" Nigel asked.

"It's not quite the same for me. But, seeing as you have asked, I must tell you about when I swam out to the rocks on my own."

"Must you?" asked Nigel.

"Yep. It will help you in your search for the truth of life, and your sexuality."

"Go on then."

He proceeded to give Nigel a graphic account of his experience on the rocks. Nigel just sat there not interrupting Mike.

"It was hot. There was nobody around for as far as he could see. I was feeling quite randy lying there naked.

"I looked down into the river, and I swear there were twenty or more large fish swimming around me. I eased myself into a comfortable kneeling position, and worked myself off. I made it last a bloody long time, holding back just as I was about to come each time. Then, when the moment came, and I couldn't hold back any longer, I shot my load. I swear to you, it was the most I had shot in my life. It was a great feeling being free outdoors, just me, my hard on, and the fish. They loved it."

"Loved what? You don't mean they gobbled up your…bloody hell," Nigel said, with an excitable tone to his voice.

Mike fell back onto his bed laughing. "Can you believe that then. I have never felt so good having a wank. The funny thing is, I took Ariel to the same rocks, and I never got a hard on with her there. Isn't it bloody strange how some things can arouse you, and just when you think you are onto a good thing, the little fucker lets you down."

Nigel was feeling good now. At last they were opening up with each other, and exchanging their life experiences. He doubted that these experiences could have been talked about back at home.

They gave each other a friendly thump on the arm, both feeling good that they could relate like this.

After lunch, they went down to the river again. Nigel said he was glad that the river flowed in that direction.

"Why is that?" Mike asked.

"Well at least this part of the river we are swimming in will not get polluted with your sperm."

"You're only jealous." Mike said.

They sat at the waters edge, kicking their feet around in the river. They took in the scene. There were some attractive people around.

"What do you think of Josh?" Nigel suddenly asked.

"I quite like him. He seems very quiet though. Haven't seem him with a girl yet."

"Don't think there is a chance of that He's gay."

"Never." Mike exploded. "So that's why he left the disco early last night. Bloody difficult to make friends I bet."

Nigel agreed.

Their conversation was brought to a halt. Erik appeared almost from nowhere. He walked through the grass towards them. First he asked how they were getting on with their new lifestyle.

"I won't interrupt your afternoon, just thought that you might like to join us for the evening. You can bring your friends along, and a bottle of wine to help out. See you about nine." He gave a wave, and was off back through the long grass again.

"That was nice of him," said Mike.

"Nice people. That takes care of another evening." Nigel said.

The sun was now very hot, so they moved into the shade. Mike crashed out on his towel. Nigel was deep in thought, so Mike being asleep was not a bad thing.

He went over all the things that he had been carrying around in his head about his sexuality for ages, yet bit by bit, he was finding that some of the questions were finally being answered now. He knew that soon he would find the confidence to enter into deeper conversations with Mike, he was truly a nice guy, and a good friend. He had loved the body contact they had had earlier.

He turned over and lay alongside Mike. He didn't know why he felt he had to, but he could not help putting his arm across Mike's shoulders. He just rested his arm there just wanting to have that contact with him again. Mike stirred. Opening his eyes slightly, he had a slight smile on his face. He gave Nigel a wink that seemed to say, 'all is well in our world.'

They lay there together, sleep overtook them again. They had been sleeping for a least an hour when Nigel sensed a movement at his side. His arm was still across Mike's shoulders, and with a rapid movement, he removed his arm almost feeling guilty that they had been found like this.

Lifting his head, he stared into the sunlight. It was Nina. "Have you been there long?" he asked.

Nina avoided the question. "I have been looking for you everywhere."

"We have been in and out of the river most of the afternoon. We only fell out of our camper about lunchtime. We have been shattered." Nigel said.

"Have you looked around the campsite yet?" Nina asked.

"We had a quick look at the swimming pool when we first arrived, but that's all."

"Come on then, sleepy head, I'll show you around." Nina held her hand out to help him up.

Nigel rolled over to whisper in Mike's ear. "Won't be long, going for a walk with Nina."

Mike raised an arm in a form of a wave to them both, but remained otherwise motionless.

Nigel caught hold of Nina's hand, and they headed off up the steep road that weaved its way around the campsite.

There was a small supermarket and a collection of small shops just by the main reception. Nigel looked at the postcards on a stand outside one of the gift shops. He thought that he should send one home. Then he remembered he was naked, with no pockets for money. Nina laughed at his expression and the way he just walked on up the road ahead of her, slapping his sides like a penguin.

As they approached the bar area, where last nights disco had been held, they found that many families had gathered at the tables and chairs outside the bar. The grass lawns were quite packed with youngsters playing. Nigel thought this was great to see. There were portrait artists sketching away, with interested onlookers. Youngsters were standing around waiting their turn to have their faces painted by a couple of talented artists. Nina told him that these artists stayed there all summer, and although they didn't earn a lot of money, they loved the freedom of being with the naturist families.

Nina grabbed his hand, pulling him away from the scene. "Come on, there are other things to see." Nigel kept turning to look back at the scene. "If you thought that that was great, wait until you see what's ahead." Nina said, giving him another tug on his arm.

They rounded the next bend in the road. Nigel could hear voices. There were twenty to thirty naturists standing in a line doing archery. There were a couple of instructors going along the line of nude people, making adjustments to how they held their bows, or as to how they were standing. Nigel found this amusing to watch. The targets were set back in a huge cut away in the mountainside. They both watched for a while. Nigel thought that he might have a go at this later.

They walked on again. Nina said that they were nearly at the top of the mountain road now.

It had been quite a climb, but worth it. He could already hear the laughter of youngsters and the sound of water splashing around. They walked over a slight banking and stood to take in the view. Here they were, on top of a mountain, and they could see for what seemed miles across mountain ranges drifting off into a misty blue skyline. Just in front of them was a swimming pool that had been sculptured into the mountainside. This was an amazing sight to see. All around the pool there were naturist families sunbathing on the surrounding pastel coloured paving terraces.

"There, wasn't that well worth the walk?" Nina suggested.

"It's got to be the most beautiful sight that I have ever seen. You can see for miles, and you can feel the air is so fresh. And just look at the kids enjoying the pool. Oh, where have I been all of my life?"

There were groups of youngsters, some just sitting talking on the sunbathing terrace. Others just seemed to form a production line, with the routine being to jump or dive into the pool, then after a few goes at this; they would join their other friends to sunbathe.

Nina had been watching his face. "This is all new to you, isn't it?"

He just gave a nod to this statement, and carried on looking.

Something was falling into place in his mind. At last he was beginning to see through the mist. Here he was, standing looking into another world. A world that allowed the freedom of being nude with others. Here he was, mixing freely with people that cared about the more simple pleasures of life. There was a bond between them. He looked at the kids. They would surely grow up wiser about life than he had. He only wished that he'd found this lifestyle earlier in life, as he was sure that he would not be so mixed up in his mind as he was.

Nina gave his arm a nudge. "Hi, remember me?"

"Sorry. I just can't believe this afternoon. You were right this is all new to me. I hope you can teach me more."

"I think you will find out more later. You wait until we all sit around talking in the evenings. People will talk about life. You will learn a lot."

"How long have you been a naturist?" he asked.

"Since I was born."

They started to walk back down the steep road. He was feeling content. Nina put her arm around him again, giving him a smile.

"I just want to show you one more thing." Nina said, leading him towards a clearing just off of the road. They opened a rustic gate and entered a clearing. Nigel could hear joyful voices chattering away through the trees. They came to a small battered caravan. Outside it, leaning against the sides, were several well-worn wooden stacker shelves full of pottery and little sculptures. Ahead of them they could see about twenty youngsters. Most of them had smudges of clay over themselves where they had wiped a hand across their faces.

"This is the kids own pottery club." Nina said.

"No kidding," he laughed.

Nina gave him a kick with her bare foot. "This is a place that the parents can leave their kids while they go away to enjoy themselves. This club has craft teachers that spend the whole summer here showing the youngsters how to make pottery and things. They love it here."

They watched for a while before heading back towards the caravans. Nigel was again deep in thought. Here he was walking naked, arms around Nina, without a care in the world. He felt so free.

When they arrived back at the camper, Mike was found to be well recovered. He waved as he saw them approaching. "The beer is cool. Do you want one?" he called out.

Nina gave a wave back. She excused herself, and on giving Nigel a peck on his cheek, started to walk away to her caravan. Mike shouted to her to tell her that she had been invited over to Erik, their friend, for the evening. Just bring a bottle of red."

"Can I bring Josh as well?" she shouted back.

"Sure." Mike replied.

Nigel sat down next to Mike after grabbing a beer. He went over what he had seen. Having given Mike a verbal tour of the campsite, he went on to tell of his thoughts whilst at the swimming pool.

"You should have seen the scene. I've never had my eyes opened like this before. The kids just mixing together, nude and free with no inhibitions. When I have kids, that's how I'll bring them up. I'm sure they won't grow up so confused as I am at this time."

Mike just looked at him. "I see you have been educated today.

Let's hope you can have kids first. We might find that you are more suited to settle down with say, someone like Josh. Mind you, you could still count me in a being your friend."

"Don't laugh and take the piss. Really, I think I have found some of the answers. Life seems a lot clearer after seeing what I've seen today. Sure beats the hell out of what's going on at home."

"See, I can't leave you on your own for a minute." Mike said, patting him on the leg.

"How about tea?"

Mike pointed to the camper. "It's already cooking."

CHAPTER 12

Having finished their meal, they decided to take a shower. As usual at this time of day, the showers were quite full. They hung up their towels, and stood awaiting their turn. As the draw seemed to work out, Mike jumped into the first one available. Josh suddenly joined Nigel in the queue. They nodded to one another. Josh asked if he'd had a good day, Nigel nodded.

A couple finished showering, so Josh and Nigel found themselves next to each other. The water was hot as usual. Nigel smiled at Josh, who was not at his talkative best. Having long hair, he hid behind this. It was his protective shield, thought Nigel

"I wish I had long hair like yours," Nigel said, shouting above the noise of the showers.

"It creates a few problems. I have to wash it after every swim, so I wish that I had your type of hair."

"You look good with short hair anyway." Josh gave him the once over look, and smiled.

As the person the other side of Nigel finished their shower, Mike, seeing the space, joined them. "What sort of day have you had then?" Mike asked Josh.

"I've been fishing with a friend, but there were too many swimmers to catch anything. Fish don't like swimmers much, so they stay under the rocks." Josh said.

Nigel, sporting a smile, asked if the fish were big and healthy, and if the rocks were a good feeding place for them. He looked direct at Mike.

"Sorry, I don't understand your question."

Mike quickly told him that he was not alone, as neither did he.

Josh looked a little confused. He managed a smile. "I think that this must be an English joke." With that, he disappeared under his hair again.

As they stood there drying off, Mike told Josh that he was invited to join them later on.

"Thanks, I'd like that."

"Your fishing friend is welcome to join us as well." Nigel said.

Josh smiled. "Thanks."

They walked back towards the camper. Josh was invited to have some wine with them.

"Grab a chair," Nigel said to Josh.

"Can I be nosey a take a look inside your camper?" asked Josh.

"Sure." Mike replied.

He stuck his head inside the camper door. "Cosy for two I bet," he said looking around, "where do you both sleep?"

Mike said that he slept down there, and Nigel slept on top. He wished he had not put it quite like that. He saw Josh smile as well, then slipping under his hair again said, "that's nice."

Mike changed the subject. "Red or white?"

"Red for me thanks." Josh replied.

"Where are we all sitting?" Nigel asked.

"Can we sit in here, I like the inside of your camper, wish I had one," Josh said, still looking around inside.

They offered him a seat. Mike and Nigel sat together on one of the bench seats. Josh sat on the other, and placed his legs across to their seat, making himself comfortable.

"You seem to have selected the girls well. I had bets with myself as to who was going to go with whom," Josh smiled, looking at both of them for a reaction.

"Did you win?" Nigel asked.

"Yes. But I think it would have been more fun if one of you had chosen Jodie."

"Why is that?" asked Mike.

"Well, she is gay."

They both fell about at this news. Once again, Mike fired a remark out, and then wished he kept his mouth shut. "Gay...So are you, aren't you?"

Josh sat there for a moment, pulling his long hair back from his face. "I'm bi-curious."

Nigel told him that he thought that he was sitting on the fence.

"Maybe, but I have a feeling that you are too." Josh stared straight at Nigel, searching for a reaction.

There was an uneasy silence at this statement. Mike put his hand over his mouth, holding back on a laugh. Nigel looked down at the floor and away from Josh who was still staring at him. Slowly looking up again, he looked direct at Josh. "What makes you think that?"

"Just a feeling I have about you. Nothing wrong in that."

Josh remarked.

Mike came to the rescue of his mate. He told Josh not to pursue that line of talk. "Nigel is out here in France, trying to find himself."

"Sorry if I hit on a nerve," Josh said. "However, if I can help Nigel by talking about it, no problem, glad to help."

Mike suggested that they drop the matter. Nigel was not so sure. "Can I ask you a direct question then Josh?"

"Surely."

"How old are you?"

"If that is the best direct question you are going to ask, easily answered, I'm eighteen."

Nigel smiled at this. "No there are others." And without letting Mike in to stem his flow now, he asked. "Have you ever made love to a woman?"

"Yes."

"And what about another guy?"

"Yes."

"That sounded very cold and direct." Nigel suggested.

Josh agreed. He suggested that the question had not been put to him the right way. "You mentioned the word love. And although I answered, I should have corrected you on the use of the word love. You see, I have had sex with both, but not love with both. So lets understand that first."

"But surely this has lead to love?" Nigel asked.

Mike decided that this was too deep for him, so he was off to have a pee. He didn't really want to have one, but he just had to escape. He grabbed his towel and climbed out of the camper.

They were about to continue the conversation, when Mike stuck his head back inside the camper again. "I've taken my towel with me, so if you feel you want to join me, I'll be at the bar."

"Right, where were we?" Nigel asked.

"Love or sex." Josh smiled.

"Explain. I'm very interested to hear what you mean about this."

Josh, taking a deep breath, sat back and started to explain his thoughts on life. He'd had sex with women, and a couple of girls of age. He had had many offers, and it was good at the time, and he had no regrets. Then he had gone to a party. He hadn't known many people there, and he was on his own. A guy had made a pass at him. He had not been sure what to do or how to react. His first reaction was to thump the guy.

Nigel's thought went back to the nightclub scene with Wayne.

Josh continued. "Some time later I met this guy again. I was not on drugs, and I'd only had a glass of wine, so I knew what I was doing. It was my suggestion to go to my flat. My friend being away, we had the place to ourselves. We had sex, not love, and it was good. I was truly sexually aroused by him. He lifted me to heights that I had never experienced before. He stayed the night, and we had sex again. It was even better. When he had gone, I tried to work out why I had enjoyed sex with a guy. It had been sex not love, but I was still confused at the time.

"I have since got it together. The sex was better with a guy, but I know that a woman has love to offer, and the sex side of the deal is in the mind."

Nigel looked confused still. "So how do you explain how you reached better heights sexually with a guy. What about the women?"

"Because a guy knows exactly what can switch you on for sex. He just knows the things that can please a guy…because he has experienced them himself. Sex with a woman…how can she know as much as a guy when it comes to the finer points of arousal?"

Nigel listened to all of this. He had nothing more to ask. His thoughts were all over the place now.

"There, that's where I think you are at in your life," Josh said, and with that he made a move to leave. He stood there stretching his lean body in front of Nigel, and just for a moment he felt the temptation to run his hands over this tanned lithe body, but he resisted. Nigel looked up at him. "Thanks a lot."

Josh told him that it would all work out in the end. It was no great deal. "I was going to give you a kiss, but you might think I'm making a pass." With that, he climbed out of the camper. "See you later then," he shouted back.

Nigel watched him walk towards his tent. He was looking for any effeminate signs in the way he walked. There were none. If Josh had not told him about himself, and from watching him walk, he would have thought that he was some form of athlete, a runner at least. His body was well toned. It was only the way he ran his fingers through his long hair and the head movement that went with this action that showed any signs of him being gay.

Nigel's thoughts raced away with him. Josh had been very

open with him. He had voiced his views on life. In a way, he had made a lot of sense. But surely, even Josh would have to decide which side was up. Pity that Mike had not stayed to listen.

With that, he picked up his towel, climbed out of the camper, and headed towards the bar.

He found Mike chatting to a group of young naturists. They were sitting around a table outside the bar. There had been some serious drinking going on, Nigel thought.

"Well, well. Here comes the guy himself." Mike said to his newly found friends.

"What has this guy been saying about me then?" Nigel asked.

There was a little laughter around the table. "Nothing but good," one of the group answered.

With introductions and handshakes all around, Nigel sat down. "Sorry, I will never remember everyone's names," he said.

"So you are the great tennis player? England needs you badly," said one of the group. The guy then sat back in his chair; arms folded, and legs apart.

Nigel smiled at him. He had the measure of him. Not only was he good looking, but also he had the type of body most other guys longed for. He must be German, thought Nigel.

"I bet you're a tennis player. I also bet you are about to challenge me to a game. Am I right?" Nigel asked.

"That's correct. But please, I was only joking with you. I don't want you to take it out of me on the tennis court as I have heard how good you are."

"See how I have been building you up. One day you will want a manager." Mike said, giving a wink at Nigel.

"Well, the first thing in the managers handbook is...how to buy the drinks." Nigel laughed.

"Please, let me get you one," said the German guy, as he stood up. "My name is Hault." He then offered his hand. Nigel shook it. It was a firm grip.

"Thanks. A beer would go down well."

Two beers were ordered. Hault asked if they should have a table or sit on stools at the bar. Nigel said that stools were fine. "Better get our towels then. I'll get them. Is yours the dark blue one on the chair?" Nigel asked. Hault gave a nod.

Nigel returned with the towels. Hault had pulled up a couple of stools at the bar.

"Your beer is getting cold," he smiled.

Nigel asked him about his tennis. Hault had played for his

area back home. He called it a zone. Nigel told him that this would be called a county in England.

Hault asked how long he and Mike had been a naturists. Nigel thought, here we go again. Hault listened to the story and found it amusing.

"I like your friend. He thinks a lot of you. You must get on well."

"He's not bad either. He's great really; I'm lucky to have him as a friend. When you're sharing a small camper like ours, you have to get on well."

"What happens when you bring girls back for the night then?" Hault asked. He had a slight grin on his face. "It must be exciting?"

"Not having had this problem yet. I'll let you know when it happens."

"What about you then. Are you in a caravan, tent, or what?"

Hault gave a giggle at this. There was a slight froth of beer on his lips. "I share a small tent with my friend. We have got to know each other very well this holiday." His eyes were smiling. "We even share a sleeping bag. But it has been too hot at night, so we lay on top, it's better for sleeping, and also better when making love."

Nigel's head buzzed for a moment. Here was a guy telling him about love. These continentals have very open minds. He had only drank half of his beer, and has already told him that he sleeps with his mate, and in the same sleeping bag. This was too much for his head to get round. Nigel thought he would have to delve more into this. Surely this was going to be his chance to find out about gay friendships, and what they do.

He told Hault that he had been talking to someone about love and sex that afternoon. He then went on to tell him about the bi-curious part of the conversation. He thought that it best not to mention who he had been talking to.

Hault listened intensely.

"Can I ask your views on what I have just told you?" asked Nigel.

Hault placed a hand on Nigel's leg. It was nearer his groin area than his knee. He felt a slight movement of Haults hand, more of a stroke really. Nigel looked around him. Shit, if anyone happens to see this, he thought, what the fuck will they think? With luck they were facing the bar, with their backs to everyone, so surely nobody could see this.

"You were asking my views about your friends sex life. Well, I think, that he might think, he is a lucky guy, and I'm no judge. You see, with having Marie to share my tent with, I don't need a guy to bunk up with." With that, Hault gave a slight rub of his hand on Nigels leg, then withdrew it. He had a broad grin on his face.

Nigel went bright red. Hault held on to the bar with laughter.

"Sorry, but you did ask for that Nigel. But don't worry, you can trust me not to let on. It was only a bit of fun. But, just to make you feel better, I have to tell you, I have slept with a guy. So you have that to hold against me if I tell our secret."

Nigel started to laugh with him. Christ, he had got that wrong.

Hault, putting his arm around Nigel's shoulders, said he thought they could become good friends over the next few days, even on the tennis court. "Drink up, and let's join the others."

"What a fine good looking couple of hunks you make," Mike shouted out on seeing their return. "Come on, I've been sitting here waiting for you for bloody ages." He stood up ready to go.

Nigel was pleased to be going back to the camper. He'd had quite a day, and what's more they had a heavy evening in front of them.

CHAPTER 13

Nigel pleaded to be taken to the showers. He was not even going to start to tell Mike about his day.

They collected their toilet gear from the camper, and made their way to the showers. Mike trying to draw him out about his chat with Josh, but he was having nothing to say. He just kept telling Mike that he would save it for another time.

The subject being dropped, the conversation now being about the evening ahead.

"Nina said we don't have to put on any clothes. Glad she told me that, else we could have made another cock up of it. I'll be glad when we've got the rules sorted out." Mike laughed.

Showers over with, they returned to the camper. "It's feeling more like home. I could live like this given the chance," Nigel said.

"Some people do, I expect. I'm not sure if I could live like this all the time though," Mike said.

"Well I could."

"Better take a couple of red wines with us tonight," Mike said, as he looked vainly in the mirror.

He kept asking himself aloud, "Do I look good, or do I look good? Christ we are looking brown now old mate. Shit I feel great, don't you?"

"If I could get a look in at the mirror I would tell you. Move your bloody big head," Nigel said, pushing Mike aside.

They decided to take their towels and sweaters, as it was bound to get a bit nippy later in the night if they were just sitting around drinking.

They walked at a fast pace to join their hosts. Mike continued to try and draw Nigel out about his mind bender with Josh, but it was a *no go* from him.

Erik greeted them. With introductions all round, they were offered a couple of chairs to sit on. Mike handed over their wine, and they both received what was to be the first of many glasses of wine.

Anita started by asking what they had been up to all day. Nigel looked around quickly; Josh had not arrived, so he quickly gave an account of his days events. He decided to leave out the time he spent with Josh. He smiled across at Nina as he spoke. She blew him a kiss across the table of wine bottles.

Mike had to admit that he'd slept a lot, had the odd swim, then a drink at the bar. Everyone gave him a clap for this. He was announced as being on the right track to becoming a naturist now. "This was the lifestyle of true naturists," Erik told him.

The conversation got into second gear now. Nina asked Mike if she could change places with him so that she could sit with Nigel.

Mike thought this to be a good idea, as he would then be sitting next to Ariel.

Everyone was talking. Nigel looked around deep in thought. There were nine of them sitting around a couple of low tables, some were sitting on the ground, others on chairs. The awning of the caravan was the only shelter from the sun, which was still quite strong. Candles had been lit ready for when the light would start to fade. There was a guitar perched against the side of the caravan. Nigel guessed that Erik would be entertaining them later.

A week ago he thought, he would have placed a heavy bet with anyone if they had told him that he would be sitting around with a group of new friends, talking and drinking wine, sitting outside in the evening sun as naked as the day he was born. Never, he thought. But here he was, doing just that.

His thoughts were broken as Josh arrived on the scene. His hair was drawn back in a ponytail, which suited him, he thought. He had arrived with a friend. Josh introduced him as "Ian."

Anita turned to Mike and Ariel, asking them to make space for the two new arrivals.

Josh settled down crossed legged on the ground, Ian sat close to him. Jodie was the only loner in the group. She had seated herself next to Ariel.

Erik, pointing to the stock of wine bottles, suggested that everyone helped themselves.

Anita, leaning across to the wine, turned to Nigel. "So, tell us what you think of our lifestyle now that you have been with us for a little while. Have you had any problems in mixing in?"

"Not at all. We 've found everyone very friendly." He gave her a hug.

"Come on, you must have more to say on this." Anita suggested.

The conversations seemed to stop. Everyone was keen to hear

what Nigel had to say. He looked across to Mike for support.

They both talked about their reactions. They told their story about not dressing for the disco, and how they ran back to the camper to get dressed. Everyone laughed at this. Ariel said she had seen them.

"But you never told me that." Mike said, looking at her. "You sneak."

Erik asked what was the most difficult thing they had had to cope with so far.

Nigel and Mike almost spoke together. Nigel said it was the thought of everyone sharing the same showers and toilets. Mike nodded in agreement.

"And how do you feel about that now?" Erik asked.

"No problem," Nigel replied.

Nigel then went on to say he felt that it was good to see families growing up like this. "It must be good to bring them up this way."

Mike said that he had never felt so free before, and that he would never have dreamed that there were places like this around. "It's a good way of living." Anita gave a little clap to this statement.

Nigel asked Erik if he could ask him a question.

"It depends how personal it is," Erik replied.

"So how did you become a naturist?"

"Well, I wanted to be free. My work dictated how I should look and dress. It told me when to get up, and when to go home. I just started looking for a better way of life. I also wanted to grow up with knowing my family, and my family knowing me. You see, the real me was under the clothes as well as the one the world saw."

"Do you and Anita walk around naked at home?" Nigel asked.

"If the weather is nice for the garden, and if the house is warm enough." He then looked at Anita. "And we go to bed like that also."

"What do your children think about that?"

"Well they are in the caravan pretending to be asleep. We have no secrets from them. They are growing up in a healthy way."

Nigel looked across at Mike. "Come on, you haven't joined in yet."

"You are doing just fine yourself," he replied.

Nigel was feeling confident enough now to ask more direct

questions. He asked for some more of the wine. "Erik, can I ask you a more personal question?"

"Try me, I will decide if I will answer it."

Nigel cleared his throat. "I am just over eighteen, and like most, I am trying to find my way in life."

He was trying not to look at anyone direct as he declared this. He could sense Josh staring at him. Mike had fallen back on his elbows, which left Ariel without his arm to support her.

"Do you mean that you are fighting your sexual feelings?" Erik said. He did not appear bothered with the subject.

"I suppose I am really."

"You are not alone at your age on this one." He looked over at Josh. "I'm sure Josh will not mind me bringing him into this. He had better not mind, he's taking his fair share of wine."

Josh said he didn't mind at all, as he could take cover under his hair if it got too heavy. With that he untied his ponytail, his hair falling over his shoulders. Everyone gave a round of applause, and Ian just sat watching, with a smile on his face.

Erik continued. "I met up with Josh two summers ago. He had a young girl friend with him then. This summer, here he is with his boyfriend. And what's more he's is drinking my wine. So why do you think I allow this?" Erik asked.

As there were no answers, he continued again. "Josh has the right to choose his way of life. He is the same guy I met two years ago. Just as long as he doesn't offend anyone here, I do not... sorry..." he looked at Anita, "we do not, have a problem with being friends with Josh and his friend Ian."

Josh gave a shake of his head. His hair parted just enough to show that he had been moved by Erik's comments.

"So you approve of Josh being gay?" Nigel asked.

Anita leaned forward suddenly in her chair. "Approve. That's not the word. We accept Josh for who he is. It is not for us to judge him, or question what he does with his life. We would guide him if he started to get lost in a world he could not handle. But he is happy, so there is no problem."

Nigel felt a lot better for hearing that.

Jodie spoke up. It was the first time she had spoken. Her voice was a little manly. "I expect you all know that I am gay too, but I don't feel that I want to have this talked about tonight. Just in case someone was about to ask me something."

Ariel then decided to speak up and explain the set up. Nigel was now totally confused.

She told them that Josh and Nina were brother and sister. Jodie and herself were sisters. Their parents had been married before, "So there," she said.

Nigel looked across at Mike. He was mouthing, "*Bloody Hell.*" across the table to him.

Erik decided that a few words were required by him to sum things up a little.

"Well," he said, "I think this goes to show you two guys, life is for living. We should all try to understand other people's feelings. And as for us older people, we should lead by example." With that he stood up and kissed Anita. He then went around the table kissing each one in turn. "You may stay as long as you wish, but we have to make love tonight."

Anita slapped his backside. "I'll take him home," she smiled. "Goodnight."

Everyone said goodnight in return.

Mike was the first to make a move. He stood up, and taking hold of Ariel's hand, helped her up as well. Jodie moved off quickly, giving a wave to all. Nigel watched as Josh and Ian slipped away through the trees into the darkness of the night. He watched as they at first walked along side my side, then when they felt that they were far enough away, held hands. He felt sorry for them as they were obviously keen not to upset people, yet they must have felt so restrictive in their feelings for each other in company.

Nina suggested that they made a foursome. The night was still very hot, so they decided to take a quick dip in the river before going to bed.

The girls ran ahead. Mike and Nigel walked together in silence, deep in thought. Mike put his arm around Nigel's shoulder as they walked along. "How are you old mate?" he asked.

"Confused, but glad that you're here."

Mike gave him a slight hug of the shoulders. Nigel felt that this was a special moment, the body contact was brief, but bonding. It was a nice feeling he thought.

The water was rather on the cold side, so the four of them splashed around trying to warm up.

The girls picked on Nigel first, and together they hung onto him ducking him, only allowing him to surface for air. He was able to call out to Mike for help. He had been standing in the shallow water watching his friend being dunked. His thoughts at the time were affecting him strangely. Nigel was very special to him, and he saw the two girls as just passing friends in the night. Nigel, he was a friend forever. It was a strange feeling that suddenly came across him. He quickly cleared his thoughts, and swam with huge splashing movements to his friends rescue.

"Hey, go easy on him, I want him whole." Mike shouted.

Nigel heard this, and although he was enjoying the fun of body contact between himself and the girls, his thoughts were with Mike. Why? He thought to himself.

Mike asked the time. Nobody had a clue. Nina told them it best to keep the noise down, as they could disturb everyone around the campsite. She then swam over to Nigel and without even being led on by him, wrapped herself around him. She kissed him, and it was not a goodnight kiss, it was one of those deep throat, let's get laid type.

He responded. Her hand started to caress his nipples, he had a thing about having his nipples touched. Her legs were now draped around his waist, and her tongue ventured deeper into his throat. He felt her hand now searching downwards towards his thighs. His mind raced away. Panic overtook him. He was thinking that if this was happening at home in his bedroom, or at the club with Sue, he would have had such a hard on that Nina's eyes would have been watering by now. He felt her hand groping for his penis. To her surprise, and to his embarrassment, he was only half erect. All kinds of thoughts raced through his head. It was just as well he was in this state, because he had not come prepared. But what would a condom do for him; he was in the bloody river. At home he would be carrying one with him. Oh, shit. What must Nina be thinking?

After a while, Nina released her body lock on him. Her hands had tried to arouse him, but she gave up. She took hold of his hand and led him towards the riverbank. They picked up their towels to dry off, and there was a long silence.

"Sorry." That was about all he could mange to say.

"Don't worry. It quite often happens like that in the water." Nina said.

It flashed though his head, this means that she has tried this with other guys before. He might have guessed by the forward way she acted that he was not the first.

Mike and Ariel were still playing around. They were not in a lovelock situation though. Nigel shouted to them to come out now.

It was past midnight now when they reached their caravans.

Mike had another kissing session with Ariel. Nigel not wishing to watch walked towards the camper. Nina had already headed off towards her caravan. There had been no chemistry between them.

He climbed into the camper and crashed out on top of Mike's bed. Just to be able to put his head down somewhere was enough, as he was not sure he could even climb onto his own bed. The events of the day were catching up on him fast. The first part of the evening had been good, but what a fucking mess he had made of being with Nina in the river. Was he demanding too much of himself? How many blokes could get a hard on under-water? Could it be his fault every time? Or was it her fault this time? Questions kept flashing up in his head. He was drifting off into a deep sleep. He was on top of Mike's sleeping bag, yet he couldn't manage to get up top into his own bed, the effort was too much.

Morning came around. The sun was streaming into the camper. Nigel stirred. His eyes were still half closed from his deep sleep. For a moment he could not clear his head. He could have been at home, his mind playing tricks with him.

Suddenly he remembered where he had crashed out. He looked around, his eyes now beginning to open. Turning his head to his right, he was greeted with the smiling face of Mike.

"How long have you been there?" Nigel asked.

"If you don't mind me bringing this to your attention, it's me that should be asking that. You are on my bed mate."

"Christ, how did I get here. You know what I'm asking, how long have you been awake?"

Nigel was now aware that he had his early morning erection as was his usual way of greeting the morning. He rolled over onto his front to hide his manhood.

Mike was laying there, hands clasped behind his head. He looked comfortable. "Don't bother to roll over like that," he said. He then looked down at himself and said, "Snap!"

Nigel turned over on his back again. "Don't tell me you have been laying there judging which one of us has the best." He smiled with inward relief.

"Sorry, no contest. I think I might just beat you past the post by a short head." With that Mike rolled over on his side. His face now all smiles, he placed an arm across Nigel's chest, and just rested his hand there.

Nigel was not sure how to react to this. "Have you been awake

long? How long have I been like this?" he said, looking down at
his manhood.

Mike gave a rub of his hand across Nigel's chest, and then
patted it. "Nigel old mate, you must stop this stupid reserve you
seem to have with me at times. I'm your mate. We are healthy,
fit and wise. We shouldn't have secrets, or be fucking coy about
having a hard on. It doesn't bother me. All you have to worry
about is getting it back to normal before you get outside the
camper."

"But this is normal size for me. Are you telling me you have
a hard on now. Shit, it's you that has the problem," Nigel laughed.

Mike thumped him on the arm. "You sod. I'll get you for
that. We'll have a competition one night, we'll see who the winner is then."

"You had better get in training then," Nigel giggled.

They both lay there feeling that this was the turning point in
their relationship. The sun was now very hot, so Mike leaned
forward to pull the camper door open. He was still sporting his
erection.

"Watch out, you might be seen," Nigel said.

"Balls, to them," Mike replied.

"Yours or mine?"

"Once again, no contest," Mike added.

"Didn't hear you come in last night. Did you get lucky?"

Mike thought about his reply. "I could have, but somehow it
didn't seem the right time or place. It's strange. There seems to
be a moral issue that stares you in the face at a place like this. I
felt that I was taking advantage of the situation. Do you feel the
same?"

"Christ, am I glad you feel that way about things."

"Oh, I'm so pleased you are glad for me. Bloody hell, I can tell
you, I'm not too pleased. I feel like some nookie, we are surrounded by crumpet, my balls are bursting, and I fail at the last
hurdle."

"I tell you what, when we have our mind bender evening, I
just hope some of this gets sorted out, because it's hurting my
head."

There was a knock at the door. It was Hault. "When are you
going to let me thrash you at tennis?"

Nigel had just returned to normal now, but Mike was still
enjoying his erection. He made a grab for a towel to place over
himself and trying to arrange it as casually as possible. Nigel

told him it didn't look natural, so he rolled over onto his stomach.

"Hi, good morning," Nigel said, climbing out of the camper. Hault was sitting on a chair, looking fit and relaxed.

"Do you know what time it is?" asked Hault.

"Not got a clue."

"Well, it's gone eleven o'clock."

"But we've only just woken up." Nigel grinned at the thought.

"Then you must have been having a good time last night?"

"You couldn't even start to guess how good a time we had. And it went on all night, well, nearly."

"So you won't feel up to playing tennis. I have booked a court for twelve thirty."

"No problem. But I haven't a racket to play you with."

Hault said he could borrow one of his. "You can use my best one as you will need all the help you can get."

"Well we'll see about that. I'll meet you on the court then," Nigel said, scratching his hair to help get his head clear. "See you."

Nigel watched Hault walk away. He had the build of a body builder. Christ, I bet he can thump a ball all right, he thought.

He climbed back into the camper. Mike was still laying there, his hand on his erection. He smiled. "Sorry," he said.

"Put it away. I've got to have something to eat. So if you don't mind, I would prefer not to have things like that hanging around, it puts me off eating."

Mike smiled, and rolled over on his stomach again. "Isn't it great to be like this. When you think back to our life at home, and how we had to conform to everything. I'd come to your house, knock on your bedroom door, and you would cover up. And at the swimming pool we'd shower with costumes on. Christ what a laugh. Look at us now, we haven't hardly worn anything for days."

Nigel sat there thinking on this. "Bloody great," he agreed. "Shall we eat?"

Breakfast revived Nigel. They sunbathed outside the camper until it was time to play tennis.

Nigel laughed at the thought that all they had to wear were socks and trainers. They looked fit and well sun-tanned as they made their way down to the courts.

Hault was sitting with a few friends waiting for them to arrive. They moved to make space on the bench seat for them.

There was quite a gathering of people sitting on the lawns around the courts.

Hault suggested a doubles. "By what you told me Mike, you are as good as Nigel."

"I never said that, honest," Mike said, turning to Nigel, "but it would be great having a doubles."

There was a quick discussion in the Hault camp. He introduced his partner. "This is Boris."

"Not the...?" Mike was cut short with his question.

"No, he is a reserve today. He's not playing at his best at the moment," Hault laughed.

They watched the end of a match being played on their court. Nigel thought that it was a bit much playing with your private bits swinging around. The women didn't have the same trouble, yet the busty ones could do with some support. He quite enjoyed watching.

Hault asked if they had played nude before.

"No, there has to be a first time though."

The players came off. Hault asked them to select their rackets, as he pulled six out of his sports bag for them to choose from.

They tossed for ends. The sun was high and across court. They had a long knock up. Hault had won the toss, and elected to serve first.

As Nigel had expected, Hault was strong and fast, and Boris was just as solid with his game.

The pairs were well matched. Naturists seemed to be coming from all around to watch.

Nigel was suddenly aware that his manhood was getting smaller. It was a strange feeling. At the change of ends, Nigel mentioned this to Mike. "Glad you have the same problem; I thought it was just me." They looked across at their opponents, and it was reassuring to see that Hault, who was well blessed in that department, was also reduced in size. Nigel felt better about this now. Must be the lack of support around the crotch, he thought.

They laughed at some of the things you don't think about until you play nude. You don't have a pocket to put the second ball in. Nigel held on to his ball, whereas Mike tossed his to the back of the court if his first serve went in. There was no shirt to wipe your brow on, so there were many breaks to grab a towel from the side of the court.

The match reached a stage where it was one set all, and Nigel was serving for the match. Earlier he had been amused at the sight of Mike's bum when at the net. Mike always bent double, keeping his head down, and his bum stuck in the air. He would have his legs wide apart, ready to launch himself across the net to cut off the return. It was not a pretty sight at times.

As he was serving for the match, he tried to block this from his mind. He powered his first serve down and advanced to the net. Hault powered the return, which Mike cut off at the net. The return from Boris was driven directly at Nigel. His reaction was to defend his manhood and managed to get his racket to the ball and cut off the drive deep onto the baseline. Boris attempted a lob. Mike, calling for the ball, waited for it to bounce, then smashed it away to win the point and the match.

The four shook hands. Hault paid a compliment. "That is one of the best games I have ever played, and just to make you feel really good, I have to admit that this is the first time we have been beaten for ages." Boris nodded. "And I hate you for it. No, I was joking, I enjoyed it very much, but we will beat you bastards another time."

The four of them took a shower at the side of the courts. It was a cold one. This did nothing to help his manhood, thought Nigel. But looking around, he was not the only one.

Hault thought they should go and get some liquid inside them, as it was steaming hot. They headed for the bar. Nigel was aware that they had attracted a small group of people who were following them.

Boris asked what they would like to drink. He took the orders and wandered away towards the bar. They found a table, and then collected some chairs. They were quite worn out after the game, so they sat there for a while, not speaking very much.

Hault asked them how they felt playing nude. Nigel gave this some thought. "Strange at first," he said, "but now it would be hard to play back home because I felt so free and relaxed."

Boris returned with the drinks. He had made quite a mess on the tray. Hault complained that he would have liked his glass refilled.

The conversation soon got around to girls. Hault said that he had seen that the two of them had already got fixed up with a couple of girls. Mike told him that it was early days yet.

"It is OK for you Hault. You are lucky by having your girl-friend from home with you."

"I think it is sometimes better to be free on holidays. I don't

137

know."

Boris said that this was his first time at having a naturists holiday. "I find it easier to make friends." And as for girls, he found that he had found girls sexier in summer clothes, but at a naturist holiday, take the clothes away, then you see the true person. "That's why it was easier to make friends here."

"That's very true." Hault agreed.

Boris continued. "You also find out much quicker if you are meeting up with a natural friend. By that I mean you get what you see. But when they are wearing clothes, it takes you quite a while to find out what type of girl you are trying to chat up. Quite often you find you have been fooled by the way she dresses. In the meantime, some other bugger has pinched the girls that could have been right for you."

"What about sex?" Mike asked. "Surely half the fun is in taking her clothes off to have sex?"

"Here we go again," Nigel said.

Hault suggested that they'd had too many textile holidays. "You see, when you are a naturist, firstly you come to places like this to relax. You will always find that friendship comes before sex. Maybe Mike has a point. Without the challenge of undressing each other, the sex side is less important in the end, if at all."

"So you come to a place like this for a whole week without wanting sex?" Nigel asked.

"No, you are missing the point of what I am saying. Wanting sex, and having it are not always possible in such a short period of being on holiday," Hault replied.

"Is that why you bring your girlfriend with you?"

"Nigel, you have it wrong again. I bring my girlfriend to have love. I love her."

"So what about you then Boris?" asked Nigel, who was not giving up his search for facts of life.

"I don't come here expecting to find love. It is not possible in such a short time." Boris answered. "All you can hope for is to make new friends."

"What about sex then?" Nigel was still not giving up.

"Nigel. You have too much sex in your head. Boris has a very good right hand," Hault answered. He looked at Boris. "Sorry."

"Right now you have been asking all the questions, how have you found it since you are new naturists?"

"I think I have found sex, but I have not been able to do anything about it," Nigel answered.

"See, it is not easy is it? People come to places like this, thinking that it happens all the time. But it is not so. You have to respect the lifestyle. It takes a long time to find love, but a short time to make friends. It is not so easy to have casual sex, for many reasons. That's why most come with a partner or friend."

"I think I'm beginning to see the whole picture at last." Nigel sat back, taking in Haults words. Mike announced that he was lost.

"Why is that?" asked Boris.

"Well I'm here with my friend Nigel."

"Then your secret is safe with us." Boris said.

"No I didn't mean it like that." Mike appealed.

"Let's leave it there." Hault suggested. "What are you both doing this evening? We will be at the bar if you want to join us."

Mike said that they might do that. "Thanks for the invite."

They waved goodbye as they walked back to the camper.

After having a shower, they collected a few bottles of wine to replace the bottles consumed the night before. Mike cooked a larger meal as Nigel was complaining of getting thin with all the exercise he was getting.

They lazed outside the camper to top up their suntan in the late afternoon sun. The view they had was beautiful. There was a small track between their camper and the riverbank. There was a line of trees that they could see through which gave them a clear view of the river. They lay there watching the naturists swimming and the canoes that paddled past. Nigel thought about his own reactions when they discovered that they were canoeing in naturist waters. It seemed a long time ago now.

Mike asked if he had any regrets about being at this camp-site.

"None whatsoever. I think I have learned more about life and myself in the past few days than I would have done in a year at home. This is what life's all about surely."

"What did you make of last evening?" Nigel asked.

Mike thought that it had been great to be able to talk like they did in company. "Well, it was you doing most of the question and answer bit really. But it had been a good evening. It was a bit of a sad ending, but that's life I suppose.

"I enjoyed the tennis today.' Nigel said.

"Yes, and I thought that Boris talked a lot of sense too afterwards. "What was it he said, something about not being possible to find love in such a short time on holiday?"

"It was a bit deep for me, but I think it made sense too," Nigel said.

"I have a feeling that there is something going on between Hault and Boris though." Mike smiled.

"Yes, I had a feeling about that too. I bet there is more going on than his right hand. It seems a funny set up with the three of them. Could you go away with your girl friend, and have your best mate tag along as well?"

"I don't know, it could be fun," Mike said.

At this remark, Nigel went into thought mode again. With all these things going on around them, at least he was learning about life by watching and listening. But he wasn't getting any physical satisfaction, well only self-help. He left these thoughts, smiling to himself.

"What are you smiling about?"

Nigel started to open his thoughts to Mike. He asked him to explain some of the frustrations he had experienced during the past week.

"Such as?" asked Mike.

"Well surely you don't have a girl wrap her legs around you when you're naked without getting a hard on. Come on, that's surely frustration?"

"But Boris explained that one for you."

"All right then, so that was sex. But my fucking dick never got the message, did he?" He then went on to question the conversation he'd had with Josh.

"Refresh my memory." Mike asked.

"Josh had made some sense at the time. He admitted that he was bi-curious. He'd had sex with girls, and also with guys."

"So what are you getting at, and what conclusion had Josh come to?"

"He had said that he found having sex with another guy was better, as a guy knows how to switch another guy on, so it made for good sex. Can you understand that?" asked Nigel.

"Yes I can. I've never put it to the test, but yes I can understand. So what are you getting at? *Are you suggesting that we should put it to the test?*"

Nigel suddenly became red in the face. He asked for another wine. He wanted time to answer.

"Come on mate. You brought the subject up. You're stalling

for time now."

"Too bloody true," replied Nigel, "because I could loose a friend over this in the next few minutes, and I don't want that to happen."

"Don't you want to follow this through then?" He put a hand under Nigel's chin, lifting his red face. "Look at me. I'm saying *yes* to your suggestion, you have to answer my question at least."

"But you are not gay," Nigel said.

"No, but then neither are you. But I don't think you'll get to know your true self until you experience this for yourself. What's more, I'd like to think you could trust me. I think it would be good for both of us. And I would be happier finding out the answers together sooner than getting involved with someone say like Josh."

Nigel now overcame his blushing. He raised his head to return Mike's look. "Do you really feel we could come out of this still remaining friends, if we did make love?"

"It wouldn't be love. Remember what Boris said?"

"Yes." Nigel muttered. "Christ, he was right."

"I know he was right. We'll see later. And if he is wrong, what have we to loose?"

"Our friendship," Nigel suggested.

"Wrong again. I believe that if we don't get in too deep, we could come out of this with a much stronger friendship."

Nigel thought about this. Suddenly he was feeling a little insecure. It would soon be time to go to bed. How was the night going to turn out now? Christ, he wished that he had never brought up the subject now.

Mike, seeing his friend was uneasy now, suggested that they should go for a shower, then settle down for the night.

"You don't have to go through with this." Nigel stuttered.

"True. But if we do, it will have to be in the right place and at the right time, nothing crude."

Nigel felt a lot better for that statement.

They took their usual end of day shower. People were already settled for the evening, so the showers were empty. The jet of hot water hit Nigel in the face, reviving him back to a sane mind again. His heart was beating faster at the thought of what they had agreed to. Without thinking, he found himself soaping his manhood area more than usual. Stupid what the mind will do to you, he thought.

Mike was watching this, but decided not to remark on it. He

just gave Nigel a reassuring wink.

Nigel was confused, worrying as to what their friendship would be like afterwards. Should he really go ahead with this? He must be mad. Surely though this would sort out the confusion over his sexuality. He should not worry so much he thought, just let it happen.

They walked back to the camper. Nigel was head down and deep in thought.

"There you go again," Mike said. "Nigel old mate, you really must learn to relax more. Life is for living. We are having a bloody good time, but if you don't want go through with it, just say so."

"Not at all, but it is a first for me." Nigel said.

"Well I've not exactly put myself around. Anyhow, we've agreed that we won't get in too deep."

It was still very warm, so they decided to sit outside the camper with their wine. Nigel was pleased about this, as it would put the arrangements for the night off a little longer. He was beginning to feel a surge of excitement run through his body.

Mike broke the silence. "Do you know, we must be the cleanest guys on the whole campsite. We take showers as if they are going out of fashion."

Nigel could not add to the conversation. He was still letting his mind stray.

"How long shall we stay at this campsite?" Mike asked. "Shall we try and head for the South Coast?"

Nigel at last snapped out of his thoughts. "Erik told us that the West Coast was good for surfing." He got up to find the map. He found it in the glove compartment. "Christ, the camper needs a bloody good clear out," he called out to Mike. In trying to find the map and handbook on campsites, he came across the packs of condoms. His mind flashed back to home. He could hear his father's words of advice on the subject.

He found one of the packs had been opened. Bloody nerve. Mike had not let on that he had been using them. He put the packs back in the cupboard, and sat down again with the map.

He passed the map over to Mike. As this was being unfolded, he posed the question of the opened pack of condoms. Mike continued to unfold the map. Looking up just for a moment he said, "Yes I did take one, but I didn't know that I had to sign for it though."

"So when did you use it then?"

"Last night, but I needn't have bothered." He started to laugh. "You were so far gone last night when I came into the camper feeling my way about trying to find them, you never stirred."

"You sod. You had sex, and you never told me?"

"Well I'll tell you now."

"That's a bloody annoying habit you have. You sit there, smug look on your face, and then you laugh to yourself. Fucking annoying."

"Sorry."

"Well come on, tell me all, you smug bastard."

"There we were, Ariel had been making all the right moves. She was really up for it, so I came back to the camper to grab a pack. I looked all over the bloody place, trying to find them. I couldn't put the light on because you were asleep, and the curtains were still open, and everyone would have seen my panic. Somehow I found them, grabbed a pack, opened it and took one out."

He started to laugh again. "Sorry, but you should have seen me. There I was, treading all over the bed looking through the cupboards like crazy, and all the time you slept through this."

"Yes all right. But the fact is you never told me you had had it away. If I had, I would have told you before now," Nigel said, trying to put on his hurt look.

"Do you want me to continue or not?"

"For fuck sake go on."

"Well picture the scene. Ariel was wanting it, and there I'd been, thrashing around in the dark, with a hard on up to my neck, trying to find the bloody things. I fell out of the camper, and tried to find Ariel. She had got some towels, and laid them out at the other side of her sister's tent. I remember thinking how bloody great it was going to be having sex outside in the warm midnight air, naked and free."

"So?" Nigel urged him to go on.

"Well I thought that the towels were too close to the tents for any grunting and groaning that would be going on, knowing me. So we picked up the towels and moved them behind the camper."

"Why the camper?"

"Well, I knew you wouldn't wake up."

"OK, so you are behind the camper...what then, was it good?"

"Not at all. The little fucker went limp on me."

"You prat. What happened then?"

"Well Ariel tried to restore some life into it, but it wasn't having it."

"So what did Ariel do then?"

"She left me standing there. I remember looking down at my dribbling dick. I tell you mate, it was a sad time. She could have waited a while, but no, she just left me. She's a prick teaser."

"I think we found a couple of them." Nigel said.

"So that's why when we clear out the camper, you'll find a condom tucked under the drivers seat."

"So why did you take so long to tell me all this?"

"Because I didn't want my image shattered."

Mike poured some more wine. They both sat there, Mike giggling, and Nigel trying not to laugh.

"Well at least your dick is in prime condition still by the size of your stiffy on display in bed this morning."

"Yes, but that's what the little sods do. When you want them to perform they let you down, and when it could take a rest, bingo, it becomes larger than life."

Mike then got back to reading the map again. He didn't want to dwell on his failure.

CHAPTER 14

The evening was coming to a close. It was still very warm. Mike having given up on his map reading had made coffee, so they sat there on Mike's bed drinking this together.

As the sliding door was open, Nigel thought that he still had time to collect himself before they settled down for the night. Once the door and curtains were closed, there would be no going back.

His mind was still in a muddle. Was this right was, and would he be able to live with himself afterwards?

Mike put his coffee cup down on the worktop; Nigel passed his over as well. This, in some strange way, was the signal that they were about to prepare for their next experience of life. Mike started to close the curtains as it was dark outside, and for sure he didn't want to be on show. Nigel closed the sliding door. The lights were switched off, and within a few moments their eyes became accustomed to the mellow moonlight that lit up the camper.

They both lay there side by side. Both unsure as to the next move. Nigel's heart was pounding as Mike rolled over closer. Their bodies touched. Nigel could feel the beginning of an erection. Mike smiled, as he was feeling aroused as well. Nigel made the first move. His hand reached down towards Mike's erection. Already he could feel the juices that start to flow on arousal were there. He withdrew his hand once he had felt Mike's hard shaft. He had never held another guy's penis before, but it felt good. Mike took hold of his hand as he tried to remove it.

"Its OK, don't hold back now."

Nigel felt a sense of relief. He hadn't been rejected by making the first move.

He felt Mike's hand on his shaft now. It was strange to feel the firmness of his grip, yet it was not his hand that was stroking his shaft into life. The movements were slow. He thought that Mike just knew how to hold and stroke with feeling. He held Mike's erection, and returned the strokes with the same amount of feeling, both raising the tempo and holding back when they felt the time was right. He followed the moves that Mike seemed quite expert at making. Mike groaned a little at the feel and touch of his strokes. He felt Mike change the rhythm, and he did the same for him. They remained pleasing each other this way for what seemed ages. They both knew when to ease off sensing when a climax was near.

Josh had been right Nigel thought, as he found that Mike knew just what to do to please. He had never had this feeling before. His sexual feelings were being taken to new heights, and then gently eased down. Mike seemed to know just the right touches to make.

Mike made a slight move. He told him not to move for a moment. Mike moved down the bed on to his knees. He was now holding his own shaft, giving it slight strokes to keep it active. Nigel was not sure what to expect now.

"Just lie there and enjoy." With that he took Nigel's shaft into his mouth. Nigel's body shuddered at the sensation. Mike rolled his tongue around the head of Nigel's penis, his lips sucking around his hard erection. This was mind blowing, and exactly what he had dreamed it would be like.

Mike gave this as a sample of what was to come. He stopped his blowjob, and return to lie at Nigel's side. He whispered that he would like him to do the same in return. Nigel needed no prompting, and took up the same position on Mike. He took great care that he followed the same routine. Nigel took Mike's shaft into his mouth. Mike groaned with delight. Nigel couldn't help thinking about the taste; it was strangely pleasant he thought. He worked his mouth around the shaft until he could sense that he would take Mike past the point of no return, so he gave a few moments of rest. He stroked his own shaft, keeping it in prime condition.

He returned to take Mike's shaft again, thrusting it hard into his mouth and throat. It was a mixture of tastes.

Mike made a move to try other positions that would heighten their excitement. They were exploring each other and they felt wildly free.

Mike directed a new position. They both lay back head to toe the full length of the camper bed. Just as Nigel was trying to work out what the next move was to be, Mike, with knees bent and legs apart, eased himself between Nigel's legs. Both with bent knees they over-locked each others leg's, Mike pushed himself closer so as their arses and balls came into contact. Nigel felt Mike's hand take hold of his erection. He then felt the sensation of their two shafts being held in Mike's hand. His head was spinning. Mike worked the two shafts together in a dual wanking motion. At the same time he sensed the feeling of their balls brushing against one another. He started to push his own arse against Mike's. The sensation of these movements was beyond anything he had experienced before. They were now locked together in a sexual fever.

Nigel felt that he now wanted to take his turn to work them both off. Their balls and arses were now moist with their combined juices as they rotated around with their sexual drive.

Mike was the first to give a body movement that alerted Nigel that he was almost ready to shoot his load, so he eased off. Mike pleaded for him not to stop now.

The strokes now were becoming more rapid. There was a tremor through Mike's body as Nigel's firm strokes, of their linked shafts teased the bursts of Mike's load to shoot across both of their bodies. He could hear the moans of pleasure coming from him as he continued to stroke the remaining spurts from his shaft. He now felt his own eruption imminent. Mike sensed this too, and took over from Nigel with the wanking movements. Nigel arched his back, so as to gain as much pull against Mike's strokes. He felt a sudden surge shoot though his body as he reached his climax.

Mike held a gentle grip on both their erections, easing the final spurts of cum from Nigel.

They lay there, exhausted with their efforts. Nigel reached down to their erections. His hand joined Mike's around their shafts as he felt the warmth of their combined love juices which had flowed over their bodies.

They both lay there for ages, not a word being spoken.

Mike was the first to make a move. He climbed alongside Nigel, and placed a gentle kiss on his cheek. Nigel responded. They were not kisses of passion, but just a seal of approval as to what they had just done together.

"Shit, that was something, wasn't it?" Nigel said.

They lay in silence again, both within their own thoughts. Mike eventually stirred himself.

He grabbed a towel and started to clean himself up a little, then passing it to Nigel, asked him if he was OK. Nigel smiled and nodded his reply. "Great, and how about you?"

"Great." He said, grinning his pleasure.

Nigel just wiped himself with the towel, the effort almost too much. He looked down again at Mike, who was already half asleep. He then laid down alongside him, almost asleep himself.

He heard Mike say, "Goodnight old mate."

Nigel gave a giggle at this. "Yes, it was. Talk in the morning."

With that, they drifted off into a deep-contented sleep. Their two bodies bronzed by the sun, resting side by side in their naked togetherness. They had just experienced a new level of sexuality. The morning would extract their feelings. Guilt or pleasure? Would this end their friendship, or would it deepen the bond between them?

Nigel was awake first. Looking at his watch, it was quite early. He squinted to make sure he was right. Yes, nearly seven thirty. Mike was still asleep.

He lay there hearing sounds that he would never have tuned into at home. He listened for quite a while to the birds calling each other. He could even hear the river flowing. The whole area was alive with peaceful calm. The sunlight was streaming through the curtains once more. He sat up, trying not to disturb Mike. Pulling the sliding door of the camper open in slow silent movements, he lay there soaking up the early morning sun.

Mike began to stir. He looked up. "Hi mate."

"Hi to you too."

Nigel put the kettle on. He sat on the edge of the bed. Looking down at Mike, he asked if all was right with him?

"Great," he replied, offering his hand to give a friendly clasp of hands.

Nigel felt that they had come out of their night of male bonding, and they were released from the pressure that had been building up since they'd left home.

Mike laughed as he looked down at his groin. "You messy bugger."

Nigel looked down at himself. He picked at the crusty remains of their cum which clung onto his pubic hair. "You didn't do so badly yourself."

The kettle boiled, and he made the tea. Mike took his mug, and sat up crossing his legs.

"So how do you feel now?"

"Fine."

"And have you had some of your questions answered now?" Mike asked.

Nigel thought this over for a while. This annoyed Mike at

times, but this time he was prepared to wait for his answer.

"I think what we did was good for me. It sure has taught me something about myself, something that I would have carried around in my head for a long time. We had good sex. Everything was just perfect. I don't think I could have done it with just anyone though. It felt right with you."

"Well thank you *Sir*. At your service, anytime," Mike laughed.

"You bloody well know what I mean. It wouldn't have been right with say…Josh!"

"How do you know that? Josh might be just the guy to complete the job for you," Mike suggested.

"I would not like to go any further than we did last night. In my mind we went as far as we should have. But fuck, it was good sex."

"So what do you think will happen when you are in the same situation with a woman?"

"I just don't know. I'm still bi-curious, and I would like to think that we could do that again."

"Would you like to take it further, if we did?"

Nigel gave this some thought again.

"Come on, give me a straight answer."

"Yes. How about you?" Nigel asked, searching for a sign of rejection in Mike's eyes.

Mike did a Nigel. He thought this through in his own time.

"Come on then, you give me a straight answer now." Nigel demanded.

"Well, for sure I enjoyed the experience last night. But I don't think we should plan to do the same each night from now on. Let's just enjoy what happened, and if it happens again, then great. But it has to be natural, and not planned. Last night was just for you."

"Ho, bloody ho! You can't tell me that you didn't enjoy it as well?"

"Well, it was quite good," Mike admitted.

"Shall we start the day then?" Nigel suggested.

As they walked towards the showers, Nigel felt a sense of guilt come over him. He tended to cover his groin area with his towel, as naturists looked and nodded early morning greetings.

Even in the shower he felt that all eyes were on him, as if they could tell what they had been up to during the night.

He told Mike about his guilt feeling on their walk back to the camper.

Mike smiled at this. "I suspect that almost every adult in the showers with us had some form of sex last night as well. So I think we were in good company."

Nigel felt better for hearing this.

Mike cooked some breakfast which they sat eating outside the camper as it was already hot. They caught sight of Ariel. She was with another guy now. Nigel thought that he had seen him crawl out of her caravan. Ariel had no choice but to walk past them, but she never glanced their way. The guy looked as if he'd had a rough night. Mike remarked that he thought that he was the sort that one found on every campsite. Blonde streaked matted hair, lean tan body, and wearing shorts that came down below the knees, the ones that this type of guy put on at the beginning of the holiday, and were never introduced to a washing machine for weeks.

Nigel told him that he thought he was being a little hard on the guy. "Could it mean that he wished it had been him crawling out of her caravan?" Nigel smiled at his own question.

"The guy looked a prat." Mike said. He gave another look over his shoulder just to confirm his opinion.

Nigel told Mike that he thought that he was better off without getting involved with Ariel. Mike agreed.

"What about you and Nina then?" Mike asked.

"I don't have any real feelings about her. I think I have been looking for love. Boris was right. You should only expect friendships to develop on a week's holiday."

"Talking of which, how long are we staying here for?" Mike asked.

"Let's give it another couple of days."

"Have you seen the notice board? It's full of events that are going on for the rest of the week. Maybe we should wander down and have a look." Mike suggested.

Nigel ran his finger over the programme of events that they found pinned to the notice board outside the reception. "Look, they have yoga," he said.

"Do you want some of that then. If you do, it starts in about twenty minutes time." Mike said, checking his watch.

They hurriedly found the yoga group. They had all grouped together in a well-chosen setting in amongst trees that seemed to form a circle around them. The sunlight streamed through the trees which made nice patterns across the naked bodies as the naturists sat on their towels awaiting the instructor.

There were about twenty in the group. They all sat around in a circle. Nigel had already made eye contact with a girl opposite him. She had a beautiful impish body. He guessed that she was about seventeen or eighteen.

The instructor arrived and was keen to start. Nigel was trying to pay attention to what was being said, but he could not take his eyes off the girl.

Mike got right into the session. His eyes closed, back straight, and with his breathing being corrected by the softly spoken words of the instructor, he looked the part.

Nigel was not doing quite so well. It took him a while to relax. He could sense a calm drifting over him, and he no longer allowed his eyes to roam the circle. He did however allow himself just quick glances over to the girl just to make sure he was not dreaming.

The session went on for just over an hour. They were told to sit for a while to allow their bodies to regain a level. After a while they started to stand up and mix together talking. Even this was in low key.

Nigel slowly moved towards the girl, not wishing to appear too keen to make contact. He opened his mouth to say something, but she spoke first.

"Hi. I've seen you around the campsite with your friend over there. I watched your tennis match. It was a good game."

"Sorry, I didn't see you there. Where are you camping?" Nigel managed to blurt out.

"Oh, over the other side of the camp with my parents and friends. Your camper is down there by the river isn't it?"

"Yes. Sorry, I'm Nigel, and you are?"

"Vikkie. They call me Vik, for short."

"Why? I like Vikkie, it suits you."

"I think that's good old English charm you are giving me," she said, smiling at him.

"I don't think so. Just the truth. I like the name."

Nigel looked around for Mike. He was walking away and gave a thumbs up sign to him. "See you at the camper, I'm going for a beer."

"Is he as nice as he looks?" Vik asked.

"They don't come any better than him," Nigel replied. "Can I walk you back to where you are camping, that's if you're going back now?"

"Sure you can."

On the way along the river footpath, Nigel found out that she hadn't a boyfriend with her. She laughed as she told him that she'd had several offers to go out drinking and to the disco since she arrived, but she hadn't met up with the right type for her. Her father tells her she's fussy.

"That means I stand no chance at all then?" Nigel looked straight at her with this question.

"I don't know. I have been watching you and your friend, and I think you might be in with a chance, as a friend." Vik smiled.

The words of Boris flashed through his head again.

They walked along at a slow pace. Every now and again, he acted the gentleman by holding back the odd overhanging branch of a tree for her. She thanked him each time.

Vik asked him how long he had been a naturist. He relayed the story so far, leaving out the more personal encounters though.

Vik told him she had been a naturist all her life. "I was born like it." Nigel thought that this was a nice way of putting it, as it seemed to put life in perspective a little more. He felt that he was going through a rapid learning curve about life. Just try explaining this at home, he thought.

Here he was, walking in the nude, with a cracking looking girl, who was also nude, and he had only just met up with her. Big Dave would never believe this one back home. He smiled at this thought.

He asked Vik why they camped so far up river and away from the social area.

"We always do, it's much better, just wait and see. There are naturists that we meet up with every year. I have been coming here with my parents since I was three years old."

"Don't you get a bit bored?" he asked.

"Not at all. It's such a change from everyday life. Here you're so free."

They walked past the part of the river Nigel had been coming to daily. This point of the river he believed was the end of the naturist area. Vik laughed at this. "No. You are about to enter a part of the campsite where true naturists come to rest."

As they rounded a bend of the riverbank, Vik pointed ahead. "Here we are. This is where we get back to nature."

Nigel could see that this was a more basic camping area. There were many small tents. Vik explained that they were for the youngsters. "This is their own little campsite. Here they learn to grow up together. They even cook their own food."

"What by themselves?" Nigel asked.

"Well, they do have one parent on duty each day, just to keep an eye on them. The youngsters love the freedom."

Nigel stood there for a moment looking down at the scene. There must have been at least thirty youngsters playing around their tented village totally naked and free. It was as if they were a native tribe, he thought.

"What a way to bring up kids," Nigel remarked.

"The only way." Vik said. "Here they learn about life at an early age. By growing up together like this nude and free, most of the problems in life are sorted out, and there are very few questions left that parents have to answer."

Nigel could see another camping area through the trees. "Are they the parents' tents?"

"Yes. That's what I told you. This is where true naturists come to rest. Parents can relax all day knowing that the kids are safe and happy."

As they walked closer, Nigel could see that there was a mixture of tents and small caravans. There seemed to be a central area based around a Bar-B-Q. There was a trail of smoke drifting from the wood fire they cooked on.

People just sat around together, some reading, others just lazing in the sun talking in soft tones.

Nigel felt that he'd just entered a time period, one that had stood still in time.

Nigel was introduced to the parents. They shook hands, but gave him little attention. He had been made aware that he was the intruder, not in an unfriendly way, but he knew that he had to earn his place with these naturists, as this was their own private world. He was welcome, but aware that he should not disturb the scene.

Vik invited him to sit down on one of the wooden benches, the type that had a table between two bench seats.

"What would you like to drink?" she asked.

He felt that he should ask for water, but she reeled off a list, and he settled for a beer.

Vic returned with his beer and sat down next to him. He was feeling very relaxed in their company. Maybe it was because nobody was taking much notice of him being there. The scene was also very different from the rest of the campsite.

He could see several teenagers around who seemed to have formed their own groups as well.

He tried to count the numbers, must be at least thirty or so. They looked almost black in colour from living in the sun. They all seemed happy just to sit around talking and laughing together.

One of the group was playing his guitar. He had long hair, which was pulled back into a ponytail. He had a small group of friends sitting around listening to him play. He was very talented.

Nigel felt he had to pinch himself just in case this was not for real. Everything around him seemed so peaceful. Could it be true?

Vik had been watching him. She smiled. "Welcome to the real world of naturism. I can see you like what you are seeing around you."

"It's just that you all seem a little remote from the rest of the campsite."

Vik explained that there were different types of naturists. "All naturists, but with different ways of living. Where you have your camper, they are mainly holiday naturists. The ones that have the mobile homes up by the pool, they are the ones with money. We don't have a problem with that."

"So what do you call yourselves then?" he asked.

"Naturists."

"But you said the others were naturists as well."

"Yes, but some of them are nudists as well," Vik replied.

"I'm confused now."

"Well nudists are those who are free to take their clothes off, but some wear rings and things on their bodies as well. Naturists tend not to, whereas nudists do."

"And naturists?"

"Naturists are sitting all around you, look. We are the ones that are close to nature and the natural things of life. We come here every year to meet up with the same people and their families. I've been coming here since I was a baby." She smiled at the thought of this.

At this point the father came across to their table. He shook hands again, "You are welcome to stay and eat with us."

Nigel thought that although this was nice of him, he had hardly spoken to him. He looked around him and he could see that the mother had already prepared the food. Plates were being passed around and large wooden bowls of salad prepared. He saw a chain of teenagers carrying plates of cooked meat that were placed on the table. Then came the bread, followed by red wine. Hardly a word was spoken during this preparation of food. It seemed that the teenagers role was serve at the table before they sat down to join their elders.

"So where are you camping?" asked the father.

Nigel pointed back towards the trees. "Along the pathway near the clubhouse. We have a camper which we have parked down by the river."

"He is a holiday naturist," Vik told her father.

"You will learn," the father smiled.

"I'm learning already," he replied.

Nigel was about to start his meal when he suddenly thought of Mike. He will be on his own for most of the day, unless he could break away to tell him where he was.

He explained to Vik that he should really contact his friend.

"Why not bring him over," she said, looking at her father for approval.

"Sure," he nodded.

Nigel excused himself. "I'll run back and collect him. Thank you."

He raced back to the camper, arriving out of breath. Mike was not there. Shit he thought, where could he have got to. Dashing back through the trees and along the riverbank, he spotted him. He had been swimming alone.

He shouted out to him. Mike heard him and came swimming back to the riverbank, and climbed out. His walk towards Nigel seemed a little slow, and he looked dejected.

"Where the hell have you been?"

Nigel, still out of breath, tried to explain. He told Mike that he thought they should move their camper over to the other side. "They are great people, and so laid back that you'd think they would fall over. They have invited you back to have a meal with them."

Mike, having heard the word 'food' demanded that he should be taken to the feast.

Nigel chatted all the way back. He told Mike what he had seen. "It's a whole new-world," he said excitedly.

They parted their way through the trees. "There, look through there," Nigel said, pointing ahead.

Mike looked around. He was seeing the same scene that Nigel had earlier. "Christ, even the tents look the older types. This is like walking into the past. Fuck me, what have you got us into now?"

MICHAEL KEENE

As they walked through the long grass, Mike wanted to scratch his balls as the long grass tickled him in that area. Good manners stopped him. Instead, he used his towel, pretending to wipe away sweat from his body.

Nigel introduced Mike to the family. They just said,"Hi." There was a strange peace about the whole situation.

"Sit down, sit down and eat," the father said.'

The food was passed around to them, and the red wine poured into pottery type wine goblets.

Vik was the first to break the silence. "Do you have a girl-friend here with you?"

He told her that he found it easy to make friends, but he didn't want to get involved.

The meal seemed to go on for ages. The wine flowed well. It seemed that the father always encouraged the meal to be the meeting point for all the family. The rest of the day they could find their own entertainment. This part of the day was set aside as being his way of showing he was head of the family.

For the first time, the father spoke. He turned to the two newcomers to his world. "So, you are from England then? Not much sunshine there?"

"No, that's why we are in France," Nigel replied.

"Why did you come to a naturist camp. Was it to have a laugh?"

"Not at all. We were out on the river in a canoe. We had no idea that the camp was here," Mike said, almost sounding annoyed at the question.

"So now that you are here, what do you think about us then?"

"I think it's great." Nigel then went on to explain that he was trying to get away for a time, just to find his way in life. He thought that this might lead the father into giving his own thoughts on the subject, as he was keen to learn. At last he was finding respect for his elders on this trip.

"You are right to want to find your own way in life," the father said. "You have to decide what is right, and what is wrong for you, and those that are close to you."

"Have you found this yourself then?" Mike asked.

"Yes I have." He then went on to say that this was his way of showing his family there was more to life than society would let them know about. Nature had the final answers to life. Science makes advances in one direction, as is doing a lot of good for people. But science was also destroying nature. So he was giv-

156

ing his children a chance to live with nature, before the trees were destroyed. "It is a vicious circle," he added.

Both Nigel and Mike listened to the father's statement. The silence around them was enough to prove that the father had got the message across.

"So are you suggesting that everyone should become naturists?" Nigel asked.

"It would solve a few of life's problems," the father said. " You have to decide many things during your life. But it comes down to simple facts. Money will not buy you life or friends. It will provide a style of life for you, yet the friends that it brings along with it may not be the ones that you would have chosen to have without money. Naturists find that a peaceful life makes you far richer than money. This way you find true friends.' The father sat back watching their reaction to this.

"What about life then?" Nigel asked. He felt he was on a roll now.

"Love of life comes first. Love is what you share with another. This in turn gives you and your lover, a life worth living."

"How do you find love then?" Nigel asked again.

"You earn it, and you know when you have found it. It comes in many ways."

Nigel was suddenly aware that everyone had gathered around to listen to the conversation. Their faces reacting to the father's statements. Mike suggested that he gave it a rest. Nigel just grinned at this. There was no way he was going to give up at this stage. Shit, he thought, the old man is talking sense. If only dad could have opened up like this.

"Could you explain what you mean by that," he asked.

"Well, do you like your friend, or do you love your friend, or is it both of these?"

Mike, looking across at Nigel fluttered his eyelids at this.

The father continued. He had caught sight of Mike's reaction.

"Do you love your parents, and are they also your friends? Do you like Vik, or do you love her?"

"Oh dad, that's not fair." Vik interrupted the conversation, looking sternly at her father.

Nigel asked if he could answer the last question first. The father suggested any order he liked.

"I can't love Vik, because I have only just met her. I think I like her, and I think Vik likes me as well. As for my parents, I love them to bits, and they are my friends as well."

Looking at Mike, he added, "as for this one, he is my best friend, and I love him also."

Mike hung down his head. A huge smile spread across his face.

The father said he would pass on his views about love and sex another time, but right now he was going to his tent to have a sleep. Without even looking back, he walked away from the group and entered his tent.

After a moments silence Vik told Nigel he had asked for that. "My father has strong views about life, and they are good ones. He hardly talks about them, only to people that he feels are interested. You were very honoured."

As most of the teenagers had gathered around to listen, Vik started to introduce them. Mike laughed. "I'll never remember them all."

The conversation got around to the evening and what everyone was going to do. The suggestions ranged from having a log fire, some beer and wine, and round it off with a midnight swim.

Some of them wanted to have a beer at the bar, but they didn't want to get mixed up with the group from the other campsite.

"Why?" asked Nigel

"We prefer to be with our own kind. Over the other side, they dress up for the evening, we don't." said one of the lads.

"They are more textile than us," added another of the group.

Nigel was now beginning to understand. The people around him were true basic naturists.

"Do you live like this all year round?" Nigel asked.

There was a hurried answer from one of the young guys. "Whenever we can."

He was about eighteen. His body was dark brown through being in the sun for long periods. There was not a white patch to be seen on his lean frame. His shoulder length hair had a natural wave in it, and there was just the sign of a goat's beard, and when he smiled, his teeth were so white. Nigel envied him in a way. He then tried to pair them up. Who was with whom? He gave up and asked Vik.

"Difficult to say really. We are all friends together and tend not to pair up."

Nigel smiled at this.

"I know what you are thinking," said Vik. "and it's not about free love. You see, we have all been coming here since we were little kids. It's hard to explain, and maybe hard for you to understand. As we live together, play together, quite often we all sleep together."

"Well in England we would call this free love."

"See, you have the wrong idea. The girls sleep together, and so do the boys."

"And how do you go about having a little sex then?" Nigel asked.

Mike told him that he should quit while he was loosing.

Vik told him that he should work that one out for himself.

Nigel smiled at his thoughts.

Mike interrupted. "Don't you think we should be getting back. It's our turn to entertain some of our friends this evening."

They headed back; Vik walked part of the way with them. She stopped at the edge of her camping area. They parted, Nigel giving her a peck on her cheek. "If you want to come and join us in our little commune, you are welcome," she said. With that she waved goodbye. Nigel watched her walk away.

God, she had a super little figure. Mike pulling his arm said, "Come on lover boy."

They slumped down in the camper. Mike burst out laughing. "Shit what was that all about? Pass me a beer."

Nigel opened the fridge, and took two bottles out, passing one to Mike who was stretched out on the bed.

"Another fine mess you have got us into," said Mike.

"I had no idea that the day was going to be like that. All I was interested in was Vik. She looked bloody lovely working out at yoga. I thought that I was on a good thing there."

"I think we would both be on to a good thing if we went over there to stay. Shit, I bet there is plenty of free love going on there," Mike said.

"I can't believe that the girls are with the girls, and the boys with the boys all night."

Mike laughed again. "Christ you would have to have a diary on who you were with last."

"Don't mention the word diary. We shouldn't laugh really. It seems they have a good lifestyle. It's just that we don't understand them because it's not the way we've been brought up. To them what they do is perfectly natural," Nigel said.

"I really do believe that they can sleep together, and sex doesn't really come into it. I bet the old man was right. When they find love, they know they have found it," said Mike.

"It makes sense I suppose. There's us, we have just started to experience the freedom of being nude. This brings on the horny thoughts in the beginning. But now look at us, we walk around as if we've been doing it for years. The scene is great, and I'm learning more about life than I would at home now. Shit, I want some more of this," Nigel said, falling back on the bed to reflect on his life. He now had a more open mind. Mike was helping him to come to terms with his sexuality. He was still bi-curious though, and he thought he should trust his inner feelings and experiment more. Shit, supposing he found out that he was really gay? How could he tell his parents? Not worth thinking about that...and what about Big Dave? He sat upright at this thought.

"Welcome back." Mike said. He didn't have to ask where Nigel's thoughts had taken him.

"Hi, sorry, I was miles away. Just thinking about life and me. I'm beginning to find another side of me."

"Thank Christ for that," said Mike. "Are we going to stay another night here to find this other person, or shall we move on?"

"I think we should stay another night at least," Nigel suggested.

"Then I think it's up to the bar tonight, I could do with a few beers inside me."

Mike prepared the meal, while Nigel wrote up some more in his diary. He had quite a lot to enter this time. He didn't hold back with writing down all his feelings, including the night with Mike

They stood at the bar looking around. It was late evening now, and quite crowded. They had already seen Josh and his friend Ian, who were with a few other guys that they had not seen before.

Nigel couldn't help staring at Josh and thinking how good he looked. His suntan was now almost black compared against Ian's more bronze colour. They were both wearing the same gear, loose white vests, in the style that gave more arm space than normal. Their shorts were loose fitting, yet showed off their bums with their every movement. There I go again, he thought. He was clearly attracted to them or else why would he notice details like this? He looked around the crowded bar and caught sight of the girls.

His mind raced away. He challenged his feelings towards them, each one in turn.

Ariel was standing there with her textbook model pose. Her slim body covered by a longish, light cotton T-shirt style top, and nothing else. Her movements showed off the curves of her body to the full.

Nina had a silk sarong tied around her waist. She was not wearing a top, yet he could see that she was holding one in her hand. He thought that this wasn't quite fair on the guys. She had nice firm breasts, not very large, but firm. He knew this from his brief experience with her, but he thought that there were a few other guys around that could claim they knew this at first hand as well.

His feelings were still very much the same. Both the guys and the girls caused the same reactions within him. So maybe he should stop thrashing his mind all the time, and accept that he was 'bi'.

"Watch out, you're spilling your beer," Mike whispered in his ear.

Erik and Anita had caught sight of them. They made their way through the crowd to join them.

"So how are you finding things now that you are one of us?" Erik asked.

Nigel told him that he was still finding it all too much to sort out. He then went on to tell of the day's events.

Erik smiled. "So you have met up with the nature lovers have you? They are very nice people. They keep themselves to themselves, and they are very communal in the way they live together."

"I quite like that," Mike said, much to Nigel's surprise.

"If you join them for any length of time, you will soon become one of them," Anita added.

"Would that be a bad thing then?" asked Nigel.

"Not at all," she replied.

"You have been listening to what I was telling you the other evening then." Erik said. "Life is for living, and you have to experience life to the full. And at your age, this can be very exciting for you."

"Nigel's doing his best," Mike said, looking at Nigel and winking.

The conversation went on, but Nigel once again drifted off

into his own world. Life was not easy for him at this age. He had not been a hit with Nina. Maybe it was because she would have been too easy to sleep with. There was also Josh at the back of his mind. Josh had made a move to become friendlier. Perhaps he should have taken advantage of this. Then there was Vik, she was offering him friendship, but there were no sexual vibes from her. Maybe this was telling him something. Was it because he was the one that was thinking about sex every time he met someone? The words of Boris once again echoed through his head.

Mike dug him in the ribs. "You are being asked if you would like another beer."

"Sorry, who was asking?"

Erik asked him again. "Would you take beer with me?"

"Yes, thank you. Sorry I was miles away."

"He travels a lot, in his mind of course, but he does travel," Mike laughed.

"And he shares my experiences with me," Nigel quickly added.

Erik collected their beers. Anita said that they should be getting back to the youngsters. "Enjoy your evening." Anita held onto Erik's hand as he made way for her through the crowded bar.

Nigel felt a tug on his arm. "Hi, won't you join us?" It was Josh.

Nigel looking at Mike gave a nod to the invite.

Josh introduced them to his friends. Nigel told them that he would never remember names.

To his surprise, Boris was one of the group. He smiled across at them. He then moved around the edge of the group to join them. "Nice to see you again. So, you know this lot then?" he said. "Only two of them," Nigel replied. "Who are you with?"

"Nobody really, I just like the company."

They got into deep conversation, mainly about tennis. Mike excused himself, and headed for the loo.

Boris and Nigel continued their conversation. Boris had turned to face Nigel and stood quite close in order to talk over the noise of the crowded bar. Nigel felt a positive movement of a hand on his bum. Boris kept on talking. He was looking directly into his eyes and his expression never altered. Thoughts raced through his head. This was a repeat of the nightclub scene. For a moment he had a vision of Wayne's face flash through mind. He was not sure that he could handle this. How could a guy talk to you keeping a straight face, and caress your arse at the same time? Where was Mike? He always goes off at the wrong moments.

The bar was now very packed. Nigel managed to get his arm around his back to remove the hand off his bum. To his relief and surprise, Boris was not the owner. Looking quickly around, he found that it belonged to Josh. Still holding Josh's hand as he removed it, he tapped Josh on the shoulder. "Is this yours?" he asked.

"Yes. Can I have it back now?" Josh smiled over his shoulder.

Boris asked if everything was all right. Nigel laughed, and tried to explain. Boris found this amusing.

"Don't be mad, they are a nice crowd, quite harmless really."

Mike returned. "Shall we get out of here, it's too bloody hot for me, and look at you, sweating like a pig," he said, running his finger across Nigel's brow.

Boris asked if he could join them if they were leaving the bar. The three of them pushed their way through the crowd. As Nigel passed Josh he said, "I'll get you for that." Josh smiled, "Yes please."

The three of them walked towards the river to cool down. They had not gone far when they heard the rest of the group running after them. Josh was carrying a ball. "Water polo everyone," he shouted.

The scene that followed would have been hard to explain back home, thought Nigel. What small amounts of clothes they had on were peeled off each other as if they were all wrestling. One by one they jumped into the river with squeals of laughter. Mike and Nigel joining them. The river seemed to be awash with naked limbs.

CHAPTER 15

Nigel lifted his head a little to ease his stiff neck. He felt a slight pressure across his chest. He managed to open his eyes just enough to confirm that he was in the camper. His mind was not in gear at all. Slowly he worked out that the pressure on his chest was Mike's arm resting across him.

The camper door was open, and as usual the sun was streaming through the windows. He was in no hurry to remove Mike from his position. His thoughts raced back to the evening before. He remembered playing around at water polo in the river. They had played for a long time. He remembered getting out of the water after the game and climbing up onto the riverbank where they all lazed around drinking. The rest of the events that followed were far from clear. His mouth felt as if it had been filled with sand. Mike was still in a deep sleep, but his arm had to be removed. Nigel sat up slowly, the arm slid away onto the bed. What a scene, he thought. Two naked bodies just dumped into the camper. The camper was nothing to be proud of, he thought. What would his parents think of the scene?

Mike stirred. His eyes were just slits. Not a sight to write home about either.

"Shit," Mike uttered.

"I take it that was your early morning greeting to me, and the world in general."

"It's the best I can come up with at the moment."

They both found it an effort to move. There were lots of questions to be answered; yet neither being able to string more than a few words together.

Nigel broke the silence first. "What happened after we got out of the river, and how did we get back to the camper?"

"Hold on. That's two questions in one. I can't handle that at the moment. I can remember being helped up off the river bank, I think it was Josh and his little friend."

"Well who helped me back then?" Nigel asked.

"I seem to remember Boris having a hand in that."

"What the hell were we drinking?"

"Not a clue old mate," Mike said, sporting a grin, "but I think we should get some of it for the rest of our trip."

They both tried to remember the river scene. Nigel said he had though that it was going to be one of those boys' type sessions. "You know, like the gay scenes you read about."

"Well I was out of luck then," Mike laughed.

Nigel decided that he wouldn't start a heavy conversation at this point. He crawled to the edge of his bed. On looking at the time, and not feeling like breakfast, he decided that it was time to take a shower, or go back to sleep.

Mike asked for a towel to be passed to him.

"Bloody hell, where are the things we were wearing last night?" Nigel asked.

"Still down by the river I expect."

Although the showers were hot, Nigel elected to take a cold one this time. Mike made a remark, which Nigel assumed to mean he was brave. He ignored this.

After about ten minutes under the shower, Nigel started to feel a lot better. The world was not such a bad place after all, he thought.

Leaving Mike standing under his shower, and looking down at his manhood, which had decreased in size with the cold water treatment, muttering "Oh shit," and shaking his head in a sad fashion, he took his towel outside to dry off in the sun. Looking around, he caught sight of Ian. He was sitting on a bench under a tree in the shade. He waved to Nigel to join him.

Ian was smoking. He patted the bench next to him, and offered Nigel the thinly rolled joint. Nigel shook his head at the offer; he was not in the habit of smoking joints, or in the mood.

"Did you enjoy last night?" Ian asked, looking into Nigel's eyes.

Nigel explained that he didn't remember much about it after about the third drink.

"Well you were well gone when Josh and I left you. We got Mike back to the camper and laid him out on his bed."

"I think Boris got me back." Nigel said. Ian gave a nod to this.

"Not sure who won, but did you enjoy the water polo?" asked Ian.

Nigel laughed at this. "I wasn't sure what to expect."

"Not sure what you mean by that remark. It's good to have a mess about like that with the boys, it's a nice form of bonding."

"Is that what you call it then?" Nigel said, with a hint of a smile.

"Yes. What would you call it then?" Ian snapped.

Nigel could see he had hit a nerve and tried to change the subject. Ian was not so keen to give up. His smile changed to an aggressive look. It was a complete mood swing.

"Listen you little shit. I know what you were expecting last night. Sorry you were out of luck my little fucked up friend," Ian snapped again.

"What was I expecting then?" asked Nigel. His face was now quite red.

"I'll tell you what you were expecting. You thought that as you were with a bunch of gay guys, we were after your arse, didn't you?"

Nigel tried to say something that would calm the situation. Ian was in full flight now.

"Well old fruit, being gay doesn't mean we have no morals. We were all down at the river to have a bit of fun. We leave the fucking of nice guy's arses for times when we are in private. You guys are all the same. It's OK for you to shag your girlfriends, not that I know much about that, but like you, we have our sex in private. The river is far from private."

"I never thought that at all."

"Balls. You thought just that. We are gay, but we have some respect for naturists we meet up with. You may like to remember we come from homes and families too. It's not all about fucking. If you really think that, then you might like to know that Josh and I have not had sex since we arrived here." Ian's head sank down at this statement. Nigel thought he could sense tears arriving.

"Sorry."

"That's OK." Ian replied.

Nigel sat a little closer to Ian and put his arm around him. Ian looked up and smiled. There was a warm feeling between them.

"Watch out, we may be seen." Ian laughed. "Then what will people think?"

Just at this point Mike appeared from the showers. Nigel decided not to remove his arm from around Ian. Right or wrong, he felt it right to react to Ian this way, and if he had to explain this to Mike…tough.

Mike sat down with them. Ian then told the story about how he and Josh had carried him back to the camper.

"Did you get into bed with me then?"

Nigel advised him that this was not he time to ask stupid questions.

Ian broke the ice by saying, "No, but it had crossed my mind."

Nigel stood up. This was getting too heavy for his liking.

Ian got up as well. "See you both later. Have fun."

The rest of the day consisted of having lunch at the bar, followed by a slow walk down to the river to see if they could find their clothes. There they were, neatly folded and placed at the foot of a tree in the shade. Nigel remarked that they would not have stood a chance of finding them again if they had been left on a 'textile camp'.

They swam in the river. It was refreshing. After their swim, they topped up their suntans some more. They both fell asleep, and it was late in the afternoon before they awoke.

Mike didn't stir from his position; he just placed his hands behind his head, and felt quite content with life. Nigel rolled over close to him, so that their conversation would not be over-heard.

"Is all well in your world then?" Nigel asked, whispering in Mike's ear.

"Give us a kiss and I'll tell you."

"Don't you start that again," Nigel insisted.

"Well I saw you with your friend Ian. It was a very romantic scene."

Nigel told him the facts surrounding the scene. Mike listened, trying not to smile.

"OK, I believe you."

"So what do you feel about all this?" Nigel asked, trying to get Mike to open up a little on the subject.

"I think the lifestyle is great. A fucking great holiday."

"Yes, but what about us?"

"Us, you and me. Well I think we are just beginning to find our true selves. I'm not scared or ashamed about what we have got ourselves involved in together, or about my feelings towards you. It means a lot to me to be able to share experiences together like this. We'll find ourselves before we get back home. I'm sure about that."

Nigel was quite touched by this statement. He wanted to react, but was aware that there were people fairly close to them. Sad, he thought. Why couldn't he respond? Girls can.

Mike gave him a dig in the ribs. "Go on I know what you

wanted to do, but you backed off."

"Yep, you're right. Shit, who would want to be our age?"

"My dad, for starters," Mike replied. With that, he got up. Leaning down, he gave Nigel a sly peck on his cheek as he picked up his towel to move off.

Nigel watched him walk away down the pathway. Christ, I only hope I look as brown as he does. He's a good-looking sod too.

He followed Mike back to the camper. The usual routine was carried out. Food first, then a shower, shorts on, then carrying their T-shirts, they headed for the bar.

Everyone seemed to be there. Mike sneaked in a beer for both of them. Ian was the first one to greet them.

"I just want to say sorry for the way I acted earlier. I'm not having a very good time at the moment." He went on to say that Josh had started to make friends with another guy. "I don't like him. I hope Josh doesn't bloody well get into trouble."

Nigel looking across the bar saw the blonde guy with Josh. He was dressed a bit OTT for a naturist camp. He seemed to be all over Josh, so he could see Ian's problem.

"Don't worry. He'll be back with you, you'll see," Nigel assured him.

Mike caught sight of Ariel across the bar and made his way across to where she was sitting. Nigel felt annoyed about this seeing as she had not got a good track record with him.

Nigel felt that he should chat with Ian for a while. Every now and again he would glance across at Mike. He could see him laughing and putting his arm around her. She had got him under her spell he thought.

As the evening went on, Josh came over to join them. "Sorry about that guy, I think he thought that he was onto a good thing," he smiled.

"And was he?" snapped Ian.

"Oh, do I detect a little sourness in your voice?"

"Yes," came the reply. They both laughed at this then moved their chairs closer together. Nigel felt he was now on his own.

Mike was still involved with Ariel and it was getting late, so Nigel decided to make his way back to the camper. He bought a couple of beers at the bar as he left.

He opened the camper door with a bang. He could feel the frustration rushing through his body. Without a thought, he cracked the bottle top down onto the edge of the cooker lid. This removed a chunk of wood from the edge. The beer tasted better for this action. He was in a foul mood.

What the hell was Mike doing? Ariel, of all people. His head went spinning around at the thought of them being together again. She must be a prick teaser.

He fell back on Mike's bed. It was hot in the camper, so he pulled his shorts off and the used his T-shirt to wipe his face.

The beer tasted good as he drank it down. He opened another and started to calm down. Maybe he was going a bit over the top, after all it was only eleven o'clock.

Perhaps he should go back and see what the scene was now. Maybe Mike was looking for him. Shit no!

He had gone off with Ariel, leaving him on his own. Why the fuck should he feel guilty. I'll drink to that, he thought.

He opened the fridge door. Fuck, no beer or wine. He sat there for a moment thinking. It's back to the bar if he wanted more beer. He kidded himself it had nothing to do with what Mike was up to. The bar was full now. People were drinking to overcome the heat. He pushed his way up to the bar. Turning as he waited to be served, he saw Josh and Ian. "Have you seen Mike?" he asked.

There was a silence. "Not for a while," Josh muttered.

With his vision now blurred, he pushed his way through the crowded bar. There was no sight of Mike. Should he take a few beers back and get smashed, or stay and wait for Mike to turn up?

On his way out he ordered a six-pack, costing him a fortune. He wasn't bothered about the money, he was feeling hurt about Mike.

He found his way back to the camper, the beers now having an effect on him. This was their home, and Mike had left for Ariel. His mind was now a mess. Stupid sod he thought, pull yourself together. Opening the camper door ever so gently now, he climbed inside and just stood there just looking around. It was now that he caught sight of what he had done to the cooker top. Stupid idiot! There was no reason to take it out on Mike's dad's camper. He was not going to sleep on Mike's bed tonight. He would climb into his own bed up top. It seemed ages since he had slept up there.

Once again he removed his shorts and just spread himself out on top of his sleeping bag.

He had only been asleep for a short while, or so he thought. Looking at his watch, it was nearly half past four in the morning. Leaning over the edge of his bed, he half expected to see

Mike asleep below. But no, he wasn't there.

He made no attempt to move. His body began to hurt with tension and his mind so full of frustrations as his emotions ran riot. He was now missing his mate, and as stupid as it felt, this was almost the same feeling he'd had over a girl a couple of year's back. A friend at the time had told him that this was down to being too young, and he would soon learn about the feelings of love when he was older. He was older now, and he had the same feelings running through his body again. But Mike was a guy. Why was he feeling the same way now?

Sleep overtook him again.

It seemed as if he'd only just closed his eyes when he heard the camper door slide open. He was not going to show Mike that he had been waiting for him, or even concerned. He kept his eyes almost closed, but open just enough to watch Mike's movements.

Mike took his shorts off, then very gently eased himself up into Nigel's bed and just lay there at his side. He'd never done that before. Mike gave him a pat on his shoulder. "Sorry old mate", he whispered, "I'll tell you all in the morning. Goodnight mate."

A great feeling of relief came over Nigel. He never spoke a word as he moved his body closer to Mike's. They both drifted off to sleep.

Nigel was aware the he was being rocked slightly as he lay on top of his bed. There was a hand on his chest. "Cup of tea old mate." Mike stood there holding a mug of tea.

Nigel turned over taking the mug in his hand. The two faced each other. Mike had a smile on his face, and Nigel put on one of his best-hurt expressions.

"Did you miss me then?" Mike asked.

"Not at all," lied Nigel.

"Did I wake you then?"

"Never felt you get into my bed."

"Then you did know I slept next to you, else you wouldn't know if or when I got to bed. Ha, Ha, got you, you bloody liar."

"Where the fuck did you get to?"

"That's more like my old mate talking."

Mike then went on to explain his evening's events. He had given Ariel the same treatment she had given him. She had made a pass at him, he had strung her along with this.

"But it was gone four in the morning, I remember looking at my watch, so cut the crap. Just tell me if you had it away with her or not?"

Mike looked down at his manly pride as it hung proud amongst a bush of pubic hair. "Do you really think I would let her enjoy the pleasure of his company?" he said, stroking it proudly.

"It's a little early in the day to be looking at one of the ten wonders of the world." Nigel said.

Mike reminded him that there were only nine wonders of the world.

Nigel pointed to Mike's pubic patch. "That's the tenth, but sadly unrecorded. The reason it's not made it's way into the history books is that its not been seen by many people."

Mike smiled at this. "Do you want to hear the rest?"

"Let me guess. You took her for a walk, she offered herself to you on the riverbank, and you refused, swam out to that rock again and gave the fish another breakfast. How's that then?"

"Almost got it right."

"OK, I give up."

"Well, she did want it. We spread out on the bank and she made all the right moves to have it away with me, the master of sex. I led her all the way to the stars, dived into the river, swam to the rock, and tossed myself off. And do you know what?"

"No, tell me more. I can't wait for this fucking story to end. God, I hope it's got a happy ending."

Mike fell back laughing. "The bloody fish had already had breakfast." With that he grabbed his crotch, dashed out of the camper saying, "I've wet myself. Just look at your face."

On his return from the toilets, Mike admitted that he'd had too many beers, and was given the push by her. "The next thing I knew was waking up on the river bank, alone and cold. So I came back to sleep with my old mate. Is that a happy ending or not?"

Nigel rolled over on his bed, letting out a girlish giggle. "Stop it, you are tearing my heart out."

"Drink up your tea you silly sod and pass me your mug."

Nigel drank the remains of what was now cold tea and handed his mug over. Mike's smile said everything. They were now much closer friends.

As they sat down to breakfast, which was well overdue as they hadn't eaten for a long time, Mike suggested that it was time to move on.

Nigel gave this some thought. "I think you could be right,

but I couldn't stay on a 'textile site' after being as free as we have been here. Christ, it's going to be hard wearing clothes again when we get back home."

They both gave this some thought. There was a silence as they both reflected back on their newfound lifestyle.

"Let's stay one more night. We can pack in the morning and leave," Nigel suggested.

"I think we should both phone home tonight and let them know our plans," Mike said.

The map was once again spread out. They cross-referenced this with their book of naturist camps.

Nigel drew a finger across the map and pointed to the West Coast. "See if there is a naturist campsite there." Mike flipped through the pages. "Yep, there are a few along the coastline."

"Great. Must feel great swimming in the sea naked." Nigel sounded excited at the thought.

The day was spent in and around the river. They swam and enjoyed the freedom that they had taken for granted during their stay at Barjac. There was something different about their friendship now.

These thoughts raced through Nigel's head. He felt that at last he had started to find himself. Was this due to being with Mike, and the new level of friendship they were reaching? What was for sure, was that for the first time in his life, he was beginning to find himself. His thoughts were now about what was going to happen between them on the next stage of their adventure. Could he really carry through with their plan? What if he found that he enjoyed having sex with Mike? He suddenly started to feel cold in the water.

Mike swam across to him. "What's the matter old mate, you look as if you've seen a mermaid and can't speak to her."

"Oh, I'm just thinking."

"That's half your problem, you think too bloody much. Come on, let's get ready to break the news that we're leaving tomorrow."

"Tell you what, I'm going to find it hard to say goodbye," Nigel said.

"Well I won't find it hard to say goodbye to Ariel," Mike added.

They swam back to their side of the river, climbed the bank and strolled back to the camper to have their last meal at the campsite. They hardly spoke.

At the bar that evening they looked around trying to find people to tell that they were leaving. They only had to mention this to Josh and Ian, and the news was spread around within half an hour. Nearly all the friends that they had made during their stay gathered around, and the drinks flowed.

Erik and Anita suggested that they all should join them at their caravan. There was a mass exodus from the bar. The only person not to be seen at this party was Ariel. Mike felt a lot happier for that.

Nigel felt that he should make a speech. Mike was heard to say, "Oh no."

Clearing his throat, Nigel, rather unsteady on his feet now, started to say a few words.

"Erik and Anita. You were the first people to make us welcome. I would like to thank you for that. You may not know it but, in a way, you have changed our lives."

"You were the first to be honoured to see us without our pants on," Mike shouted out.

"Yes, thanks Mike, I'm sure that is a sight that they will remember for life," Nigel said.

"We will try." Anita shouted back.

Nigel tried to continue, but there was a lump swelling in his throat. Mike, sensing that Nigel might crack up, got to his feet to take over.

Putting his arm around his mates shoulders he continued. "My friend here isn't the type to be lost for words normally. What he is trying to say is, it's been bloody great to meet up with such a fantastic bunch of people. Tomorrow morning it's going to be hard to leave you all."

"Sit down," Erik said. "You have not been here long, but you have been two nice guys to know. We will miss you both. You can take home the nice thought that we will be here again next year, same time, and same place. You will be welcome to join us again. Nothing will have changed, apart for Josh and Ian; they will have found themselves, as you two surely will. So drink up. Cheers to Nigel and Mike."

There were lots of handshakes and hugs, a few kisses and a lot of laughter as they all talked about the events of their stay.

The farewells lasted well into the night. Nigel and Mike left Erik's caravan, sad but content.

Chapter 16

Mike was the first to wake up next morning. Looking at his watch, it was only half past five.

He decided just to lie there on top of his sleeping bag. Nigel was still a million miles away. When they got to bed last night there had hardly been a conversation between them. They were both not sure that they were doing the right thing by moving on. Mike thought that it was the right thing to do, seeing that Nigel was still fucked up in his head about his life and sexuality. He had told Nigel, that in his humble opinion, although he had made some good friends where they were, there were more important things for them to explore together. Nigel knew what he meant by this.

Mike lay there just thinking. The very reason they had ventured into France was to help Nigel sort himself out. Doubts now started to enter his own head. Had he gone too far in offering to help his mate?

Shit, they had nearly gone all the way in allowing themselves to express their sexual feelings together.

He glanced at Nigel. He was a really nice guy and had everything going for him. He could have any girl he wanted...if he wanted. Yet, when he had it in front of him, he backed away. With his good looks he was always being approached by gay guys. Nigel had a problem, and he had agreed to help him.

They should move on now, that was clear to him. They needed some time to themselves. The people they had met and enjoyed had all helped in different ways, but now it was up to the two of them to sort it out. They needed space to be together.

The only problem he had was in dealing with his own feelings towards helping Nigel. He had to be honest; he was beginning to enjoy the experience himself. Could this now affect his own life?

Nigel stirred. He rolled over onto his stomach in an attempt to hide his usual morning erection from Mike. He turned his head to face Mike. "Good morning."

"I can see that."

Nigel nestled his groin into the bed with a contented smile on his face.

Mike asked if he would like some tea. A nod indicating yes,

was all that Nigel could muster up.

There was a long silence between them. This was not going to be an easy morning for them to get through.

Mike made the tea and sat down on the bed next to Nigel. "Here, sit up and take hold of this," he said, waiting for Nigel to sit up.

"Sorry, but my middle stump has not gone down yet." Nigel said, placing his hand over his erection, making an attempt to sit up.

Mike handed the mug of tea back again. "For fuck sake, why do you still find it difficult to relax with me? Don't forget, I've seen it enough times and been much closer to it than this . Sit, drink up, and shut up."

"Oh we are in control this morning, aren't we," he said, as he settled down with his tea. He smiled at Mike, and then looked down at his flagging erection. "See what you've done, you've upset it now, and it's going away."

"Hard to tell the difference," came Mike's reply.

They both sat crossed legged on the bed with the map once again spread out in front of them. They decided that they would head for Biarritz or a little higher up the coastline. At this point there was a knock at the camper door. As it was already open, a head popped round. It was Josh.

"I know it's only early, but I thought you'd be up and about. I see I'm wrong, you lazy sods."

He climbed into the camper, and sat on the edge of the bed to join them. He curled his long legs up resting his chin on his knees.

Nigel felt good about being free like this together. Where else could they relax like this without people getting wrong ideas?

"Are you really going today?" Josh asked.

"Yep, very soon." Mike replied, in his best-upset sounding voice.

"I'm going to miss you both."

"Oh, you've got Ian." Nigel winked at Josh.

"True, but that won't last forever," Josh said, pulling his arms tighter around his folded legs and rocking himself on the bed. His face was very sad. "Shit, I'm not very good at saying good-bye."

Mike detected a watery eye. Josh heaved himself up. Then with one quick movement, leaned his lean body forward to put his arms in an embrace around Nigel. He then did the same to Mike.

"Have a safe journey. Hope to see you next year." With that he had gone.

"I could swear he was crying," Mike said.

"So am I." Nigel said, wiping his eyes. "Fuck me, that was nice. I wanted to give him a hug too."

"Why didn't you then?"

"Because being British it's not the right thing to do."

"What a load of crap."

"Oh God, I wish I'd hugged him, he must think I'm cold."

Mike thought that if this were going to be the same with all the friends they had made, he wouldn't be able to handle it.

"Come on, let's get packed up and move on. This is getting to me." Nigel cried out, his voice shaking.

There was a hectic half-hour. Beds pulled down and folded. Coffee and toast was all they could manage. With the cupboards secured, they were now ready.

They made a quick dash to the showers to shower away the results of their efforts, then back to the camper ready for the off.

After a quick check around their pitch, they took up their positions in the front seats. Mike turned the key in the ignition, and to his delight, the engine fired first time.

"How's that then?" He smiled.

"I really thought that they would all be round to wave good-bye." Nigel said, looking out of the window.

"Maybe we're too early for them all. I can't say that I was looking forward to all the fuss anyway." Mike remarked.

With that, the camper lurched forward, the engine eager to perform. They headed towards the main reception area to check out. Nigel had the money at the ready, plus his cash card.

The camper climbed the steep hill to the main gate. Mike shouted out. "Fuck me, look up there. They have all got up early to see us off."

"To your invitation, no thanks not just now." They both laughed at this, which helped to overcome their emotions. Parting from these folk was not going to be easy.

Mike pulled on the handbrake. Erik opened the camper door. "So, you thought you could slip away without being noticed?"

Nigel dashed into the reception to pay up for their stay. Mike was left to handle the situation.

The camping being paid for, Nigel returned to the scene. They were all embracing each other, and lot's of shaking of hands and a few kisses too. Mike was in the middle of this. Nigel thought that he should get some attention too, so he entered the arena. To the outsider, the scene of naked people embracing each other would seem odd, but to naturists, so very natural.

Josh had turned up for a second go. He never said alot, he was too emotional. "Have a safe journey," he said, giving Nigel a warm hug.

"Now you be good." Nigel managed to croak out. "Take care of yourself." This time he did return the hug.

After a while they managed to retreat into the camper. Once again the engine started with a roar. There were lots of shouts from their new friends as they slowly moved off.

Nigel stuck his head out of the window to give the final wave. He gave a sudden tug at Mike's arm. "Stop," he shouted. He opened the door and leapt out.

Mike pulled up once again. Looking in his wing mirror, he could see Nigel with his arms around a girl. He watched the romantic scene. It reminded him of a film he had seen. It was Vik, coming to say goodbye. That'll make his day, he thought.

Mike kept the engine running. Their friends were still waving in the distance.

After what seemed ages, Nigel returned to the camper, all red in the face.

"Drive on fast," he shouted. Mike responded. The camper lurched away again.

"Shit. I never thought that Vik would have known we were leaving. What a bloody good time to tell me she could fall in love with me. Look, she has given me her address." A piece of screwed up paper appeared in his hand.

"Well if that's all you got out of her, what a week you've had," said Mike, with a smile.

"Shit. She kissed me."

The camper had travelled a few miles with both of them in complete silence. It was the way in which the silence was broken that caused the camper to swerve.

Mike was deep in thought when he felt the sensation of a hand touching his balls. One hand made a natural reaction to protect himself and the other hand remained on the steering wheel trying to keep the camper under control around a bend in the road. He didn't challenge Nigel on the stroking of his balls, he just laughed. Nigel was already falling about laughing. They had just driven several miles without remembering to even put on a pair of shorts. They were driving along stark naked.

With that he dived over the back of the camper, bum in full view to a tractor that was passing in the opposite direction. The young guy tooted his horn as they passed.

Nigel found their shorts. It was easy for him to pull his on, but was amused to watch Mike trying to drive and manoeuvre his legs into his.

They had needed that to relieve the tension.

The camper was running well. Nigel sat there, with bare feet up on the dashboard, arms folded and feeling good. The music they played was relaxing and well selected to suit their mood.

They had driven about a hundred and fifty miles. The sun was hot. Mike thought that it was time to stop for a beer. "Let's stop at the next town or village and mix with the natives," he suggested.

Nigel was the first to spot the sign. "Looks as if this could be our village square coming up."

Mike eased the camper into the car park in the square.

"Got your shorts on this time?" Mike asked.

"Yes, and it feels bloody strange doesn't it?"

Mike pointed to a bar across the square. They both headed towards it. They were just wearing their shorts, without T-shirts or anything on their feet.

They ordered two beers, and sat down outside in the sunshine. The beer tasted good. They relaxed back in their chairs to observe the scene.

"Just take a look at all the people walking around in the heat. Just a few hours back, we were able to sit and drink our beers starkers. What a tosspot world we live in. If only they could see life in Barjac," Mike said.

"I think we were bloody lucky when we took out that canoe, we could have paddled in the other direction and missed out on a fantastic experience."

Mike nodded his agreement. "Are we having a good time, or are we not?"

"A bloody good time." Nigel held his hand out for Mike to clasp.

"Let's drink up. I'm feeling a little uncomfortable sitting here like this," Mike said.

"You don't have to bribe me either. Let's go man."

They set off on the road again. "There are a few naturist campsites around this area." Nigel pointed to Albi on the map. "Do you think we can make it before tea?"

"I hope so, but I'll have to push the camper a bit harder now."

"Fancy Vik liking me that much. She should have said so earlier and then maybe we would still be there."

"For fuck sake, let's not go down that track again," Mike pleaded.

Nigel sat back, lost in his thoughts. There was still something not clear in his head about his reactions to people that he makes contact with. It must be me, he thought. The next few days alone with Mike will sort these feelings out surely.

It was now four in the afternoon and the sun was still beating down on the camper. Nigel removed his feet from the dashboard.

"What the hell do you think you are doing?" Mike asked, as he watched Nigel struggle to pull his shorts off while still sitting on his seat.

"Well I've just looked at the map, and it seems that we have about a couple of hours of straight road through the countryside ahead of us, so I wanted to be free again. I can always cover up if I have to."

"Right, if that's the mood of the day, I'll join you." The camper came to a halt and Mike removed his shorts as well. "Shit to the world," he shouted.

They drove for several miles like this, naked and free. They felt good about flirting against all social standards. The music was played loud, and they sang even louder. They felt alive.

As they got nearer to Albi, they decided to pull their shorts on again. Mike continued to drive as he struggled into his. Nigel leaned across to help. Just for a moment his hand brushed against Mike's pubic area. Mike gave a smile. "Steady on, save it until later," he said. Nigel had to check himself from making anything out of the situation. He sat back in his seat again, with Mike's words echoing in his head.

Nigel saw a FFN sign at the side of the road. "Look! And there's another."

Mike pulled the camper into the side of the road. There was a small lane to their left. "Must be down there," he said.

As the camper headed down the small narrow lane, it demanded a lower gear. There were bumps and ridges in the rough track. The pots and plates started to jump around in the cupboards. "Steady on old mate, this is our home that you're trying to bust the guts out of,'" Nigel pleaded, laughing at the way the camper swayed around.

They pulled up outside some huge double gates, about eight feet high and painted blue.

"What happens now?" Mike asked.

Nigel got out of the camper, and pulling his shorts up, went over to the wall supporting the gates. He found a bell, pressed it, and waited.

After a few moments he heard footsteps on a gravel drive the other side of the gates.

"Are you English?" Nigel shouted.

Mike thought that this was a stupid question, but then it was Nigel.

The gate swung open. A little old lady stood before Nigel. She was nude, but had silk cloth draped over her shoulders. She must have been a beautiful woman when she was younger, Nigel thought.

"I hear you speak perfect English," she said. "Do you want to join us then?"

"We would like to stay just overnight, if that's possible?" Nigel was using his best tone, and a smile to match.

He thought the scene was rather funny. A couple of hours ago, both he and Mike were sitting in the camper in the nod. Now here he was, standing wearing his shorts, talking to a little old lady who was wearing just a silk cloth across her, knowing that there were people just the other side of the gate leaping around naked.

The old lady told him that they were welcome to look around. Mike joined them, leaving the camper where it was parked, the old lady assuring him that it was quite safe there.

There were only a few people around in the evening sunshine. She showed them the pool first. "It was only finished this year," she told them. There were several caravans dotted around, and all had their own gardens neatly lined by neat hedges. They passed the clubhouse. "We all meet in there in the evenings," she told them.

Mike pointed to a tennis court. He remarked that it looked shorter than usual.

"It's a Mini-ten court," said the old lady.

"What's Mini-ten?" Mike asked.

"It's like a game of tennis. You will see it played later," she said.

They passed the showers which had just four showerheads.

The walls and floor were tiled in blue. There was no shelter apart from a plastic roof. It was very basic.

"That looks like a whole lot of fun," Nigel remarked.

"It is around November time," smiled the old lady. "You can park your camper by the Mini-ten court if you like. Have you got membership cards?"

"Yes. They are in the camper." Nigel told her.

"Meet me in the office once you have parked your camper then." With that she walked back towards the office.

They parked the camper, and with shorts removed again, they walked through the campsite to book in.

Once the official forms were signed, the little lady started to give them an insight into the club.

She said it was not very large. Some of the naturists lived in their caravans most of the year. They even go to work from the club each day.

"What do they do in the winter?" Nigel asked.

"They have flats or homes in and around Albi. Even on a nice weekend in the winter they come to the club."

What a nice way to live Nigel thought. Then turning to the little old lady he said, "Sorry, we didn't ask your name."

"That's all right, its Ariel. I know your names, that's what's nice about being in the office, I get to know everyone first."

Mike, who had been looking at the magazines that were scattered around, gave a cough on hearing her name. This turned into a coughing fit. With his hand over his mouth, he dashed from the office.

Ariel looked concerned. "Is he well?"

"Yes, he will be OK. He suffers with his chest; the medication helps him through the rough times."

"Well you know where my caravan is, so if he wants anything, just send him over to me, poor lad."

Nigel hurried outside. He was almost having a coughing fit himself. Mike was making his way to the camper holding his chest. Nigel caught him up.

"Well you lucky sod. Ariel says that if you want anything at all this evening, just knock on her caravan door and she will do anything for you."

Mike, now in fits of laughter, just had to sit down on the grass. Nigel walked on towards the camper. He opened the sliding door. There was no point in putting the roof up for his bed, he thought, as they would only be staying the night.

He opened up a couple of beers from the fridge, looking at the damaged woodwork of the worktop. He felt guilty about this now, but Mike had not mentioned it. He told himself off about getting so strung up about things.

Mike joined him and fell on the bed. "Thanks. I could do with a beer. Oh God, what a laugh. At least I have a choice tonight. At long last I could spend the night with Ariel, or I can sleep with you again. Shit, I'm living it up."

"I'm not sure that you would get what you are looking for from either of your options," Nigel said.

"So I should rule out Ariel then?" Mike smiled.

Nigel just smiled at the implications.

"Is it still about finding ourselves then?" Mike asked, looking directly at Nigel. "If so, I think we will find ourselves. Some guys would give anything to be in our position. There are so many questions to be answered, but nobody has the balls to be open about them themselves. The world is full of our age group, mostly fucked up with trying to find themselves. Put it there mate," Mike offered Nigel his hand to shake. "We have it right."

"So it's to be me then?" Nigel smiled.

"Afraid so old mate, but must have some food first." They sat outside the camper to eat. The sun was still very warm. It was nice just to sit and relax for a while. They heard voices coming from the other side of the camper mixed with the sound of a repeated thumping noise.

"What the hell's that?"

"I can hear a tennis ball bouncing away. You see, that's professional knowledge for you, I know these things," Nigel said, sitting back and looking smug.

They finished their meal and walked around the back of the camper to see what was going on.

There were two couples on the court, thumping a tennis ball across the net just like tennis. Instead of using rackets, they had their hands slotted into what looked like blocks of wood.

"Bloody hell," muttered Mike.

The ball was being hit at high speed across the net. The players were nude, apart from wearing trainers.

They sat down to watch. Just in front of them were a couple of spare bats. Nigel picked one up to hold. It was made with just two pieces of wood about eight inches square, with a grip like piece of wood, wedged between them which was the handle.

"Feel that," Nigel said.

"Feel what?" Mike asked.

"This you sexy fool."

Mike took the bat to hold. "What a weapon. You could go to war with a weapon like this. We could be witnesses to murder."

With the players locked in combat, they went back to finish their meal. They were well into their third beer when the players passed the camper.

"Hi, I see you are English?" one of the players called out.

"Does it show that much?" replied Mike.

"No. But we read your numberplate. Do you play?"

"Tennis, but not Mini-ten. Looks too dangerous," Nigel said. He moved his hands to cover over his manhood. This bought laughter from the players.

"What are the bats called?" asked Mike.

"Thugs."

"Good name for them," smiled Mike.

"English humour, I like it. See you at the bar tonight? We could do with some more English humour." He introduced the other players. Their names were too difficult to remember, thought Mike.

The party moved on. "See you."

"Nice people. We have been lucky to meet so many friendly people," Nigel said.

"Are we going to join them tonight?"

"I don't think so," Mike said. "Do you feel like going?"

"Not really. Shower and bed for me I think."

They decided to go and freshen up. They grabbed their towels and made off towards the showers. They passed several caravans with couples sitting outside in the warm evening sun. It all seemed so peaceful.

"I think I could live like this forever," Nigel said, looking around him.

"Yep. I'm feeling so relaxed," Mike said, looking at both their tanned bodies. "Look at us, we're almost black now, and we've still got a couple of weeks left." Nigel suddenly grabbed Mike's arm. "What are you on now?" Mike asked.

"Look ahead of you mate." Nigel pointed towards the showers. There were three girls already using them.

Mike's eye's lit up at the sight. They were around their own age group, with lush bodies and beautifully tanned. All three had long black hair. There was something quite sexy in seeing nude females with water flowing over her bodies, and the way they held their heads back, running their hands through their hair. Mike just had to get off this line of thinking. It was not easy to control a guy's reactions to scenes like this.

Nigel gave him a nudge. His towel was his only defence between him and being asked to leave the campsite.

"We can't just stand here looking. Let's get under the shower," Mike suggested.

"There's only one problem with that, there are only four showers," Nigel said, still holding his towel in defence.

"That's quite bright coming from you. You even worked that out without your calculator," Mike laughed.

They walked over to the wooden bench to place their towels on. The girls remained under their own shower. One gave a nod, and another smiled at them. This didn't help them to make their next move.

"You go first," Mike suggested.

"No, after you," Nigel smiled. He was in two minds about picking up his towel again, as he tried to relay a message through to his over active penis. 'Behave you bastard.'

They both made a dash to get under the fourth shower together. The girls giggled at the sight.

"Christ, the water's bloody cold," Mike shouted out. They both moved around each other, rubbing the soap over their bodies in the hope that this frantic exercise would help warm their bodies up. As they were sharing the plastic bottle of liquid soap, this led to them starting to fight for ownership of it. Their footing, not being too secure on the wet tiled floor, made them slip around trying to grab anything that stood still. Mike was the first to slip. He made a grab at Nigel, who in turn lost his footing. The girls looked on laughing at the scene.

They all started to talk at once. Mike decided to remain seated on the wet floor letting the cold water splash over him. Nigel placed a hand on the wall to help steady himself as he tried to understand the questions that were being fired at them.

"I think they have worked it out that we are English," Nigel shouted down at Mike.

"You are, aren't you? Tell us you are from England," one of the girls asked.

Mike gave a nod. Nigel said, "Hi, I'm Nigel and that wet thing on the floor is Mike."

The girls introduced themselves. Jill, Wendy, and Nicole. Two of them came from England, and Nicole from France.

Nicole left her shower to towel off, offering the shower to Nigel.

It turned out that the two from England, Jill and Wendy, were backpacking around France and Spain. Nicole lived on the campsite. She went to work outside the campsite each day in the local village.

"What goes on at this campsite?" Nigel asked, from under his shower. He was not having problems with his penis now; the cold water had reduced it to a small protrusion appearing through his thick bush of pubic hair.

"Not a lot, but it is nice and peaceful here. We like it that way," said Wendy.

They were now all towelling down together. It was as if they had all known each other for ages.

"Are you going to the clubhouse tonight?" asked Nicole.

"Mike is going to have an early night tonight. He's been driving a lot today."

"No I'm not. That shower has done me a power of good. I'm ready to attack the bar."

"Good. Then see you about nine then," Nicole said, as she walked off with the other two.

On the way back to the camper, they found it hard not to look back at the girls.

"For fuck sake, keep walking towards the camper, and close your mouth, and it's not natural to dribble like that when you see women," Mike said.

Nigel put his hand to his mouth. "Was I dribbling then?"

"I wasn't referring to your mouth." Mike said, looking down at Nigel's manhood.

"Does this situation remind you of anything?" Mike asked.

"Yes, we're back to the threesome again."

"Which one is the lesbian then?"

"Yours of course," Nigel laughed.

Following that remark, Mike made a grab at Nigel's balls as they fought for the mirror to shave in.

As they wrestled around the camper together Nigel was aware that he was having a reaction to their body contact. He could feel the beginning of an erection coming on. Mike sensed this, and pulling them closer together, told him to save it for later.

"Fuck, I'm sorry, I'm just feeling randy," Nigel said, drawing himself away from the situation. Mike, not wishing to break away like this, held on and pulled Nigel down onto the bed with him. They lay there together not speaking for a while. Nigel's thoughts were racing away again. What Mike had just said about 'saving it for later,' and his feelings getting stronger towards Mike each day. How much longer could he hang out with these mixed emotions before he found the answer?

There was a moment of a vivid picture gallery of faces flashing through his mind. Wayne, Josh, Mike. How could he have feelings towards them, yet here he was getting ready to strut his stuff with the three girls this evening?

"Where are you floating off too now?" Mike asked.

Nigel wanted to suggest that they stayed in tonight, but this might be wrong just in case he was seen as forcing the sexual act he wanted to experience with Mike.

"Sorry, you know me, I was everywhere." Nigel answered after a pause.

Mike offered him a wine. "Cheers old mate," he said as he raised his glass to Nigel. "Here's to a good evening. Don't forget that if we strike lucky, this is my camper."

"Well, as you stand no chance of getting your end away, you might just as well pass the keys over now."

"Bollocks," was the reply.

They dressed in jeans and tight fitting T-shirts. "Fuck, do we look good, or what?" Mike laughed, as he gave him a hug. Nigel felt the mood coming on again and wished they weren't going out.

There were a few people sitting around outside the clubhouse drinking as they arrived. Nigel thought that it was now becoming very natural seeing people enjoying their nakedness together.

Nigel stuck his head around the door and peered inside the bar to see if the girls were there yet.

"Shit man, oh shit," Nigel said as he took a step backwards. He lost his footing on the top step. Mike made a grab to support him.

"What was that all about then?" Mike asked.

"Take a look in there," Nigel said, removing himself from the steps.

Mike poked his head inside. "Fuck, we've done it again." Everyone inside the bar was in the nude.

They quickly retreated to the camper to get their clothes removed. With just T-shirts flung over shoulders, they returned to the clubhouse pretending that they were just arriving for the first time.

Nicole was the first to see them. She gave them a wave to

join them. They juggled themselves around the table. Nigel found himself sitting next to Jill. Mike as usual elected to sit between the other two girls. He had a contented look on his face.

"Let's put some money in the kitty," suggested Nicole.

Mike was keen to part with the money that was screwed up in his hand. "There," he said, "straight from my pocket."

Nigel took the orders and went to the bar with Nicole.

Standing waiting for their order to arrive, she asked him where they had been for the last couple of weeks. Nigel decided not to let on that they were new to naturism.

"We have been travelling around in the camper. We met up with some nice people in Barjac."

"So what happens there?" she asked.

"Quite a lot really. We swam in the river most of the day, and in the evenings we went to the bar, just like tonight. Well not quite, they all dressed for the evening there."

"Do you find it strange here then?" she asked.

"Not strange, just nice."

The young guy behind the bar made eye contact with Nigel. "Will that be all you're wanting?"

Nigel smiled at this remark. It was a positive attempt to make contact. "Yes thanks," he replied.

God, he was making a pass at me, and he was bloody good looking as well. Oh shit, he thought, here I go again.

When they got back to the table, Mike was well into his usual chat up lines.

Nigel passed the drinks around. To reach his chair he had to squeeze past Jill. He almost had to sit on her lap to pass her. She was more than willing to give him a helping hand to steady himself.

Nicole turned to the girls and told them what Nigel had told her about Barjac. "They all get dressed in the evenings," she said.

"Why get dressed if you don't have too?" said Jill

"Ah yes, but how long have you been naturists?" asked Nigel.

"Since I was born. How about you two?"

"Well to be honest, we only found out about this lifestyle a couple of weeks ago," Nigel answered.

They then went on to tell the story to the interested girls. There were no funny remarks or giggles from any of them.

"So is that the truth, and nothing but the truth?" asked Wendy.

"Well there are a few minor things that we have left out,"

Mike said, giving a wink to Nigel.

Nicole asked Nigel if he had a girlfriend. He glanced across at Mike before he attempted to reply.

"Well sort of." His mind raced away to think of a name.

"It's Sue," Mike said quickly.

"Yes, Sue," Nigel repeated.

"What is she like?" Nicole asked.

Before Mike could say a word, Nigel spoke up. "Nicole asked what was she like, not what she liked.'

"You read me like a book," said Mike, smiling.

"Now stop it you two. Is it Sue, or is it not?"

"Not." Nigel said, looking sheepish now.

"Then are you gay?" questioned Wendy.

Mike leaned across the table, and taking hold of Nigel by the neck, planted a kiss on his lips. He then turned to Wendy and said, "Yes."

"Oh, for Christ sake, can't we get off the subject," pleaded Nigel.

"The truth always hurts," Mike teased.

The evening passed without the subject being raised again, yet there must have been doubts planted in the minds of the girls, Nigel thought.

They all left the bar together and went their separate ways.

Mike pulled open the camper door. Nigel brushing him aside flopped down on the bed.

"Well that went down fucking well. You big prick, fancy saying that. They believed you. Fuck me, we can't stay here."

"I have a strong feeling that you are not too happy with me," Mike said.

"Too bloody true. You went over the top a bit, I felt a right prat. Why bring up Sue?"

"I think I've touched on a nerve," Mike suggested.

Nigel didn't answer this. Instead he opened the camper door and went for a pee. On his return he grabbed his sleeping bag and flung it up onto his own bed, then with one big leap, hauled himself up to lie on his bed.

Mike sat there sitting on his bed. He looked up and muttered, "Goodnight."

It was not going to be one of those nights for sleeping. Mike lay there, his thought's raced away with him. Maybe he had gone over the top a bit. Maybe the morning would see Nigel in a better frame of mind.

Nigel just couldn't sleep. His mind was full of his problems. This was the first time that he had fallen out with Mike this holiday. Why was he still so confused about his sexuality? Yes he had found a new way of life; he was comfortable with it. But why was he so touchy with Mike over the evening's events and his remark. Had Mike now just accepted that he was gay? Am I?

Sleep overtook them both eventually. The night saw two restless guy's turning in their beds. It was the first time that they had slept apart since their first week together. Mike was the first to wake. The sun was streaming into the camper. He looked at his watch; it was nearly seven thirty.

He tried not to wake Nigel. He rested his folded arms on the edge of Nigel's bed looking at his sleeping mate. Christ, I annoyed him last night, but he is a mixed up guy, he thought. Was he right in agreeing to help Nigel sort out his sexuality?

He was very close to Nigel's face now. He just stood there looking at him.

Nigel stirred. He managed to open an eye to see Mike. "Morning. Fuck, I'm sorry about last night."

Mike placed a hand on Nigel's head and ruffled his hair. The mood suddenly changed.

"What a couple of pricks we are," Mike whispered. "Shit man, I hardly slept through the night."

"Me neither."

"Tell you what. Let's get the hell out of here and find some place where we can just be us."

"Oh man, that sounds good to me." With that Nigel slid down from his bed to sit with Mike.

They made some tea and then some toast from the stale bread they had lying around before heading for the showers. Cold or not, they just had to have one to revive themselves for the journey ahead of them.

CHAPTER 17

They hurried their escape. The camper roof was lowered, the two sleeping bags where rolled up together again, and the dirty cups and plates were just dumped in the sink. Mike leaped into the driver's seat and started the engine. It raced away as he put his foot down. Nigel gave a quick check around the camper, which had now become routine for him. With that mission over, he jumped in alongside Mike ready to do some map reading.

They arrived at the gates. Nigel got out to open them giving a wave to the person on duty in the office. Mike put his foot down hard, making it difficult for Nigel to jump back into his seat again.

They were in a better mood now. Nigel gave directions. "Turn left, and keep on this road for about four miles."

Mike suggested that they stop at the nearest town and pick up some fresh food and milk.

"The town should be about there," Nigel said, pointing to the map. "What do we have to get?"

They both compiled a shopping list just as the town was coming into view. Mike pulled the camper over to the side of the road.

"I'll get the grub and you keep an eye on the camper," Nigel suggested. With that, he jumped out and started to run towards a little supermarket ahead. He had only run a few yards when he heard the camper horn being tooted.

He stopped and looked back. There was Mike waving a pair of shorts out of the window.

Nigel, hands covering his private parts, ran back, opened the camper door and fell across the seat to hide. Looking up he shouted, "You bastard, you've been waiting for that haven't you? This is the second time you've done this to me."

"Well, if you insist on being an exhibitionist, don't get me involved," Mike laughed.

Shorts now having been pulled on, he set off again. Mike tooted once again. Nigel gave him the one finger sign in return.

Basket in hand, he raced around the little supermarket. With his mission completed, he arrived at the checkout. The young girl cashier kept smiling at him. She gave him his change and smiled again. "Have a good trip," she said in perfect English. "You shouldn't spend so much on food, then you could afford to buy some clothes."

"Thank you," he said, "but why mention clothes?"

"Well it's best not to roam the streets around here without them."

Nigel's face turned bright red. She must have seen him. He gulped a "Goodbye," and dashed back to the camper.

"Well Tarzan does run well," Mike said, laughing at the scene.

"Next time, you can do the shopping. I seem to attract too much attention." Nigel held his hands out ready to receive a comment.

"Well, if you go around showing your little pisser off every time we stop, you can't expect much more than laughter."

"I don't think my pisser, as you call it, is anything to laugh about."

"Pass," Mike said.

They both sat there laughing at the situation. It was great to be back on good terms again.

Mike started up the camper, and they drove off. Nigel started to stack the food away while the camper was on the move. Mike seeing this, started to sway the camper around. Nigel lost control, and the food started to fall on the floor, with Nigel joining it.

"Whilst you're down there, pass me a beer old mate."

Nigel finished stacking the food away, grabbed a couple of beers from the fridge and joined Mike in the front again.

"I think we should push on until about four o'clock, then we could look out for a spot to stay the night," Mike suggested.

Looking at the map, Nigel pointed out a couple of blue areas on it. "These must be lakes, shall we try them?"

"Yes, why not."

The beers went down well. The sun was beaming down on the camper. Nigel sorted out some tapes from the glove compartment and they sat back listening to a selection of his music. Nigel was feeling that finally they were free to express themselves. With luck, they would find a remote spot to settle down for the night. Maybe this was going to be the time that they had planned for.

Suddenly he became quite nervous at the thought. How would he react?

Mike looked across at him as if he knew what was going through Nigel's head. "You're not smiling," he said.

Nigel snapped out of his thoughts and tried to give a smile. "I'm trying, honest," he said.

It was coming up to four o'clock. Nigel started to point ahead. "Did you see that sign, we must be getting near the lakes."

Mike tugged at the wheel and swung the camper into a small track off the main road. "I guess this is the spot."

The track was at least half a mile in length and full of potholes. Both began to doubt that this was the right place, but just as they were about to turn around, they saw the lakes ahead of them surrounded by pine trees.

"This looks good to me," Mike said, bringing the camper to a halt.

They both sat there for a while. The scene looked ideal. The lakes were tucked away amongst a Pine forest, and miles from anywhere.

"Let's take a walk around and see if we can find the ideal spot," Mike suggested.

The lakes seemed to stretch for some distance. "Look. If we park over there, we can't be seen by anyone. What's more, we will be able to spot anyone from a hell of a distance away."

"Perfect." Nigel agreed.

"What about water?" Nigel asked.

Mike assured him that they had plenty in the containers for a couple of days. "Anyhow, we haven't looked around yet, we might find a tap somewhere."

They decided that the perfect spot was over by the trees. It would give them some shade, as the days seemed to be getting hotter. They were also then only about twenty yards away from the lake.

"Do you think the lake is OK for swimming in?" Nigel asked.

Mike started to walk towards the waters edged. He removed his shorts and flung them back towards the camper. "I hate wearing those bloody things now."

Nigel trotted down to catch him up, having removed his shorts as well.

"Looks clean to me," Nigel said, scooping up a handful of water. "Looks clear enough to drink."

"You can," Mike said, "but I'll stick to the beer."

They decided to lock the camper up and take a stroll around their newfound piece of France.

"Best take our shorts with us, just in case we meet up with someone."

Mike agreed. "I think we should head over there in that direction" he said, pointing through the trees.

A few minutes later they found themselves amongst the pine trees. There were shafts of sunlight streaming through. They danced from one stream of sunlight to the next like a couple of kids.

"Christ this is great. I feel bloody free at last. Just you, me and the fresh air." Nigel gave another little dance to this.

Mike's way of rejoicing was to have a pee. He stood there, hands clasped behind his head letting the jets swish from side to side as he rolled his body from the hips. Nigel watched, amused by the scene.

"I can honestly say, that's the best piss I've ever had."

"Well, it certainly lasted long enough." Nigel commented.

"That was a man's piss. Beat that if you can," Mike laughed.

They came to the edge of the trees. All they could see were green fields in the distance, and in the field they were standing in there were rolled bales of hay.

"I think we've chosen the right place to park the camper. Look, you can't see it through the trees." Mike said, pointing back in the camper's direction.

Way over to their left they could see the top of a church spire. "At least we have natives in the distance," Mike said. "But they are too far away to worry us I think."

Having surveyed the countryside around them and agreeing that they could not be seen from any direction, they headed back to the camper.

"Well at least we've got food, beer, wine, water, and a lake to swim in. I think this is the right place where we can sort things out for you mate," Mike said.

Nigel felt a little flushed at this thought. He could not back off now, as he had been the one who had suggested it, and Mike was prepared to go all the way with him. Was this the right time and place?

"Are you sure that you want to go through with this?" Nigel asked, hoping to be reassured.

"If it is to be, then I think that this is the place where we can be free to enjoy the experience together."

They had reached the camper now. Nigel thought that he would have a swim to help clear his head.

Mike, being the practical one, had collected a couple of bottles of wine and some beers to place in the water to keep cool amongst the reeds.

Nigel swam out into the lake a little way. The water felt warm. He stood up with the water being at waist level. Mike waded out to him carrying a bottle of wine that had been opened the night before. Raising the bottle to his mouth, he swallowed a large mouthful, and then handed it to Nigel. "Here you are sir, room temperature."

The sun was still very warm as it was beginning to set. There was a silence that fell over them as they stood there, side by side, taking it in turns to take a slug of wine.

Mike took the last swig, holding up the bottle to shake the last few drops from it. He then flung it into the centre of the lake. They both swam after it as it floated on the surface, splashing and pushing each other away from getting hold of it.

They both made a grab at it together. Breathless they stood up with the water level was around their chests. They both stood there holding the bottle between them. Nigel suddenly became tense. He felt that this was going to be the moment of truth. Mike made the first move, and Nigel froze. He was suddenly unsure that he wanted this to happen. Mike, now with his arm around Nigel's neck, checked back. He looked into Nigel's eyes.

"Come on, you know you want to follow this through, so why chicken out now?"

"I'm not sure," he replied.

Mike withdrew his arm completely. They both stood there looking at each other. Nigel with one gliding move wrapped his arms around Mike's neck and entwined his legs around his waist. He then laid his head on Mike's shoulder. Neither of them moved for a while.

Nigel's head was spinning. Christ, was this right, he was thinking. Mike's only move was to place his arms around Nigel. The two of them stayed locked together like this for what seemed an eternity. Nigel was the first to unlock the bonding. He turned and started to swim back towards the camper.

He walked across the grass and sat down. Mike was still standing in the middle of the lake. He slowly swam towards Nigel. As he passed the spot where the beers were cooling, he picked hold of a couple of bottles and a bottle of wine.

He slumped down at the side of Nigel. "Well that was a disaster, was it not?"

"Yep, my fault," Nigel said. "Can't we have a long chat, sooner than getting involved?" he asked.

"Shall we eat first?" Mike asked.

"Sure, but you haven't answered my question."

"If you only want to talk, it's a fucking long way to have come for that. We could have had a chat in the pub back home," Mike grunted.

"Sorry. You're right."

Mike prepared the meal and placed it on the table. Nigel had been sitting there deep in thought.

He looked up and thanked the chef. He then filled up the wine glasses again. Mike thanked him for his contribution.

"You've been doing a lot of thinking whilst I slaved over a hot stove. Do you want to go on this mind bender now?"

Nigel, picking at his meal with his fork, nodded. "I just hope that this doesn't end our friendship. I have so much bottled up inside me, I think I'll explode if I were to hold back any more."

"Look, we've met a lot of people over the last couple of weeks. I don't think you've been listening to them," Mike suggested.

"Yes I have."

"Well then, is it all about your sex life?" Mike said, leaning across the table on his elbows to stare at Nigel.

"Yes, in a way. Have you ever felt that you would prefer sex with another guy sooner than a girl?"

Nigel's face was now quite red. His question demanded an answer.

"I think we have been down this avenue before," Mike sighed. "Shit, we've fooled around together, and came so near to having it away."

"I know, and that's the point, I have never gone all the way."

"Do you want to?"

"I don't know. Yes. What I mean is, I would like to find out, but I'm scared that you might regret agreeing to this."

"Oh, fuck me. Pardon the expression. It's not as if you're going to make me pregnant and commit yourself to being married to me." Mike laughed at his own remark. "Let's clear up and relax down for the evening." He stood up and started clearing the plates.

"You didn't eat very much. You can't have sex on an empty stomach."

Nigel, not knowing what to do next, shuffled around the table. He poured another wine for both of them, and took Mike's into the camper.

"Thanks. Look, if we are going to carry this through, let's go and have some fun over there in the cornfield, it's still quite hot out there. If we are going to have some fun, let's have some real fun."

With that, Mike stood up taking hold of a blanket and stepped outside the camper. "Oh, bring the wine and a couple of condoms."

Nigel hunted in the glove compartment for these. He also took some towels.

"What are you bringing those for?" Mike asked.

"Just so you don't get pregnant," laughed Nigel

"No, the towels, you bloody fool."

"So we can have a swim afterwards."

As they made their way through the trees Mike asked him if he was still sure that he wanted to go through with it? Nigel looked down at his rising erection. "I think so, or at least part of me is."

They found a spot in the middle of the cornfield. Mike spread the blanket out and sat down. He patted the blanket at the side of him. Nigel, feeling a little embarrassed, knelt down next to him holding the wine bottle. He took a large swig from it, then passed it over to Mike.

"Here, sit behind me, so that I can rest against you," Mike suggested.

Nigel moved around, spreading his legs apart so that Mike could nestle between them and lie back.

Nigel could feel the sun, which was still quite hot on his back, making him feel rather horny.

Mike could sense this. He was aware of Nigel's firm shaft throbbing away against his back now.

Nigel placed his arms around Mike's chest. "That feels good," Mike whispered in his ear.

Nigel's hands brushed against Mike's nipples. He knew the feeling of this. Mike groaned with pleasure. Nigel could see that he was getting aroused.

Mike began to work on his own erection now, giving himself long slow strokes. Nigel could feel the juices from his own erection beginning to leak out onto Mike's back.

"Christ, this feels so good man," Mike said. He then made a move to turn Nigel over and lie on his back. Mike then spread his body on top of him and started working his erect shaft against Nigel's, in slow left to right movements, their juices now starting to mix together. Nigel slowly placed his hands on Mike's bum, parting the cheeks in time to Mike's movements.

Nigel just faintly heard Mike asking him to finger his arse. He didn't need a second request. His finger found the moist entry, and with slow movements, his finger entered the unexplored area. Mike gave a groan to this feeling. The thrusting of one finger then became two. Nigel was now aware that the entry was able to take more than just two.

Mike made a move to kneel down away from Nigel. This was the moment that Nigel had been dreaming and waiting for.

The condom rolled on with ease. Nigel's shaft was rock solid now. Mike, as if by magic, produced a tube of love joy jelly from under the blanket.

"You sod, you had this all planned," Nigel muttered.

With a fair amount of the lubricant on his fingers, Nigel once again entered the virgin area.

Mike made moves that were a sign of approval of Nigel's tender fingers searching him. He was still working on his own shaft with slow strokes to keep it active.

Nigel felt that he was now ready for the final act. He'd had dreams about similar situations to what he was about to experience now.

He held Mike around his waist. His fingers started to dig into his flesh. There was a slight groan of expectancy released from Mike. Nigel raised himself up onto his knees. His body lay across Mike's firm back. Every muscle in Mike's body seemed tense. Sweat was running from Nigel, the constant flow dripping onto Mike's body. Nigel tried once more to enter his fingers into Mike's now moist rectum. He could feel the mixture of love jelly and sweat mixing together.

He raised his body ready to make his entry. He'd never viewed an arse quite like this before. It was inviting him to enter.

His thoughts now were very mixed and confused. His head was thumping. Fuck, what was going on, he thought? His shaft was becoming less ridgid. It was loosing its firmness. He took a grip on it trying to arouse it back into life.

"Oh shit, I can't do it," he shouted out, "come on you bastard." He continued to take hold of his penis working it with hard and fast strokes, hoping that it would respond. The harder he worked it, the less it responded.

Mike rolled over onto his back, his hand still working himself off. On seeing Nigel's state, he stopped his own actions and moved towards him, putting his arm around his shoulders.

Nigel fell to the ground. He had given up on himself. "Fuck," he yelled out, almost crying.

They both lay there for a while, without a word being spoken.

Nigel broke the silence first. "Fuck, I'm sorry. I fucked it up."

Mike gave him a reassuring look. "Don't worry, it was good while it lasted." With that, he got up quickly and ran through the cornfield a little way. Then there was silence.

Nigel sat up, pulling the condom off his now limp penis and he tossed it towards the trees.

He couldn't see Mike so he stood up. He could just see Mike's head and shoulders above the corn. His body movements told Nigel that he was tossing himself off.

Nigel sat down again so as not to intrude on Mike's moment of pleasure. He had let him down. He must have so much frustration inside his body, he thought.

Moments later, Mike appeared through the corn. "Sorry about that, but it was needed."

Nigel sat there feeling rather stupid. "I wish I could be like you. I can't get the little sod to raise itself. Fuck, what's the matter with me?"

Mike moved towards him to kneel down at his side. He placed his hand on Nigel's chest, teasing his nipples to a firmness. His hand searched down Nigel's tense stomach muscles, to run his fingers through his bushy pubic hair to take hold of his penis. Slowly he felt a reaction. Nigel tried to move away.

Mike assured him that it was all right. Slowly, Nigel found his shaft respond to Mike's touches. He soon became aroused to a level that he had long forgotten he could reach.

"Just lie back and enjoy," Mike whispered, as his hand worked on him with smooth, firm strokes.

Nigel's hand reached down to join his. The two stroked away for a while. Nigel was happy that he had played a part in this as well, but he now let his hand be removed. Mike, sensing that the climax was near quickened his strokes. Nigel lay back groaning with delight. Mike watched Nigel's stomach muscles tighten, and his back arch off the blanket. "Oh shit" shouted Nigel, as his penis head shot streams of spunk up onto his chest. Mike had never seen such a fountain of spurts before. He felt proud for Nigel.

They both collapsed back on the blanket. Mike lay there resting on one elbow looking at his contented friend. "Well, I never thought you had one as large as that. Thank the fuck you didn't get that lot inside me after all." They both laughed at the thought.

Nigel felt like crying, but held back his emotions. "Shit, I'm sorry I let you down all the same."

"We will make it next time, you wait and see," Mike said, pretending not to see the tears forming in his friend's eyes. "You're just an emotional sod."

"Come on, let's go for a swim," Mike suggested, patting Nigel's pride and joy.

As they ran through the trees heading for the lake again, Nigel's thoughts were still very mixed, but he felt much more relaxed now. Yet still running through his head was the question as to why he had backed off.

Mike was also thinking. *What would it have felt like if Nigel had performed?*

The water was still warm, and the sun was setting behind the trees, casting shadows across the lake. They swam until they were in the sunlight again. Mike found a spot that he could stand up in, and Nigel swam towards him. He flung his arms around Mike, more in relief than a sexual embrace. Mike held him tightly. It was a wonderful feeling as their two bodies came into contact. Nigel felt that maybe it had turned out for the best, and their friendship was even stronger for the experience. They messed around in the water for a while before heading back to the camper.

Mike collected the wine and beers from the edge of the lake "These should help us through the night," he said, plonking them down onto the table.

They lay together on top of Mike's bed. The beers were the first to be attacked. Neither had mentioned the failed afternoon and the attempt to sort our Nigel's problems. They both talked around the subject, even to the point of talking about cricket, a sport that was not high on their sporting list. Nigel was the first to raise the subject. "I don't know what happened to me. I just lost my nerve. Sorry old mate."

Mike lay there for a while without saying a word. Then, with rather a sheepish look on his face told him that he thought the role has reversed.

"What do you mean?"

"Well, I think I would like this adventure between you and

me kept just to us. We are getting involved in things that should remain private, just between us."

"Well you have my word on that point." Nigel said, raising his hand as a matter of oath.

Mike asked for another beer. Nigel passed it to him. "Don't you think you are drinking too much?"

Mike smiled at the same time as taking a large swig at the bottle. Then clearing his throat as if he was about to make the statement of the year said. "I have never offered my arse to anyone before. And to be honest, I would have thumped anyone that suggested they were after it."

"So why did you set the whole thing up this evening?" Nigel asked.

"For you mate. For you."

"Oh come on, I would never have let another guy toss me off in a cornfield like that."

"Then why did you let me do it?"

"Because I think I owed it to you for me letting you down."

"Bollocks. You enjoyed it, so don't give me that crap."

"So what are you getting at then?" Nigel asked.

"Well it all started off in the aid of science. We both knew what we were getting into. But you still haven't had your questions answered yet."

"So why the big issue then?"

Mike looked almost embarrassed. "Ok," he said, then he coughed to clear his throat. " When you gave me the full treatment, you touched me in all the places that when I'm with a girl, my mind is begging her to touch. You just knew how to arouse me."

"Was I that good then?" Nigel asked. It was his turn to ruffle Mike's hair this time.

"Well I know now this is what *you* have been trying to experience."

"Go on tell me then," Nigel said.

"Well, unless I'm wrong, you've been busting your arse to find what it's like to have full sex with another guy, right?"

"Yes, because I believe that a bloke can have better sex with another guy. Women can't possibly know what a guy wants to satisfy him. And I bet that's the same for women if they were honest about it."

Mike sat back to think about this point. "Well, I think I'm the one that's been the nearest to finding out, so we have a lot of research to do yet. Christ, I can't believe that I'm doing this."

"But do you regret it?" Nigel asked.

"For you, No. I'm not sure I could have done the same for say…Josh. What I do know is that what little sex I've had with girls, it's been nowhere near as good as going just half way with you today."

"I'm flattered," said Nigel.

"Don't take the piss."

"So how did it feel then?"

"Well, there you go. You won't know until I return the favour." Mike smiled.

"Yes, but I've not fucked you yet, so how would you know the complete answer then?"

"I don't believe that we are having this conversation," Mike said, smiling at the situation.

"So what now then?" Nigel asked.

Mike gave a yawn, and suggested bed. "But no exploring of the unknown tonight."

Nigel stood up. "Help me raise the roof up so I can get to bed then."

"Don't be daft, sleep down here tonight." Mike said, patting his bed. "I think we have passed that stage in our friendship now."

The camper even seemed different now. They had the curtains closed and the door firmly locked. But for all of this, the single light gave them a sense of being comfortable in their own company.

As it was warm, they lay on Mike's bed, naked, together. Nigel was still eager to continue the conversation.

"Tell me, what touches and feelings did you miss out on when you had sex with a girl," Nigel asked.

"I think I've been frustrated when making love to a girl. All the time I was wishing she would touch and explore me more. The final act is better than a wank, but she didn't know how to arouse me. There is an art in that."

"Listen to you. An art," Nigel teased. "But I know what you mean."

"Do you. Then tell me."

"Well, as I've said all along, a bloke just knows what turns another guy on, but you have to explain this to a woman, because how can she even start to know?"

"So that's what you aim to find out this holiday, is it?"

"Yes. But the only doubt I have is, am I gay by thinking and feeling like I do?" Nigel asked.

"OK. Let's suppose you are gay. So what?"

"Fuck. What would my parents say to that?" Nigel said, looking thoughtful.

"Well, first of all, we have to find out if you are."

"Yes, but you see, I didn't find it wrong in trying to fuck you, even if I never made it. Surely, if I were straight, there would be no way that I would have thought about shafting you?"

"Listen," Mike said, sitting up sharply. "Did you hear that?"

"What?"

"Someone is out there."

Nigel sat up to listen. There was a movement outside. There was knock at the door.

Mike made a grab for his shorts while Nigel struggled into his sleeping bag. Mike slid the door open a little way.

He was blinded by a torchlight, but could just make out an old man standing there holding a piece of wood and waving it around as he shouted in rapid French.

Mike kept repeating. "We are English. I don't understand."

"What's he on about?" Nigel asked.

"I think he is telling us to piss off of his land."

"I got the word 'private' I think. So I guess you're right."

"Christ, education is a wonderful thing. Your understanding of French is beyond belief." Mike said. "Why don't you have a chat with him?" "And don't poke me with that stick you bloody idiot," he shouted at the irrate man.

The old man kept pointing down the lane, and repeating, "Allez-vous."

Mike shouted back at him. "OK, you prat, we're leaving." With that he got out of the camper, and flung the two chairs inside. He did a quick walk around the to see if they would be leaving anything. All the time the old man was shouting at him, and pointing to the way out of the lane.

Nigel remained in his sleeping bag as the camper was started up. Mike drove off at a fair rate. The camper bounced and bucked around the rough track as Nigel was tossed around on the bed. "For fuck sake slow down, I can't get any sleep like this." he said, laughing at the situation.

They found the road again. The night was creeping in fast now. Nigel had managed to find his crumpled shorts, and got out of bed to join Mike up front.

"Well that was a quick exit," Nigel said, trying to get his legs into his shorts.

As it was ten o'clock, they stood little chance of finding a camp-site now. They decided that they would park anywhere, even a carpark would do.

They drove for about an hour. The skyline was lighting up. "This must be a fairly big town we are heading into." Nigel suggested.

"This will do," Mike said, as he turned the wheel to bring the camper to rest in the well-lit carpark. He backed the camper against the wall that ran alongside a river.

"There. That's as far as I'm driving tonight. I'm fucked. It's been quite a day."

Nigel climbed into the back of the camper and fell onto Mike's bed laughing. "Look we've been driving with the roof up all that way."

They checked the curtains just to see that there were no gaps in them. Mike climbed onto his bed, and climbed under his sleeping bag, still keeping his shorts on.

Nigel sensing that Mike wasn't in the mood for talking lay down on the bed, almost going to sleep as he closed his eyes. He heard Mike mutter, "Night mate."

Nigel just gave him a pat on his back. "Good night."

CHAPTER 18

Nigel turned his head on his pillow. He was far from awake, but was suddenly aware that there were movements outside the camper. Just for a moment he was trying to figure out where he was.

Sitting up slowly, he pulled the edge of the curtain back. There were cars being parked and loads of people in business suits buzzing around in the car park.

He looked at his watch. It was only just six o'clock. Falling back onto the bed, he turned to ruffle Mike's hair to wake him.

"What's going on?" Mike moaned.

"We've parked in the middle of a bloody city car park. There are loads of strange looking people out there all walking around wearing clothes."

Mike leaned across to look through the curtains. "I see I selected a good spot. Don't try to open the door just yet, I don't think they could handle the scene in here."

"I want a pee," Nigel said, holding his crotch.

"Well you can't just go outside. Remember where you are."

"What am I going to do? I'm bursting."

"Oh, lob it in the sink," Mike suggested. "I think I'll join you. I'm breaking my neck as well."

They both stood at the sink stretched on tiptoe so they could reach over the edge. An endless stream of pee passing from both of them brought relief to their faces. They laughed at the situation they were in as Mike gave a shove of Nigel's shoulder, trying to throw him off balance.

Mission over, they both sat on the edge of the bed again, listening to the sound of their pee still flowing down the narrow drainpipe landing directly onto the carpark.

This seemed to raise the tones of the voices from outside. They were not too sure as to what was being said, but the commuters were clearly concerned about the liquid that was leaking from the camper and creating a steaming puddle in the car park.

Mike suggested that they kept a low profile at this point. Nigel giggled saying, "It could have been worse. We could have been wanting a crap as well."

They decided to make their exit, the camper was started up,

and Mike drove at a slow pace out onto the main road.

Nigel was busy in the back trying to prepare a jam sandwich for both of them. Mike commenting that he wasn't too happy that Nigel had been holding his penis just prior to this.

"All part of the service my man," Nigel said, as he joined Mike at the front.

Mike took his sandwich with a look of disgust on his face. Nigel assured him that he had only touched his pride and joy with one hand.

"How the fuck can you make a sandwich with one hand then?" Mike demanded, with a smile, awaiting the reply.

"I used my dick to spread the jam."

Mike said that they should be able to reach the West Coast by the end of the day. "It will be good to get our kit off again. It's getting hotter the closer we get to the place."

The camper motored well. They stopped for some lunch, checking the map again.

"Look, if we hang in there, we could reach Arcachon," Mike suggested, pointing to the map.

"It's right on the coast. Do you know what, I'm so looking forward to running along the beach nude and free. God, it must be a brilliant feeling," Nigel said, smiling at the thought.

"Do you know what though, it's going to be bloody difficult to go back home and conform to the way we've lived up until now."

"Not worth thinking about," Nigel said. "It's a laugh really. Just think how we've changed towards each other even since being out here. Can you remember coming to my bedroom and me covering up so as not to embarrass you. Look at us now, we eat, drink, and sleep together in the nude. Our mates back home would never believe us."

"I notice you don't mention the sex side of our adventure now so much either," Mike added.

"It's always on my mind. You have no idea how I feel now that the pressure is lifting. Yet, if I find out that I am gay...what sort of pressure will that bring?" Nigel asked.

"Just relax and enjoy finding out first."

Nigel gave Mike a wink at this suggestion. "I'm bloody pleased that I'm finding myself with you though and not someone else. But, I'm still looking at guy's as well, so there's definitely something that attracts me to them."

"Then I'll have to try harder over the next couple of weeks," Mike laughed.

"Yes, or I'll go back and chat up Josh."

"Come on, let's get on the road again, you're trying to upset me now." Mike gave a mocked crying session and staggered to reach the driving seat.

Mike decided that he could make the distance. He put his foot down hard, and the engine responded.

Nigel shouted out, "Arcachon, here we come."

It was about seven thirty. Nigel pointed to a sign at the roadside. "Look, there's that welcoming sign again FFN."

The camper pulled into the main gate of what seemed to be a very large campsite.

"This looks bloody good to me." Nigel said, as he released himself from his safety strap. "I'll do the honours," he said.

With that, he started to trot towards the reception.

Pulling up his shorts to adjust them after the long journey, he entered the reception area. It was busy with people booking in and out. There seemed to be an endless flow of questions being asked across to the team of nude staff. As he heard English being spoken by most of the staff, he set his mind on selecting which one of the girls he was going to book in with. He leaned on the counter to wait his turn. He could not help but notice that the guys were good looking as well as the girls. This was good for passing the time, he thought.

As the girls were all in good shape, he decided he would take his chances with any of them. He noticed a girl, her hair cut quite short. She had a nice figure, with the type of breasts he liked, not too big, and with neat tight nipples. Christ, I'm glad I've got shorts on, feeling a slight erection coming on.

She had a nice tight bum as well, the firm type that you can fit into the palm of your hand as you walk along together...Shit he thought. I must stop this line of thinking. He was getting aroused.

"Yes Sir. Can I help you?" It was a young guy's voice bringing him back to earth.

"Err, yes. I would like to camp here for a few days. Is it possible?"

"All is possible if you have your INF card with you."

Nigel handed over the cards to the young guy, who smiled at him. "So you are with a friend?"

"That's alright isn't it?" Nigel asked, looking the guy straight in the eyes.

"Do you have a tent or caravan?"

"Camper."

"Does it sleep two or four persons?"

"Four, but there are only the two of us."

Nigel was asked to fill in a form. The young guy proceeded to walk across to the other side of the reception.

Nice bum, thought Nigel. He tried to concentrate on the form in front of him and not the form of the guy.

Names, addresses and other information jotted down, he placed the pen and form across the counter to wait.

His thoughts raced away with him once again. The guy must be Dutch and about nineteen. He was quite tall, with short blonde hair. He had to be Dutch.

Nigel watched him return to the counter. He was quite slim, and quite well hung. Shit, should he notice these things?

"Thank you. Have you completed everything on the form?" The young guy checked it over.

"Well Nigel, you have a choice of areas to camp in. You can either get away from the crowds and stay there," he said, pointing to a map of the campsite, "or you can stay there by the main bar area."

"By the way, my names Gusta. Don't laugh, it's just a name they gave me for the season here. You would laugh at my real name though, so I prefer Gusta."

Nigel studied the map. "I think we will settle for the one away from the crowds. We can manage to walk across to the bar."

"Good, then that is lot 124. I'm sure you will both be happy over there," he smiled.

"I hope so too."

"Just drive your camper down the road to your left, and keep going until you pass the toilet block. Just past there, a little further to your right, you'll find your place to rest with your friend." Gusta smiled at this. "I trust you will both be able to stay longer."

Nigel smiled back at this last comment. Gusta had hung onto the word "stay" he thought. "Thanks a lot, hope we meet up with you during our stay here. I'll buy you a beer."

"That would be nice," Gusta said.

Nigel gave a nod as he headed towards the door. He had almost reached the first step outside when Gusta caught him up. Looking Nigel up and down he said, "I'm sure you know the rules, no shorts to be worn whilst you are here, only in the bar area at night. They are the rules, and I also agree with them" He gave one more look at Nigel, turned to walk away, wearing a cheeky grin across his face. "See you."

"Cheers," shouted Nigel. "Where the fuck have you been. I could see you chatting up the blonde guy. Have you scored again?"

"He was a nice guy. Very helpful."

"I'm sure he was. I like the way you toss me aside as soon as you get picked up."

"I was *not* picked up. He was just being helpful." Nigel thought that he could drag this out longer if he wanted to, but chose not to.

"You should have seen the talent in there. Christ, there was one girl, she had the kind of boobs that I like, and a bum to match."

"So why get off with the guy?"

"I didn't get off with him. For fuck's sake, he was just a nice guy." Nigel was letting this get to him now. Running through his mind was the same old problem. There he was, the choice of a guy or girl, and what was he attracted to most...the guy. Oh, for Christ sake, he thought.

Nigel gave directions to the camping area and found 124. The camper rolled along at a slow pace.

Both took it in turns to comment on the talent en route.

It was a very large campsite. Nigel had seen on the map how close they were to the beach. The camping area was protected from the Atlantic Ocean by a line of pine trees. Although it was hard to judge from the map, the beach stretched at least for over a mile. He relayed this to Mike, but he was not really listening. Maybe he was more interested in the talent, Nigel thought.

The camper came to rest amongst the pine trees. The ground was far from level, so Mike had to reverse several times to get it reasonably balanced. "There, that's the best I can do."

Removing their shorts, they clambered out of the camper to stretch their legs.

Their next-door neighbours had been watching the action. "Would you like a beer?"

"Thanks, that's the best offer we've had all day," Nigel called back.

'You bloody liar. What about the blonde guy at reception?' Mike thought.

"Take a seat. You are English? We can tell. Have you been travelling long today?"

"Quite a distance," Mike answered.

The couple introduced themselves as, Vicky and Jon. They both came from Holland.

"So how do you find the campsite?" Nigel asked.

Jon thought for a moment. "I think it is nice for young at one end of the camp, and good for the older people at the other end. However, it's good for everyone in the bar in the evenings." Jon said.

"What's the sea like along this coastline?" Mike asked.

"Quite cold at times to swim in, but great for surfing in. There's so much sandy beach, most of the time everyone plays volleyball."

"That sounds good to me. We could do with some exercise. We have been either sleeping or sitting around most days," Nigel said.

"Oh, come on, we have been quite active in the evenings," Mike added, giving Nigel a wink.

"You mean the discos and things?" Jon said.

"Well yes, that as well," Mike replied.

"So how long have you both been together then?" Nigel was now fighting for conversation.

"Thirty one years."

"Well you both look well on it."

Mike stood up. Looking down at Nigel he said, "Well I think I should prepare our meal. You can stay if you like."

"No really, you have had a long day, and I think I should help you prepare the meal."

They thanked the couple, and moved to leave.

"You bastard, you tried to leave me to that couple, didn't you?" Nigel said, as they walked towards the camper.

"Would I do a thing like that?"

"Yes."

Pulling the camper door open, the heat hit them like an oven. "Should have left the door open to let some air in," Mike muttered.

They hunted for their towels to go for a shower. The camper was now beginning to look like they had been travelling for weeks. The bed was still down with both their sleeping bags screwed up in the back. The sink was full of dirty plates and mugs. Mike suggested that they should do something about the mess they were beginning to live in. Nigel tutted and gave a nod.

"Shower first," Nigel said.

The shower block looked quite rustic for such a large campsite.

"Bet it's been here for years." Nigel said, as they entered.

There must have been at least twenty teenagers in the showers enjoying fooling around. One of the girls pointed to their feet. "You must leave your footwear outside."

They removed their trainers, and placed them outside amongst a line of assorted footwear.

Mike grabbed a shower between two girls. Nigel landed up at the other end between a nice looking girl, with a nice smile he thought, and a good-looking young guy. He thought he had seen the guy working in the reception.

He gave the guy a nod. 'Hi." The girl spoke first. "You have just arrived today?"

"Yes, with my friend Mike." He pointed him out at the other end of the showers.

"I know, we have been talking about you both."

"Really. All good?"

"Oh yes. I think you made quite an impression on your arrival."

"We always do," he laughed. "You wouldn't like to know about some of them though."

It still seemed strange to be talking to a complete stranger, and a girl at that, while he stood there washing his private parts. But nobody even bothers to look, or even cares...it's all seems so natural to them.

"By the way, I'm Nigel. So, what goes on at this campsite then?" he asked.

"I'm Rachel." They shook with soapy hands, and laughed.

"Sorry, I heard your question," said the young guy. "We spend our time together from sun up, until it goes down...and even later. We talk a lot about life, we drink a little, we swim in the sea, surf the waves, sit out under the stars, then sleep a little...until the sun comes up again."

Rachel laughed as she watched Nigel's face as he listened. "His name is Urk."

Nigel looked back at the guy again. "Hi Urk, I'm Nigel." This was followed with another soapy handshake.

Nigel, having been under the shower long enough, made a move to collect his towel. Both Rachel and Urk joined him. Mike having already towelled himself down, stood waiting to be introduced.

Introductions over with, Urk suggested that they meet up later. "We could all have a drink before we hit the beach."

"Sounds good to me," Nigel said. "How about you Mike?"

"Yep."

They all parted. Nigel and Mike returned to the camper to tidy it up a little.

Nigel elected to do the washing up. There were sinks across from where they were camping. It made him smile as he thought about what his folks would say, seeing him standing there, out in the open, washing up whilst totally naked. A splash of hot water soon made him return to his chores. Shit, he thought, that could have been nasty, that could have scalded my dick. He had a mental vision of a nurse tending his injury. With just a towel and T-shirt each, they headed for the bar and restaurant. They walked along a sandy pathway through the pine trees finding themselves in a large clearing. They were taken back by the sheer size of the place.

"This is like a small town in it's own right," Nigel remarked.

They looked at the menu, it was very inviting. Steak and salad seemed to be their choice. It felt strange standing there together, just wearing their T-shirts, waiting to be served.

The guys doing the cooking wore striped trousers and small white jackets. They all looked very hot as they rushed about tossing the deep-fry chip pans around as they passed each time. They settled down at a table with their trays. Towels being placed on the chairs, as was the custom, and, having checked what most others were doing, they removed their T-shirts.

Mike looked across at a guy on the next table. He was pouring himself red wine from a jug, and then topping it up with what looked like water from another jug.

"Looks as though it's strong wine that guy's drinking."

"That's a carafe of wine and one of water. I know these things," Nigel said, in a superior tone.

Nigel couldn't help looking around at the people eating. It was still very warm. He felt good sitting outside in the open-air. The restaurant only had a large wooden roof covering the whole seating area. He estimated that it seated about eighty people at a time, and most were sitting there eating in the nude. Funny, he thought, each camp must have a different style.

He felt quite comfortable sitting there without any clothes on. It felt good. He could live like this forever.

They had nearly finished when their friends from the showers joined them. They just gathered around. Some sat on chairs, some on the floor.

"Please finish your meal. Don't mind us, we have all evening to spare." Urk was heard to say.

They were passing cans of beer around. Their mood was light and friendly.

Mike was the first to finish. "Lead us to the beach," he demanded, jumping to his feet.

The group cheered at this, and in one mass they headed off with arms linked together. This would have seemed weird to people outside the campsite. There they all were, as naked as the day they were born, walking linked together as if they were in another world of their own. As they passed through the pine forest the group thinned out. Nigel and Mike kept together within the group of newfound friends they seemed to have acquired.

The sand was soft underfoot, and still warm from the days sun. The evening was closing in fast.

"Look at that sunset," Nigel said, as he stopped for a moment to take in the scene. The beach seemed to stretch for miles. Mike stood at his side. Not a word being spoken. The sight was amazing.

They were suddenly jolted into moving again. "Come on you two, we have to collect driftwood. You can't drink our beer and eat our food unless you work your passage." It was Urk again, shouting from down the beach to them.

They collected the wood, and watched the experts light the fire. Before long the flames cast a glow over the naked bodies as they sat around chatting as they watched the last of the sun go down. The voices were lowered, almost as if they were all waiting for the start of an event. It was strange. Nigel began to feel an inner peace sitting there.

Once the sun had finally set, they were just being warmed by the fire. Nigel had expected to be feeling the cold, but it was really very warm and comfortable sitting around as they were. Mike gave him a nudge in the ribs. "Here, this is the first of the food," he said, passing a couple of chicken legs and what seemed like the worlds largest sausage to him.

The talk was about life. Everyone spoke in English, although at odd times they broke away into their own languages when they got excited. It seemed that they were all agreeing that the way they were living was as near perfect as they could want for. Someone fired a question at Nigel. He was asked what he thought of their way of living.

"Well it's great. But it is only a holiday, so it can only last for a short time." He felt that this was quite a bright reply, seeing that he had not been listening too hard.

"Why not?" Someone shouted across the fire.

Nigel peered through the flames to see who was firing the

MICHAEL KEENE

questions at him. He could just make out the figure on the other side. He had short fair hair. Yes, it was Gusta.

"I knew that you would be trouble," Nigel shouted back.

"But you haven't answered my question."

"Because we all have to go home and go to work. It's only a holiday."

"Work for what?" Gusta asked again.

"To live." Nigel was now fighting for a good reason as to why he had to go back home to work when life could be more basic and simple for him out here.

"I can't agree." Gusta added. "I have seen my parents slave to make a living back home. They will end up with nothing or very little. They have no idea about this way of living. They have been trying to become rich, but money isn't everything. This is being rich...Life.'

Everyone had tuned into the conversation now. There was a silence around the fire.

"Could you survive here then?" Nigel asked.

"Yes. I work a little. Get paid a little. I have a small caravan to sleep in. I live under the sun, and swim in the sea. I drink a little, love a little, and I don't need clothes. Well, only for the winter, but then that's only for two months."

Mike gave Nigel another nudge. "I think you should give up. I'm sure you're not winning."

There was a lot of laughter around the fire at this point. Nigel went within himself. Gusta had a point. The evening went on like this. Questions were thrown into the arena, mainly about life. Many views were exchanged.

It was nearly midnight when the group started to split up. Couples started to drift away from the glowing embers of the fire. It had been a good evening.

Mike and Nigel made their way to the camper. Mike had been in quite a good mood he thought.

They decided to have a quick wash, and a pee, before slumping down on top of their bed.

"Christ, that was a nice evening," Mike said. "Do you realise that we didn't even have to put our T-shirts on. I'm still glowing."

"I'm glowing too." His voice trailed off as he drifted off to sleep.

Chapter 19

Nigel woke up early in the morning, the sun streaming through the curtains. He eased himself up off of his sleeping bag, not wishing to disturb Mike.

Pulling the camper door slowly open, he peered outside for a moment. It seemed very peaceful.

The rays of the sun were streaming through the trees. Their camper seemed to be standing in a pool of sunlight, almost as if a huge torch was being directed down on them. His thoughts raced back to last night on the beach. Had Gusta got it right?

He lay down on top of his sleeping bag again next to Mike. His mind started to wander in all directions again, but his eyes were drawn to Mike as he slept there, nude and relaxed in his sleep. He started to explore Mike's body with his eyes, trying to resist the urge to touch him.

Mike had strong legs, with dark hairs that added to the strength of his muscles. He gazed at the hairs that curled on his thighs and up to his buttocks. There was a shaft of sunlight that helped sculpt those two mounds.

He couldn't help but notice the sight of Mike's balls being forced through the gap between his parted legs. His eyes lingered on this area for quite a while. How could a body look so…there was no other word to describe this…so beautiful? Was this a homosexual reaction to be looking at Mike like this?

The short dark hairs around his arse were almost tempting him to touch. His gaze followed a thin line of darkish hair which trailed upwards through the dip in his back from just above his bum.

His back muscles, although relaxed, showed his strength. His neck picked up the defined line of hair again. If the hair had been longer, it would have surely curled.

With his head turned to one side, he studied Mike's features. This was one good-looking guy, and he's my friend, he thought. The tanned features were well defined, almost Greek like.

Nigel's thoughts turned to his own life. He lay onto his back, with his hands supporting his head. He tried going back in his mind as far as he could.

He could remember his first erection. It almost frightened

him at the time, but it was a strange and somewhat nice feeling. He smiled at the recollection.

He remembered having the urge to play with his new toy. It produced a feeling that distanced himself from everyone. Only his bedroom had shared his secret. Christ, his room had been good to him, over the years it had kept all the secrets well hidden. He had felt secure in his room.

He remembered the first time he had played with himself and finding that he had a sticky trickle on his hand, thought that he'd injured himself. How he had panicked.

Then there was his first experience with an older boy at school. Yes, he could remember that. It was during cricket. What was his name? He could only have been a couple of years older than him, but bigger. They had been standing in the outfield and somehow found themselves in the bushes together.

He remembered the boy putting his hand inside his shorts and touching his cock, and him getting a swift erection. He had wanted to pull away, but didn't. This was to be the start of several get togethers. In time, they found it boring.

Mike made a sudden move to roll over onto his back. Nigel thought that this was good of him to let him explore his frontal regions. He only had a few hairs on his chest, and his nipples were neat and tight.

God, nipples fascinated him.

His eyes wandered down over Mike's six-pack, which was firm but relaxed. His pubic hair was quite a feature, dark and bushy.

His penis was half-erect. He watched it move, laughing to himself as it slowly stiffened. He looked quickly back at Mike's face. He was still asleep, but there was a hint of a smile appearing.

He had just spent the last ten minutes looking at the naked body of a guy, yet he had never done this to a girl. Was it because he was a bit scared of females, or was it that he was more attracted to males?

For sure, he felt comfortable with a guy…Or was it just with Mike? Mike now placed a hand over his erection. It was almost a pat that he gave it.

Suddenly he stirred, making a funny snorting noise as he opened his eyes to the world.

"I've been watching you," Nigel said.

"Well, I hope you enjoyed the experience. I could have arranged a full erection if you'd asked me before." He placed both hands over his privates now.

"Too late, I've seen it all mate."

"I've read about guys like you, and to think I've been sleeping with one for a couple of weeks."

"Piss off staring, and make the tea."

Nigel turned around, leaning over to put the kettle on. He felt a hand caress his bum.

"Do you know, you have quite a nice arse?" Mike laughed.

"Thanks. I've been thinking the same about yours." He then farted. "There, and mine speaks as well." Nigel giggled.

With that, Mike returned the compliment. This sent Nigel into fits of laughter. Leaping out of the camper and falling onto the grass and at the same time trying to restrain himself from giving a succession of loud farts caused by laughing too much.

"Get your own tea," he managed to shout out. The grass was still damp with dew. He rolled over and over. The feeling was something that he had not experienced before. He felt fresh, clean and alive.

His naked body, now wet with fresh morning dew felt injected with new life. He had never felt so free. He rolled himself over in the grass some more. In the distance he could hear the waves pounding the sandy beach. It was as though it was calling him.

He shouted to Mike, "Won't be long." He stood up and started to jog towards the beach.

Running through the pine trees, he caught his first sight of the sea.

The feel of running bare foot through the grass, the sea breeze and the warm early morning sun caressing his body, gave him the feeling of floating on air.

He suddenly remembered a poetry book he had read…what was the poets name again? Yes, Steve Loxely.

'Now I understand his poems. How well he had captured the feelings of freedom and written about them so well.'

He started to run faster across the sand and into the crashing waves. With one mighty dash, yelling out aloud, he entered the sea. It was brisk and refreshing. Diving under the waves, he swam with pure naked freedom.

He eventually stood up, waist high in the water with the waves crashing over him. He couldn't see anyone for quite some distance. He felt free to shout at the top of his voice.

"Christ, this is living," he shouted. "I want to stay here for ever."

He dived under the waves again, trying to rid himself of all the frustrations in his body. He found that he could stand again, the water lapping waist high.

Turning towards the beach again, he shouted aloud. "Fuck me, this is my world. So fuck the rest of you."

He slowly made his way to back to the beach to sit down. He was now feeling quite exhausted, but good.

Sitting looking out to sea, with elbows on his knees, and his hands supporting his head under his chin, he began to take stock of his life. He reflected back to the way he had been looking at Mike in the camper earlier. Maybe it was the fresh sea air that was helping to clear his head. He told himself off for allowing himself to doubt his reactions.

This was his life. Who were the others to tell him the rights and wrongs of living?

He thought over his doubts of his own sexuality. He simply had to find out what it was like to make love to a woman, and how he would react. But supposing he failed?'

His thoughts went back to what happened in the camper with Mike this morning. One thing was for sure; he didn't get an erection, or felt that he wanted sex with him. So, would he have had the same control if it had been a woman?

What was it like to have sex with a woman? Surely the feelings were the same when you shafted away. Let's be crude about this for a moment, in the aid of science, he thought.

It was the sensation of having his erect penis pounding away in a moist hole that gave the pleasure surely? So, if he closed his eyes, what was the difference? It was purely sex.

That's what he had to find out about, the difference between sex and love. Could he love a guy? He rolled over onto his stomach. To his left he could see a young couple walking in his direction. It was a nice scene he thought. They were naked and holding hands together. This painted a nice picture in his mind.

As the couple came closer, he could see that they were in love. There were short bursts of laughter followed by soft tender kisses.

Nigel watched as they drew level. They gave him a nod and smiled. Nigel returned this with a wave. He watched them walk away into the distance. Every now and again, the guy caressed the girl's bum. It was a nice sight.

Now that was surely love, he thought. Nothing to do with sex. Surely *this* was what he was getting confused about.

He didn't love Mike. Well, not in that way. Not the sort of

way that the couple had been showing towards each other or the sort of love his parents had for each other.

He thought on this for a moment. How did he know he couldn't love another guy? He had never allowed his feelings to test this out. The norm was boy and girl...and it was not quite right to have the same feelings for another guy.

Oh fuck, he thought, I'm confused again.

One thing he was clear in his mind about, was that he was sure that the naturist lifestyle was right for him. He just had to find a way to live like this. It had nothing to do with love or sex; it was just a natural way of living. He felt comfortable with this.

So what was his next move? He had to wander into the world of unknown.

Mike had given him the chance to experiment with his sexuality, and he had cocked that up. He hoped that he would have the chance to try again.

How the hell was he going to find a girl that he could have sex with, one that would take him to the heights of sexual pleasure he desired? Mike could do that, but could a girl do the same?

He entered the sea, letting the cold water clear his head again. After a while he felt that he could face the world once more. He was ready for the challenge of sorting out his sexuality once again.

He started to return to the camper, walking, not running this time, giving himself time to collect himself. His thoughts were now centred on Mike.

How and when would be the right time to follow through with the experiment? He would have to find the right mood.

Mike had prepared breakfast. "It's nearly cold," he said.

"Thanks old mate."

"Where the fuck have you been?"

"Just playing with myself."

"So what's new with that?"

"Oh, quite a lot really," Nigel smiled. "I just wanted to have some space for myself." He then went on to tell Mike about his thoughts on the beach. Mike listened. He showed no signs of reacting to what he was hearing. He had been listening to Nigel, but his own thoughts were racing away.

Although Nigel was the one who was thirsting for the sexual answers, how could he tell Nigel that he was bursting to have sex with him? Nigel had aroused him, and he wanted more.

"You haven't heard a word I've said, have you?" Nigel demanded.

Mike blinked several times, touching his brow in a salute. "Yes Sir. I heard every word."

"Well you could have fooled me."

"Come on let's leave the washing up and go down to the beach. Maybe I can find myself down there as well."

Mike stood up to grab a towel. "Come on show me the way. Maybe we could walk along holding hands, like that couple you met. Would that make us in love according to your books?"

"It would make us look a couple of prats," Nigel said.

The sun was hot as they hit the beach. They hadn't even bothered wearing anything on their feet. This made them hop around on the hot sand and head straight down to the waters edge.

"Shit that was hot," Nigel said.

They walked along the water's edge for about a mile. Small groups of naturists were starting to gather together on the beach. "Nice to see families like that," Mike remarked, looking around at the kids playing together in and out of the water. They turned around and headed back. When they arrived back at the spot where they had run down to the beach, they could see some of the group that they were with the night before.

There was a lot of waving signaling that they were to join them sunbathing. Now it was daylight, it was possible to make introductions. Mike admitted that he would never be able to remember the names, but he would try.

Nigel couldn't help glancing at a very attractive girl. She had been passing looks across at him also.

"Surely you were one of the girls in reception when we arrived? How is it that you aren't on duty?" Nigel asked.

"We do get the odd day off. Come and sit down, it's hurting my neck looking up at you."

She patted the sand at the side of her. He sat down on his towel next to her. "I'm Nigel." he said.

"They call me Jo. I don't like my real name."

"Jo sounds fine to me. Where do you come from?"

"Sweden."

"Nice."

"So what do you do in England?"

Nigel explained that he was at college. "I'm not sure what I want to do for the future. I think I would like to stay in France and find a naturist place to settle down in."

"So you have taken to the lifestyle?" she asked.

"Very much so. I like the freedom."

"What will your family and girlfriend think about that then?" Jo asked, searching for a clue.

"My family will freak out. But as I don't have regular girlfriend back home, no problem on that front."

Jo turned over on her stomach. Nigel remained sitting.

Jo looked up at him. "No girlfriend. I can't believe that. Does that make you a little bit...?"

"Gay?" Nigel suggested.

"Yes, gay."

Without thinking, Nigel said. "No, but I am a little bi-curious."

"Sexy then are you?" Jo asked, with a smile.

"Healthy," he replied.

"I'll buy that," Jo said.

"What about you and your boyfriend then?" Nigel asked her.

"Had a few, but I am curious like you. Do you have a problem with that?"

Nigel gave this some thought. "Not at all."

Jo spread her arms and body out. "Do you mind if I get some serious sunbathing in. Don't go away, I like you."

Nigel continued to sit there. Jo looked relaxed and comfortable as she lay there, drifting into a sleep.

He found himself wanting to explore her body as she lay there. Twice in one day he thought.

Jo had the sort of body that he liked. Her legs were shapely, with firm calf muscles. His eyes examined her thighs, then her buttocks. They were nice and firm. There was a nice dip in the small of her back. Her short hairstyle suited her. She was a natural blonde. His eyes roamed back downwards to her arse. It was a nice arse. He wanted to touch it, but didn't dare.

All these thoughts started to have an effect on him. He was feeling aroused, so he quickly turned to lie on his stomach.

Yes, he was having an erection and a half. Well deserved he thought, smiling at the feeling.

He heard Mike's voice. "What are you smiling at?" he asked.

Nigel put two fingers up.

He lay there enjoying his erection. I bet she won't turn over for the second part of my survey, he thought. It had been easy with Mike.

He must have drifted off to sleep for a while. He felt the sensation of someone blowing in his ear.

Turning his head, it was Jo. "Welcome back," she said.

He had lost his erection by now, and felt safe enough to sit up again.

Jo was now lying on her back. Was this the time to explore her frontal regions? If only she would lay still.

He looked across at Mike. He was chatting to a couple of girls as usual, so he was quite happy.

"Well we both needed some sleep. Always find the sun does that to me," Nigel said, turning to Jo again.

She put her hands up to her eyes to protect them from the bright sun. This gave him the chance to give her a quick once over.

She had the type of breasts he liked. They reminded him of Sue's back home. Not too large, but firm with tight nipples.

His eyes ran down to her pubic area. This appeared like a small mound, surrounded by dark curly hair. This was an area he had never explored with a girl. God, it looked inviting. It would be good to nestle into that, he thought.

He drifted back into the real world on hearing Jo asking if he found her suitable enough.

"Sorry, I couldn't help looking at you like that. Sorry, hope you aren't going to be mad at me?"

"I'm not upset."

"Shall we go for a swim?" Nigel asked, trying to get out of his embarrassing situation. "I think I need to cool off."

Jo jumped up quickly. She started to run towards the waves. "If you beat me, you can take me out tonight," she shouted as she ran.

Nigel raced after her, and quickly passed her. She was not running very fast, he thought. She was making it easy for him.

They swam and played around in the water. Jo entwined herself around his body several times. It felt good. Nigel's thoughts flashed back to Barjac and the river.

This time though, he did get a reaction. It became rigid, and there was nothing that he could or wanted to do about it. He was going to enjoy this one.

Jo sensed this, yet didn't tease him about it. She just smiled.

It felt bloody good swimming with an erection, he thought, but what was he going to do about it if Jo decided to go back to the beach?

After a while they reached shallow water, which reached up to their waists. The waves were thumping them on their backs. Jo fell forward, letting the waves crash over her. She tumbled her way to a point where she could lay down, letting the waves drift over her back. Nigel followed.

They lay there with the water moving the sand around them like a gentle massage. This took his mind off his erection. He had a feeling that Jo knew what to do to help in situations like his. She must have experienced this with other guys. She knew that if they lay there long enough a guy could get himself under control.

"Thanks," Nigel said.

"For what?"

"You know," he smiled. Now fully recovered, he attempted to stand up again. He held his hand out. Jo took hold of it, and he pulled her up. They held hands as they walked up the beach to rejoin the group again.

"Well that looked very romantic," Mike said.

He smiled at Mike's remark. "Doesn't look as if you've done so badly." Nigel nodded to the girls either side of Mike.

Jo sat down next to Nigel. He could feel the vibes. It was a feeling that he hadn't had with other girls. But it was too early to say if this would lead to anything.

"Look I have to work this afternoon at reception. I finish at eight."

"Can I walk you to work?" he asked.

"That would be nice. I have to take a shower first though."

"Then I'll join you, if that's OK with you?"

"Sure."

They walked away from the group, giving a wave back to them. There were a few remarks flying around, but he decided to ignore them. He was feeling good.

As they walked past the camper so that he could grab a towel, he asked Jo if she would like to borrow a towel of his.

"No thanks I can pick one up on the way, as we have to pass my caravan."

"You are very nice. I have never been with an English guy before."

"You don't know what you have been missing then."

"I hope to find out later," she smiled. "Sorry, I'm not really like this with a guy so soon after meeting them."

"Not a problem, I feel very comfortable with you as well. Can't be bad." They entered the showers. There were only a couple of other people in them, so they settled for showers next to each other.

Nigel soaped himself down. He almost felt shy washing his private parts, yet in a strange way it now seemed quite natural.

Jo offered to soap his back. He turned for her. Her hands ran across his back, it felt good. He offered to do the same for her. She stood just outside the jet of the shower as he washed her back for her. He felt the urge to let his hands go around the front of her. Those breasts were so inviting.

They towelled themselves down. Jo had to hurry up now.

Knowing that she was going to be late for work, they hurried themselves, and arrived at reception with only a couple of minutes to spare.

It seemed strange, both standing there, nude and holding hands.

"See you at eight then," Joe said. She gave him a quick kiss on the lips. Nigel went for another kiss, but she placed her hand on his chest. "Later," she told him.

With that, she dashed into the reception, giving him a wave and blowing a kiss over her shoulder.

Nigel stood there, his legs unable to move. Christ, he thought, it used to be his arms that froze, but now it's his legs.

He walked back to the camper. He had mixed reactions as to how he felt. Here he was, just about to get involved with a girl he had only just met. She was nice and she had the looks that appealed to him...but she was bi-curious.

What would this mean to a relationship? Well it was certainly going to interesting at least, but surely it was going to add to his confusion about his own sexuality? As he approached the camper he could see Mike stretched out on the grass.

"So where are the girls then?"

"Oh. I can't be bothered. I'm sure they're all just prick teasers. They seem too experienced for me to handle. How about you then?"

Nigel told him about having a date later that evening. "She's bi-curious," he said. He then went on to tell Mike of his concerns.

Mike smiled at the situation. "We do pick them. Might just as well have stayed at Barjac."

With that, he sat up and yawned. "Fancy a game of tennis. Let's take it out on the balls."

"Great. We could have a couple of hours play, have a shower then something to eat, then I'd be ready for Jo.'

The tennis courts were top quality. They sat there on the

bench putting on their trainers.

Four out of the six courts were being used. They sat there watching for a moment.

It was something quite special watching tennis played in the nude. The bronzed bodies looked good in action.

Nigel couldn't help but watch a couple of guys playing. They were about twenty. There was something quite graceful in the way their bodies moved around the court. His eyes became quite fixed on them.

A tennis ball came rolling across to Nigel's feet. He picked it up looking for the court it had come from. He saw one of the women players walking towards him, so he rolled the ball back to her.

She gave a smile and waved as she picked the ball up.

Now why had he not noticed the women's foursome being played? Why had he only noticed the two guys?

"Come on you dreamer." Mike called out.

The games between them were always close. Nigel was seeing the ball like the size of a football. Everything he touched seemed to be a winner. He was feeling good.

Mike was the sort of player that made several spurts in a match and could raise his standard under pressure.

They did the usual handshaking bit at the end of the game. The usual chatter between them was always amusing as they walked off court. Mike had thought that Nigel had been bloody lucky again. Nigel saying that it was just down to pure talent. With their bodies hot and sticky from playing in the heat, a shower was the order of the day.

Heading towards the shower block, the two guys that had been playing were just ahead of them.

They went through the usual routine. Trainers off at the entrance, towels hung up on one of the hooks, and then a look around the steamy shower room for a vacant shower.

The two guys were already waiting their turn. One turned to speak. "You both play a fair game of tennis. We were watching you. How about a foursome some time?"

Nigel looked at Mike, they both nodded approval at the challenge.

"Fine, that would be good." Nigel said.

They were just in the middle of exchanging names when two showers became free. The two guys dashed under them. Moments later two others became free either side of them.

Although the noise of the showers restricted conversation, introductions were made in a more formal manner. They laughed as they exchanged handshakes under jets of water. The two guys names were Neil and Fredric. They both came from Holland. Like Mike and Nigel, they too were travelling around France.

With the four of them now towelling themselves down, and the noise level now at pitch where they could hear one another, they were able to have a conversation. They started to exchange stories about the past few weeks of travel

Fredric told of how he froze when they arrived at their first naturist campsite. Neil had to sit in the car with him, waiting for the whisky to kick in. And when eventually it did, Fredric could hardly stand in the reception to sign in for nerves. They fell about laughing at this

Nigel then asked about their reaction to seeing all the naked women.

Fredric looked amused at the question. "I was only concerned that I didn't have a reaction at all." Neil was the same. He looked at Fredric saying, "But that's normal for you."

They left the shower block, and before parting they agreed to have a beer at the bar later.

"They're a nice couple of guy's. Should be fun drinking with them," Mike said.

"But I have a date with Jo."

"Well you could come for a drink first, then pick Jo up and join us later."

"Not a good idea. I have a feeling that I'm in luck this evening."

"I hope you haven't any thoughts of using the camper to break your duck?"

Over their meal, Nigel thought out the evenings timings. "Mike, I think you should have your drinks in the bar without me. I'm picking up Jo at eight."

"Well you could at least have a swift half. The bars next to the reception. Fuck me, you haven't far to walk. I doubt if one half of beer is going to have an effect on your action man."

Nigel reluctantly agreed. He then started to prepare himself for his big night out. Mike watched his every move.

"I see you aren't going to wear any briefs under your shorts then. What's that for, instant action?"

"Trust you to see a crude side to everything I do. But just

look. Am I good looking, or am I good looking?'

"You look so good, I wish I was going out with you myself," Mike said, as he licked his finger and brushed it over his eyebrows.

"Mike. Can I be serious for a minute?"

"You can, but can I?"

"If I do get lucky tonight, can I use the camper?"

"Yes."

"Fuck me. That was easy. Thanks mate."

"Are you coming to the bar first though?" Mike asked.

"Only if you get your shorts on quickly."

Mike grabbed his shorts and T-shirt. Hopping out of the camper and trying to pull his trainers on at the same time, shouting to Nigel to slow down.

He caught Nigel up. "Nervous?" he asked. "Shit scared really." Fredric and Neil were almost the only ones in the bar. They had seen the two of them arriving and ordered the beers.

"Thanks," said Nigel. "Shall we go outside? It's still very hot." He moved towards the door.

"Don't worry about him. He's on a promise this evening." Mike said, as he joined them outside.

"Thanks a bunch. We should put a notice up around the campsite? Nigel's on a promise."

"No need, every one can tell. You have that animal look about you. You also look too groomed to be just drinking at the bar tonight."

Nigel looked down at himself. "Fuck me, I've only got a pair of shorts on."

"I don't see the point in even wearing those. They won't be on you for long."

Fredric had been smiling at their conversation. "Are you always like this?"

Mike reassured him that it was only in fun.

Fun it might be, Nigel was thinking, but I'm that close to bottling out of seeing Jo.

Mike sensing how Nigel was feeling, got serious for a moment. "Listen to me. This is the moment you've been waiting for since we arrived. Don't blow it now."

Neil questioned the remark. "What has Nigel been waiting for?"

Nigel looked at Mike. "Don't you dare say a word."

Mike just shook his head. "Why don't you get going. You will only get in deeper if you stay drinking with us. Go on. See you in the morning."

"Yep. You're right. Nice meeting you both. I'll make up for lost time some other time.'

Mike watched his friend walk off in the direction of the reception. He felt a lump arrive in his throat. Stupid he thought, feeling this way about Nigel. But it was something that his friend had to sort out for himself. Christ, it was going to be the end of Nigel's virgin life.

CHAPTER 20

Nigel was early and Jo was busy with new arrivals. She saw him, and gave him a wave.

Nigel, not wanting to be seen as being too keen, walked out of view. He sat down on the wall that ran the length of the reception entrance.

His thoughts started to race away with him. This was not going to be love. It was going to be an introduction to manhood. This was to satisfy his sexual feelings towards women. But how would he feel afterwards, and was he just using Jo? Was this right? Should he make the first move? With all the books he had read, and all the videos he had seen, how was it in real life? Could he even stay long enough to perform this sexual experience? Would he fuck it up right from the start? Would he be able to satisfy her? Would he be able to...? God this was too much. His head was spinning. Should he go through with it?'

"Hi."

It was Jo standing there in front of him. *Oh God.*

"Hello. Where did you appear from?"

"Well you wouldn't have seen me from the distance you were at. You were miles away."

"Well, where shall we go?" he asked.

"Let's go down to the beach. It's great at this time of the day. Most of the naturists have gone back to eat, and the beach is almost empty. Have you got a towel?"

"I can pick one up as we pass the camper."

They walked hand in hand towards the camper. Mike gave them a wave as they passed the bar.

Nigel had no idea what made him stop to remove his shorts, but he did. Maybe it was because Jo was not wearing anything. Bloody hell, she looked good he thought.

Jo peered into the camper as he hunted for a clean towel. Mike's bed was a mess.

"So this is home. Who sleeps up top?"

"We both sleep down here together," Nigel said, regretting this as soon as the words left his mouth.

"So what you were saying this morning, you are bi-curious then?" She smiled at this.

"Confused, I think is a better way of putting it."

He sat down on the edge of Mike's bed and invited her to sit with him.

"Look," he said. I'm not sure that I should be talking like this to a girl. But you see I have to tell you, I have never had real sex with a girl before. Shit, why did I have to tell you that?"

"And what makes you think you're going to have it with me then?"

"Sorry. That didn't come out right. You know what I'm trying to tell you."

Jo smiled, but never replied. They sat there in silence.

"Have you?" he asked.

"Have I what?"

"Made love to other guy's?"

Jo laughed. "Yes, and with women as well. Does that shock you?"

"No."

The conversation came to a grinding halt. "I think we should head for the beach,' Jo said.

The sun was still very warm, and the beach almost deserted apart from a few people in the distance leaving for the day.

"Let's go up into the sand dunes." Jo pointed to their right.

They spread the towels out. Jo opened her sling bag she had been carrying.

"Do you smoke?" she said, offering him a cigarette.

"No, not really. But could I?"

Jo flicked at her lighter and lit her cigarette first then passed it to Nigel. He lit his, giving a cough on his first intake of smoke.

They both sat there looking out to sea. The sun was warm, and the sand dunes cut out what little breeze there was.

Nigel's thoughts raced away again. Fuck. He had left the pack of condoms back at the camper, and all that talking to by his dad as well. Shit he was going to have unprotected sex.

His thoughts and worries were cut short. "Shall we go for swim then to freshen up? I've had a long day at work."

With that she started to run down the beach. By the time Nigel caught her up she was already splashing away in the waves as they crashed down onto the beach. He passed her at speed, diving into the waves. God, the water felt good, it cleared his head. He swam towards her, then stood up in the water which lapped around his chest. He looked around, but he couldn't see her. She appeared out of the water right in front of him. They shouted out aloud, excited about their freedom. There was nobody around to hear them.

Jo went under the water again, diving between his legs. She brushed her hand over his pubic hair and caressed his balls on her way through. He looked over his shoulder to see her emerge. She stood there wiping the water from her boyish face. She smiled.

He made a backward dive between Jo's legs. He had a feeling that she wanted this to happen. Her legs were parted just enough to allow him to brush against her pubic mound. His head had to squeeze through first, giving him enough time to kiss her mound. Just for a moment she tightened her grip on him with her thighs, just long enough to enjoy the sensation.

Nigel, running short of breath had to force his way free. He surfaced gasping for air, but happy.

They swam together. Their arms locked as they embraced each time they got close and were able to stand. His hand felt for her crotch. Jo rotated her pubic area around on his hand. Her head rested on his shoulder. He could hear her breathing, fast and uneven. "Don't stop," she whispered.

Nigel was now well aroused by his moves towards her. His erection stood proud, even in the cool water. He longed for her to take hold of his shaft and work hard on it.

"Let's go back to the dunes," she said.

Nigel released his hold on her and followed her out of the water. His erection was still hard, but he was not bothered as the beach was deserted.

They ran hand in hand up the beach. She looked down at the stiffness of his erection. "God, that looks good to me," she said, trying to take hold of it as they ran.

'Wait till you feel it inside you, and then you will know how good it really is,' he was thinking.

Jo lay back on her towel, raising her arms up to him inviting him to lie with her.

Once again his mind raced away with him. How should he start? What should he do now that he had the chance? He settled down at the side of her. Leaning over her they started to kiss. Their tongues were starting to explore and excite. He moved his hand across her breasts. They were firm and just as he liked them, not too full, but ones that you could hold firmly in your hand. He could feel her nipples standing firm and hard.

He wanted her to touch him now. If only she would caress his nipples as well. He felt her hand grasp hold of his penis. Her hold was firm as she worked him with strokes that were a little too fast for him.

He kissed her nipples. They tasted of the salt from the sea, yet added to the sensation. He now moved on top of her. She was still working away with rapid strokes on his shaft. He placed his hand on hers, trying to slow her strokes down. This led her to letting go of her hold and placing her arms above her head.

He raised his body a little, and slowly ran his hand down to her pubic area. He could feel her juices moist and inviting to his touch. His finger searched for the magic spot he had heard about.

After a few moments of searching, Jo's movements of joy helped him find heaven for her.

She lay there breathing heavily. Her expression was of sheer delight.

He was now in a state of high excitement. But he was craving for her to touch and explore his body. He longed to be driven to new heights, but could he hold on much longer?

Jo was now just lying there giving herself to him, but with no reciprocation.

He moved down her body, searching with his tongue her deepest hole. He wanted to experience the excitement he had read about.

It was a mixture of sweetness mixed with a tang of sea water. This aroused her. She cried out with joy as he kissed and extended his tongue into the moist cavern. His breath seemed hot as his mouth fought for air amongst her pubic hair. He felt her hands at the back of his head helping to thrust his tongue into her. God he could hardly breathe.

He held and squeezed onto his erection to hold back from releasing his load prematurely. He dare not stroke it now.

Jo begged him to enter her. She was ready for him. Nigel slumped onto his side, removing himself from her pubic mound.

"I haven't anything to put on. I should have brought them from the camper," he muttered.

Jo pointed towards her bag. There's a pack in there, in the back pocket."

He raised himself to stretch over her. Jo took hold of his erection for a moment. Her lips kissed the tip of it. The love juices were now flowing from him. She had her eyes closed as she tasted them. He remained in this position allowing her to take his shaft into her mouth.

He wrestled between trying to search through her bag, and

enjoying the blowjob she was expertly giving him. Shit he thought, I can't hold out much longer.

Jo released him from her mouth, and turned to rummage through the bag herself.

She passed him the pack, and watched him fumble with opening it. He rolled the sheath down his shaft, aware that Jo was watching him. This added to his nervous state.

Jo lay there waiting for him to enter her, arms stretched above her head again.

God, this was the moment he had always dreamed about. All the times he had acted out this part in various ways in his bedroom were now playing their role. But this was for real...He looked down at himself as he entered her. Bloody hell, he thought, I have never had a hard on like this before, would Jo be able to take it all in?

His head went back, his back arched and tense. He felt the sensation of sliding his shaft full length into her, slowly, but with one full movement.

Jo groaned, raising her hips towards his thrust. He worked in slow movements, as he felt Jo tighten her muscles around his shaft.

He bent forward to kiss her quickly. She held his head in her hands. Christ, I wish she would let her hands explore him in action, he thought in his thumping head.

Oh, to have her stroke his balls, or have her finger enter his arse to work it in time with his own thrusts. All this flashed through his mind, as he fought for control of shooting his load too soon.

Jo still lay there with arms and hands laying outstretched on the towels.

He looked down to enjoy the sight of his shaft entering her moist love hole. With his strokes now becoming more rapid, he placed his arms around the small of her back, pulling her towards his thrusts.

He could hold back no longer. His thrusts became faster, as the load he had been storing suddenly shot with firm bursts from his shaft. His head was now spinning. He was almost at the point of passing out, yet he kept thrusting away, as he felt the sensation of his balls slapping against Jo's love juices. God, I'm going to pass out, he thought. But it was all over now.

He withdrew himself, and lay at her side, breathless, and with his body running with sweat.

They both lay there motionless and without speaking.

After a while he opened his eyes to look at Jo. "Hi," he managed to say.

Jo sat up and lit a cigarette. She placed a kiss on her finger and placed it on his lips.

Nigel tidied himself up, and then pinched another cigarette from her pack.

They both sat there watching the sun go down on the horizon. Still not a word being spoken.

Jo flicked her cigarette stub into the sand as she stood up to collect her things together. It was obviously all over with now.

He passed her the remaining condoms. Not knowing what to do with the used one, he shuffled it into the sand feeling a little embarrassed by not knowing what one does with them after use.

They headed back towards the campsite, hardly speaking. He wanted to ask if he had performed well enough for her, but was frightened to know the answer.

He was in a world of his own. He had just lost his virginity. At least he didn't make a fuck up of it. Most guys would have shot their load within the first few seconds, but he had lasted the pace. He felt good about this, yet there had been something missing.

For a moment he mused with the thought that it had been better than a wank, but he had expected to have feelings running through him at the time that would have blown his mind. Sure, he had entered the mystical love cove, shafted away, and then the final trust. Shit, it had felt good...But surely there were more feelings and sensations that went along with this.

"You are miles away," Jo said, tugging at his hand. "Didn't you enjoy it then?"

"Sure, it was fine," he said, trying not to look into her face. "Do you want a drink at the bar?" he asked, trying to change the subject.

"No thanks. I've got to be in work early in the morning."

"Can I kiss you goodnight then?" he asked.

She pulled their bodies close together. They were still warm from their exertions. She kissed him on the lips, but put a finger up to them as he tried to have another.

"Thank you, you were good," Joe said.

"Well thank you," he said. Fuck me she's giving him points out of ten, he couldn't help thinking.

He watched as she walked back to her caravan.

The camper seemed a million miles away. His legs suddenly felt very weak. Sliding the camper door open, he fell on top of Mike's bed, in a daze.

It was still very warm, and he felt it would have been easy just to slip into a sleep. He snapped out of this feeling. Best take a shower, he thought, and tidy myself up. The showers were empty. His legs still felt very unsteady. Is that what happens to everyone, or was it because it was his first time?

He showered himself down, with extra attention to his private areas. He cleaned his teeth at the washbasin to rid himself of the taste. Funny he thought it tasted good at the time, but now all he wanted to do was wash it away. His mind flashed back to some of his bedroom antics. He had quite often excited his mind whilst masturbating with the thought that he would taste the cum off of his fingers after the event, but quite often the urge to do so left him as soon as he finished. Same thing now I suppose?

He got back to the camper. He was gasping for a beer.

His thoughts kicked into gear again as he lay on the bed.

The evening had been nothing like he had expected…well sort of. He questioned himself about having sex with Jo so soon after meeting her. How many other guys had she taken to the dunes?

He sat upright at this thought. Was this why she had just laid there letting it happen? It must have been just a routine for her. But fuck, this had been his first time. Bugger me, how many pricks had been there before his?

He reached for another beer. He looked at the time. It was almost eleven o'clock. Where was Mike?

That's a thought. Mike was bound to ask all the questions. What should he tell him?

He lounged there with his beer, reflecting over his sexual experiences with women. Sue's face flashed before him. Then there was the blowjob at the badminton club. He had caressed and kissed women's breasts before. And now with Jo he had gone all the way. He had just fucked a woman. *'Come on man, you have just shafted your first woman,'* he said to himself. Yet surely there must be more feelings that he should have experienced during their sex act. It was a let down.

He took down another gulp of beer. He had been expecting more. His hand reached for another beer. Steady he thought. But then, no, fuck it, he needed it.

He lay there taking the beer down in huge gulps. The bottle, now empty, rolled away from his grasp as he fell into a deep sleep.

He became aware that he was being rolled over onto his side, and Mike whispering in his ear.

"Come on mate move over. I sleep here too."

Nigel was not sure if he had been asked a question, but he muttered softly, "I'll tell you about it in the morning."

Mike smiled at this. He had not asked the sixty four-dollar question. He looked down at Nigel and removing the beer bottle away, tucked himself up alongside him, and fell into his own dreamworld.

Mike was the first to stir in the morning. The sun, as usual, was warm and bright. As the curtains were still open, he could see movements going on outside, people going to the shower block, and others hurrying to collect their bread. It was a scene that he was beginning to take for granted. It was like living in another world, a very basic form of living in a way. It was beginning to feel very natural living in the nude now.

He looked around at Nigel. They had only been away for a couple of weeks, yet their minds were much broader for the experiences they had been through so far. There was no way they could have gained so much from being back at home.

He was hoping that when Nigel awoke he was not going to tell him that it had been a failure with Jo. Nigel needed the answers to his sexuality. If Jo had not provided some of the answers, he was prepared to go all the way to help Nigel and his bi-curious hang up. He knew what Nigel wanted, and it was up to him to take the lead with their experiment.

He sat back to think ahead a little. Now supposing that it had been a disaster with Jo, and just supposing they had completed their act at the lake…would that mean that they were both gay? He gave a little chuckle at this thought.

Nigel began to open his eyes. They were just slits in the sunlight. His hand shielded his eyes from the sunlight.

"Good morning. I never heard you come in last night."

"Well you were dead to the world, and full of beer."

"Shit, yes, I remember knocking a few back."

"Well did you get your end away?" Mike blurted out. *'Well there goes my big mouth again,'* he thought.

"Be more direct with your questions, why don't you!" Nigel snorted out, as he tried to sit up.

"I didn't mean it to come out like that, believe me.!

236

"Well it fucking well did."

"Well, did you?"

"Yes."

There was a silence for a moment, followed by a fit of laughing together. Mike said that he would make some tea first before he heard the sordid details.

"I could do with that. My mouth is as dry as a sandpit."

"Here grab hold of that," Mike said, passing him his mug of tea. "I could have told you that you had had it away before you told me."

"How?"

"Well you didn't have your usual erection to greet me with this morning."

Mike stretched himself across the bed trying not to spill his own tea. "Now tell me every thing."

Nigel had decided to leave out Jo's lack of skills in touching him in the right spots, and how he had mentally been screaming out for those sensations. He felt that if he did get into detail, when they eventually did get together to have a sexual session, Mike would remember and try extra hard to satisfy him. He wanted to find out without prompting. He told Mike about the way in which they fooled around in the sea. Mike making a remark that it was a replay of the film, Blue Lagoon.

When it came to having sex in the dunes, he gave Mike the impression that he had it away twice, and within minutes of the first orgasm. He watched Mike's face as he told him this.

"You lucky bastard," Mike remarked. "How did it all end. I thought you were going to use the camper to lose your virginity in."

"Oh, I think I was just one of many that she had taken to the dunes. She seemed too cool about it all. It was all too rehearsed for me to have been one of the first."

Nigel told him the bit about not being prepared by taking any condoms down with him, and how she provided them. "Another reason to think it was all pre-planned."

Mike nodded in agreement. "Another prick teaser."

"I think I'll give her a miss," Nigel said, looking a little sad at the thought of what it should have been like on his first attempt.

"Listen. Somebody's coming," Mike said, looking out of the window. "Christ, it's Jo."

"Shit no."

"Only kidding!"

"Very funny. Who is it then?"

"Fredric and Neil. I bet you feel like playing tennis?"

"No I bloody well don't. I don't think I could even stand at this moment."

"Shouldn't think so. Twice in one evening. Fuck me," Mike said, looking up at the camper roof.

"I was only kidding. It was once."

"Bastard." That was all Mike had time to say as there was a knock on the camper door.

"Hi, come in, take a seat," Mike said, clearing a space for them.

Fredric looked around. "So this is home? I like these campers."

"It's good fun," Mike said.

"I hear you went out with Jo last night. Did you have a good time?" Neil asked.

"Who told you that?" Nigel said, looking at Mike as he passed coffee around.

"Well it wasn't me. These two guys knew way before me even."

"It did get around the camp a little," Fredric laughed.

Neil told Fredric not to be a bastard.

"OK, you tell him then," Fredric said.

"Well, most new arrivals have been out with her."

"Have you been with her?" asked Nigel, looking a bit pissed off on hearing this.

The two guys looked at each other and laughed. "Yes, Neil was first, then I was next."

"Fuck," exclaimed Nigel.

"Yes, she had us both," Neil said grinning from ear to ear.

"Do I read you clearly?" Mike asked, wide eyed.

"At the same time?" Nigel spluttered.

"Yes, afraid so," Neil said, looking pleased with himself.

"Did she take you to the dunes?" Fredric asked.

Nigel nodded his reply. "She looks so nice. I could have taken her as being a virgin."

"She's far from that. But it's what we both thought at the time."

Mike moved closer to Nigel without it being obvious while Neil and Fredric talked away in Dutch.

Mike placed a hand on Nigel's shoulder. "Never mind mate, at least you have broken your duck."

"What is a broken duck then?" asked Neil, on hearing this.

"Never mind. It's too hard to explain."

Noel attempted to explain in detail what happened when they

went with Jo. Nigel soon closed the subject. It all sounded a little too crude to be talking about something that should really be private. Christ, we hardly know them, he thought.

"Have you had many women?" asked Neil.

"Quite a few," Nigel grunted back.

Mike sensing that Nigel was getting embarrassed changed the subject. "Look, do you mind if we give the tennis a miss?"

"No, we are feeling a bit shattered as well."

Fredric, sensing the tension building up, stood up ready to leave. "Cheers. See you both later I expect."

After they had left, Nigel asked why Mike had cancelled the tennis.

"Because I felt they were trying to take the piss out of you, and I'm fucked if I like that."

They lazed around for most of the morning. A beer at the bar was suggested, but Nigel hesitated.

"What if Jo is there?"

"Fuck her." Mike replied.

"You amaze me," Nigel said. "You have a terrible memory. I've just told you I did that last night, and you've forgotten already."

"Is that the way you see last night with her then. Just a fuck?"

"Well it wasn't love. Remember what Boris was saying."

They were nearing the reception, when they heard shouting coming from the office. They walked slowly to get closer. They sat on the wall outside the office trying to listen in, but it was mainly in Dutch.

After a few minutes, Jo appeared on the steps. She was dressed, and carrying a travel bag. Her face was bright red. The shouting still continued as she walked away in the direction of the gates. She raised one finger up in the direction of the office... Then she was gone.

They both stood there with mouths open.

Mike was the first to speak.

"And she never said good-bye to her lovers," he said, looking around at a group of guys just standing and looking dazed. "She must had most of them I would think by the looks on their faces"

"I think they are done with her services in the office though," Nigel said.

Mike decided to go into the office to see if he could find out what it had been all about. He met Fredric inside. He'd heard it all from the beginning.

Mike rejoined Nigel who was sitting on the wall. He explained that the owners had heard of her exploits, and sacked

MICHAEL KEENE

her on the spot.

"She had taken advantage of her position." Mike laughed.

"Who writes your script?" Nigel said, reflecting back on last night in the dunes.

As they started to walk towards the bar, there was a shout from the office. It was Fredric.

"Nigel. Sorry, I nearly forgot. I've got a letter for you. It arrived this morning."

"Thanks," Nigel said, taking a look at the postmark. "Who the hell is writing to me from Barjac?"

"It's a little love letter," Mike said, as he gave Nigel's cheek a pinch.

"Shove off."

"Well go on, open it, and read it to me."

"No way. It's addressed to me, so you stand no chance of reading it."

They got back to the camper. Nigel sat on the ground while Mike got a couple of beers from the fridge.

"Well go on, open the bloody thing. Don't just sit there sniffing the bloody envelope."

The envelope was slowly opened. Nigel's fingers pulled the letter out with great care. Sitting upright, he started to read it to himself. Mike tried to position himself with his beer, so that he could have a sneak preview, but he was out of luck as Nigel rolled over onto his back and holding the letter up shielding his eyes from the sun.

Mike watched, smiling at the scene. "Who's it from then?"

There was a long silence. "It's from Vic."

"Well?"

"She's got the hots for me. Fuck, she has the bloody hots for me. And I'm bloody well stuck here."

Mike sat there wondering why when a guy lay on his back, one hand always seemed to take hold of his balls. Nigel finished reading, and lay there with a lost look on his face.

"Well can I have a read of it?" Mike asked, taking another swig of beer.

Nigel, now on another planet, handed it to him. "Go on then, take the piss out of that."

Mike proceeded to pull faces as he read it. He picked out little snips and read them aloud.

"I think she's asking you to call back before you return home."

"How do you feel about that?" Nigel asked. "She is going to be

240

there until the end of September."

"Fine by me. I'm only the driver."

Nigel took the letter back and read it again. She was in love with him. Maybe this is what he had been looking for. Yet how can you fall in love within hours of meeting someone? Was he in love with her though?

They decided to have something to eat then go down to the beach.

The sun was even hotter today. The sand was scorching, and they rushed down to the waters edge as fast as they could to avoid their feet being burnt.

"Isn't it great being free like this. How are we ever going to cope when we get back home again?" Nigel asked.

"I'd like to stay here forever, just you and me. Sod the women. I'm enjoying the freedom," Mike said, as he pulled Nigel under the waves.

Nigel surfaced. "Why sod the women?"

"Well they are nothing but trouble."

"Blokes can't do without them mate," Nigel remarked.

"Do you want to debate that?" Mike asked. "I thought you were out here to find yourself. And what happened. It only takes one letter from a girl you have only known for a couple of days, and you loose control."

As they stood there in the water, Nigel went into his thoughts once again. Mike had a point. Was it that he had fallen for one of the oldest moves in the book, by being led to believe that someone loved you?

He decided to play around in the sea with Mike so that he could get relieved of his frustrations.

They had mock fights, taking turns to duck each other under the crashing waves. Their bodies locked in a show of strength, the feel of Mike's naked body against his which Nigel found enjoyable, and having no inhibitions to hold them back in their naked combat.

After a while of exhausting play, they retreated to their towels and stretched out on the golden sand.

They lay there for a while, without a word from either of them. Nigel started to dwell on Mike's comment about women. Then his thoughts went back to home again. He thought how differently things would have turned out if he had brought Dean with him. God, it certainly wouldn't have been the same, for sure.

He looked over at Mike. He was asleep already. Must be the

sun that makes you tired he thought as he drifted away too, into his dreams. He couldn't have been asleep long. He felt his shoulder being shoved. "You can't lie there like that. Turn over or something," he heard Mike saying.

He suddenly understood what Mike was on about. He was lying there with an erection again, something that he was prone to when lying on his back.

"How long have I been like that?" he asked, rolling over on to his stomach.

"Well I've been admiring it for about ten minutes, but as we have a few people approaching, I thought that they could be spared the thrill."

Once the group of people had passed, they decided to make their way back to the camper for some food.

With the meal over, they sat down outside the camper to plan their route back to Barjac, only this time in reverse.

There were the odd jokes to help the wine down. Mike suggested that Nigel could do a hand-stand in the front seat to read the map upside down. He thought it would work as long as Nigel remembered to get his shorts on, just to save attracting attention.

They drank well into the night. It was after the third bottle had been opened that Mike decided they should hit the sack.

With that, he clambered into the camper, flopped down on top of his bed, and calling out through the door, "Good night, sweet dreams mate."

Nigel stayed outside in the warm night air to reflect over his life. He thought back over the past weeks, from the time he announced to his parents about the trip, and up to the last few days.

He felt that he had suddenly grown up in a very short space of time. He had been lucky to meet some great people since they arrived in France. He was glad that he had found this naturist lifestyle.

The question though, was he doing the right thing by going back to see Vik?

He had accepted Mike's offer whilst at the lake but cocked it up. Maybe there would be another chance? As Mike had said, it had to be at the right time, and the right place.

His head started to spin again. He poured another half glass of wine, sank it back, then crawled onto the bed at the side of Mike.

CHAPTER 21

Once again, Mike was the first to wake. Nigel turned on his bed, eyes squinting against the sunlight streaming through the camper windows.

"Shit this is boring with sun every day. I don't think I can handle much more of this."

"Wait until you get back home, you won't be saying that then," Mike said.

"It's a good job we've been sleeping on top of our sleeping bags, or else they would have been humming by now." He also reminded Nigel that it was his bed that was always being used.

"Don't you like me sleeping down here then?"

"Love it."

As they were eating breakfast, they checked the money situation. After laying out all of their Euros and loose change on the table, they decided that the situation was tight, but not impossible.

"I think we could last out about another ten days," Mike said.

"How do you make that out then? We only have 1,500 francs left."

"Well my little friend, I have some in reserve. It's been in my toilet bag since we arrived."

"You lovely sod." Nigel laughed.

Once again the camper was made tidy for the journey ahead. Mike started up the engine and it roared into life. Nigel did the usual check around just to make sure nothing was left behind.

"Hold it," he shouted out to Mike. "We've done it again, the roof's still up."

They got inside again, and with one good tug, the roof dropped down into position.

"It's so good to get on the open road again," Mike said, as he wiggled the steering wheel around.

"Steady on, I want to arrive in Barjac in one piece if you don't mind."

They put several miles behind them before stopping for a midday break. They pulled into a slip road which displayed a sign for picnics.

There were several lorries parked there already. Mike pulled the camper into a space between them.

Nigel opened the sliding door, while Mike raided the fridge for a beer. They sat on the step of the camper staring into space.

Mike glanced around. He noticed that they were attracting attention from the lorry drivers who were standing in a group, talking and drinking. There were bursts of laughter as they kept glancing across at them.

"Don't look now, but we are being watched by those guy's over there."

Nigel stood up to stretch himself and turned to glance towards the drivers. Mike was right.

"I think it's because we're just wearing shorts, and they're after our bodies. They must think we're gay."

Mike thought this was funny. "Give me a kiss then," he said, laughing at the situation.

"Don't laugh, it will make things worse," Nigel said, looking concerned now. "I think we'd better get on our way."

"Shit. Sod that lot. I'm hungry. Do you think it's because we're English? Remember the trip down when we went into that bar?"

Nigel thought for a moment, and smiled. "Seems like ages ago, doesn't it?"

Mike climbed into the drivers seat, started the engine, and they hit the road again.

They motored on, passing the lake that they were evicted from. "I don't think we'll stay there tonight."

Nigel glanced at the spot as they passed. His thoughts went to his failure to perform. He'd had his chance. *Doubt if I will have another chance now. I would've known by now if I were bisexual or not.*

His thoughts were broken. "Tell you what, how about stopping at a small hotel tonight? It would make a change. We could have some proper food, and a bath. How does that sound to you?"

"Have we got enough dosh to afford that. Maybe a B&B would be cheaper?" Nigel replied.

"B&B it is then."

"Right then pick a place on the map. Not a big town though, maybe a small village."

Nigel spread the map out across his legs, ran his finger along the route they were taking, and with a thrust of his finger selected a spot at random.

It was about five in the afternoon when they arrived at the elected spot. It looked fine. They drove the camper around the square looking for rooms.

"There." Nigel shouted. "That looks the place for us."

It was a small hotel. It had shutters at the windows, and a balcony that overlooked the square.

They pulled up outside. Slipping on their trainers and T-shirts, they got out of the camper, locked the doors, and strolled inside.

A little old lady appeared from behind curtains that divided the office and reception area. She was all in black. Her face was a mass of wrinkles, but her eyes were alive.

After they had exchanged the greetings of "Bonjour" between the three of them, the conversation seemed to dry up.

Mike leaned on the counter. "Parlez-vous-Anglais?"

"Non."

'Well that's fucked it up,' thought Nigel.

"Avez-vous un lit?" Mike asked.

Nigel looked at him, mouth open.

"Oui." The old lady said. She then pointed to a book for them to sign in.

Mike waved his hand. He then pointed to his eye with one finger. He then pointed up to the ceiling. "Can we see the room?"

With that, the old lady turned, and went back through the curtains again. There was a lot of shouting in French, and moments later a young lad appeared.

He was about sixteen. He smiled as he walked past them and down the hallway towards the stairs. He turned, looked back, and with a movement of his head, suggested that they follow him.

Mike gave Nigel a shove forward. "Go on then, I've done my bit."

They were shown a couple of rooms. Both had single beds in, a wash hand basin plus a shower.

"What's that?" Nigel asked, with a smile on his face.

"A bidet. It's where you wash your privates," Mike whispered.

One of the rooms had a balcony overlooking the square. "I think we'll have this one," Mike said, turning to the boy.

"Good choice," he said.

"Oh, you speak English then?" Mike said.

"A little."

They found out what the room was going to cost them. About 170 Euros each. The evening meal was going to be extra.

Mike asked if the camper was safe where he had parked it. Having had the assurance that it was, they went down to collect some clean clothes to wear for the evening meal.

Nigel elected to have a bath instead of a shower. The bathroom was just along the hallway. Mike asked him to leave it clean for him, and not to use up all the hot water. Nigel gave a two finger sign behind his back as he headed off.

He filled the bath right to the top, and relaxed in the hot water. It was the first bath since leaving home.

Although the bath was nice, somehow he felt very enclosed. He suddenly felt a strong desire to get up and run free outdoors. He thought it strange. He had to blank this from his mind.

He quickly got out of the bath and towelled himself dry. He tossed up whether he should wrap a towel around his waist, or get dressed again. Stupid he thought, at the campsites he would have walked back with the towel over his shoulder. Daft old world. He opened the door to the room. Mike was stretched out on his bed.

"You were quick. I see you remembered to cover up then."

Nigel then told him how he'd felt. "It must be a reaction to all that fresh air we've had."

Mike got off of his bed and headed to the bathroom, leaving Nigel to his thoughts.

Nigel removed the towel from around his waist and stretched out on his bed. He was feeling restless. He got up and went to the open french windows leading out to the balcony.

As he had nothing on, he just took a peep outside first to see if he could be seen by anyone. As the balcony was quite large, there was no fear of being seen from down below.

He stretched his arms above his head. Taking in some fresh air again he started to feel a little more relaxed. He stayed there for quite a while.

Mike returned, slamming the door shut.

"Shit. I felt the same as you," he said, joining Nigel.

They both stood there watching the people below going about their lives.

"Come on mate. I could eat a horse." Mike said.

"We might just be doing that."

They got dressed, both feeling uncomfortable in shirts and jeans again. "God, I feel really enclosed." Nigel muttered.

It took them a while to read the menu. The young guy that had shown them their room was also the waiter. He helped them select both the food and wine.

"That was nice of him to do that," Mike said.

"Wait 'til you get the bill," Nigel replied.

With the meal over with, and both feeling better for having some good food inside them, they sat back not knowing what to do next.

"I hear the bar calling," Mike said.

"How much was the meal then?" Nigel asked.

Mike passed the bill across to him. "Christ, that was good. That means that we'll have more to spend at the bar." Nigel grinned.

They decided to tuck themselves into a corner table in the bar, having ordered some wine.

As they made their way across the bar, they were once again aware that they were being stared at.

"Must be your after-shave," Mike said.

"Never. It's the way you walk."

The bar was quite full. Everyone seemed to be smoking. Mike remarked that he wished at times he smoked too.

The young guy was now serving behind the bar. He made his way through the tables with the wine for them to taste.

"That's fine, thanks," said Mike.

"Is there anything else that I can arrange or get for you?"

Nigel looked at Mike. "How about a smoke? It's a long time since I had one."

The young waiter, giving them a nod, told them that this could be arranged. He hurried back behind the bar and through the curtains.

They were in deep conversation when the waiter returned. He placed a small pack of what they thought was tobacco on the table. He then gave them a packet of cigarette papers and matches.

"You can pay for these quite separately." He gave a wink at this, and left them to it.

"Shit. I think we have just been sold some funny fags."

"No," said Nigel.

"Yes," said Mike, grabbing the package and quickly putting it into his pocket.

"Have you ever had these before?" Mike asked.

Nigel smiled. "Yes I have. And they do make me funny."

"Let's take the wine and get ourselves up to our room," Mike suggested.

247

"This isn't the same as being in our camper is it?"

"Not quite," Mike agreed, shoving the door closed with his foot.

He handed Nigel a bottle of wine that hadn't been opened.

"I suppose we'll have to drink from these plastic cups. Pass them over."

Nigel decided to get out of his gear. He pulled his jeans and T-shirt off hurriedly. "Christ I'm glad to get out of these things. Talk about feeling trussed up."

"When you have a moment, would you pass me the bloody cups?" Mike asked.

Nigel passed them across the bed. "Do you object to sharing a room with a naked guy? If you are shy then I'll cover up with a towel or something for you."

"There's a box of tissues at the side of you. One should be enough to cover you." Mike laughed.

Nigel ignored the remark. "Just pour the wine."

Mike stripped off his clothes first, and then passed the wine over. "Cheers."

With an air of excitement, Nigel asked to have a look at the package from the waiter. "Have you really smoked a joint before?"

"Yep," said Mike.

"I'm not sure that I really want to have one." Nigel remarked.

"Here pass me the stuff. I'll roll one up and we can share it."

Nigel watched as Mike struggled to roll a slim joint. "It looks nothing like the ones you see guys smoke at the clubs. It looks more like a cigar." Nigel taunted.

"There, I've done my best. Pass me the matches."

Nigel watched again as Mike lit up. There was quite a flame appear. "Shit, I nearly lost an eyebrow."

Nigel just looked on.

"I don't think you've quite mastered the art of this, have you?"

Mike inhaled the smoke, taking it right down. This resulted in a coughing fit.

"Christ that was good," he said, his eyes now watering.

Nigel rolled around his bed laughing.

Mike then passed the joint over to him. Nigel took a short swift draw on it and coughed his lungs up.

"Well you're not going to get high on that are you? Pass it back."

Mike took another few drags of it and passed it over to Nigel again. As he inhaled deeper, he could feel the effects now. He had heard about people saying 'spaced out' and that was what he was feeling now.

He took yet another draw on it before handing it over to Mike again.

"More wine?" Mike offered.

"Yep, fill it up man." He had a silly smile starting to spread across his face.

Nigel was being offered another drag on the joint. He raised his hand. "No thanks, I'm fine." He was feeling very relaxed as he lay on his bed with his thoughts running through his head.

Mike was chattering away. Nigel could hear him, but it was as if he was talking from another room.

He lay there for a while before he became aware that Mike was shaking him on the shoulder.

"You haven't heard a word I was saying, have you?"

"Funny, but I have." Nigel said, as he laid back with his hands behind his head. "I was miles away."

"I know the feeling. I'm feeling relaxed, so move over, make room for me."

Nigel moved without giving it a second thought. Mike grabbed his pillows and stretched himself out at Nigel's side. The touching of their naked bodies felt especially good, Nigel thought.

Mike turned onto his side letting his arm rest across Nigel's chest. Not a word was spoken.

Nigel knew that this was going to be the moment that they'd been building up to. At first he didn't move. He could feel his heart beating faster as Mike's hand brushed over his chest searching for his nipples. He loved the sensation. At this moment his mind was now clear as to what he was doing. He turned so that their bodies could embrace together.

They took it in turns to explore each other. It was as if Mike would find an area of Nigel's body which he knew his friend would long to have touched and caressed most himself.

Nigel would then explore Mike's body in the same way. Each of them finding the exact places to caress.

Their erections became solid. The juices of their excitement left wet patches across their bodies as they continued to explore each other. There seemed to be no end to this slow, sexual arousal. Nigel was groaning with pleasure. Mike gave little gasps with each intake of breath.

Mike was the first to utter a few words. "Man is this good."

Nigel moved down the bed to take hold of Mike's erection. He slowly started to work on the strong, hard, shaft with firm, steady strokes. The love juices appeared like teardrops as he stroked and squeezed the sturdy rod. He kissed the throbbing head as he eased it into his mouth. The taste was as good as he had remembered it from last time. He ran his tongue around the rim, and then took it deep into his mouth again.

He could feel Mike's desire to make thrusting movements. Nigel felt Mike's hand at the back of his head in order to create the right length of stroke, whilst his other hand took hold of Nigel's erection, keeping it firm.

Without a word, Mike eased himself around on the bed so that he could take in Nigel's shaft in order to give the same sexual pleasure in return. They both lay there in a head to toe position, each taking in the other's erection.

Nigel knew that if he continued taking Mike's shaft into the depths of his throat any longer, Mike would shoot his load. He eased off, and Mike followed by gently holding Nigel's shaft with a firm grip, holding back the flow that he knew Nigel was ready to release.

"Bloody hell, you know how to get the best out of me," Mike said, with a smile. It was a smile that said all was well. Nigel smiled back in contentment.

They exchanged a quick kiss. Nigel was not sure in his mind that this was the right thing to do. He wasn't in love; he was just experimenting with sex.

Mike was keen to get to the heights of their sexual encounter. "How are you feeling now?" he whispered in Nigel's ear. "Do you still want to go through with it?"

Nigel was now too far down the line to give up this experience of life. His mind quickly focused on what they were doing. All doubts were now cleared from his mind.

"Don't stop now," was all he could manage to say.

Mike got off the bed. Reaching into his bag, he tossed a condom to Nigel, having taken it out of the foil for him.

Mike watched as Nigel rolled the sheath over his erection. His thoughts were focused on how he was going to take this inside him. Could his arse take that shaft? What was it going to be like? Was it going to hurt?

Mike returned to the bed. He lay there on his back, bending his knees towards his chest; he was ready to take Nigel. He passed the tube of gel from the side of the bed to him. "There, use that please."

This was it, Nigel thought. He tried to clear his head from all thoughts. He wanted this to work this time.

He eased his finger into Mike's anus. He did this as though he had done this so many times before. Mike was already moist and ready for him to enter. With his thoughts now driven from his head, he drifted into this new sexual experience. Mike groaned as Nigel's fingers entered him. First one, then two. Mike moved in time to the thrusting of them. With his other hand Nigel caressed Mike's nipples. Mike groaned with joy and excitement. He was ready to receive Nigel's shaft.

There seemed no need for the gel to be used, but Nigel smeared some in and around the point of entry, mixing it with the natural juices that were already there.

Nigel, taking a deep breath, eased his erect shaft into the warmth of Mike's anus. He entered only the head of his throbbing shaft at first, easing it around. Mike groaned his approval.

Their bodies were now bathed in sweat. Nigel leaned forward onto his hands. Slowly he entered his shaft inch by inch into the unknown depths. Mike uttered "Yes, that's beautiful. Fuck me, go on, yes I can take all of you."

Nigel increased the force of his thrusts. He pushed harder as Mike urged him on with shouts of "Yes." The muscles of Mike's arse tightened and relaxed as he shafted in and out at a controlled pace. The sensation was something that Nigel had never ever experienced before. The feeling was beyond belief.

Nigel leaned back now. Mike placed his legs over Nigel's shoulders in order to allow him to enter even deeper.

The more Nigel leaned back, the more he enjoyed the pressure on his shaft. This was heaven, he thought.

He looked down at his own shaft. He loved the sight of his penis entering and retracting. All the time he felt his balls thumping against Mike's arse. It was mind blowing.

Mike teased Nigel's nipples, and in return he took hold of Mike's erection. Mike groaned with pleasure as he felt Nigel's wanking strokes.

Nigel was now working himself to a frenzy. His head began to spin as he worked himself almost to the point of passing out with exertion. He was nearing the point of shooting his load. He withdrew just in time, gripping his erection tightly to steady himself.

He heard Mike pleading for him to go on. Nigel eased his

shaft into the depths again. He felt good about being able to control himself like this. His strokes started slowly at first, then increased to rapid thrusts. Mike seemed a master at tightening and relaxing his anus muscles, adding to the sensation.

Nigel was now nearing the point of no return and almost passing out with joy.

With one final thrust he felt the force of his load shoot from his shaft.

The force was like nothing he had experienced before. God, he had never shot a load like this, ever.

He leaned backwards again, putting full pressure on his shaft forcing every last drop of fluid from his penis.

He stayed like this for a moment, and then fell forward onto Mike's sweating body. They lay there, their beating hearts pounding away through their bodies.

It was ages before either spoke.

"How was that then?" Nigel whispered.

"Fucking great."

Removing his sheath with a tissue, Nigel placed his load on the floor between the beds.

Mike rolled over onto his side. His hands roamed Nigel's body, Nigel knew that this was the moment he had been preparing for mentally.

Mike placed his finger into Nigel's anus. Like most guys, this was a feeling he'd experienced when playing around with himself. But the feeling of someone else doing it felt really good.

Mike played with this area for a while. It became moist and ready to enter.

Mike got onto his knees, and rolled Nigel over. Placing his arm under his waist raised him to his knees.

Nigel held on to the headboard. He exposed his arse towards Mike, who had continued playing around with his fingers in the hole of mystery. Nigel was ready to be entered.

Not a word was spoken between them. Mike spread the gel around the entrance. Nigel tensed for a moment as he waited for the feel of Mike's shaft entering him.

Mike gave him an assuring pat on his back. Then slowly Nigel felt the head of Mike's shaft ease into him. He tensed again, and then relaxed. Mike entered a little more, withdrew then entered again with slow and deeper thrusts. He had never experienced a sensation quite like this before. He felt the firm length and rounded erection reaching deep inside. It felt so good.

He had often wondered what the feeling was like. And now he finally knew.

Mike moved the pace up a little, shafting him with longer strokes. Nigel's own erection was on the decline. Mike sensing this, held a firm grip on it to ease it back to life.

Mike withdrew, and turning Nigel over onto his back, took hold of his legs and placed them over his shoulders. Mike then did something quite unexpected. He eased Nigel upwards, and then placed his head between Nigel's legs.

He could feel Mike's hot breath as he kissed and tongued his arse. Mike's moist tongue entered him. Nigel felt as though he was about to blow his mind with excitement.

Mike worked his hands all over Nigel's body, who, in return teased Mike's nipples and caressed his body as well. Mike took hold of Nigel's solid erection and rapidly tossed him off. His load shot across his body and up to his chest, some spurted within the reach of his tongue. He had tasted his cum before, but it tasted much better this time.

He felt Mike's shaft enter him again, this time with more force behind the thrusts. These became rapid. There was a moan from Mike. "Fuck, I'm coming." Nigel was ready to receive whatever was coming.

He felt the swift sharp shooting of Mike's load inside him, together with the throbbing of his shaft. Sweat was running off of Mike in rivers. He stayed with his back arched for a while. Nigel placed a hand down to caress their balls together. Mike slowly withdrew his erection. Nigel held on to it as it left him.

They lay there together, neither wanting the experience to end.

CHAPTER 22

Nigel woke up to the sound of the shower. He continued to lay there. He felt strange. It was a mixture of feeling good, yet quite knackered.

He had managed to throw a sheet over himself during the night, but he couldn't remember going to sleep.

Looking across to Mike's bed, it had not been slept in. Either that or he had made his bed before taking a shower.

His mind went back over the past evening's events. Bloody hell, that was something else. He slid his hand down under the sheets to check over his balls, they ached, and so did his arse. He give a pat to his dick. It had done well. He smiled as it showed signs of movement again. Suddenly a black mood swing came over him. He started to question the rights and wrongs of what he had got involved in. He had fucked a bloke. Friend or not, he had fucked a bloke.

This was not natural surely. What's more he thought, I have been fucked by a guy as well. I must be gay because I enjoyed it?

He then thought back to Jo. He had fucked her, and he had enjoyed that as well, not as much as last night, but he had enjoyed it.

This was crazy. He had set out from home being bi-curious and now he had dabbled in both worlds.

So what did that tell him? He was bi-sexual?

Mike appeared out of the shower rubbing his hair dry with a towel. He was looking good even after a hectic night.

"Morning," Mike said. "Did you sleep well?"

"I don't remember."

"And how do you feel this morning. Is there anything that I can do for you?"

"I don't think so, you did it all for me last night."

Nigel pulled the sheet off of himself, putting one leg on the floor.

"Hold it," Mike said, "can I give you a hand."

"You can piss off. I had the services of both your hands last night thank you very much."

He brushed past Mike to get into the much-needed shower.

Mike stopped him in his tracks. Placing both hands on the shoulders of Nigel, he looked into his eyes. Neither spoke a word, but both felt the warmth of the bond they now had. Mike embraced him, then let him go. It was a moment to be treasured. They both knew that this was their world, and their secret. Nigel was in the shower when Mike shouted out that he was going on ahead to order breakfast.

Shower over with, having given his private areas extra attention with the soap, he towelled himself down.

His penis was feeling slightly sensitive. It had been rather overworked last night. He consoled himself with that thought. He sat down on his bed. *'I can't believe I did that. I must be fucked up more than I thought.'*

Pulling on his shorts and T-shirt, checking that it was clean enough, he made his way down to breakfast.

Mike was already drinking his coffee and had poured one for Nigel.

"It's the traditional French breakfast," Mike said.

"So where are the plates?"

Mike took hold of his bread and tore it into pieces. The crumbs showered over the marble table.

"Oh, very French I must say."

"I have given the guy six packs of durex for the funny fags."

"Did he mind having them instead of money?" Nigel asked.

"I don't think he was too pleased, but I told him to go fuck himself."

"You didn't?"

"No." Mike laughed. He was quite happy about it."

They paid the bill and collected their things from their room. Nigel took a long time standing at the door looking back at the scene. The memory would remain with him for life, he was sure of that.

The camper pulled out into the stream of early morning traffic. Mike turned on the radio. "Find us some descent music to listen to."

They had travelled several miles before they touched on the subject of last night's performance.

Nigel was the first to broach the subject. "How do you feel now that we've done it?"

Mike sat there twisting the steering wheel around a bit more than usual as he thought over the question.

"Tell you the truth, I feel bloody good about it. What about you?"

"I feel a bit odd, well sore really, but it was better than I expected it to be."

"But did you enjoy it?"

"It was quite an experience."

Mike asked him if he had expected more. "Come on mate, loosen up a little, it's me you are talking to. I'm involved too, so I'm not likely to go shooting my mouth off about it, am I?"

Nigel felt relaxed after that statement. "To be honest, it was bloody great."

"I'm glad about that."

"But sorry, I have been trying to compare you with Jo."

"Thanks a lot."

"Well you did ask. With Jo, she never did any of the things...you know... the things that can turn a guy on. She just lay there, waiting to be fucked. That's what I gave her ...that's all. There was nothing more to it than some of my better wanking sessions."

"And how about us then?"

Nigel didn't reply straight away. He coughed to clear his throat. "Well, I feel a bit of a prat saying this, but, somehow you knew just what would turn me on, and the right spots to touch and caress. What's more I've never ever shot a load like that in my life...It was great."

"Was it love?" Mike asked.

"No. It was just a good evening of sex. Nothing more than that for me. It just blew my mind."

"If we pulled the camper over later, could you do it all again?" Mike asked.

"I don't think so."

"Why not."

Nigel patted his his penis. "I don't think he could come out to play just yet."

"Then I stand no chance today then?" Mike asked, smiling at Nigel's actions in describing his wellbeing.

"No, but as you have been asking all the questions, how about you then?"

"Well, as you know, I have shagged a couple of women before, but I never rated them. But last night, and I'm being very honest here, last night was really all about helping you sort your mind out about your sexuality. Yes?" Mike said, glancing across for a reaction.

"Yes."

"Well, I bloody well enjoyed it. I could pull the camper over right now and continue where we left off."

Nigel's face turned from a smile to a grin. "Really?"

"Yep. At this moment I would rather fuck a guy than the women I have had."

"I feel deeply honoured," Nigel grinned. The conversation seemed to die at this point. They had come to a roadwork junction which demanded the full attention of Mike's driving skills.

This gave Nigel time to think and clear his mind a little. He'd now had sex with both sexes, and out of the two, he'd had better sex with Mike, his friend, who was a guy. So what was the difference?

He was now being crude with his thinking. It's only the thing between his legs that gave him the pleasure. That was purely sex...not love.

What bothered him most was something that he'd believed for a long time. He had proved to himself that a guy could satisfy his needs better than a female. A guy just knows what another guy wants, more than a woman could ever know. A woman could only know these areas if you told her. And to be able to tell her, you would have to be in love. Casual sex was not about love.

Mike had helped him see the difference between love and sex. He knew that he couldn't love Mike, so how was he to find love?

Mike, now having fought way through the traffic asked for directions. "There is a turning on our left we should have taken. I would be grateful if the co-pilot could redirect."

They motored on. The conversation returned to normal, with the previous evening not being mentioned. They came across signs for Barjac. Nigel started to get nervous at the thought of meeting up with Vik again. Would it be the same second time around? And what about Mike? Good old Mike, he'd driven the camper right across France for him. He'd also shown him what sex was, and now he was taking him back to Barjac in the hope that he would find love. He went quite cold at the thought of failure.

What would Mike do while he spent time with Vik?

Too late to ponder now as Mike was pulling the camper into the lane leading down to the campsite. They drove down the steep little track that twisted down to the main entrance. They caught their first sight of naturists walking around. "God this feels like home again," Mike said.

Mike pulled the camper up and turned the engine off. The

routine started all over again with Nigel getting out to take care of the booking in. He returned five minutes later waving the documents in his hand. Mike started the engine up again. "Now where do you want us to park?" Mike asked.

"You decide."

He gave it some thought and decided that it would for the best if they stayed clear of Ariel and her crowd. "Let's stay down by the river nearer to your loved one."

The camper bumped its way down the rough track that led to the other side of the campsite. Nigel pointed to a spot near the riverbank.

Mike reversed the camper trying to find level ground. After a few goes, he gave up. "That will have to do."

They opened the camper doors and windows, letting what little air there was flow through the camper.

Nigel, pulling off his shorts said, "Christ that does feel good, I'm going for a swim."

Mike who'd already got one leg out of his shorts was also on the run towards the river.

They both dived in, swimming nearly the entire width of the river before surfacing. It was good to be back again. It felt like home thought Nigel.

They swam down river in the direction of where Vik was camping. The flow of the river helped them cover the distance without too much effort. As they rounded the bend they could see the camping area.

Nigel swam to the other bank and climbed onto the rocks, trying to get a better view. Mike joined him. "Do you know, I feel a bit nervous meeting up with Vic again. Suppose she's changed her mind? Maybe she's found another guy? Let's face it, she wrote that letter days ago now."

"Come on, she wouldn't have written like that if you weren't her number one guy."

"I know that, but I still feel on edge. I could do with having a beer."

"Me too," Mike said.

They swam back to the other bank again, climbed out and started to walk along the narrow pathway in the direction of the camper. Nigel kept looking back over his shoulder in the hope of seeing her.

Mike grabbed his arm. "Unless I'm mistaken, isn't that Vik down there ,sitting on the rocks?"

"Where?" Nigel asked. His voice sounded nervous.

"If you stopped looking backwards, you would have fucking well seen her first."

"Shit. Yes that's her. Oh fuck, what shall I do? She looks beautiful sitting there."

"Now I'm going to disappear back to the camper. Take it easy man, and for fuck sake, don't go getting a hard on. See you later."

"Piss off. You know I'm not like that."

Mike looked down at Nigel's groin area. " There, I saw it move."

"Bugger off will you, I'm nervous enough without having to worry about that."

Mike hurried away after giving Nigel a friendly pat on the shoulder. "See you."

Nigel stood there, not knowing how to play this one. He couldn't help staring at her. She looked great sitting there with the sunlight shining on her body. She was all alone with just her thoughts.

He decided to slip into the water and swim around the rock she was sitting on. This would give her a surprise, she still thinks I'm miles away. At least she's not with anyone else, he thought.

With silent, steady strokes he swam towards the rock hoping that she would not turn her head in his direction. As he got closer he could feel his heart beating faster than normal in his chest.

He got within a few strokes and called out. "Hi, are you waiting for someone?"

Vik heard him, and looked around for a moment, almost in panic.

Nigel was now hanging on under the rock face. Vik would have to look over and down to see him. He laughed with nerves. She could hear him but not see him.

He popped his head up over the edge of the rock. "Hello, are you looking for a boyfriend?"

Vik looked down at him. "Nigel. Oh God. Nigel," she cried out. With that she eased herself into the river.

Moments later they could be seen hugging and kissing, with frantic thrashing of the water around them.

They kissed laughed and embraced each other. Nigel's fears had now deserted him.

"You got my letter then?" Vik asked.

"No. I just knew that you were willing me back here."

"You fool. I love you for coming back. I have been so un-happy."

Nigel thought on his reply. He felt he couldn't say the same after last night in the hotel. "I've missed you too." He felt that was the right thing to say.

They climbed up onto the bank. "You look different," she said, as they lay there looking into each other's eyes.

"I think I have grown up a little since I left here." His mind raced back over the past few days. He smiled at the thought.

"What are you thinking?"

"I'm thinking what a lucky guy I am having someone like you caring for me. You have changed too. You are looking even more beautiful than ever."

"Stop it, you are making me blush."

"How could I tell, with a suntan like yours?" he said, running his hand across her back. God, she feels good, he thought.

"Tell me about your trip since you left here."

Nigel had to think sharply on this. He told her about reaching the coast. "Well you already know that don't you? You wrote to me there.'" He told her about staying near the lake, and the old boy moving them on.

Vik lay there listening to all the parts he felt he could tell her about.

"So it was just you and Mike really. Didn't you meet up with anyone interesting?"

"Not really, only the tennis guy's I told you about." He thought he should try and get off the subject fast.

"What about you then? Have you done anything exciting?" he asked.

"Not really. I've told you, I missed you too much, and didn't want to do very much. My father kept telling me off for brooding about you."

"You were in a mood then?"

"Most day's. Not in a mood, but just couldn't settle," she said.

"Didn't you go to the bar in the evenings to chat up the guy's?"

"No. Come on let me show you to my dad again. He didn't believe that you would come back."

They walked hand in hand back through the trees into the camping site where her parents greeted him.

"Sit down, sit down. So you have come back to learn a little more about life?" her father said.

Nigel gave a nod at the remark. He thought back to his last conversation with him. He now felt wiser for his experiences with Jo and Mike.

"Get him a beer," her father shouted to Vik. "How have you been since you left us?"

Nigel started to tell him the bits that he could. His mind became active as he skipped over some of the events of the past week.

Vik's father asked to be called Uric. "Everyone calls me that."

As they sat and talked, they were joined at the wooden table by some of the teenagers. They looked even more tanned than when he had last seen them.

Uric stood up and took hold of Nigel's arm. "Take a walk with me."

Vik looked amused at this. Nigel was not sure what to expect, and felt a little uncomfortable.

They walked quite some distance away from the others. "Let's sit here."

Nigel sat down on the grass. Uric sat crossed legged facing him. His skin was more like leather and his face was stern.

"So you think you are going to be more than friends with my daughter?" Uric asked, staring directly into his eyes for a reaction.

Nigel thought that this was a shit question to start with. "What do you mean?" he asked in return.

"Look, I will ask the questions. You must remember I'm her father, and she is very special to us."

"I'm sure she is."

"Are you liking her more than a friend?"

Nigel thought on this question. "I'm not sure that I understand you."

"Oh, I think you do. Vikkie has not stopped talking about you since you left. I think she is in love with you."

"I'm glad," Nigel said, blushing at the thought.

"I will say this to you, so hear me good. I like the look of you, and you have good manners."

"Thank you."

"I haven't finished. I trust you with her. But if you ever break that trust, I will break your bloody neck even if I have to come to England to find you."

Nigel thought that this was a bit hard on him. "Don't worry; I think I know what you mean. You have nothing to worry about, and I will remember your words, and respect them."

"Good, because I don't want to harm you," he said, with a smile creeping across his face.

Uric got up. Nigel followed. As they walked back to join the others, Uric put his arm around Nigel's shoulders. It was a firm shrug of friendship Nigel felt.

"Don't worry. One day you will be saying the same thing to a young man about to go out with your daughter."

Nigel smiled at the thought. "It might also turn out to be your grand daughter." The words had hardly left his lips, when he wished he were dead

Vik looked up. "Dad, what have you been saying to Nigel, he looks very red in the face."

The teenagers all laughed at this. Nigel felt that he was on show now.

Uric said he had only been making a new friendship of understanding. He gave Nigel a thump on his arm.

"Give the man from England another Dutch beer." With that, Uric turned and walked away back towards his tent. He turned to wave. Nigel felt that this was directed at him. He began to feel that he understood the old man.

"Don't worry about dad. He is a lovely man." Vik said, taking hold of Nigel's hand and squeezing it.

"Come on, let's go and swim round to your camper," she suggested.

"Prefer to walk, if that's alright by you."

"Fine."

Instead of walking along the footpath, they went through the trees. They passed small groups of naturists sitting outside their small tents, tucked away in the shade of the trees.

"They seem very private," Nigel said.

"That is how I would like to be with someone." Vik said, as she glanced at a naked couple lazing outside their tent.

Nigel felt that this could have been them if they had met up earlier.

She asked him how long he would be staying. He thought that this had a meaning behind it.

"As long as I wish and the money lasts. Why do you ask?"

"I just feel comfortable with you. I look at some of those couples back there, and I would like to be like them. With you of cause."

"But we hardly know each other. And what would your father say?"

She put her arm around him. He felt he hand searching his back. This felt good.

He did the same to her. He was tempted to feel her plum shaped bum. Why should he hold back, he just knew that she would love that? He wanted to lie down in the grass and make love to her. Easy man, you have to prove yourself first. But it was not easy to control his feelings for her. He began to feel a movement in his penis. God, don't let that happen, he thought. Control it man.

Vik smiled. "Am I teasing you by doing that, sorry, it must be hard for a guy, as everyone can see if you get aroused a little." She kept her hand still on his back for a while.

He regained his control. I hope that when the time comes, she will know all the right moves and touches, in the same way as she sensed his arousal, he thought.

It felt good walking through the long grass, nude and free. What's more, he was with a girl who seemed to be floating on the same cloud as him. He had never felt like this before. Was this to be love?

They stopped to look at the birds flying around. Vik told him that they were swifts. "If they are flying high the weather is going to be fine, and if they fly just above the water, this means that there is going to be a storm. I think I've got that right," she laughed.

She told him the names of some of the wild flowers around. "Some of these are protected flowers. See those, they're wild orchids."

"Do you know that since I have been here, I've learned that there is more to life than those back home could even start to understand."

"Do you mean your parents?" Vik asked.

" Not really. Just about everyone. This is a whole new way of life for me, and it's going to be hard to explain it back home."

"Does it please you?"

"Very much so."

They could see the camper through the trees. As they approached, Nigel was sure he had just seen Josh disappear through the bushes. He wondered what Josh and Ian had been up to while he had been away?

They found Mike lying outside the camper. He looked up at the two of them. "Hi. So you found each other then?" He got up to greet Vik.

"Nice seeing you again. This guy, he has been on edge since he received your letter. Can't see what you see in him really?"

"Thanks a bunch," Nigel said, giving him a playful punch on the arm.

Vik told Mike she thought that he was looking well. He thanked her, telling her that he thought she looked good also.

"Well now that we've established that we are all looking good, what are the chances of getting a drink?"

"Sit down. Beer, wine or orange juice?" Mike asked.

Both Vik and Nigel went for orange juice and Mike had a beer.

"Did I see Josh just now?" Nigel asked.'

"You did. He isn't with Ian anymore, he's gone home."

"So who is he with now?" Nigel asked.

"Himself," Mike answered, with a smile.

"Don't be crude. We have a lady with us."

"What are you both doing this evening?" Vik asked. "Why don't you join us for a Bar B Q?"

"What time's it going to happen?" Nigel asked.

"Oh, it won't get going till about nine. Are you going to join us as well Mike?" Nigel thought he looked uneasy about answering this.

"If you don't mind, I'll give it a miss. I've had a hard days drive just to bring this guy to you."

"So what will you do then? You can't spend the evening on your own." Nigel said.

"I'll survive," Mike assured him.

"As it's your first night back here, I'll send him back early for bed," Vik joked, patting Nigel on his bum.

"No, really, I'll be fine." Mike assured her.

"Well I'd better get you back safely." Nigel said, turning to Vik.

She insisted that she would find her own way back. "You don't have to dress for the evening, we have the fire to keep us warm, and we aren't in England you know, it stays warm through the evening."

"Shall I bring a towel?"

"Yes, and maybe a T-shirt."

Nigel took hold of her hand. "See you in a bit then Mike, I'll just walk Vik part way back."

On his way back to the camper, after seeing Vik to her campsite, he had time to think about events. He walked slowly through the trees with his mind drifting away again.

He was feeling rough about leaving Mike on his own for the evening. This is where friendships suffer between guys. Women always come between them.

Mike looked up as Nigel returned. He had already taken a shower. The table showed signs that he had eaten something as well.

"Have a wine," he said, holding up the bottle for Nigel.

"Thanks."

"Well, do you think you will get your end away tonight?"

"Strangely enoughVik isn't like that," Nigel said. "You are so bloody crude at times."

"Fuck off. She will be all over you mate."

"I don't think so. I think this time I have found someone that believes in love. Sex doesn't come into it."

"Oh sod me then. So this is the one is it? Tell me more."

"Do you mind if I go out this evening? Why don't you come as well?"

"What and queer your pitch. No thanks, I'll have an early night."

Nigel sank his wine. It went straight to his head. "I'm going for a shower. Won't be long."

The shower was hot. He stayed under it for much longer than usual. After towelling down, he shaved and splashed after-shave about his body and promptly wondering if he'd overdone it.

As he returned to the camper he could see Josh sitting there with Mike drinking wine.

"Hi. How are you then Josh?"

"Fine thanks. How about you?"

"Yep, fine."

"Sod me." Mike said. "Let's not have another one of those sessions."

"I hear that you are out with her this evening. Are you staying overnight?" Josh had a sly look on his face as he'd asked. Nigel was not sure what was behind the question and the way it was put.

Nigel went into the camper to grab a clean towel and T-shirt. He could hear Mike and Josh laughing outside.

"Well I'll be off then." Nigel said. "See you later mate." He turned to Josh. "See you around."

CHAPTER 23

The Bar-B-Q turned out to be a friendly affair. Nigel felt it was like being back in the scouts again as they sat around the huge campfire. He was enjoying the simple evening's entertainment.

There was quite a mixture of naturists sitting around the fire, just telling stories. Some stories true, and others a bit hard to believe.

Vik sat very close to him all evening with her arms around his waist giving him little hugs. Their bodies warm from the fire making him feel quite romantic.

He was aware that her father was watching his every move and expression.

"Come on Nigel, tell us about your travels." Uric chanted to the campfire crowd. "It's our friend from England's turn to entertain us now."

Nigel, now with a few wines inside him, had half expected this to happen. He gave a cough, to clear his throat. Vik gave him a kiss on his cheek just to give him support.

He told them that he came from just outside London, and that he was one of England's most promising tennis players.

Someone shouted from the group. "Have you played at Wimbledon?"

"No."

"You can't be very good then," came the shout back.

"I'd thrash your arse," Nigel responded. There was a lot of laughter at this. Vik gave him another hug.

Nigel thought that he was doing quite well so far.

"Go on. Take no notice of him." Uric shouted.

Nigel then went on to tell of their journey across France. He was about two thirds of the way through his story when a guitar started to be played, very softly. This seemed to add to the story telling. So when he started to come to the end, the guitar player sensed this, and provided a perfect strumming of his guitar.

There was shouting and clapping, with chants of "More." Nigel stood up, and applauded them back. He had just made many new friends.

He sat down again as the clapping started to die down. Vik gave him a kiss. "I love you," she whispered in his ear. "They

267

love you too, but not in the same way as I do."

All that Nigel could utter was "Shit, that was something." He put his arm around her; he just knew that she was the one for him.

Vik whispered in his ear. "Let's take a break away from all this. I could do with a swim, I'm so hot."

"I have that effect on women." He was trying to stand up as he spoke. The wine had taken its toll, but he felt oh so good.

Vik, putting her arm around him to steady him, led him towards the river. They could hear shouts coming from the naturists around the campfire. As most of the shouting was in Dutch, he was not aware of what they were saying. He smiled a stupid smile, and waved back to them.

"Come on, the river will do you good," Vik said, as she led him towards the water's edge.

He stood on the bank for a while, then just fell forward doing a belly flop. Vik dived in and swam towards him. The water was still warm but felt cool compared to the heat of the fire. This cleared his head.

He felt Vik's arms wrap around his legs as she began to surface. He waited for her to pop her head out of the water. Their bodies entwined, and he began to feel aroused.

Vik was content to just embrace and kiss, but he felt the urge to make love, right there in the river.

She took hold of his erection. He mobed his body in such a way that encouraged Vik to respond with firm strokes.

He lay back against the riverbank with his back arched and tense as he felt her kiss his now throbbing erection. Before she took him into her mouth, her hand eased its way down between his legs. And with a gentle teasing of her finger, she toyed it into his rectum. The sensation increased the firmness of his erection.

He felt the warmth of her mouth around his shaft as she took him deep into her throat. He wondered if he was hurting her. The groans were simply of pleasure though. Her hands searched his body. All he could do was lay back and enjoy the experience.

He wanted to enter her. He started to explore her in the same frantic way that she was searching him.

Her nipples were erect. He licked and sucked at them. She moaned her delight as they exchanged caresses.

He tried to take hold of his erection as he wanted to direct it into her and let her enjoy his shaft.

His head was spinning. He was aware that she was saying something to him. "Don't try anything now. You're not pre- pared. Just let me make you happy. My turn will come soon."

He could not hold on any longer, and he felt the spurts of his cum shooting into the river.

Vik was expertly holding his erection with one hand, and with the other giving small strokes over the head of his throbbing penis. The spurts of his love-juice seemed endless, he watched them shoot across her breasts and neck.

They lay there on the bank trying to regain their senses. They kissed with softness now as they showed each other they had enjoyed the experience.

Nigel slipped back into the river to wash himself clear of the love-juices. He took handfuls of water to wash his cum off of her breasts. This almost drove him to another session.

He leaned over her. "You were wonderful," he whispered. "You did everything that I had hoped for. When will you let me make love to you?"

"I don't know. I made a promise to myself. I promised that when I met the right guy, I would let him take my virginity."

Nigel didn't move. He kept looking into her eyes, searching for signs that would tell him that she was teasing him, but no.

"You are a virgin still?" He said, as he tried to clear the lump in his throat.

"Yes. Does that shock you?"

"No...well, in a way, yes. But the way you made love to me...how, where did you get the experience from?"

Vik smiled at the question. "Well I read, and I have a brother and we are very close. He loves me asking questions about lov- ing a man."

"Didn't you get embarrassed in asking him, and how would he know anyway?" Nigel asked, with a quizzed expression on his face now.

"No I didn't get embarrassed because he's *gay*."

Nigel sat up sharply. He suddenly felt that he had come full circle now. Vik smiled at his reactions.

"*Gay?*"

"Yes. Do you have a problem with that?"

"Not at all. You have no idea how well I understand that one."

Nigel thought that he would like to get back to his original question. He looked down at her again.

"When will you let me make love to you? I just know that I am in love with you."

"That's why I wrote to you. I knew then that you were the right person for me. You see I have grown up in a very close family. We share our feelings and emotions. My father has always told me about life."

Nigel's thoughts flashed back to home. His family was close, but he could never have asked his dad to talk openly about love and sex. Dad would have died at the thought.

"You are lucky then," he said.

"I think so. Even having a gay brother helped. He was able to explain his feelings about love making from a man's point of view."

Nigel was hearing her talking, but his thoughts were about her being a virgin. Shit, a virgin.

"Are you sure that I'm the right guy to...well you know?"

"As sure as I will ever be. I only hope that we remain friends afterwards."

Nigel rolled over to kiss her. She held him in her arms and whispered. "Let's make love tonight."

His head went into a complete spin.

"I'll have to go back to the camper to get something," he said.

"What?"

"You know."

"No, you don't have to do that, I'll ask my brother for some."

She held out her hand to lead him back to the campfire. He felt a little red in the face in having to let her brother know that he was about to take his sister's virginity. And what's more he was going to have the use of his condoms. He smiled as he thought of his situation.

As they got within sight of the campfire, Vik suggested that he stayed where he was and she would talk to her brother. He felt relieved about this.

Sitting down in the long grass, he watched as she approached the group. He peered over the top of the tall grass. He felt this was a nice shield from his embarrassment as Vik approached them.

So that's her brother. Who would have thought that he was gay? He watched her brother's reactions. The first thing he did after listening to her was to stand up and kiss her. He then leaned down to the guy he had been sitting next to and said something to him. They laughed, and slapped each playfully.

He watched as her brother walked back towards the tents. He returned holding a rolled up towel which he handed to Vik. She gave him a kiss, turned and ran back to Nigel. He could see she was happy as she ran though the long grass towards him.

"There, I knew that he would agree." Vik said.

"Agree what?"

"Well my brother joked when I asked him. He told me that he felt happy for me. And if I hadn't have had you, then he would have been tempted to."

"Well, that's nice of him...nice to think one's wanted."

Vik took hold of his hand again. "Come on. I have the keys to my brother's boyfriend's caravan as well. It's very posh...is that how you say it in England?"

They were walking towards the clubhouse and bar area. People were still sitting around outside drinking.

As they continued to walk, Vik pointed ahead through the trees to the luxury caravan, which was to be theirs for the night.

Nigel unlocked , opened the door and peered inside.

"This isn't a caravan, it's a palace."

Vik laughed. "He's a very rich guy. But he can't get his caravan over to the other side of the campsite, the road's too narrow. He spends his nights with my brother in his tent."

"But the tents only small surely?"

"Yes, isn't love a funny thing?" Vik added.

There was that '*love*' word again, he thought.

Once inside the caravan, he began to feel very nervous. He felt that he had placed a lot of pressure on himself, he had to perform a love act...this was not sex, this was to be love. Mentally he had to prepare himself...She was a virgin for Christ sake.

He watched as Vik opened cupboards and doors, looking for drinks. Nigel told her not to bother; he didn't really want to drink at this time.

She went to the bedroom at the end of the long caravan. He saw her pull the bedclothes back, then turning towards him she smiled and beckoned him to join her. She looked beautiful.

They both sat on the edge of the bed, which was made up with silk sheets and pillows.

"Are you sure you want to go through with this?" he asked.

Vik put her hand on his chest and pushed him back onto the bed. "I'm as sure as I will ever be. Please be gentle with me," she whispered, as she placed a kiss on his cheek.

He pulled her on top of him. He was already erect. He knew he had to master this, as it was all about control, and he wanted to make it last.

They kissed with warmth and passion. They took it in turns at first to explore each other's bodies, searching for the areas that excited them most.

Nigel gently turned her over onto her back. Then, kneeling between her outstretched legs, he took the condom and rolled it onto his erect penis.

Vik watched. He felt nervous now.

He placed a pillow under the small of her back, raising her into a comfortable position. He leaned forward on his hands to support himself, and was now ready to enter her. He felt her hand take hold of his penis, and together they guided it into the moist pubic hair zone.

Gently he eased his shaft into her. She groaned as he entered her. He watched her face, concerned that he might be hurting her. She raised her legs to help him ease himself even deeper into her. Her hands took hold of the cheeks of his arse, and then using her finger, gently eased it into his anus, then entering and withdrawing in rythm to his thrusts. Oh God, it felt good, thought Nigel.

He started to gain confidence and entered her even deeper with each thrust. There was a muffled cry from her as he claimed his first virgin. Looking into her eyes, he saw signs of tears. He eased back, but her hands pressured him to continue.His firm thrusts brought gasps of joy from her. He was reaching the point of no return. She brushed her hands over his nipples; something that she had already found pleased him and added to his excitement. He leaned over her body gently, their nipples brushing against each other. His strokes slowed down so that they could enjoy the feel of their bodies against each other, but Vik was ready to climax. He suddenly felt her loves juices oozing from her, making his thrusts easier. He'd liked the tightness of her before her climax, and Vik sensing this, tensed her muscles to grip his now fast thrusting shaft. He was almost ready to eject his load when her body eased back from his thrusts. He waited, and then withdrew from her. He knelt there, entering his finger into her love nest. This pleased her and she swayed her body to his movements.

At first he was not sure that he could contain himself any longer. He was surprised that he had maintained his erection whilst at the same time give her pleasure with his fingers.

She had another climax. He felt it with his hand. It was an exciting and wonderful experience.

His erection had not left him, so he entered her again. "This one is for you, my lover," he heard her whisper. The pace had now reach fever pitch, with his shaft pumping away inside her. He could hardly breath. The pace quickened. And in one blinding flood, he felt his manly load spurt out time and time again. Vik released another climax with him. They had made it together.

They both fell back onto the bed, their bodies dripping wet from their act of love.

Vik pulled the silk sheet over them. She kissed him gently. "Thank you, my lover."

Nigel awoke. His left arm felt dead. Vik was laying there, her body draped across him. She looked beautiful and content. Removing his arm from under her, he eased himself out of bed. He put his foot down onto something wet. Looking down at the carpet, he had trodden on the spent condom. Smiling, he picked it up, not remembering having removed it. In fact he couldn't remember having gone to sleep.

He made his way to the toilet, had a pee, flushing the condom away at the same time. Looking around at the little maze of doors, he found the shower. Turning on the taps, he heard the gas boiler ignite.

The water showered over him, he felt good, yet sad to be washing away the remains of his night of love.

He had almost finished when the door opened. Vik smiled. "Good morning," she said, as she joined him under the jets of hot water. They embraced.

He asked if he'd made her happy. She smiled. "You were so gentle with me. I love you for that." He felt that he had become a man overnight, and kissed her as he cuddled her under the shower to thank her.

They decided that they should not be seen leaving the caravan together. Nigel went first so that she could lock up and take the key back to her brother's boyfriend. They parted company, both feeling that they had entered a new stage of their lives.

The early morning sun was breaking through the trees. He looked at his watch, it was just past seven o'clock. He was tempted to take a swim as he was feeling so free and happy, but breakfast was needed, as he was feeling hungry as well.

His thoughts then turned to Mike. Bloody hell, what must he

be feeling? This made him feel guilty leaving him for a night with Vik. What could he say to Mike to make up for leaving him for a night of lovemaking?

He began to feel worse as he approached the camper. What a shithead he'd been, dumping his best mate like that. Maybe he should go for a swim and wait for breakfast? No, he thought. Best face the problem now. Maybe, if he was quiet, he could get the kettle on and make coffee and toast without waking Mike? He took hold of the sliding door. Pulling it open very slowly, he put his head inside the camper.

"Fuck me," was the greeting. "When did you get back? I wasn't expecting you back until much later." Mike said loudly, as he made a grab at his sleeping bag in panic.

Nigel looked down at the bed. His mouth dropped open wide. There at the side of Mike was a body, which he tried to cover up.

"Let me explain," Mike blurted out.

Nigel stood there, mouth still open. The body moved and spoke. "What the hell's going on?"

"Josh. What the fuck are you doing in the camper?" Nigel screamed out.

Josh looked guilty lying there on the bed. Mike fell backwards onto his back, hands behind head. It was if he was giving in to the situation…Game up.

Nigel was lost for words. He turned around in a hurry to get out of the camper. His eyes couldn't focus in his blind attempt to get away from the scene he had just witnessed.

He ran in the direction of the river. He fought his way through the branches of the trees and bushes in his escape. He had lost all sense of direction in his blinding rage. He staggered towards the bank and with a flop into the water, he swam as if he was half-crazed towards the rocks on the other bank. He clambered up onto them and lay there. His heartbeat was thumping away, his mind in a whirl. He lay there, deep in thought. Was he mad at what he had seen, or was he just hurt with Mike? Was it that he was jealous of Josh?

He tried to clear his head by thinking of his own experience last night. Had he at last found the answer to all of his questions about his own sexuality

He should be lying there feeling free and full of love for Vik. He started to compare the three sex acts he'd been involved in since leaving home. Maybe he should be giving them marks out of ten.

First, there was his time on the beach with Jo. That was pure sex. She had no feelings for him, but he was able to release his pent up feelings. No there was more to it that that. Then there was the night he'd shared sexual exchanges with Mike. He had enjoyed that. Mike had taken him to new heights of experiences by just knowing the right places to caress and touch. Mike had understood his sexual needs. But this had not been love. So what was the difference between Mike and Jo? Mike had given him more pleasure. He thought on this for a moment. Yes, Mike scored more points.

This left Vik. This had been an exchange of feelings. He had enjoyed giving her pleasure, just as much as he'd enjoyed receiving it... So surely this was what love was about?

He lay back again to think on this. His thoughts were broken by the sound of splashing in the river. He looked up and across to the other bank. He rolled over to look. It was Mike thrashing his way across the water to join him.

"Hi. Can I come up and join you?" He looked uneasy with the question. It was as if he were pleading.

"Please yourself."

Mike tried to clamber up. He held one hand out to Nigel to help him. Nigel refused. With a bit of an effort, Mike made it. He sat down beside Nigel.

There was a long silence. They both looked away from each other.

Mike broke the silence first. "Can I explain about what you saw back there?"

"I don't think you really have to."

"But I'd like to."

"Would you really. Not sure I want to hear though."

"Josh slept with me last night. You were away for the night, and I met up with him just by chance."

"Really, you don't have to explain." Nigel said, turning to look at Mike now, searching for the truth.

"I don't know why I let it happen. Josh just turned up at the bar. God, I don't know how to tell you this. We came away on this trip to help you sort your head out didn't we?"

Nigel raised an eyebrow.

"Well I think it's done the same for me as well."

"What are you trying to tell me?" Nigel asked, with a puzzled look on his face.

"Well I got to the bar thinking that I could chat up a girl."

"And did you?!

"No. Instead I found myself looking at some of the guy's instead. There was one guy there that I couldn't keep my eyes off of."

Nigel rolled over to look at Mike as he stumbled over some of his words. "I know what you mean. I've had the same feelings this holiday."

"You're only saying that to make me feel good," Mike smiled.

"No, really I'm not."

"Well I tried to get interested in some of the women there, but this guy kept attracting me. I couldn't keep my eyes off him. Shit, I started to have feelings towards him in a big way."

"So how did you land up with Josh?"

Mike thought for a moment. "Somehow he appeared at the bar. We got talking. I suppose we were both feeling a bit pissed off with our lot at the time. Anyhow, Josh rolled me a joint, and I suppose it went from there."

"Who suggested that you slept together?"

"We just had the feeling that we were going to spend the night together right from the point when I told him you were going to be out all night."

"Do you want to tell me more, or are you going to let me guess the rest?" Nigel asked, not knowing if he really wanted to hear more.

Mike turned to lie on his stomach as Nigel turned on his side to face him.

"Well we had a couple of glasses of wine and shared another joint. It got quite late, and Josh went to make a move to leave. It could have been easy to let him go, but something inside me was telling me that I wanted him to stay. I don't know if I wanted to have sex with him, or it was just that I was feeling pissed off with you being with Vik."

"So he stayed the night?"

"Yes."

"And did you?"

"Not really," Nigel was lost at this point. "What do you mean by that?"

"Well we never had proper sex." Mike laid his head on his arms, trying to cover his face with his next part of the answer. "We just had some fun."

"Fuck me. What do you mean by fun?"

"We just had mutual wanking sessions. Just a couple of times during the night."

"So you never had proper sex with him them?"

Mike looked up now. "No."

"But you could have?"

"Yes, but the timing wasn't right, and somehow it would have felt cheap."

"And how do you feel now?"

"To tell you the truth, I had been hoping that you were going to have the same feelings for me as I've had for you all the time. But now that you have found Vik...I suppose I have lost out."

"So what you are telling me is that you prefer guys to girls."

"Yes, but not just any guy. It's you I really have strong feelings for, but now that's not possible, I must admit though, I think I could go all the way with Josh."

Nigel stared at Mike for a moment, then placed his arm around his shoulders. Mike turned his head away. Nigel sensed that it was to hide the fact that he was trying to hold back his emotions.

"What an adventure this has turned out to be." Nigel said, pulling himself closer to Mike.

"Do you think I'm gay?" Mike asked.

"I don't know anymore. All I know is that I think I have experienced love." Nigel said. He then went on to tell Mike about his night with Vik. He went into great detail.

Mike listened with a bland expression on his face. "So are you telling me that you have found yourself at last?"

"Yes, I think so. How about you?"

"I think I have as well. But as you're not available now, it makes it difficult to handle. You see, although I get aroused by other guy's, I have strong feelings for you."

"I don't see this as a great problem. I'm sure we can work something out," Nigel said, not really believing he had said this.

"How do you work that one out?" Mike asked.

"I've enjoyed making love to a girl...but it still leaves me unsure as to which kind of relationship I like best. We have had some good sex between us since we agreed to free ourselves from all the rules that others make up for us."

"So what are you suggesting?" Mike asked, with a look of hope appearing on his face.

"Well I think it makes me bi-sexual. But I don't think I could be like that with everyone, only with those who I can get close to."

Mike turned and smiled. "You're not mad with me then for

getting involved with Josh?"

"As long as you're not mad with me getting involved with Vik."

"If we weren't out here and so exposed to everyone, I think I'd show you my feelings about what you've just said right now. Shit, what a funny fucking world we live in. Do you think there are others like us around?"

"I think so. Maybe not quite like us. I think we have something more special than most," Nigel said, leaning over to plant a kiss on Mike's cheek, having looked around to see if they could be seen.

"Come on let's get back, I'm hungry," Nigel said.

They dived into the river and swam to the other bank. There was a lack of conversation between them as they walked back to the camper, both deep in thought.

Mike poured some water into the kettle, lit the gas burner to make tea. Nigel had slumped down on one of the bench seats.

"Bloody hell, I feel quite at home in here," Nigel said, as he laid back, hands stretching above his head. "Don't you?"

Mike reminded him that it was not him who had stayed out all night.

"That's more like the old Mike I know. Never missing a trick."

Breakfast went down well for Nigel. He was aware that he had not eaten since the previous evening. There was little talk about the situation they found themselves in. Nigel was thinking that he'd been a bit hasty in deciding that he was bi-sexual. He should have thought this through before saying it to Mike.

And as for Mike, well he seemed to have no doubts that he was gay. Funny, Nigel thought, he had never shown any signs of that back home. What's more, they still had days before they returned home.

Mike broke the silence. "Are you shocked now that I've told you about my feelings?"

"A little. But you seem to have made up your mind about...well, you know...things."

"I was only telling you about how I felt about you. I must confess, I feel a bit fucked up in my mind over it though."

"I don't know about you, but I'm knackered. I'm going to get some sleep," Nigel said, curling up on the bed.

Mike settled down at the side of him. They slept till the early afternoon.

The camper was hot inside. Nigel was awake first. He looked

down at his sleeping mate. What a turaround it had been. He'd had no idea that his mate was like that at all. And there he was all the time scared to even mention his own screwed up feelings for fear of being taken the wrong way and possibly losing a friend for life.

Mike stirred. "Hi. How are you feeling now?"

"Much better for the sleep. I needed that."

"Tell you what, I've got to get outside in the fresh air. This camper's got no air in it." Mike climbed off of the bed, and sat down on a chair in the shade outside.

Nigel prepared something to eat, and the beers began to flow. They were not in the mood to do anything active. They were both spent of energy. Later that afternoon Josh joined them outside the camper. Nigel tried to keep his head down.

Mike greeted him, but Nigel could tell there was tension in the air.

"Hi," said Josh. "Just thought that I would call and help explain about last night Nigel."

"You don't have to. Mike's done that already."

"I hope you don't feel that I was trying to come between you and Mike?" Josh said.

Mike stood up. "Nobody's going to do that, believe me."

Nigel felt a lump arrive in his throat. "Mike's right on that score."

"Can we at least remain friends then?" Josh asked.

Mike and Nigel gave a nod to the question as they exchanged glances.

"Oh for fuck sake. Sit down and have a beer," Nigel said.

As Mike entered the camper for some more beers, Josh quickly said in a hushed voice, "Nothing happened between us last night, honest."

Nigel gave a wave of his hand. "Forget it."

They sat around talking. It got to the point as to what they were going to do in the evening. Nigel explained that he would be over on the other campsite with Vik and her friends.

"Why not join us?"

Mike looked at Nigel. "Were you directing that at me, Josh, or both of us?"

"What I meant was, we could all spend the evening around the campfire. It's quite good. Not a lot goes on, but it's good."

"But surely you'll be spending the night with Vik?" Mike

suggested.

"I don't think that's going to be the right thing to do. I don't want to get in too deep. Vik is nice but…I don't want to get committed."

"I think you'll want to sleep with her again tonight." Mike said, giving a glance across to Josh.

"I might want to, but I don't think it's going to happen somehow. We'll see."

As if the timing had been arranged to fit in with the conversation, Vik appeared.

Nigel leaped up from his chair as she walked towards them. She looked so good. What a lucky bastard I am, he thought.

Mike and Josh turned to look. "What a fucking gentleman our Nigel is," Mike said.

Nigel landed a kick against his leg. Josh laughed at the scene.

"Hello," Vik said. "Can I join you, or is this all mans talk?"

Nigel walked a few steps towards her, they embraced each other and exchanged lingering kisses.

Taking her hand, Nigel introduced her to Josh.

"We've met before," Vik said.

Josh smiled. "Yes, I know your brother."

Mike looked from Josh to Vik, just to watch their expressions. He then offered her a chair.

"Would you like a drink?" Nigel asked her.

"Thanks, water would be fine."

Nigel went inside the camper to get the bottled water from the fridge. He looked out of the window.

Vik was looking beautiful. I would be a bloody fool not to follow up on last night. He then put his head into gear. No, that wouldn't be love. It would mean he was only out for sex with her. He stood there at the window just staring at her.

"Come on Nigel, have you got stuck in the well?" shouted Mike.

Nigel placed the bottle on the table. "Would you like a glass?"

"No thanks, the bottle's just fine" she replied.

"We thought that it would be good if we could all meet up at your Bar-B-Q tonight," Nigel said.

"Why not. I think my father has a meeting of officials," Vik said. "But that won't stop us enjoying ourselves. Anyway, Josh has been to them before. They are good fun, better than staying on this side of the camp."

"Oh, I don't know about that," Mike laughed, looking at Nigel.

Nigel blushed. "You just can't help it can you. You never miss a trick. You don't do so badly when you are left on your own over here."

It was now Josh that looked embaressed.

Vik looked confused. She stood up saying, "Look Nigel, why don't you come across with me now, and let Mike and Josh join us later. I think my father want's to have a word with you anyway."

Mike looked amused at this. "What have you been getting up to then?" he asked Nigel.

"The way the conversation is going here, I think it's best if I came with you right now." He stood up, grabbed his towel and T-shirt and made ready to make a move. Vik took hold of his hand, and they made a rapid retreat.

Nigel looked over his shoulder back at Mike. This was the parting of the ways that he had been dreading.

He was leaving Mike in the hands of Josh. And here he was with Vik, heading into a love affair if he was not careful. Christ, how things have changed almost over night. What Mike had owned up to was playing on his mind. He really wanted time with Mike to sort it out. He felt he was being torn in two directions.

"Come on. You seem miles away," Vik said, tugging at his arm.

"Sorry. Yes I was."

"Thank you for last night." She put her arm around his waist, giving him a hug.

"No, thank you. You were so good…I mean you were all that I had hoped you would be," Nigel said.

They stopped and kissed under a tree. Nigel leaned back on the trunk of the tree, pulling her towards him.

Their naked bodies moulded together. Nigel could feel himself being aroused again. Vik sensing this took hold of her towel to cover his rising hardness.

They remained like this for quite sometime. They were alone in their own world.

"I think we shouldn't get too involved, someone might come along," Nigel said.

Vik broke away. She smiled. "You had better carry both our towels in front of you then, you naughty man."

They approached the campfire area. The teenagers were collecting wood for the fire. Nigel was getting concerned as to what

Vik's father wanted to speak to him about. Surely he didn't know about him making love to Vik?

"What does your father want to see me about?"

"I don't really know. He just said he wanted a word with you. He has a lot on his mind at the moment."

CHAPTER 24

The bonfire was shooting flames high into the sky. There were quite a few naturists gathering, waiting for the food from the Bar-B-Q to be prepared. The wine was already flowing.

Nigel could see Uric seated at a bench surrounded by official looking men dressed in shirts and ties.

"Looks very serious," Nigel said. "What's going on?"

"He's meeting the officials tonight. He has plans to start a naturist campsite just upstream a little way. Tonight is the final meeting. He will know if he can have permission or not." Vik told him.

It looked funny seeing men in suits sitting with Uric who was sitting there with them still naked.

He remarked on this to Vik.

"He's a true naturist. He is very comfortable as he is. They are the ones that are feeling uncomfortable, you watch them," Vik laughed

"Starting a naturist campsite up. Bloody hell, will you be helping him then?" he asked.

"Yes, and all the family."

"So what will you be doing for work?"

"Oh, I expect I shall get the job of being in reception."

Nigel's mind flashed back to Jo.

The food started to be passed around. Nigel was hungry so Vik piled his plate up for him.

He had no sooner started than Mike and Josh appeared. He felt a strange feeling come over him as he watched them both laughing and placing hands on each other's shoulders. God, was he jealous?

Vik had been watching his face. "Don't worry about Mike, Josh is a nice guy," she said.

"That's what worries me."

Vik snuggled up close to him. He felt comfortable in her company. He then started to think where he was going to end up sleeping. Supposing Josh slept with Mike. Shit, that would mean he would have to sleep up top in the camper. He couldn't even start to think how he would feel about that. How could he sleep, knowing that they were down below and maybe having sex together?'

He couldn't expect to sleep with Vik again. So what the hell was he going to do?

"You are doing it again," Vik said. "You are off into your little world aren't you?"

"Sorry."

He looked around at Uric and his meeting. Someone was walking across to Vik. It was one of the youth's. He sat down and whispered into Vik's ear. She nodded, and he walked away.

"My father would like to speak with you soon. Is that all right?"

"Oh, what is he going to see me about. It wasn't what we got up to last night is it?" he asked.

Vik laughed. "I didn't tell him anything. But I have a feeling that he knows about our love."

"Then your brother must have told him."

"No. But he knows we made love. I share everything with him. We have no secrets."

Josh and Mike came over to join them.

"Hi," Mike said. "Haven't we met before?"

"Yes." said Nigel. "Who's your friend?"

Vik, sensing the tension, suggested that Nigel went across to see her father. "The officials have left now."

"Aren't you going to come with me?" Nigel asked.

"If you like. I want to know if he has permission to start the campsite as well." Uric looked up. He looked tired, but happy. "Welcome young man. Sit down."

He kissed Vik on her cheek. "She is now happy again. I think it is you that makes her happy."

Nigel was relieved to receive such a welcome. He had been expecting the worst. Even so, he felt guilty sitting there with Uric having made love to his daughter. It must be the same for all parents though.

"How was your meeting?" Vik asked.

"Fine. The French make hard work over the smallist of detail, but they have agreed to my plans. So my little daughter, it looks as if we are to spend a long summer here. And it is going to be hard work through the winter."

"Oh, I'm so happy for you." Vik said, throwing her arms around Uric's neck.

"Enough of that. Save all that for Nigel," he said.

"Shall I leave you to talk?" Nigel asked.

"Not at all. It is you that I wish to talk to. So, Vic will go and join the others at the campfire for a while, won't you my dear?"

Vik gave Nigel a kiss on the cheek. "Be sure you listen. And be double sure that you give the right answers." With that she turned and ran to her brother and his boyfriend at the campfire. Uric spread a plan out on the table. "Come, sit here next to me. I'll show you a future beyond your dreams."

Nigel felt strange being left with him. Why would he want to share his plans with him? Uric talked at length about a dream he had for the future. He had dreamt of having a naturist camp-site alongside the river. He pointed just up-stream on the map. "I want to have tents in that area there, all along the riverbank. Then just through those trees, there will be space for over twenty family caravans.

You know the large ones that sleep six or more. And this area will allow naturists to bring their own caravans and park them all around that area there," he said, pointing each area out in detail.

Nigel wanting to appear intelligent pointed to an area printed in blue. "Is that a swimming pool then?"

"Yes for adults, and a little one at the side of it for the children, see there."

Nigel nodded. "And what is that area there?"

"That's going to be tennis courts, mini-ten courts, badminton, and next to them the clubhouse and a Bar-B-Q centre, a big one. And just over there, see the shaded area, that will be for the youngsters to play ping pong."

"Looks good to me," Nigel said.

"Wait. See that area way over there at the top of the map? That is going to be a clubhouse for the teenagers. And all around the clubhouse will be a tented area for them to have their own space to grow up in together."

"Great," Nigel added. "I am pleased for you. It looks just right for a natural campsite for everyone."

"I'm pleased for you too," Uric said, smiling as he did so.

"Me?"

"Yes, you." Uric smiled.

"Why me?"

"I have been hearing a lot about you and how good you are at sport. I would like to offer you the job of running that side of the campsite next summer." He looked directly at Nigel for a reaction.

"You are offering me a job out here in France. I can't believe it," Nigel spluttered.

"Well you had better, because I won't be offering it twice to you. It offers you a good future. In fact it offers both you and Vik a secure future together."

Nigel fumbled for words. "But you hardly know me. And I am not sure that I am the right one for Vik."

"I do," was the quick reply.

Nigel just sat there dumbstruck.

"Go away and think on it, and let me know your answer."

"Thanks. I am very honoured, but I would like time to think on it."

"Yes, I think so. Have a good evening."

Nigel stood up and shook Uric's hand. He then turned and walked away, not really knowing where to go.

He quickly told Vik that he wanted to be alone for a while. She nodded her understanding.

He had to talk to Mike. He also wanted to talk with Vik as well, but Mike was his best mate.

He started to walk away from the campfire area. Maybe he could sit by the river and think this one through. Fuck, what a switch around life he was having, and all within a month.

It seemed cooler away from the campfire. He decided to go back to the camper, at least he could think in comfort.

Pulling the camper door open wide, he slumped down on the bed. A beer was needed.

What was he going to tell his parents if he took up the offer? But then, if he went back home, what would he be doing as a career. Which lifestyle was he suited to best? Shit, this was too much to take in. He had ventured away to find himself, let's not loose sight of that, he told himself. It was question-and-answer time for him now.

He had found love with Vik. But he had only just got to know her. If he took up the offer Uric made, maybe he would have time to get to know her better. At least it would be a smashing life together if it all worked out. Christ, living as naturists together all year round. That had to be better than the expectations of his parents. They would have him go into computing or something like that.

Well that was one question answered already. He felt pleased with himself. There was still the question as to how he would tackle telling them back home. He could just picture his mother's face as he tried to explain what he'd been up to in France. It made his walking from bedroom to bathroom in the nude quite funny now. And if she would often question him on doing that, what the hell was she going to say about him being with naturists for four weeks? He smiled at the thought.

As for his brother, well, he would get some mileage out of this one. Boy would he have fun?

Dad would want to know about Vik. Now there's a thought. He would have to invite Vik home to introduce her to the family. What would they think of her? Dad would see her as a stripper from a nightclub. Shit, what a laugh. He would expect her to arrive on the doorstep naked.

He would have to go into the offer Uric had made in detail. But on the surface, it sounded great. At least he would be able to play a lot of sport... and what a lifestyle. His thoughts were broken by the sound of someone approaching outside. Vik's head appeared around the door. She looked concerned.

"Are you alright?" she asked. "You dashed off without saying anything. Are you alright?"

"Come on in. Yes I'm OK really. Just wanted to be on my own for a while."

"Sure, I can understand that. My father does like to hit people with ideas he has in his head. Not many of us can keep up with him."

"That includes me," Nigel said.

Vik sat down with him. She placed her arm around his shoulders and snuggled up to him. He laid his head on her shoulder.

"What are you going to do then?" Vik asked.

"Well it's all hit me at once, but I think I could love you enough to come back and live with you and your family."

"You think? Well I just know that it would work out." Vik said.

"How do you know?"

"Because I love you. I have never felt like this before. I know it's only been a short time that we have had together, but I just know it's right for both of us."

"What are my family going to say? I have to go back home and explain so much to them. And you would have to meet them as well. That's if you would like to?"

"Let's not worry about all that just now. The question is, do you want to come to France and work for my father and his project?"

"I can't believe that this is happening to me. Hell, it sounds brilliant. I would be able to play tennis and other sports, and be outdoors all day with other naturists…what more could a guy wish for?"

"What about me?"

"I think I'm lucky in finding you also. I think our love would grow, and I feel that you, the lifestyle and the offer your father has made me, are what dreams are made of."

"What about going home to tell your family. Will they understand?"

"That's what I've been thinking about."

"Don't worry about all these things tonight." Vik said, giving him a kiss just to stop him talking anymore.

They fell back onto the bed. They caressed and explored each other's bodies again.

Nigel became aroused and was eager to make love once more. He got off the bed and reached across the passenger seat to find the condoms in the glove compartment. Vik teased him whilst he stretched himself across the back of the seat. He felt her hands between his legs as she caressed his erection. He managed to grab what he was looking for, and while he tried to tear the foil he felt Vik trying to turn him towards her.

He stretched back against the seat as she took his shaft into her mouth. He sank to his knees as she continued to tease her newfound pleasure toy. He was just about reaching cloud nine…There were sounds of someone approaching the camper.

Too late. Mike's head appeared through the door. The sight amused him, yet he stayed there looking.

The scene before him was that of Nigel holding a condom in one hand as he knelt down with Vic still holding his erection like an athlete's baton.

There was a brief pause of silence. Then Nigel, coming down to earth in rapid fall shouted, "don't you ever think of knocking?"

"Please carry on," Mike said, his face full of amusement. "Oh by the way, this is Josh." Another head appeared through the open door.

Vik slid back onto the bed and sat there curled up with arms around her legs. She was slightly amused by the scene. Nigel stood up and joined her at her side to sit in the same position. His erection had taken a rapid decline. He tossed the used condom at Mike. He caught it, and held it up to show Josh, who then in turn took hold of it with two fingers. "What is this?" he asked, smiling at the situation.

"Can we join you?" Mike asked, entering anyway.

"Why not. Let's make it a foursome," Nigel sniggered.

Vik cuddled him. "Come on Nigel, you must laugh at it. It's quite funny really."

Nigel thought for a moment. "Oh come on in Josh."

They decided that drinks were in order all round. The four of them sat there on the bed drinking.

"Why did you dash away from us all. Did you get a telling off from Uric?" Mike asked.

Nigel thought that this was a good time to explain what had been proposed to him. Mike listened with a look of disbelief on his face.

"Shit. How are you going to explain this at home?" Mike asked.

"Don't know."

Josh, who was sitting there rolling a joint said. "Easy, just tell them straight. After all, that's what Mike is going to have to do."

"Do what?" Nigel asked.

Mike looked uneasy at this question. " Well...Oh Josh, you tell them."

Josh took a drag on his weed. "When Mike gets back home, I'm going to join him in England. I would like to see London, and find out if I can get a place in the London College of Art and Design. I'm into fashion you know."

Nigel looked at Josh as he sat there naked on the bed. "Don't think much of your latest creation."

"Josh. You can't let him get away with that remark."

The news of Josh joining Mike back home hit Nigel like a thunderbolt. "What are you going to tell your parents?"

"Like you. I don't know."

At this stage, Vic sensing that Nigel and Mike needed some space to talk, got off the bed, held her hand out to Josh. "Walk me back would you."

"Sure said Josh."

Vik giving Nigel a peck on his cheeks, pulled Josh off the bed and went to the doorway saying, "Talk it through. My father will want to know your answer in the morning." With that she walked away. Josh popped his head back inside the camper. "Have fun," he said, and then ran to catch Vik up.

"At least she will be safe with Josh," said Mike.

Nigel suddenly dashed towards the door. Leaping out of the camper, he caught Vik up, having passed Josh in his hurry.

She turned. They kissed and embraced. "I love you," Nigel said. Looking into her eyes, he could see tears. "Don't cry, you should be happy," he said, as he cradled her in his arms.

"You will make the right decision tonight, won't you? I love you too, and I know we would be happy together," she said.

"I know, I know, but I have a lot of things to clear in my head first."

Josh passed them. He went ahead to sit down on a tree trunk to wait for Vik.

Nigel let go of her, and she walked towards Josh. Nigel called out to him. "Are you sure you don't mind taking Vik back?"

"Not at all, I might be lucky enough to grab some of the Bar-B-Q food. See you tomorrow."

Vik turned and waved. She looked sad. Back in the camper Mike had made coffee. "Well, I think we're in for a long night."

"Where do we start?" Nigel asked.

"How about you going over the offer that Uric made you?"

Nigel explained the evening's session with Uric and his plans. Mike listened without any humorous interruptions.

"So do you think you'll take up the offer?"

"What do you think I should do?" Nigel asked.

There was a long pause. "I think I would go for it. You like the lifestyle now that you've found it. You will be doing something with your life, and sharing it with someone that you love. Let's face it mate, long term, you could own the bloody lot. Uric will want to hand it over to Vik. And by the time he does that, Shit, you will be married with a couple of kids."

Nigel thought on this. "Fuck, am I ready for this?"

"Better than sitting in a bloody block of offices thumping away at a computer all of your life."

"Right then. Tomorrow I'll go into the details with Uric. Now then, how about you?" Nigel asked. "What's this with you and Josh?"

Mike said that he had '*Come Out.*'

"Come out from where?" teased Nigel

"Well I now know that I am at ease with a guy. I thought that I liked women, but my feelings have turned towards other guy's."

"Is that as a result of what we've been up to?" Nigel asked.

"It helped tip the scales."

"Fuck me," said Nigel.

"Not now," laughed Mike.

"But surely you won't be taking him home with you?"

"No. But he want's to join me later, when we get home."

"How will you explain that away to your parents?"

"No idea at this time. Maybe they don't have to know," Mike said, with a quizzed look on his face. They discussed the problems through the rest of the evening together. One bottle of wine had turned into two being consumed.

Nigel was now beginning to feel uneasy as to how he should handle the sleeping arrangements for the night. He thought it best if he grabbed his sleeping bag and placed it up onto the top bed.

Mike watched as he removed his sleeping bag and pillow.

"What the fuck are you doing then?"

"I thought that I should sleep up top from now on."

"Bollocks. Why the sudden change? Have you gone all heterosexual on me then?"

"No. But what do you think we should do?"

"I think we have come a long way together, and what we choose to do with our lives is up to us.'

Nigel put his sleeping bag back down on Mike's bed. It was still very hot, so he lay out on top as usual.

Mike curled up alongside him. Nigel wrestled with the situation in his mind. He felt Mike's arm across his body, pulling him closer. Should he resist him or not?

Mike muttered in his ear. "Relax."

Nigel was so tired now; he was past the point of caring

The next morning greeted them with warm rays of sunshine streaming through the camper onto their bed.

Nigel stirred. Mike's arm was still around him. He gently removed it, trying not to disturb him. Rolling over onto his back trying to clear his head, he was aware that he hadn't had his usual early morning erection.

He ran his hand down across his stomach. There were signs of crusted cum amongst his pubic hair.

At this point Mike stirred. "Morning mate."

"Morning to you."

Mike caught sight of Nigel's exploring of his groin. He smiled.

"Did we?" asked Nigel.

"No. I did." Mike's smile grew larger. As he rolled over onto his back as well, Nigel had full frontal view of Mike's early warning system.

"What do you mean by that."

"What?' asked Mike.

"By what you just said."

"Oh that. Well you were asleep, but you looked as if you enjoyed it as well," Mike laughed.

"Did I have sex with you?"

"No. I just enjoyed myself. Relax."

Nigel patted his stomach again. Is that all that happened?"

"Yes, I thought it was not one of your best performances though."

"You cheeky bastard," Nigel said, turning and getting Mike in a headlock.

They wrestled around for a while. Their laughter helping to release their tension. Mike landed up on top of Nigel and sitting across his chest. "There, that's more like we were, before others got between us."

They pledged to keep their friendship open. Nigel encouraged himself to raise an erection. Mike needed no encouragement to arouse his. They knelt facing each other, their erect shafts touched. Both of them held the two erections together with their left hands. They then raised their right hands. Laughingly Mike asked Nigel to repeat after him. "*All for one – and one for all.*" They both felt that this was daft and quite laughable, but deep down it was a bond of true friendship, whatever the future had in store for them.

"Do other guy's act like this?" Nigel asked, as they lay back again on the bed.

"I have no idea, but maybe they should."

"Well, I must get over to see Uric."

They had breakfast and then took a shower together.

"I'll meet you down at the river with Josh then?" Nigel said.

"Yep, that's my man. Be nice to Vik," Mike added, "and bring her down for a swim as well."

"I will, don't you worry. See you later."

CHAPTER 25

Nigel headed through the trees to meet up with Uric. He felt nervous, yet happy. He felt good about the fact that with all the changes that had taken place within his life in the past few weeks, he had still remained good friends with Mike. Fancy him coming out and announcing that he was gay.

He pondered on this for a moment. It takes a special type of friendship that can take that on board. It would put a lot of pressure on their relationship, but he could handle that now. It's funny, he thought, he would never have come away with Mike if he had known he was gay, well not on his own. But now he was here, he didn't have a problem with it. To think, it was himself that had come away with doubts about his sexuality, and as it turned out, they had both helped each other to find themselves...what a switch. He parted some branches from a tree and got a clear view of the camping area. It was a lazy scene. Not so much lazy he thought, but relaxed...yes that was it, relaxed.

As he approached he caught sight of Vik. She waved, and came running across the long grass towards him.

They fell into each other's arms, kissing frantically as they fell together into the long grass.

"Have you thought about staying over here? Please tell me that you are going to live with us." Vik said, almost too excited to hear his reply.

"Hey. Let me get my breath back."

"Come on...tell me you are going to take up my fathers offer."

"Well. I have given it a lot of thought...and, oh God, how do I break it to you...Mike thinks that, well we both think..."

"Come on, shouted Vik, tell me."

"Well...Yes!"

Vik gave a cry of joy. "I love you, I really love you." With that, she flung herself on top of him, raining kisses over his body.

"Stop it," Nigel giggled. "You're crushing me."

They sat up and talked excitedly.

"I think I should talk to your father now."

"He's waiting for you. He will have my brother with him as well."

"What's his name? I'm not sure that I've been introduced."

"Dan, or Daniel."

They walked over to the table cluttered with papers and plans. Uric appeared from his tent.

"Good morning. Sit down, sit down. Coffee?"

"Yes please."

"Well, have you slept on it?" Uric asked.

"Yes, very much so."

"And what is your answer?"

"Thank you. Yes I would like to think that I could join you in your venture. I would of course like to go into it in more detail."

"Good. Yes of course you have to know everything you need to know. Let me call my son out." He looked across to the tented area. "Daniel. Come and join us."

Vik made a move to leave them. Uric suggested that she stay.

Daniel, looking a little tussled, slumped down on the bench seat next to his father. "Hi," he said, extending his hand for Nigel to shake.

A man of few words, thought Nigel.

Uric went over the layout of the plans again. He thought that it would take about three years to complete as he would have wished. "The French authorities are slow to approve things."

His plan was to create a naturist family campsite, one that would attract families with teenagers. "These are our future," he said.

"You see that area there," Daniel said, "that is where the teenagers will have their own camping area. There they will have their own clubhouse. No adults will be allowed into their area."

"But there will be one adult person in charge each day and night," Uric added.

"Yes, that will be part of our jobs too," Daniel said.

"Sounds good to me" remarked Nigel.

"Happy so far?" Vik asked Nigel.

"Yes, but what will be the main job I'll be responsible for?"

"The sporting activities," Uric said.

"Where will I live?"

"To start with, you will have a caravan. See, like that," he said, pointing to one in the distance.

Nigel turned to take a look. "Looks fine to me."

"Then later, maybe at the end of next season, you might have a log cabin to live in. That depends on many things though," he said, looking at Vik.

She gave Nigel a pinch on his bum on hearing that from her father. Nigel put his arm around her.

"Right, is that all you wish to know?" Uric asked.

"How about money. Do I get paid as well?" Nigel laughed, somewhat nervously.

"Yes, of course. Let me see if I can work it out in English money. About one hundred pounds a week. But don't forget you will have the caravan or log cabin free, plus all your meals. At least you won't have to buy clothes." Uric laughed at this. "How will your parents like you being away from home?"

"I don't really know yet. They don't even know that I'm at a naturist campsite."

"I think you have a lot to explain to them."

"Yes I have. But I think I'll leave it until I get home."

"Well I would like you back here at the end of October. There is a lot to do during then, and again when we open in May. So you will have plenty of time to tell them."

They made all the final arrangements, and shook hands. "We'll see a lot of you before you depart I think."

Vik hurried Nigel away. She was anxious to have him to herself. They decided to take a swim to cool off a bit from the discussions. They were both excited about the adventure.

"You will have to come to England to meet my family too."

"I've never been to England. Are your parents nice?"

"They will love you. My brother might even like you too." Nigel laughed at the thought of the introductions. How the hell was he going to break the news to them?

Vik dived into the river. Nigel followed her. They swam upstream looking for Mike and Josh.

"There they are, over there on the rocks," Vik shouted out.

Ah, the famous rock, thought Nigel. He watched their body language as he swam towards them. They were lying close together, laughing and touching one another as if they were alone. Christ, he thought, they don't seem to care if anyone is watching. He saw Josh whisper in Mike's ear, it could easily have been a kiss. Come on Nigel, he said to himself, you're getting jealous you prat, just keep on swimming. Mike spotted Vik first. "Hi. Here come the lovers," he called out.

Josh knelt down to give Vik a hand up onto the rock. Mike offered Nigel his hand, but refused it.

After a few attempts, Nigel managed to climb up, much to

the amusement of Mike.

"Well, have you settled all of your plans?" Mike asked.

"I think so."

"So when will we be heading home then?" Mike asked, with a glance at Josh.

"In a couple of days," Nigel informed him.

All four of them sat there with something fresh to talk about in their lives. The meeting up of the foursome had changed their lives. They were very excited about the future.

"I still want to know how you are going to tell your parents?" Mike said.

"I should worry. What about you then?"

"I've told you, I don't think I will tell them straight away." Mike said. "Josh will be staying in London for a while. He's not coming home to sleep with me."

"Why not?" Josh asked with a smile. "Your parents will fall in love with me. I'm well house trained."

They sat there planning what was going to be their last couple of days at Barjac. They thought that it would be only right to spend their days together as a foursome, and the nights in their own beds.

"I should phone home and let my parents know that we are returning," Nigel said.

"This should be worth listening to," Mike suggested.

The sun was now going down in the blue sky that had been kind to them for the past month. They swam to the riverbank, and made their way towards the camper. Nigel just knew that he was not going to escape their listening in to his phone call home.

"Have you got your phone card handy Mike?"

"You can use it with pleasure. It will be worth every penny to be able to listen in. I can hear you now. 'Hi mum, I'm standing here naked phoning you to tell you that I'm going to be on my way home soon. Oh, by the way...I shall be coming back to France in about six weeks to live...'" Mike mimicked.

They all huddled together around the phone booth. Nigel dialled the number and waited.

"Hello. Yes it's me. How are you? Me...Nigel. Yes I'm still in France." He put his hand over the handset. "It's Dean. Trust me to get him."

"Is mum or dad there? Could you get them then? No...it's not because I don't want to talk to you, it's because it costs a lot of money from here."

There was a long pause. The others were holding back their laughter.

"Hi Mum. Yes I'm fine. I know I haven't phoned before...you needn't have worried like that, I'm fine."

Nigel looked at the three, raising his eyes to the top of his head.

"Where have I been? Well it's a long story, I'll tell you when I get home."

There was another pause.

"We are setting off home in a couple of days. Should be home for the weekend. What's that? Washing. Not a lot really. Only towels and T-shirts...No, not a lot else. Why do you ask, why?"

Nigel looked round at the threesome again. This was now getting to the laughing bit for them.

"Well, you won't believe this bit...but we found ourselves at a naturist campsite...Yes, that's right, where you don't wear any clothes. Hello...are you still there?"

There was now a longer silence. "Mum, Mum, talk to me."

The threesome was now falling around. "You tell them Nigel," Mike laughed. "That's my man. Your Mum's now in total shock."

After another pause. "Hi Dad, how are you?" Nigel was heard to say. "Yes I'm fine. Yes by the weekend."

"What do you mean about time? Yes, Mum did hear right first time...naturist campsite...Yes Mike as well."

Nigel turned and smiled at Mike as if to say, "You're in it up to your neck too mate."

"Dad, listen. I might as well tell you the other bit of the reason for calling you...yes, there is more. I've got a job out here as well. Isn't that great? What do you mean by '*Christ sake boy*?' I thought you would at least be pleased for me. I start in about six week's time."

Nigel looked down at the time left on the phone card. He turned to Mike. "You're a fucking mean bastard at heart, aren't you?"

"Dad...Dean, Dean. What are you doing on the phone, where's Dad gone? What do you mean he handed the phone to you...he's where, doing what? Having a scotch...He doesn't drink scotch."

With that the line went dead. "Bugger it," he said, chucking the card to the ground and jumping on it.

"Well, you handled that quite well I thought. I can see the banners up outside your house now. '*Welcome Home, and Good*

Luck in Your New Career.' "Mike collapsed to the ground holding his groin, trying not to pee himself.

Vik put her arms around Nigel. "Don't worry, I'm sure they will understand once you get home."

Josh just rolled a joint, as he sat there on the grass. "Man, I think that was real cool of you." He took a long drag on the weed, and then offered it to Nigel. He refused the offer. The evening was spent around the campfire. This time Uric had arranged a supper outside his family's tent. The table was prepared in true French style.

There were wooden bowls of fresh salad, bread, jugs of red and white wine. Uric and his wife then made a grand entrance carrying plates of meat. They placed them on the table, and in one swoop there were hands flashing around passing the various bowls and plates of food around.

Uric presented Nigel with a knife. It was like a penknife, with a blade that folded into the wooden handle. He had seen these being used by the French and Dutch before. He thanked Uric, and they shook hands.

"Now you are one of us," he said. Everyone clapped a shouted, "Welcome."

So this was going to be his way of life from now on, Nigel thought. This was the group of people that he would be sharing and working with.

He glanced around the table. He studied Mike and Josh. The only thing was, Mike would not be there for him. He felt a lump appear in his throat over this thought.

Vik, sensing his emotions, gave him a cuddle. He felt good in her company. He kissed her on the cheek, and put his arm around her waist. Out of the corner of his eye, he saw Uric's face break into a smile. When the meal was over [*which seemed to last for hours*] Vik walked with Nigel to the edge of the camping area. He rested his back against a tree trunk. Vik laid her body against his. It felt soft yet firm…God, he was lucky, he thought.

He felt himself getting aroused again. "I think I had better go now," he said. "I'm not being a good boy."

They kissed and caressed for a while. Nigel could have taken her again, but he was not prepared this time.

He was thankful in a way that Mike and Josh walked past them. They both said, "Good night."

Nigel watched them disappear down the pathway leading to the camper. "I think I should go," he said. "I'm about to loose my bed if I'm not careful."

Vik smiled. "I'm sure they will keep their word. Remember what we agreed on the rocks."

"Sure. Maybe we can climb the cliffs tomorrow and make love?" Nigel said, as he watched her face.

"That would be nice." Her hand touched his pubic area, just for a second. "Look after it till then."

With one final kiss, she started to walk back to her camp. She turned and waved back to him. He was still leaning against the tree, with his erection still hard and firm. He waved back. "See you in the morning."

He started walking towards the camper. His erection waved around as he walked. He wiggled his arse to feel the swaying of his shaft. It made him laugh aloud. "Fuck me, I feel so free," he shouted in a soft tone.

"So I see," came a voice from the trees on his right. He started to run in alarm. "Good night," came the voice again. Nigel turned. It was Daniel and his gay friend Rob.

Nigel shouted out "Good night," as he started to break into a trot, conscious that his erection was half way past it's sell by date now.

How embarrassing he thought. That's a good start to my career. He couldn't see any lights on in the camper as he approached it. Should he knock, or should he just barge in? The sliding door was open, so he pocked his head inside.

"Hi." Mike was stretched out on the bed.

"Where's Josh then?" Nigel asked.

"Gone to his own tent...I hope."

Nigel stood there for a moment. "Shall I put the light on?"

"No, I feel comfortable as I am. Coming to bed then?"

Nigel turned to the sink and cleaned his teeth. His mouth felt fresher now having done this chore. The taste of wine now gone.

Mike had been watching him. There was a shaft of moonlight that had drifted across Nigel as he stood there.

"You might tidy up in the prick department as well," Mike said.

Nigel looked down. "What's up with you?"

"I can see a little streak of dribble drifting in the moonlight. Just thought you should know."

Nigel looked down again. "Rubbish. You sod."

Nigel didn't ask this time about the sleeping arrangements.

He crawled alongside Mike on top of the bed.

"What a day?" Mike said.

"Are you and Josh hitting it off?"

"No. We haven't gone beyond that night you caught us at it."

"I asked you if you were hitting it off, not having it off. But thanks for telling me."

"So who's the bastard now?" Mike laughed, putting his arm around Nigel.

Nigel had mixed feelings about him doing this now. He was almost tempted to remove his arm away, but he didn't. It was strange. He still had feelings towards Mike. Yet somehow he could not see himself being like this with Josh, or another guy. Those feelings had gone now having found Vik.

Mike made a move to take hold of Nigel's penis. Should he resist?

He turned over to face Mike. "Let me do that to you."

Without even a word, Mike lay on his back. His arousal was swift. Nigel went about satisfying Mike with as much sensitivity as his mind would allow.

Mike, now satisfied by Nigel's touches, then cleaned up, and after a while drifted off into sleep. No words were exchanged. His face now a picture of contentment.

Nigel turned over, relieved that he hadn't had to decide if he could, or should have let Mike do the same for him. He took only seconds to drift off.

CHAPTER 26

Once again Nigel awoke to the stream of sunshine entering the camper. He looked down and went through the usual routine of hand over erection. He smiled to himself as he thought of the first few times in the camper with Mike when he'd tried to cover up, feeling rather self-conscious. What a difference a few weeks had made to his way of thinking. He felt he was going home a new man. He left Mike sleeping while he slipped away for a shower. It was early, and he almost had the shower to himself. Going mad soaping himself liberally all over, he was about to step back under the shower of hot water, when Josh appeared.

"Good morning," Josh called out as he walked towards him. "Can I assist in watering you down?"

Nigel thought he would have taken up the offer a couple of week's back. "No thanks, I can manage."

"Do you mind if I join you then?"

"Not at all," Nigel said looking at all the empty showers.

"I haven't any soap with me. That's what I meant by joining you." With that he stood underneath Nigel's shower. "Here, would you soap my back?"

Without thinking, Nigel spread the soap across his shoulders. Josh leaned over to help as he was taller than Nigel.

For a moment, he was tempted to continue soaping other areas of Josh, but he kept himself in check.

He was sure that he was being tested by Josh.

"There, have the soap, it's nearly empty anyway." With that he hopped under the next shower and washed himself down.

He had just started to towel himself down when Mike appeared. Mike looked at the two of them. Nigel raised his hands. "Not a chance," he laughed.

Mike smiled at the situation.

"I'll leave you two to it. Have fun," Nigel said, as he tried to pull his trainers on which isn't easy when you're not quite dry. He was in a hurry to leave them to it. He got back to the camper. Mike had already put the kettle on, and it was whistling away. With coffee made, he prepared a cooked breakfast. He was going to need this if he was going to have to climb the rock face, and then make love to Vik. The thought of this made him feel a twitch in his manhood. "Behave you little beauty," he told his penis.

Mike arrived back with Josh. "Is there enough to go round for three?" Mike asked.

"Yes sure."

They tucked into the breakfast. "Can I leave you two to wash up, I've got a date," Nigel said.

"Where are you going then?" Mike asked.

"Not telling. See you both later in the day. Have fun." He felt that he was getting back at Josh, as these were always his parting words to him. He walked through the trees carrying his towel around his neck. Vik came running towards him.

"Hello. What's that you have in your hand?"

"A bin liner for our towels. Don't forget, towels can get quite wet when you have to swim to the other bank."

The climb up to the top of the steep white cliffs was exhausting for them both. Nigel went first, stopping now and again to put his hand out for Vik at the more difficult parts.

After about twenty minutes they reached the top. They stood there looking at the view across the mountain range. It was beautiful. The sky was blue without a cloud in sight.

"Have you ever been up here before?" Nigel asked.

"No never."

They looked around. There were no signs of a pathway through to where they were.

"It looks as if we have chosen a good spot. Let's go back under the rocks over there." Nigel pointed behind them.

"Can't we stay here on the grass. The view is so nice. It would be romantic to make love knowing that we were not able to be seen, yet we can look down on everyone." Vik suggested.

They spread the towels out on the grass. "What else can I feel in the bag?"

"Take a look," she said.

"Food and drinks. What a bright girl you are."

"Well thank you. There's something else in the bag too, look." Taking the bag away from him, she put her hand inside and handed him a pack of condoms. "There."

"Oh Christ, I completely forgot mine. That would have finished me if I had to go back down and collect them, and then climb up again. You are an angel."

"I know," she laughed. There was something quite beautiful yet primitive about making love high up in the mountains. He could feel his whole body being bathed in sunshine as they rolled, locked together in their passions.

They laughed at the world as they broke away from their love making to look down at the very small dots of people far below them by the river. They sat there feeling as free as the birds that flew overhead. They had no need for food, only to drink the water to quench their thirsts between their bursts of lovemaking.

The afternoon passed away all too soon, yet, in that period, they had grown to know that they were right for each other. Nigel knew that he had found the meaning of love at long last. They slept under the shade of the trees, curled up together almost as one. Vik was the first to awake from their slumbers. She rained a series of kiss up and down Nigel's body trying to wake him. The sensation was too much for him. He rolled over trying to pull a towel over his head. "Don't stop," he shouted. "I like being woken up like this." She teased him until he had to give in.

The climb down to the river seemed much easier than the climb up.

They swam across to the other bank. Nigel stood on the riverbank looking up at the cliffs. Vik held his hand. "I shall always remember that spot...it must be the most perfect place on earth."

Vik gave his hand a squeeze. "Me too." There were tears in her eyes, tears of happiness.

He knew that he was making the right decision by coming back to France to live his life of freedom. He knew that he would *Return* to *Ceze*.

As for Mike... At least he had found himself as well on the trip. But will Josh be right for him?

The mood around the campfire that evening was a mixture of happiness and sadness rolled into one. Nigel had watched Mike and Josh trying to act out the mood of the evening together. It was difficult being gay in front of a crowd. He was able to show Vik his feelings towards her with the odd cuddle and kiss, but for Mike and Josh they were restricted to acts of male friendship. The fire seemed to be telling them that the evening was coming to a close as the embers began to loose their glow.

After saying goodbye to their hosts in continental style, Nigel and Vik walked together wrapped in each other's arms as they ambled along the narrow path through the trees. Nigel had seen Mike and Josh leave together with the only sign of bonding being the odd touch of the hand on shoulder. He and Vik were quite tearful as they tried to express their feelings for each other. They kissed and embraced for a while before they parted. Nigel stood in the clearing waving to her as she half ran, and half walked back to her tent. God how he wished he could have shared her bed tonight.

He approached the camper with caution. He was sure that he would find Josh inside with Mike. Tapping on the open door, he peered inside. Mike was curled up on the bed alone.

"Hi," Mike said. "How did you leave her?"

"God it was tough."

Mike smiled. He patted the bed for Nigel to join him. There were very few words spoken as they lay there together, arms comforting each other. Sleep eventually came. It had been a long day.

The next morning saw the two of them packing their gear in plastic bags and trying to gain some order in the camper as they prepared to depart for home. Their silence was almost painful. As the engine of the camper roared into life, Nigel did his usual routine inspection around the area where they had parked. It was early. They wanted to get on the road before emotions overtook them again. There was little chance of this though. The camper had only moved a few yards before a sea of naked bodies appeared through the trees. They both looked at each other and began to laugh. They had hoped that they would have received a good send off, yet, they had not expected this. Jumping out of the camper, Nigel hugged and kissed Vik. Although she had tears in her eyes, she looked beautiful in her nakedness. Nigel could see the fatherly figure of Uric, standing there smiling at the two of them. He also caught sight of Mike and Josh breaking down the barriers and attempting to show their emotions in public. There were shouts and cheers as they eventually pulled away in the camper. Vik ran alongside for a short while, holding Nigel's hand. He watched her out of the window and waved until she was just a dot in the distance.

They had been on the road for more than ten minutes when Nigel suddenly realised that they were performing one of their usual tricks again. There they both were, sitting there toally unaware of their nakedness. In an act of defiance against conforming to society, they continued for a few more miles like this before succumbing to putting their shorts on. The tension was broken between them for a while. Their conversation livened as they passed the places they had stayed at on their route down to the sun. As they passed the spot where they had parked in the fields where the owner had evicted them that night, they both went within themselves with their thoughts. That was the spot where they had started to find themselves. Neither wanted to discuss that night again, but it would remain with them for life. Now, wearing not so neat shorts, they also revisited the bars they had been in. The beer tasted very good.

It was not until they were on the ferry, crossing the channel for home, that they started wanting to express their thoughts and feelings again. In a way, neither cared if they were seen laughing and making contact with each other, for they had been on a venture of a lifetime with no regrets. As Portsmouth Harbour came into view, the mood changed once again. They both had mixed feelings about returning home. Both of them had problems to deal with. Nigel at least had the easier task by only having to tell his parents of his decision to return to France to live and work. As for Mike, how does a guy break the news to his parents and friends that he is gay?

On the motorway, with the signs to London flashing past them, these problems became closer each mile they travelled.

"Well old mate of mine, would you do that all over again?" Mike finally asked, as sight of home came into view.

Nigel turned to look at Mike. For a moment there was a silence.

"Yes, I bloody well would," Nigel replied. They laughed and shook hands as the camper wobbled across the road.

To be continued...

The second title in the trilogy
'Return to Ceze'
will be out in time for summer 2009

If you would like to pre-order your copy of the next title in
the trilogy please drop by our website or drop us an email to:
ThroughTheMist@collectivepublishing.co.uk,
with the
subject - 'Please reserve me 'Return to Ceze' -

The third (working) title in the trilogy
'Don't Josh with me'
will be out the following year
(or sooner if we can!)